· THE SIXTH WORLD OF MEN ·

A BEACON OF HOPE

WALTER E. MARK

Tate Publishing & *Enterprises*

A Beacon Of Hope
Copyright © 2010 by Walter E. Mark. All rights reserved.

No part of this publication may be reproduced, stored in a retrieval system or transmitted in any way by any means, electronic, mechanical, photocopy, recording or otherwise without the prior permission of the author except as provided by USA copyright law.

This novel is a work of fiction. Names, descriptions, entities, and incidents included in the story are products of the author's imagination. Any resemblance to actual persons, events, and entities is entirely coincidental.

The opinions expressed by the author are not necessarily those of Tate Publishing, LLC.

Published by Tate Publishing & Enterprises, LLC
127 E. Trade Center Terrace | Mustang, Oklahoma 73064 USA
1.888.361.9473 | www.tatepublishing.com

Tate Publishing is committed to excellence in the publishing industry. The company reflects the philosophy established by the founders, based on Psalm 68:11,
"The Lord gave the word and great was the company of those who published it."

Book design copyright © 2010 by Tate Publishing, LLC. All rights reserved.
Cover design by Chris Webb
Interior design by Scott Parrish

Published in the United States of America
ISBN: 978-1-61663-708-8
Fiction, Fantasy, Epic
10.08.04

Dedication

The words contained in this book would not exist if not for the encouragement of my most beloved Wendy and the enthusiasm of my dearest Winona. They gave me the courage to dream and the determination to persevere.

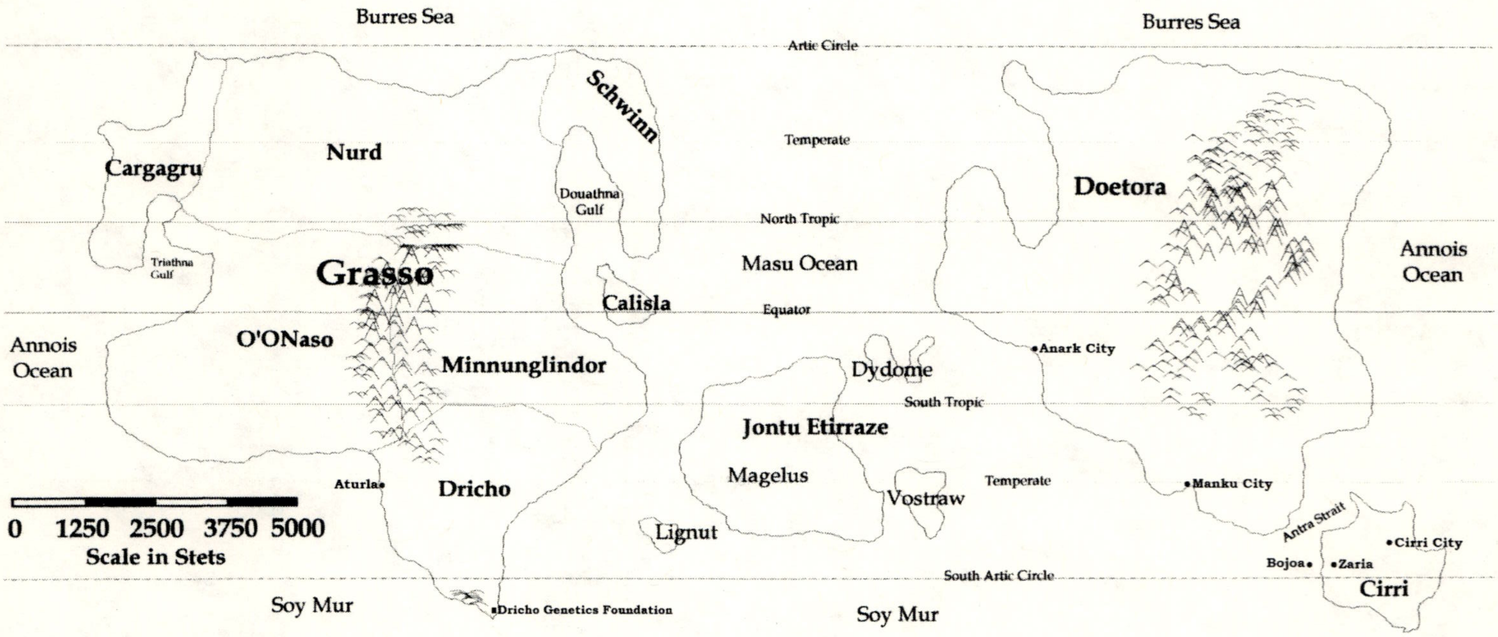
Burres Sea
Burres Sea
Artic Circle
Schwinn
Temperate
Nurd
Cargagru
Douathna Gulf
Doetora
North Tropic
Triathna Gulf
Grasso
Masu Ocean
Annois Ocean
Calisla
Equator
Annois Ocean
O'ONaso
Anark City
Minnunglindor
Dydome
South Tropic
Jontu Etirraze
Magelus
Temperate
Manku City
Aturla
Dricho
Vostraw
Antra Strait
0 1250 2500 3750 5000
Scale in Stets
Lignut
Cirri City
Bojoa
Zaria
South Artic Circle
Cirri
Soy Mur
Dricho Genetics Foundation
Soy Mur

Table of Contents

Prologue: The Visitation...................9
The Journey............................16
Bojoa..................................38
A Slow Start...........................66
The First Encounter....................75
Faces..................................80
An Out-of-Building Experience..........86
The Team...............................92
The Awakening.........................111
The Cirrian Agent.....................116
Aide to the Lord Director.............120
The Great One.........................124
A Voice Heard.........................130
The All-Council Meeting...............139

Bookshelf History	175
Confronting the Unknown	187
The D'Yavoly Reports	197
Celebration of Tryst	204
The Road-weary Inn	224
The Sealed Labs	244
A Means of Escape	254
Triumvirates	272
A Perfect Reflection	279
Civility	304
To Tell or Not to Tell	308
Mind Games	311
To Trust or Not to Trust	345
Glossary	352
Appendix	360

Prologue:
The Visitation

Jahnu propped himself up in the darkness, staring toward the foot of his bed. It all happened so quickly yet seemed to take so long. The searing light that had emanated from the face of the apparition still glowed in his mind's eye, though the room now appeared totally dark. Was it real? His eyes told him it was real. The light had seared the face of the apparition onto his vision, and wherever he looked in the room the face followed. He blinked, trying to get a focus on his surroundings; but his eyes were unable to capture enough light to make out anything in the darkness. Panic grasped at his heart as he looked to where he knew the window was in his room. Relief came as the light emanating from Cirri City greeted him, but the lights seemed so dim compared to the image still seared into his mind.

He fumbled for the lamp that he knew was beside the bed. He felt the table. He walked his fingers across the top of the table. His fingers ran across a book. Jahnu knew it was the book that was always on his night table, the book he read every night before going to bed: the Levra. Once his fingers found the base of the lamp, he waved his hand upward. The lamp clicked on.

Prologue: The Visitation

He looked about the room; but it was still dim compared to the image, so he placed his hand even with the light rod of the lamp and then slowly raised his hand. The light became stronger. He stopped when the light became its brightest. He looked straight at the light. It was strange that his eyes did not hurt when looking directly at the light. It had always hurt his eyes when he had looked at the light at its brightest setting before.

He could clearly make out the room now, but it still seemed dim. He closed his eyes, and the face was still there, nearly as bright as before. Wait. No. It was a bit fainter. The image was fading. A wave of relief rolled over him. He felt that the image might continue to fade now. He reopened his eyes. Now he could make out the light green of the walls—more relief.

It had to be real. Why else would his eyes have been nearly blinded? But it was all so unbelievable. One moment, he was sound asleep dreaming of... *What was he dreaming of?* He couldn't remember. He jerked his mind back from the search. *That's not important.* He continued his thoughts. One moment, he was asleep. The next moment, he was face-to-face with the most beautiful yet fearsome creature he had ever seen. The face had been in the image of a man, but it shone like the sun. Yet he could make out every feature of the face, and each feature was perfect. Yes. That's it. That's the only word to describe the face: *perfect.* The whiteness of the clothes that the apparition wore was more brilliant than the whiteness of sunlight reflected off new-fallen snow.

No. It couldn't have been that bright. He would have been blinded. Yet it had been that bright. He remembered it. He couldn't have imagined that kind of brightness. He had to have seen it. It was impossible, yet it must be so. His mind continued to argue with itself in this manner for some time.

He didn't know how much time elapsed as he argued

within himself; but at last, a thought came to him that made his heart end his mind's argument. *It was a miracle, a visitation from Thaoi,* exalted his heart.

There hasn't been a visitation for two thousand years, his mind interrupted again.

But one was promised, his heart reminded him.

Yes, a visitation was promised, his mind conceded, *but who are you to receive such a visitation?*

His heart had no answer, yet his heart knew that it must be true; and his mind was beginning to agree, but what should he do?

You must tell someone, a voice resounded in his thoughts.

Tell someone? No. No one will believe me. I am no one. No. This should have happened to a leader, someone of importance, or a Levra scholar. I am no one, just a lowly maintenance supervisor, Jahnu protested against the voice.

But the voice insisted. Louder and louder it repeated, *You must tell... You must tell... You must tell!*

He held his head. The voice was so loud now that it made his head feel as though it was ready to burst apart from the inside. *Axi...Axi. I'll tell. I'll tell,* he shouted back in thought to the voice in his mind. Still, the voice did not relent. *I'll tell,* he thought desperately. The voice still hammered his mind. "I will tell now! I will tell now!" he shouted repeatedly, this time aloud and at the top of his lungs.

Suddenly, he realized that the voice in his mind had stopped. He sank back on his bed in relief.

The relief was soon replaced by the worst anxiety he had ever experienced. *I must tell, but who? Who will believe me? I will be a laughingstock,* his mind groaned.

No, chided his heart. *This was a visitation. Thaoi will have prepared someone to hear. All I must do is let Thaoi lead me.*

Prologue: The Visitation

He cleared his mind of fear and doubt and called out with his heart, *Who?*

A quiet, small voice answered, *The one your heart knows.*

Instantly, a name came to him; and his heart jumped and raced. Then a feeling of calmness came upon him.

Of course, thought his mind. And with that thought, his feet took action.

Before his mind could catch up, he was in the lift. The next thing he knew, he was out of his building and onto a public overtrack. He noticed the stares of the few late-night commuters; but his thoughts were intent on his destination, so he did not bother himself to wonder why they were staring. He instead stared out the window. The overtrack was passing the Cirri City council center. He was almost there.

He suddenly realized that the image of the face was now gone from his vision. At the same moment, Jahnu realized that he was standing in front of a door and the door was all he could see. He pushed the door alert button; and after a moment, the door opened.

A gray-haired, bearded man stood before him with a look of what had to be a mixture of recognition and astonishment. He knew of this man but never met him before in person. The man's name was Odanoi. Odanoi stood motionless, staring at him, and then, without a word, motioned for Jahnu to enter.

He stood, facing Odanoi, in the middle of a great foyer for what seemed like half a lifetime. The old man seemed to know him—not by sight, but by some form of precognition. He knew that his surroundings were opulent and should have been distracted by them; but instead, he only gazed into the eyes of the elderly man. The old man's eyes screamed the contrasting emotions of dread and calmness. Although he never saw a look like that before, he understood its meaning, as he felt a similar mixture of emotions. Finally, Odanoi motioned him into a room off to the right of the foyer.

The room was a library. It was dark except for the light of a single lamp and the glow of the dying embers of the fireplace. Odanoi pointed in the direction of the fireplace. He saw two chairs, which he was sure matched at one time, facing the fireplace. One chair's soft cushions were worn while the other chair looked to have been hardly used at all. Upon approaching the chairs, Odanoi picked up a book, which was lying open and face down on the unused chair. He recognized the book immediately. It was the Levra.

Odanoi motioned for him to sit in the unused chair. Odanoi settled into the worn chair. For a long while, the two just sat there, looking at the embers of fire and stealing glimpses of each other. Finally, Odanoi spoke.

"I was just doing some reading out of the Levra. I am certain you know the book." Odanoi's voice was soft yet steady.

Jahnu nodded.

"I was reading a portion of Malluntekas. You are familiar with the prophecies."

This was not stated as a question; but when Odanoi paused and looked at him, he nodded and added, "I was reading from the prophecies before I went to bed."

Odanoi nodded as if this was expected. "I do not know your name, but I believe I know why you are here. However, I must ask your name before we continue." Odanoi paused for an answer.

"It is Jahnu, Jahnu Vija," he replied.

Although it seemed impossible, Odanoi's eyes grew even more dreadfully calm. "And…you say, 'Jahnu,' not because you feel I should know you…but because it is truly your

Prologue: The Visitation

root name?" The eyes remained calm, but the voice sounded slightly shaken.

"My father died just before my birth. My mother named me Jahnu instead of Jahn. She told me it was because I was now the dearest person in the world to her."

"I see. This follows the old custom," Odanoi said in a distant whisper.

"That is what my mother said," he said distractedly. "She said that she didn't know why she had to follow it, but she said that she had no choice. I never really knew what she meant by that."

"I am sure she did not really know either, Jahnu, but I know why," said Odanoi in a now-steady voice. Odanoi noticed the question in his eyes and continued. "It is because you were destined to have a visitation from Thaoi...and...from your presence here in these early morning parzes, I believe that you have had that visitation."

Jahnu's heart jumped. He knew that Odanoi would know why he was here, but hearing it made his heart pound like the ocean pounds the rocks, hard and slow. He managed to whisper, "How can you be so sure?"

Odanoi began slowly. "The last few nights, I have been studying the prophecy of the soulless...I was trying to understand it." Odanoi paused for a long time. When he caught Jahnu's gaze, he continued. "While studying the passage, a voice seemed to speak to me."

His breath caught, but he managed to say, "And...what did the voice say?"

Odanoi hesitated. Finally, he blurted, "That a man named after the old custom would come, dressed for sleep, to deliver a message of his visitation."

He flushed when he realized that he did indeed still have

on his bedclothes, but he quickly recovered. "How—how many nights did the voice speak to you?" he managed to ask.

"This is the seventh night." Odanoi paused and seemed to examine him with his eyes. Jahnu knew the significance of the number. It was the number associated with prophecy in the Levra. After a moment Odanoi continued, "I was up late tonight to see if the voice would speak to me for the seventh time. I was about to give up and go to bed when the voice spoke to me again and, immediately, the door alert sounded. This is the reason I answered the door at this time of night. The time of night is why I received you instead of a staff person. And your being dressed in your nightclothes is the reason I let you in."

So there it was. He could not ask for more confirmation than that. And now, the message from the visitation made sense. The message warned that a two-thousand-year-old prophecy, the prophecy of the soulless, was to be fulfilled at any moment. So he began to do as the voice had commanded him. He began to tell, "Odanoi, Chair of the High Council of Cirri, I have a message for you delivered by Mechial, High Ongiloi of our Lord Thaoi. The time has come. The Father of the Soulless is among the people of Kosundo. Only the faithful will remain."

1

THE JOURNEY

Ever since the dawn of humanity, the human mind has been at war. The mind has been the battleground for a war between the forces of good and the forces of evil. The war is an ancient war that knows no bounds. Sometimes, the forces of good prevail in individual battles; and sometimes, the victors of the battle are the forces of evil. There is only one constant in each battle: the final say who wins the battle is up to the human who owns the mind. No human is fated to do right. No human is fated to do wrong. But all humans come to a time in their existence when each human must decide between the forces of evil and the forces of good.

This is the way of every world where man exists. This battle is universal, and the universe is vast.

Scattered in this vastness are rare worlds where the precious seed of life has been sown. Scattered amongst these worlds are a very few worlds where an extraordinary seed has been sown. These worlds are the worlds of men.

On Earth, we are familiar with this war that rages on each of the worlds of men. The war manifests itself in the actions of every man and every woman. The war has many battles, and the loss of one battle does not lose the war. Yet, on one of earth's few sister worlds, the war of the mind became a war with only one battle. This world is called Kosundo.

Now, I could say that the world of Kosundo is an ancient world, but who is to say that it is more or less ancient than any of its sisters. Time exists in the universe, but who is to say that it flows in the same manner in every remote corner. The only thing that is certain is that time has flowed on Kosundo. In this flow of time, the men and women of Kosundo faced a battle for their minds unlike anyone on earth has ever faced.

Kosundo, which some say is the sixth world of men, did not start as a major battlefield. The history of the world was peaceful and not plagued by the same evil that existed on other worlds. Still, the full force of evil will find humanity wherever it exists; it just found Kosundo later than it found the other worlds of men.

Kosundo was a world consisting of only a few nations, most of which resided on the land of a huge continent. There was another nation that resided on several large islands in the midst of an ocean, while still another nation resided in a gulf of water. The largest nation of Kosundo resided alone on a continent that was nearly as large as the other huge continent. Still, the nation that resided in the most isolation for millennia was the nation of Cirri.

Cirri sat apart from other nations for so long that they developed into a race unto themselves. While the other nations fumed, fussed, and warred with each other, Cirri was left alone to develop a great technological society. Despite the advancements in technology, Cirri retained, more than any other nation, the way of their fathers. It was this old way that brought the understanding needed to recognize the evil that was growing in Kosundo.

The old way also played a key role in the life of a Cirrian man. The man was young by Cirri standards. He was already an accomplished professional, a prodigy of sorts. Although the young man didn't like to admit it, he was already an admired figure in Cirri, especially among those who knew him best. However, this young man didn't love the fame that his accomplishments brought. In truth, he shunned accolades. What this man loved was easy to define. He loved the old way, he loved his country, he loved a woman, and he loved to read.

The young man's name was Agap. His hair was a very light blonde, almost white, but then all Cirrians had blonde hair of some sort. He was tall, but not particularly tall for a Cirrian male. The sark that he wore was not overly embroidered, nor was it overly plain. His trousers were neatly pressed, but not elegant by any standard. Like all Cirrians, he was very conscious of time and thought that being late was nearly a crime. Although it could be said that he was more aware of time than most in Cirri. Yet he stood out in two ways: he had accomplished a lot for a man his age, and he was a habitual reader on any subject on which he could find a book.

This particular evening, he was reading a book about the history of his country. It was the last evening that he would be in his hometown, and the reading seemed appropriate to him. The passage he was reading was about a time in history when Cirri very nearly did get involved in war, and not just any war but the Great War:

> Cirri had nearly gone to war once in their history. The whole of Kosundo was embroiled in a global conflict caused by the assassination of Hysap, who was then

the Director of the Doetoran Edvukaat. The shooter was found to be an agent of Schwinn.

The shooter, a man by the name of Gior Tysdul, fled to Schwinn, which was secretly allied to O'ONaso. Schwinn refused to extradite the assassin to Doetora and tensions built up until Doetora retaliated by sinking trade ships from Schwinn.

O'ONaso used the occasion of the sinking to send military ships into Doetoran waters, thus maneuvering O'ONaso into a position to strike Doetora. Soon, O'ONaso attacked Doetora, which did not have a strong military. Getting intelligence from Schwinn spies, the O'ONaso forces soon gained a strong foothold in eastern Doetora. Schwinn joined in the conflict on the side of O'ONaso, and the Jontu followed on the side of Doetora. After the Jontu Alliance joined the fight, the rest of the countries of Grasso sided with O'ONaso; and the Great War was in full swing.

Many people in Cirri supported going to war because they feared the fall of Doetora to O'ONaso might upset the balance of power in Kosundo. Only the leadership of Yarukoi, a well-respected high council chair, prevented the Cirri high council from making war preparations. It would have marked the first time in history that the Cirrian government had authorized the manufacture of weapons of war.

He looked up from his reading because he wondered if he had remembered to ask the neighbors to pick up the last of the items he had put outside his door for the charity bazaar. He wouldn't be able to be there for the bazaar, but he wanted to make sure he was contributing something. A man should always look out for those who are in need. He was taught that lesson repeatedly as a child, and the lesson had taken root well. A man ought to never pass on a chance to help when he had the opportunity. As the Levra said, "A man cannot keep a clear conscience if he refuses to help those who cannot help themselves." He did his best to keep a clear conscience. After thinking about it, he didn't think he asked the neighbors. He would have to stop by his neighbors on his way to the port tomorrow. It was after nine parzes, and it was getting too late to bother anyone tonight.

Besides, it was time to relax and sit in his favorite chair. It was an old, brown, leather chair that was broken in just right. He would miss that chair. He hoped Yotux's new toy could create a chair comparable to his old chair for his quarters in Bojoa.

The book he was reading was *A History of Cirrian Leaders* written by the Magist Tutos Turies. He was a lesser-known historian that lived during the latter days of Yarukoi. Agap thought that it was often interesting to read history from the perspective of people who lived close to the time when major historical events took place.

One interesting note about Turies and some of his contemporary writers was that they sometimes referred to Kosundo as the sixth world. These writers claimed that Kosundo was the sixth world on which men lived. The writers seemed to convey that is was a popular belief in their time, but Agap didn't know where the belief had originated. He never could track down any original writings discussing the topic. Considering the tumultuous nature of the times two thousand years ago, the origins of the belief might never be known.

The section of the book that he had been reading this evening in the larger part acclaimed the accomplishments of several of Cirri's high council chairs. Yarukoi certainly was currently recognized as one of the greatest chairs in Cirrian history. Apparently, this contemporary of Yarukoi shared that opinion as well.

Turies seemed to be proud that Cirri had never been in a war or even engaged in the manufacture of weapons of war since its founding shortly after the breaking. That was something no other country in Kosundo could say.

The breaking had changed the landscape of Kosundo. Before the breaking, Kosundo was all one large landmass. Agap mused that Cirri's location after the breaking had played a large role in their ability to avoid war with foreign powers.

If the Kosundoan calendar was accurate, the breaking occurred over four thousand years ago. The current year was 4520 MENS. The calendar marked the breaking as zero MENS. MENS was an abbreviation for the old tongue phrase meaning, "period after the breaking."

The breaking made Cirri, as the land became known, drift far to the south of its original geographical location. The climate in Cirri became harsh because of the drifting. Only the northern part of Cirri could support civilization at first. Cirrians had to be tough and didn't really have much choice but to depend on one another. The southern part of Cirri had drifted into the South Arctic Circle, and it lay abandoned for centuries until innovations in technology had made it possible to conquer the arctic climate.

Cirri had drifted apart from other landmasses as well. The breaking had made several large islands in the Masu Sea. Cirri was the second largest of those islands. The other islands that were formed stayed grouped relatively close to each other; and eventually, the people on them united to become the Jontu Alliance. The Jontu had now reformed into a single country called the Jontu Etirraze. Cirri was not grouped with those islands and was separated from the Doetoran continent by a little over seven hundred stets of ocean. The nearest Jontu island was only slightly closer to Cirri than the continent of Grasso. Grasso was over five thousand stets away from Cirri. Cirri sat in the Masu Sea, isolated and cold. Agap agreed with most historians that this isolation is what enabled Cirri to avoid the conflicts that started to plague the rest of Kosundo about two thousand years ago.

There were small conflicts before the wars that started two thousand years ago, but these conflicts did not even begin to compare with the Great Wars. The Great Wars consumed Kosundo for a full nineteen hundred years. From all accounts, it was a terrifying time in Kosundo. Although Cirri never suffered any war, the threat of war was constant. Terrible war after terrible war followed the initial wars until they all stopped about a hundred years ago. Now, all of Kosundo was at peace. It was a tenuous peace at best, but any peace was good as far as Agap was concerned.

The isolation of Cirri also meant that the Cirrians did not intermingle with other people in Kosundo for centuries after the breaking. That period of isolation before trade began developed a people that had similar physical traits in Cirri, and Cirrians now regarded these traits as a part of who they were as a people.

All Cirrians tended to be of slightly above-average height with blonde hair, although not all Cirrians had the same shade of blonde hair. Cirrians had blue or gray eyes with an occasional green-eyed Cirrian.

For several hundred years before the Great Wars, all Kosundoan countries had vibrant trade relations with each other, largely due to the advent of air travel and world communications. Because Cirri had always been the leader in technology, they maintained healthy trade relations with everyone. So dominant was the Cirri economy and technology that banking for all of Kosundo became centered in Cirri. Once Cirri became Kosundo's merchant bank, it was only a few decades before all of Kosundo started to speak the Linuve language, which was the language spoken in Cirri. Ironically, Cirri itself only began to speak Linuve four hundred years before because of their heavy trade relations with the Jontu Alliance, which now had formed into a single country called the Jontu Etirraze. Before that, Cirrians had spoken a direct derivative from the old tongue called Glussi. Cirrian names for people and places still reflected the Glussi language. Of course, most other countries also tended to name people and places based on the old language of the region as well. Most settlements in Kosundo were quite old, three thousand years old or more. Still, even comparatively new settlements tended to be named after the old native language or the old tongue itself. That included the brand-new settlement that Agap was moving to today. He had named the settlement Bojoa using the old Glussi language.

 He glanced at the time. It was 9:70 already. The overtrack he was taking would be leaving at 3:10 tomorrow. It was time to go to bed. He got up and placed the book he had been reading into the box that sat in front of his chair. Agap had dozens of boxes, many of them containing books, stacked in his living quarters, ready to be picked up by the movers. The movers would arrive well before three parzes.

 He looked out the window that was in the main living area of his quarters. His quarters were in the Prutoi Memorial Living Complex, known simply as the PMLC. Prutoi was the first council member that had called his hometown Zaria. The living complex was named after him. The complex stood near the cave entrance. The area near entrances in all cave cities was always excavated since the floor of large Cirrian caves tended to drop several dets as the cave progressed underground. The excavation of the entrance area in Zaria allowed the PMLC to have seven levels of quarters. His quarters faced the cave opening so that he could see the valley and the neighboring mountain. He saw a little green growth sprouting on the neighboring mountain as he looked out his window. It was late spring in Cirri. The next month, Uchum, signaled the arrival of summer. By that time, that mountain would turn completely green except for the top third of the mountain. That part of the mountain was always covered in ice. Zaria was located about five hundred and sixty stets north of the South Arctic Circle. Summers tended to be the only time much green was seen in the Zaria area outside of the agrodyne that was housed at the back of the cave. He would miss the summer season in Zaria. That gave him just a tinge of sadness because he really did like summers in Zaria.

He stretched and yawned broadly. A tired feeling was starting to ebb its way into his body. Still, he was sort of excited. He was finally going back to his team in Bojoa. Although he wouldn't actually tell them, he missed his team a lot. It had been a while since he had been with them.

He then looked around his quarters that had served as his home for so many years. This was home long before he had started his career. His parents lived over just a few streets. He would miss this place. He knew that he would probably not be coming back to live again in Zaria, although he may be able to squeeze in a visit every now and again. Zaria was Agap's hometown and the one of the first cave cities established in Cirri some eighteen hundred years ago in one of the many caves that led into a large cavern in the Cirri mountains. Leaving was a little bit sad, but he had responsibilities now that would take him a long way from home.

On the brighter side, he would not be going alone on his journey. He had arranged for Holon to meet him at the port. It was good he was going to be with Holon for this journey. It made leaving much easier. He would have liked to spend a little more time with his parents before he left, but duty called. Odanoi had called a meeting for the fifth of Setmi. Today was the third. He had delayed going as long as he could. Since he was a council member, he had to go. Once he was there, he would have only part of the day to get both Holon and himself settled and to get in touch with his team before the meeting.

That meeting was a bit of a mystery itself. It was going to be held in Bojoa, a brand-new settlement. All of the councils would be there in person, which never happened. And then there was this Jahnu Vija who was going to be a speaker. No one knew much about this Jahnu. The name was strange being in the familiar. But that was a matter to think about tomorrow. He had a long trip on a submarine to think about the meeting and this Jahnu. Tonight, he needed to get some rest; so he headed off to bed.

Once in bed, he soon came to realize that just because he had lain down, it didn't mean that he was going to go to sleep. The same thoughts that had occupied his mind before he lay down still occupied it. His mind raced over the topics again, but the meeting preoccupied most of his thoughts. Finally, he sighed and pushed all of the thoughts out of his mind except the thoughts about Holon. He pictured Holon with her long, reddish-blonde hair down, looking at him with those wonderful blue eyes of hers. She looked heavenly, as she always did. Holon was a vision of perfect beauty. His mind quieted after thinking about her, and he soon fell fast asleep.

He got up early the next morning at around fifteen spens after the second parz. It was his habit to get up early enough to have time to read. He always read from the Levra in the morning; and if he got up early enough, like he did this morning, he could also find time to do a little extra casual reading. However, today, after he finished reading the Levra, he would pack away his casual reading in a travel bag. He would have time to read on the trip.

After he read his morning passage from the Levra and packed away some books to read on his trip, he checked outside his door. The items for the bazaar were gone. He must have asked the neighbors after all, and they must have already picked the items up. That was good. It was one less thing that he would have to do.

Soon, the movers arrived and began the task of loading his boxes on their wheeled cargo transport. There were four of them; but even so, they had to make quite a few trips up to his quarters and then back down to their transport. Still, the movers managed to load the boxes and cases Agap had piled for them in just a few spens.

He watched the movers' transport leave for the port out of his bedroom window. Once they sped away, he looked at his watch. It read 2:63. It was a little early to walk down to the rail station, and his old chair beckoned him. Yet, if he sat down in the chair to read, time would pass quickly and he would likely miss his overtrack. He took one last look at his old quarters. He would miss the old place, but Bojoa would be a great experience, especially since Holon would be there. He then turned off the lights and headed out the door.

To his surprise, Holon, complete with travel bags and cases, was at the station already when he arrived. Then he thought that he shouldn't have been too surprised. Holon had told him she was an early riser. That was a good quality in a person as far as he was concerned. Holon smelled of freshly cut flower blossoms, as she always did. It was a fragrance that summoned Holon into his mind any time they were apart. He gave Holon a short hug, and then they found seats near their departure exit and started to talk.

They didn't really talk of anything of consequence, but he enjoyed the conversation just the same. It was a pleasure just being with Holon. Before he knew it, their overtrack was announced and they were on their way to their sub and then Bojoa.

The overtrack took them to the coast due west of Zaria. When it stopped at the small port town of Paquarto, they disembarked the overtrack, retrieved their luggage cases, and waited in front of the station. Before long, a small hovercraft stopped in front of them.

"Agapoi?" asked the driver of the hovercraft.

He nodded and both he and Holon showed the driver their identity cards.

The driver scanned the cards to verify that they were indeed his passengers. After the scan was verified, he hopped out of the hovercraft, picked up their cases and said, "You may ride in the back."

Agap opened the back door of the hovercraft for Holon as the driver stowed their cases. Holon got in and he followed.

The driver then drove them north up the coast. After a few spens, he stopped at a small wooden building that was alongside the road. "This is it," said the driver as he turned around to look at them.

"Yes, I know," he said with a smirk. "I've been here a few times before."

The driver nodded and opened the storage compartment of the hovercraft from his seat. "I'm not supposed to get out of the hovercraft."

He nodded that he understood, and climbed out of the hovercraft and then assisted Holon out of the craft.

After they retrieved their cases, he shut the storage compartment. The hovercraft left, leaving them alone outside the small building.

He led Holon to the back of the building to what seemed to be an entrance to the basement of the building. Beside the entrance was an old light pole. As he approached the pole with Holon, a flash of red was emitted by the pole. This was a scanning beam that used a bio-filter to determine identity.

Shortly after they saw the flash, the ground on the other side of the pole opened up revealing a staircase. "There's the entrance to the sub bay," he said to Holon.

"I feel like I'm in a PT spy program," said Holon.

He chuckled and said, "Cirri does take security seriously, especially concerning a secret facility like Bojoa. I think I have viewed a PT program that seemed similar, though."

As they descended the staircase, the entrance closed behind them. They could now see the underground sub bay.

The bay could only accommodate one vessel at a time, but the vessel it could accommodate was a very large sub. The sub was one of the five new iri-plated subs commissioned by the council of nine. These subs were primarily used to carry passengers and supplies to Bojoa. They were the only large subs that could withstand the pressure encountered at very deep depths. The iri plating made their hulls stronger than any other sub in Kosundo.

They were met by a porter who took their luggage and gave them their seat assignments. As they were about to board, Holon stopped to stare at the sub. It was a huge vessel, and the slight yellow hue to its silvery hull made it look even larger.

"I've never seen such a huge sub. It's incredible," she said in awe.

"It's nothing compared to Bojoa; you'll see, Holu."

There were already many people on the sub. The sub had made many stops at several points along the coast, and it had more to make. Their trip would be a long one.

Once at her seat, Holon settled in for the long journey. She had brought an extra pillow and made herself comfortable. She talked with him for a little while, but then the monotony of the journey affected her. It wasn't long before she fell asleep.

He waited for a while until he was sure Holon was asleep. He then rifled through his travel bag and found a book to read. It wasn't long before he finished the first book and was looking for another. A small volume caught his attention. It was a book on philosophy. He thought that a philosophy book should keep his mind occupied for a while, so he settled in with the book. It wasn't long before he was well into the book, and he came upon a passage that seemed to capture the essence of the book:

> Life is a song. Each day that passes adds stanzas to the song. Some days are like choruses; they pass so similarly that each one is like an old refrain. Rise in the morning, get ready for the day, do what must be done, try to save some time for yourself and others that you love if you can, then get ready to rest to face another day. Some days are verses; the lyrics change, but each returns the same melody. Days such as these are marked with departures from the daily routine, whether the departures are welcome or unwelcome. Yet, these departures are minor and do not affect life's overall course. Some days are bridges to another mel-

ody, leading us to another type of life. Some days are crescendos that highlight our song, and some days are lulls where the song is weak but life manages to go on. But the day will come that is the song's finale. Sometimes, the finale is a brilliant crescendo; sometimes a gradual fading; sometimes the song just ends and the finale is cut short.

Such is life. It is a song that disrupts the silence of the universe. Like a song, it is familiar or can become familiar if you hear it enough. Life is the universe's song. The same song might affect each life differently, as one life affects other lives in varied and unique ways. Life is the great song that demands that all sing along, whether well or poorly, whether the life is considered great or small. No one can help but sing this song.

If life is the song, then we are the choir. What part of the song is sung and how well it is sung determines the strength, the beauty, and the passion of the song. So then each life that is lived contributes to the song and thus affects life, whether its effect is big or small. Even a song that is sung in a faraway place can still affect the whole choir of life. That is how it is everywhere there is life.

He paused from his reading to reflect on the passage. The book from which he was reading was *The Value of a Life* written by Vedoi, an honored ancient philosopher of Cirri. Vedoi was read in not only the country of Cirri but also widely in all of Kosundo. He respected the philosopher as everyone did, but he held all who had earned the honorific distinction of having the one formal name in particularly high regard. This was proper in Cirri, especially to those who had earned the honor to be buried with the one name as Vedoi had earned.

He himself had earned the honor of the one name, as it was called. Most people referred to Agap as Agapoi. Born Agap Virdod, he had received his third name, Jost, when he was thirty-five, quite young by Cirri standards, and his fourth name, Margon, at forty-two, which was an unheard of age to earn such an honor. He had earned the one name, Agapoi, by being appointed and sitting on the technology council. Still, he was the youngest on the council at fifty-seven and did not feel it proper to speak at an all-council meeting with the council of nine present just yet. After all, everyone else on the councils was twice his age or more. Of course, he always thought of himself only as Agap Virdod and really couldn't get used to all the formal honors that the council position brought; and he couldn't see himself as ever being able to earn the one name in perpetuity as Vedoi had earned. Sure, he had accomplished a lot in his short lifetime—most council members were first elected when they were twice his age—but he felt that he had a lot more to prove before he could even be considered for an honor such as the perpetual one name.

He brought himself again to the passage he had read and started to reflect on the significance of the thoughts behind the words. He soon found himself musing about the possibility that, right now, someone somewhere in Kosundo, maybe even in Doetora, might very well be reading this very passage and reflecting just as he was. The reflections would be different, of course, but the very fact that one passage could inspire thought, perhaps life-altering thought, was an indication that the song spoken of in the passage not only could reach across distance but it could also reach across time. Certainly, Vedoi's song is a song that has weaved its way into the very core of countless songs throughout the passing of time on Kosundo. As he mused, he wondered if it was possible that this song could even reach across the vastness of space and somehow affect other worlds, if other worlds indeed existed. After all, scientists on Kosundo were just now uncovering the fact that brainwaves, more commonly called thought waves, were indeed transmitted from every mind. We only had to tune our minds to receive such thoughts. Could another world have managed to perfect this reception to the point where even the faint thoughts of a far-off world could somehow be received and understood? Vedoi's thought waves certainly had thousands of years to travel into space.

He lost his grip on the book, and the book fell to the deck of the main passenger area, startling him out of his muse. He chided himself for being so careless with a cherished book of his personal collection.

As he bent over his seat to pick up the book, he again chided himself for allowing his musing go so far afield. Certainly, there was no evidence of life on other worlds. But then again, it was impossible to prove that there wasn't life in other parts of the universe since they were vast parts of the universe that no one on Kosundo knew anything about.

He sighed aloud as he uprighted himself in his seat. It appeared that Noso's fascination with the quest for life in space was beginning to affect him as well. Noso was a good friend, but most thought his fascination a gross waste of time. However, Noso was a brilliant man. It was he who first discovered the actual existence of thought waves. He had even built a crude thought wave receiver. His receiver did indeed seem to be able to detect thought waves. It was all quite interesting. Noso was currently trying to have a deep space probe launched with a TWR installed to see if another world out there had emitted thought waves. Such a probe was not likely to be launched anytime soon however. As much as he liked

Noso and respected his research, even he could not vote to launch such a project in good conscience. After all, council members were sworn to use all-resources provided by Cirri citizenry to best benefit the Cirri citizenry. There were many things that would benefit the Cirri citizenry more right now than Noso's project.

For now, Noso would have to be content that his TWR project was still receiving funding at all. There were many on the technology council who feared that the project might lead to a mind reading machine. For now, he was able to satisfy the council that the technology to read actual thoughts was not the goal of the project. Rather, the goal was to discover the nature of thought waves. He reasoned that this could aid emergency rescue personnel in locating disaster and accident victims as well as being useful for tracking the subjects of a security search that were hiding in remote locations. This satisfied the majority of the council enough for funding to continue, although at a slightly decreased rate.

"Now how did I get to thinking about that?" He wondered aloud to no one. He had set out to think about a great philosopher's writings and ended up thinking about Noso and council matters. He really did have to learn to focus on something beside council and team matters.

He reached down, picked up his travel bag, and placed the book inside to accompany the many other books in the bag. He had plenty more books with his luggage, and he had shipped the rest of his collection ahead. He smiled. He was probably the only person in the newly built settlement of Bojoa that had such a large collection of books. Many people in Bojoa carried only the Levra as a book due to the special respect they felt for the Levra. The rest of the literature was commonly stored on reading rods and viewed through a view screen or term of some sort. Most people had portable view screens called nonaterms. These varied in size. Some had screens the size of a small book while others were small enough to wear on a person's wrist. He preferred turning pages to scrolling on a screen. View screens were far too impersonal for him.

He knew that other people felt the same way. They just were not fortunate enough to have access to such a collection. People were constantly after him to borrow this book or that, but he found that it was a pain getting people to bring the book back. As a solution, he was in the habit of inviting interested friends over for reading sessions—not sessions where everyone would read the same book, mind you. His reading sessions consisted of him in his favorite reading chair, reading a book of his choice, while the guests sat in other chairs, reading books of their choice. Nevertheless, the sessions proved popular in Zaria.

He again mused, this time about how ironic it was for a member of the technology council to cling to the past as he did. He hated reading from those small, handheld nonaterms, or nonas for short, instead preferring books. He did not originate the idea of the nonas, but he was the head of the team that designed them. He realized that he was a creature of habit and he resisted things that encroached on what he saw as his routine. However, some things might just be best left unchanged. After all, there is definitely pleasure derived from the feel of a good book in your hands. The reading sessions proved that he was not alone in feeling that pleasure. On the other hand, he supposed that he might think of the nonas the same way he thought of books if he had grown up reading from a nona; but he had a hard time imagining that being the case.

He turned to the large window next to his seat. The window now looked out upon the new settlement he had helped plan and build. He named the city Bojoa. The word *Bojoa* was a contraction of two words in the Cirrian Glussi language. The resulting word gave the meaning of "over the under," which he thought captured what was accomplished with this settlement. Bojoa was the first underwater, domed city in Kosundo. He reasoned that the name described the city well, showing that the deep, underwater domain could be overcome with a lot a hard work and the fortuitous discovery of iri. He was excited about all the possibilities that iri promised. Really, from a strictly chemical standpoint, iri should not exist. Solid iri has a crystalline structure, making it less dense than alum, which was the lightest usable metal known only a few short years ago. But that same crystalline structure made iri strong, very strong. And whatever can be combined with iri becomes light and strong as well—light and strong, like the dome that covered the city. The outside structure of the dome was constructed entirely of firocryl, a blending of the common metal alloy firos, iri, and a few plastics and polymers. Firocryl was an extremely strong, translucent substance, which hardens at 64° K and becomes extremely strong below 9° K. The dome can withstand the pressure of water at a depth of fifteen hundred sunds when the firocryl is at a temperature below 9 degrees. Once a way was found to heat the inside of the dome without warming up the outside of the dome, the underwater settlement of Bojoa, placed on a large ridge at a depth of twelve hundred and fifty sunds, became possible. The ridge was chosen because of the presence of a large vein of iri on the slopes above the ridge. Bojoa was to be a place of discovery about many things but certainly about what wonders the newly found metal would yield next. The dome itself would not have been possible without this remarkable metal, if a metal was truly what iri was.

He emerged from his thoughts to view the city again. The city was striking. It looked like a giant, glowing, amber bell against the darkness of the sea. He knew that inside there would be gleaming silver buildings surrounded by trees. There was even some large shrub and flower gardens toward the middle of the dome. The dome wasn't finished the last time he was here. He was looking forward to seeing the completed city.

Again, he became immersed in thought. He was trying to avoid thinking about the visitor Bojoa was about to receive, but it seemed that his thoughts always were eventually drawn to the visit; and his thoughts again were drawn to this line of thought. After all, Odanoi was coming to hold an all-council session in Bojoa. These sessions were usually held in Cirri City, and then not everyone would be physically present. He was puzzled why the meeting would be held in Cirri's newest settlement instead of the council center. He was further baffled as to why the session was to be held publicly in the top floor of the recreation building, yet not broadcast outside of the dome. Still another puzzle was that the session was still considered a closed session yet open to some of the people who lived within Bojoa. Adding to the puzzle was the fact that no cameras or recording devices would be allowed in the session.

The location chosen for the session in the dome was not puzzling though. The top floor of the recreation building could seat over fifteen hundred people. It was a single room known as the viewing room, because of the large migoterms, each measuring fifty-six dets long and twenty dets tall, which dominated the walls of the room.

There was another puzzle though. he was extremely curious about the person Odanoi was bringing with him, a man called Jahnu, Jahnu Vija. He could not remember when a man was generally called by a familiar name in public. Sure, some people knew him as Agapu, but those were few and he was never publicly called by his familiar name; neither was anyone else in usual circumstances. *Unless,* he then reasoned, *a person was named after the old custom. That would be unusual. No one followed the old custom anymore. It was thought to be too personal for public display in modern Cirri society. Nevertheless, it must be.*

Questions then shot through his mind. *So who is Jahnu Vija? Why is he accompanying Odanoi? He is not anyone of major importance. That much is certain. After all, he is known only by two names. He obviously has not earned a third or fourth name. His full name would have been announced, and he certainly had not earned the one-name distinction. His name indicated that he was just an ordinary citizen of no special note. Yet he is accompanying Odanoi, the chair of the high council, the leader of the council of nine. Odanoi is the highest-ranking Cirrian. Why would he be bringing an ordinary citizen to speak at an all-council meeting?*

He never spoke at an all-council meeting—not that he couldn't. He just didn't feel that it was his place. Agap, through the earning and shedding of names, knew he had earned the right to speak but chose not to because of his youth. *What has Jahnu Vija accomplished that he should speak?* thought Agap.

Suddenly, a thought occurred to Agap. *Maybe the question should not be who Jahnu Vija is, but rather, what does this man have to say?* Agap shifted in his seat as he considered the thought. *Could he be a witness for Odanoi? Maybe that is the reason Jahnu Vija is speaking. That would explain it. Then again, why then would Odanoi need a witness? He is the chair of the council of nine.* Agap scratched his head. Then another thought came to him that made him feel uncomfortable. *Could it be that someone on the council has accused Odanoi?* His mind calmed as he thought further. *No. That cannot be. The session is semi-public. That means that the session will be used to make a public announcement. Why would Jahnu speak? Unless the announcement somehow concerns him.* Agap then straightened in his seat. *That has to be it, but in what way?*

2
Bojoa

Agap finally realized that he was not going to reason out anything more about Jahnu without more information. Everyone said that Odanoi told no one what the session was to be about, so he concluded that it was a waste of time to ponder further.

He looked back out the window. The sub was almost even with Bojoa now. It's amber glow nearly filled the window. He looked over at Holon. She was still sleeping, he hadn't awakened her. He chastised himself for being so thoughtless for a tic or two, then he said, "Holu, wake up."

"What did you say, Agapu?" said an only half-awake Holon.

Holon was his intended for all of two weeks now. She was going to be on his technology team and had quarters in the same building where he would stay. Today, she was wearing a light blue jumpsuit. The suit was made for travel and, as such, was nothing fancy, but Holon had a way of making everything she wore look like it was made for a queen. She sat up and put her pillow back into a travel bag. Then she reached back and pulled her wavy, reddish blonde hair over her right shoulder and then tossed it to her back again. He thought that her suit highlighted her bright blue eyes nicely.

"Wake up, we are here. If you look out this window, you can see Bojoa," he said, pointing to the window by his seat.

Holon moved up in her seat to look out the window. "Oh, Agapu! It's almost like seeing the sun under water! I know you said it was not going to be a dark or sterile city, but I never imagined that a deep-water city could look so vibrant. And it looks so big!" Holon was nearly breathless with excitement, which pleased him greatly.

"It is quite an accomplishment, isn't it? I'm excited to see how it turned out. Do you think you'll be able to survive, living and working down here?" He smiled as he teased Holon about her first reaction to the prospect of living in Bojoa. She had said that she didn't know if she could stand to be cooped up in a cramped, dingy dome for so long.

"Axi. You were right," admitted Holon. Then she added, "This time." Holon smiled at him and then snuggled up against his shoulder and gave him a playful punch in his side. "How long until we get to the approach tunnel?" she then asked.

"Probably about six or seven spens. The pilot will have to get the sub lined up and check for cross currents before he can approach. We have a bit more time before we need to start gathering our stuff together, so you can stay right where you are for a little while longer, my dear." He put his arm around Holon and gave her a squeeze.

Holon sighed briefly and then snuggled closer.

He reflected for a moment on how lucky he was to be able to call Holon his intended. After all, he was nothing special to look at, rather ordinary in fact. There was nothing ordinary about Holon. Sure, she had blonde hair like all Cirrians, but her hair had a touch of red in it. Blue eyes were ordinary for Cirrians, but hers were so ... alive. No. There was nothing ordinary about her eyes either. And her spirit, there was certainly nothing ordinary about that, and that was absolutely for certain. He squeezed Holon again. Holon looked up at him with those beautiful eyes. As he looked down at her, he felt some rather improper thoughts going through his mind; so he decided it might be best if he withdrew his arm. He smiled at Holon, feigned a stretch, and put his hands in his lap.

Holon sat upright in her seat again, and he turned to the window again. He hadn't told anyone on his team about Holon, even though he had been seeing her for almost two years now. He had always wanted to keep his personal and professional lives separate. As far as his team knew, he was a confirmed bachelor. At least he hoped that no one, especially not Kowtsom, had learned that not all of his frequent calls and visits to the Cirri mainland were completely about professional issues. No. Kowtsom hadn't found out. If she had, he would have heard about the rumor. Kowtsom couldn't keep a juicy, personal secret about anyone from anyone. He looked again at the dome.

What is special about Bojoa? He thought as he continued his thinking about the council meeting. *Well, there are some obvious things.* He turned from the window as he started to enumerate. *It is the newest and most modern of all Cirri settlements. In addition, there is the fact that it is a domed settlement. Then there is the fact that both the manufacturing and technology trades have set up their bases of operation here. However, none of those facts seem to matter all that much.*

Holon rifled through one of her bags looking for something, but her activity didn't keep him distracted from his thoughts long.

It must be the fact that Bojoa is the only underwater settlement in Cirri, well, in Kosundo for that matter. Yes, that must have something to do with it. So why, exactly, would the meeting be held underwater? It can't be for convenience. It takes longer to get here than anywhere else in Cirri. Bojoa is cut off from other settlements by the depth of twelve hundred and fifty sunds of water, cut off from all of Kosundo really. He shrugged his shoulders while he thought. Not wanting to draw a question about his shrug, he flexed his arms and neck for a moment. Then it dawned on him. *That is why the session is being held here. It is under twelve hundred and fifty sunds of water, and no other country has the technology to reach it and dock here. It is for safety concerns that the session will be held here. It must be,* Agap thought triumphantly.

Triumph then faded into a cold realization. *If the council is to make this announcement from the place that is the safest from outside powers in Cirri, what does that mean? Cirri had never been at war, so Odanoi must be expecting trouble as never seen before in Kosundo, and soon.* He no longer wanted to dwell on the meeting, but he knew that it would dominate his thoughts unless he distracted himself for a little while. He resolved to try to think only of getting Holon and himself moved in, at least for a little while.

Before he knew it, the sub was in the tunnel. Holon had moved forward in her seat to look out the window. He thought of how much planning and work went into the construction of the dome sub bay and the tunnel. The workers dug through solid rock from inside the dome. The depth of the cliff made any other way of working on the ledge impossible. First, the completed dome was lowered on the ledge from a surface construction ship. The water was then pumped out, and the dome was properly pressurized. The workers and equipment accessed the dome via the pressure locks from specially designed construction subs. He noticed that the workers did a great job of smoothing the sides of the tunnel, except for the very ends, where explosives were used to open the tunnel to the ocean.

The sub came to a stop. He could see the lights of the sub bay above the sub. Soon, the sub began to rise; and finally, the sub windows revealed the inside of the dome. He had forgotten just how big the dome actually was. It could be awe-inspiring for a person seeing it for the first time. He looked over at Holon, who was gaping out the window with her mouth open. There was another thing to love about Holon. She looked beautiful even with a look of astonishment on her face. He wanted to lean over and meet her open mouth with his, but that would not be appropriate. Instead, he made her eyes meet his.

"So what do you think *now*, Holu?" he asked with a grin.

Holon gave him a soft whack on the side of the head. "I said that you were right," she said, trying her best to look stern. Then her look softened to excitement. "I can't believe how huge it is." She stretched in front of him to look up. "The top of the dome looks like the sky! How'd you do that?" Holon asked as she sat back in her seat again.

"It wasn't intended," he said, still pretending his head hurt. "The dome has a layer of gases sealed in between the different layers of the dome's surface. The gas was meant to act as an insulating layer, keeping the outer layer of firocryl from heating up too much and the inner layer of polymers from transferring the water's cold temperature inside the dome. The blueness of the top of the dome when the artificial sun lamps are lit is really just a fortunate accident."

"Oh, you're good," Holon said in a semi-mocking tone. "You can create beauty by accident." Holon threw a quick smirk at him then said in a whispered tone, "Do you think the blue skies of Kosundo were created by accident, Agapu?"

"No. I believe Thaoi knew exactly what he was doing. I can only do my best and hope I get lucky."

"Well, then you must be one of the luckiest men in the history of Kosundo. It seems you've been lucky a whole lot." Holon was using a rather playful tone now.

"I must confess that you are right, Holu." He paused for a moment and then continued. "Because I am the lucky one that you chose to marry. You can't get any luckier than that."

Holon took his hand and squeezed it. "Oh, Agapu, you do know what to say to ruin a good tease, don't you?"

Passengers were starting to disembark now, and they had not even started to gather their things. So they hastily gathered their bags and carrying cases and made their way toward the exit. Holon exited first and began to wander around the bay. Once she walked far enough to see past the sub, she stopped abruptly. It was all he could do to avoid walking over her.

"Why'd you stop?" he asked in a mildly irritated tone.

She stood for a moment seemingly in awe, and then looked at him with a question on her face. "There is no way all this could be underwater!" she finally exclaimed. "I thought I was seeing most of the dome from the window, but that was puny compared to this!"

He followed her gaze to see the gigantic silvery living complex just off to their left, what looked like a whole forest to the right, and a beach directly over the bay from where they were standing. He took a second look at the beach. That hadn't been there yet when he was here last. They did a nice job. It was even complete with food-vending stands. He knew that the living complex and the arbor, as the forested area was called, were blocking their view to the rest of the city. Holon would have a surprise again once she was able to see past the living complex.

"Yeah. They did a nice job on the beach," Agap stated casually.

"The beach! What about that humongous building and all those trees?" Holon asked in exasperation.

"I know, I know. I was just teasing," he responded lightly. "It's truly hard to believe that all this could be possible on the ledge of an underwater mountain, but here it is. I don't want to cause you too much excitement, but you can get a better view of the rest of the dome if you walk to the other side of the living complex."

"There's more?" Holon wondered aloud.

"Oh yes. There is a lot more. There is an administration complex, a mining complex, and a recreation complex. There are manufacturing buildings, commercial buildings, technology buildings, and the agricultural complex that circles behind you encompasses two-thirds of the dome and houses hundreds of different agrodynes. On top of that, there is a large garden and athletic fields." When he finished, he had to admit that even his head was swimming. Holon had that stunned look on her face again. "Holu, I told you. We built a modern, self-sustaining city down here."

"I know you said that, but this isn't what I expected at all. If you didn't know you were underwater, you would never believe it. Agapu, even the air smells like the outdoors." Holon sat down on the grass that was just on her right.

"That's because of the plant and animal life that now call the dome home. Small animals, trees, and a variety of other plants live in the arbor area; livestock live in some of the agrodynes in the agricultural complex; and of course, there are the crops in the other agrodynes of the agricultural complex," he explained. "We even have a variable air circulation system that can simulate a breeze or even a wind if you like. We chose a very mild breeze for today."

Suddenly, Holon got up, left her bags behind, and darted for the beach. "Last one to the beach is a grazing koh!" she shouted.

He dropped his bags and shouted, "What about the bags?" as he sprinted to catch up.

"They'll be there when we get back, won't they?" Holon shouted back.

"I suppose they will at that," he responded.

They both ran until they reached the sand and then plopped down spread eagle. It was almost like being on a real beach. It seemed real and surreal at the same time.

They laid there for a while. Meanwhile, people were passing by, most of them seeing the city for the first time. There were many surprised faces. He also noticed quite a few people were joining them on the beach. They must have thought their bags marked a drop-off area because nearly everyone on the beach piled their bags with Holon's and his bags. It made for quite a pile. It was going to be a real challenge for everyone to find their bags after they get up from the beach. Holon and Agap looked at each other and began to laugh. They laughed for quite a while it seemed. After the laughter subsided, they both laid there looking up at the top of the dome.

"Where are the clouds?" Holon asked playfully. "We don't see too many days without clouds in Cirri."

"We thought that cloudless days were preferable," he retorted again playfully.

"Ahh... but I like to look at the clouds. Clouds can be anything you imagine them to be," pouted Holon.

He rolled on his side to face Holon and said, "Well then, we'll just have to make some clouds for you, won't we?"

He noticed that Holon appeared to have an indignant look growing on her face, as she probably thought that he was teasing her again. But when her eyes met his, the look changed. It softened.

She then turned her head toward him and said, "If anyone can find a way to make clouds in the dome, it would be you. Thank you, Agapu." Then Holon broke out in a big grin and said, "I'll expect the clouds by next Diotiri."

"Oh, and I guess you'll want me to work on them on eKureaki too," He said in feigned disgust.

Holon propped herself on her elbow to meet his face. "No, no. The weekend you will spend with me. Today is Titarti, which gives you tomorrow and the next day to work on them. You can even use part of Diotiri if you need it," Holon finished with a regal look.

"Then I guess I have plenty of time. Will there be anything else, your highness?" his tone dripped with playful sarcasm.

"Not that I can think of right now, but I'll let you know," Holon said in her best regal tone.

"Then, by your leave, I will pick up our belongings, if I can still find them, and make preparations to take residence of our domiciles," he said in an over-the-top tone of a Doetoran assistant. Then Agap strode off in very good imitation of the Doetoran strut, although it was ruined a bit by the need to shake the sand out his clothes.

Holon giggled as she watched him stride off and giggled even more as he had difficulty sorting through all the jumbled bags. Eventually, he emerged from the pile with their belongings and strode up to Holon.

Holon, wishing to extend the spoof a little bit longer, said, "I trust you did not have any trouble finding my bags. I would hate to think I would cause you any inconvenience."

Agap obliged by answering, "I am dreadfully sorry, my lady. I will try to hasten my pace. It is my pleasure to serve, my lady."

Holon looked at Agapu regally for another moment and then lost all composure and laughed hysterically. Her laugh was so infectious that Agapu started to laugh along with her. She noticed that their laughter was causing people around them a few giggles as well.

Eventually, she was able to gain enough control to say, "Oh, Agapu, just hand me my bags. There's no sense of you being a packed mowlare."

"Thank you for relinquishing your throne, my lady. I believe your bags are in my left hand," said Agapu, holding onto his tone for one last time. Agapu handed her her bags and suggested, "Why don't we go check out our quarters?—I mean—I'll walk you to your quarters and I'll check out my quarters by myself."

She laughed again. She had been still wiping away tears from her last outburst. "You can be very cute sometimes, Agapu." She noticed that he looked uncertain. He might have taken her comment wrongly.

"Don't worry, Agapu. I find it very endearing." Holon said with a very large smile. "So, lead the way," she said spiritedly and then proceeded to walk ahead of Agapu toward the towering living complex.

She looked away from the complex for a moment to her right. There she saw the arbor that Agapu had mentioned. There were varied types of trees, but all of them looked to be in perfect health. It was a beautiful sight. She turned to Agapu and said, "Let's go for a walk in the arbor."

"But what about our bags?" he asked.

"Do you have a crime problem in Bojoa already?" she asked playfully.

Agapu smiled. She loved it when he smiled. He had such a cute and wonderful smile. "Not as far as I know," he replied. He then put down his cases and bags on a grassy area near the arbor. She followed suit and the two of them walked arm in arm into the arbor.

As they walked, further into the arbor, she felt as if she had walked into a forest. It was a tidy and well kept forest, but it had everything she expected to see in a forest. There were small plants between the trees. These plants were low to the ground, the type that didn't need much sun. Some of the plants were green but many of them were dark shades of red, bright shades of yellow and many shades of blue. Together with the various trees, some of which bore colorful fruit, the scenery was breathtaking.

She looked at Agapu. He was looking back at her with that cute smile of his. She could lose herself in that smile. "It's wonderful, Agapu," she gushed. She couldn't think of anything more to say, though she felt as if she was not doing what she saw justice.

He kept that darling smile, but his answer wasn't very romantic. He said, "We found that mixing a ground iri and carbon compound with nitrates made an excellent fertilizer. The plants that you see here were only planted two years ago."

That information was fascinating to be sure, but she would have to work on Agapu's emotional spontaneity. "But, isn't it beautiful, Agapu?" she asked.

He just nodded and his adorable smile grew larger.

She smiled back and squeezed his arm briefly. She was about to try to coax something more out of him, when her peripheral vision caught sight of a darkly clothed man. The man was wearing a loose fitting hood and was behind a particularly large tree looking directly at them. "Agapu, there's someone looking at us," she said urgently pointing in the direction of the man.

Agapu turned and looked in the direction she pointed, but when she also looked back she didn't see anyone. "I don't see anyone," said Agapu.

"I don't see him anymore," she said. She thought within herself for a moment and then she said, "He must be hiding behind the tree."

"Axi, Holu," said Agapu. "I'll go have a look,"

"Not without me, you're not," she said determinedly.

Agapu nodded but let go of her arm. "Stay behind me," he said.

The two of them then walked slowly not toward the tree, but diagonal to the tree. When they reached a point where they could see the other side of the tree, she didn't see the man. She looked beyond the tree and saw motion. The branches of a low shrub were moving. The branches of the other shrubs nearby were motionless. "He went over there," she shouted, pointing toward the shrub.

Her intended picked up his pace and moved toward the shrub. She almost had to run to keep up. When she arrived at the bush a couple of steps behind her love, she saw nothing. She looked around, trying to catch a glimpse of movement, but she still saw nothing.

"I guess we scared him off," said Agapu.

"You do believe me, don't you?" she asked.

"Of course," he said. His voice was soft, but she thought she detected doubt in it.

"A man *was* watching us, Agapu," she said determinedly.

"Axi, Holu," said Agapu softly. "What did he look like?"

She had only caught a glimpse of him, but she said, "He was wearing dark clothing." She tried to picture the man in her mind's eye. "He was wearing a running hood, but I could see blonde hair under it. I couldn't tell what shade of blonde, but he was a Cirrian." She thought harder on her mind's image of the man. "He had something on his neck. I could see it under the hood. It might have been a scar," she said. Then she felt her hands starting to tremble and she felt sobs creep up into her throat.

Agapu held her closely. "It's axi, Holu. He's gone now," he said softly. She still wasn't certain that he believed her, but she loved being in his arms. It made everything seem axi. "Let's go, Holu. I need to get you to your room."

She wiped a tear from her eye and looked up at him. "You do believe me," she said with a question in her voice.

Agapu held her away from him slightly with both of his muscular arms, although his grip was gentle. He looked at her tenderly with his eyes. His eyes looked soft, as if they were puddles of blue water, not eyes at all. "I will always believe you, Holu," he said gently.

She searched his eyes and found only sincerity. His words were said with so much conviction, that it melted her doubts away. "I am sorry that I doubted," she said softly.

His next reply made her feel silly, yet she felt the love in it. "We all doubt, Holu. We must make a decision to trust," he said earnestly. "I decided long ago to trust you. I will never doubt you, Holu. Trust me.'

"How can I do anything else," she said. She meant it as sincerely as she had ever said anything.

He let go of Holon and the two of them walked out of the arbor area and picked up their bags. In front of them was the huge living complex. "Here's our new home," he said cheerfully, trying to lighten the mood.

"It's impressive," said Holon. He noticed that she said that as if she didn't think she could ever call it home.

"You'll see," he said. "You can make your quarters what you want them to be."

"If you say so, I will trust you on that," she said with a slight smile. He was glad to see that her mood had brightened.

The front complex proper was V-shaped, but in front of the complex was a lobby enclosed in a clear material known as tough glass, although the material was not actually glass at all but a clear polymer. The lobby stood about fifty dets high and ran the width of the front of the building. The lobby appeared as an inverted triangle from the front, filling in the indent of the V-shaped building behind. There were three sets of doors in the front. Holon headed for the set nearest to her.

He walked behind until Holon looked back as if to say, "Where are you?" He then quickened his pace until he came next to Holon. The two exchanged grins and then walked silently into the living complex.

Once inside the cavernous lobby area of the complex, the two slowed their pace to admire the fountains and ornate carvings that decorated all the woodwork in the lobby. Holon gave a look to him that said, "I know, not sterile," and both of them exchanged even broader grins. They walked a few more slow paces. He too was seeing the finished lobby for the first time.

"I could see myself getting lost in this place. Where to now?" asked Holon.

"Let's see..." He took out the communications he was given for their room assignments. "We are both assigned to Level Seven South Corridor One. You are assigned to room eighty-one, and my room is room seventy-seven. All we need to do is to find a lift, and there is one right over there." Agap said, pointing to the left at the black door in the wall of the building proper.

"Are you sure that this is the south side of the building?" Holon inquired as they turned toward the door.

"Actually, the front of the building faces west. That would make this half of the building the north half," he said as he hit the triangle-shaped button on the right of the door. The door opened immediately, and he motioned Holon to get on the lift.

"Are you trying to get me lost? Shouldn't we go to the other side so we arrive closer to our rooms?" Holon asked, sort of urgently actually, while she entered the lift.

He followed her on, the door closed behind them, and then he replied, "It really doesn't matter which lift door we enter. This lift doesn't just go up and down. It can go sideways too." He pointed to the control panel on the lift.

Holon's eyes followed his finger to the panel marked Translift Controls. "That is the most unusual control panel I've ever seen in a lift. It looks like a keyboard with a small display at the top," she said.

He smiled and said, "Actually, this is a translift. It doesn't have a traditional vertical shaft. The translift travels along a tube that has many junctions. Any time the lift is stationary and the doors can open, like they can now, the lift is in a junction. However, the lift can go through any unoccupied junction without stopping. The control panel lets you program in what direction to take at each junction by selecting the destination junction. You do this by typing in the junction code. Look. The code for our junction is in the communication the dome administration staff sent to us." He presented her with the two slips of paper. "Notice that our two codes are slightly different, but my guess is that they both will take us to the same junction because the rooms are so close together. The code consists of the building code, the floor number, the corridor, and the room number." He was punching in the code as he spoke. LC07S1081 was displayed on the small, elongated display. "All we have to do now is to hit the green button and we'll be off. Would you like to do the honors?" he asked her.

"Why not!" Holon said enthusiastically, pressing the green button.

The lift immediately started to go up. After a few tics, the lift shifted to the left; a couple tics later, it felt like it turned slightly; and then a couple tics later, it took a hard left. Then it stopped. The doors opened, and they stepped out into a beige hallway. The walls had colorful patterns in stripes toward its top and at its bottom. At the very top of the wall across from the elevator was a label that read, S1.

"Well, it looks like we're in the right hallway," he stated, after seeing the S1 label. He turned to find a room number at the door near the translift. "Okay. Here's room number ninety-eight. We'll have to go down the hall a little bit," he said, pointing to the left of the door he was facing.

After they walked a couple of steps, he remarked, "Drus. Our rooms will have real windows."

"What do you mean by 'real windows'?" asked a puzzled Holon.

"Well, all the rooms of a building this shape and size can't have an outside wall. This is an outer hallway, but the rooms on the side of the lift would have all inside walls. The rooms opposite the lift will have an outside wall, therefore, real windows."

They had come to the door marked "Room 81," and they stopped in front of the door.

"So, what do the rooms on the other side of the hall have?" asked Holon.

"They have simulated windows. We call them sim windows for short."

Holon looked at him quizzically.

He put down his bags in the hall. "The sim windows can be programmed to display a variety of outside scenery. A lot of people might like them, but I'd rather have a window that actually opens, one you can stick you head out of if you want."

Holon nodded her head and then looked at the door. "Umm... Agapu, there's no door handle." That puzzled look had come back to her face again.

"Just press the alert button to the right of the door. It's just like the call button on the translift."

Holon pressed the triangle-shaped button. A voice of a man said, "There is currently no one occupying this room. Please state your full name." The voice startled her slightly. It did sound like a real person. "Holon Tapienus Arkita," stated Holon after she recovered. The door slid open. She turned to him and said, "Is it always going to ask me to say my name?"

"No. Let me show you. Put your things inside the room, and come back out."

Holon stepped in, threw her bags down on the floor, and stepped back out of the room next to him. The door closed behind her. "Now, tell me that you love me."

Holon looked like she was going to ask a question.

He shook his head. "I'm serious. Say, 'I love you'," he insisted.

"I love you," she said finally. The room door opened. "I have to say, 'I love you,' to open the door? Don't you think that could be a bit embarrassing?" she asked vehemently.

He saw that he could have a little fun with this, so he tried to sound hurt when he said, "You would be embarrassed to say 'I love you'?"

"Not if you were standing out here, you lovely ninny, but what if I was standing here alone and some stranger walked by. Maybe he might think that I was talking to him. Did you not think of that?" She crossed her arms and let out an audible breath in disgust.

He broke out in a smile. "You sure are pretty when you're angry."

That, of course, made her start tapping her foot, a sure sign that she was getting angrier. He decided that he'd better stop playing around and said, "You don't have to say, 'I love you' to open the door." He stepped to the open door, stuck his arm in the room, waved it twice, and then stepped back into the hallway. The door closed. "Say anything that pops into your head."

"You're terrible," she said, looking Agap squarely in the eyes.

The door opened.

He ignored the insult and continued. "The dome computer system stores an imprint of the voice of everyone who lives in or visits the dome. You verified your identity to the computer when you stated your name. Now, when you want to open the door or program anything in the room, the computer will recognize your voice pattern and comply. In the case of opening the door, it will open as soon as your voice registers in the hall."

"Won't it open if I talk loudly in the room? That could be bad too."

"We thought of that. Go inside, let the door shut, and scream at the top of your lungs."

She hesitated. "You're not playing a trick on me again, are you?"

He feigned indignance. "May a running towrus gore my chest if I am pulling a trick on you now." He looked up and down the hall. "See. No towrus."

She smiled, maybe a bit sarcastically; but she went into the room. The door closed. Quite a few tics later, the door opened. "All I had to do was act like I was going to walk through the door to get it to open? You could have told me that. I was screaming at you to tell me how to open the door," she vented.

"Well, see? That proves my point. You can't open the door with your voice when you're inside," he said rather triumphantly.

"But why didn't you answer me?" Holon insisted.

"I couldn't hear you. We used a new sound deadening material in the doors, walls, ceilings, and floors. The room is completely soundproof, except for the windows, especially when they're open." he smirked.

She suddenly flushed. "Do you suppose someone outside in the dome heard me screaming my head off?"

"I doubt it, Holu. The windows do deaden sound pretty well, and we're seven floors up. Unless, of course, you opened a window. Then half of the dome would hear you. Sound travels pretty well in the dome at altitude," he said nonchalantly. He gave her a hug and started to pick up his bags.

She stopped him by saying, "I have one more question before you go." He straightened his back and looked at her. "The walls in the room, well, there are no walls. I mean, there are outside walls but no inside walls, nothing to separate the…" her voice trailed off then she continued in an urgent whisper, "There are no walls around the washroom." She looked up and down the hall, clearly embarrassed at saying *washroom* in public. She looked relieved when she saw that the hall was still clear, but that look faded quickly into a sort of mild anguish.

"Oh. I forgot that you said that you weren't able to check your messages yet. Well, just call me a nail and whack me on the head. I guess I do need to come in to show you how to set up your room. It won't take but a spen." He finished and then rethought and hastily added, "I can put my bags in the doorway to keep the door open."

"Oh, Agapu! You are such a gentleman! Maybe a little funny, but definitely a gentleman," she said with a chuckle. "By all means, come in and show me how to set up my room."

She went into the room, and he picked up his bags and dropped them in the doorway as he entered. The door remained open. The room was indeed completely unset. The walls were bare and colored white; there were appliances, fixtures, and the necessary plumbing but no furniture; and there were no inside walls, not even around the washroom. It was good to see that her luggage had already been delivered though.

He walked into the room reluctantly. He really didn't feel comfortable being alone with her in the room, even with the door open. It's not that he was afraid of her. He was afraid of himself. So he silently vowed to respect Holon once again, as he found he had to do from time to time. She was just so beautiful. He found it difficult to control his desires sometimes. It would be different if they were already joined, but that date was a while away yet. After he made his quick vow, he said, "To set up your room, you must activate the chomile." He walked to the wall on the right side of the door. "The center of the right side wall of each room is where the chomile is hidden." He pointed to where the chomile should be. "To activate the chomile, you must say this phrase: 'Show me the chomile.'" Nothing happened. He knew it wouldn't, but Holon had that questioning look again. "I cannot activate the chomile in your room. The room has mapped all command functions to your voice pattern. Only you can set up your room." He lowered his arm and signaled for her to say it.

She looked at him doubtfully, but then politely said, "Show me the chomile please." The chomile appeared where he said it would. She looked almost apologetically at him. "I thought it would be nicer to say, please," she explained.

He smiled and nodded in agreement. "Once the chomile is active, as it is now, you can ask it to create things in the room. We may have to move some of these boxes and bags around so that you can create things where you want them. You can use this pointing pen"—he picked up the pen that was created on the left side of the of the chomile panel and handed it to her—"to locate where you want things created."

He stopped directing her while she moved the pen throughout the room. Wherever the pen pointed, a red pinpoint of light could be seen. She seemed to be having a bit of fun watching the red light dance about the ceiling and walls.

He cleared his throat, pretending to be annoyed. "Anyway, you must say the word *create* and then say what you want created. So, if you want to create a wall, you would say, 'Create wall,' and the wall would be created wherever the red light was when you said the word *create*. Are you with me so far?"

She nodded. "Yes. I understand. If I say, 'Create wall—.'"

A loud, rather annoying buzzing sound was heard.

A startled Holon exclaimed, "What was that? Did I do that?"

An amused Agap calmly said, "Yes, you did. You had the pen pointed at me when you said 'Create.' Since the chomile could not create the wall with me as a starting point, the buzz sounded to let you know the chomile could not comply, and

I am very glad that it decided that I was not a proper starting place for a wall. So you will have to be aware of where you have the pen pointed when you say, 'Create.' Remember, the chomile will only respond to *your* voice."

A rather sheepish Holon nodded.

"About making walls. The default wall will always be created at a ninety-degree angle to the originating *wall.*" He emphasized the word *wall*, to Holon's chagrin. He smirked a little then continued. "The default wall will continue until it reaches a real wall, like the walls that divide the rooms." He saw a question on Holon's face and paused.

"Do you mean that the things you create with the chomile are not real?" she asked.

"They are real in the sense that you can see and touch them, but they are not matter. The chomile panel itself and the pen in your hand are not matter either." That brought a fully confused look to her face. He hastened to explain. "Think of the things that the chomile creates as solid energy fields. These fields can easily be manipulated to create, delete, and modify *apparent matter*, for the lack of a better term. The chomiles are a product of our research on teleportation." That explanation seemed to satisfy her. He continued on about the walls. "If you want to specify a particular angle of a wall, say forty-five degrees, you have to say, 'Create forty-five-degree wall to the right,' or, 'Create forty-five-degree wall to the left.' If you don't want a wall to continue to a real wall, you will have to specify the length of the wall, either with an actual measurement or with a fraction of the room size. All single rooms are one fet wide and one fet long. So, if you want to create a wall that is half the length of the room, you would say, 'Create one-half wall,' or, 'Create point five fet wall,' or even, 'Create fifty det wall.' Ready to create a wall then?"

She sighed, "Why don't you just create my walls for me?"

"I can't. You have to," he reminded her.

"Then tell me exactly what to say, and I'll say it," she suggested.

"Axi," he surrendered. "Just don't say the word *create* until you actually are ready to create, axi?"

She agreed.

"Point to where you want to create your first wall."

She pointed to the wall just outside the washroom area.

He smiled. "So do you want the wall to go all the way across the room, or do you just want it to enclose the washroom?"

"Just around the washroom please." She smiled shyly.

"Then say, 'Create washroom wall.'"

A disgusted look came over her face. "You didn't tell me I could do that! I thought I had to give a fractions or measurements!" She was practically shouting.

"That's true, but I seemed to be losing you, so I just thought we'd try a wall to let you see how fun and easy using the chomile is," he explained. That explanation only seemed to satisfy her partially.

She shook her head and said, "Create washroom wall." Immediately, a white wall appeared around the washroom area. "Oh, great. Now how do I get to the washroom? There's no door," she muttered.

"The chomile doesn't assume anything, Holu. You will have to create a door where you want one."

"How do I know where I want one? I don't remember where everything in the washroom is," she whined. Well, maybe it was more like a whimper.

"That's easy. Point to the wall, and say, 'Change color,'" he said cheerfully.

She gave a return look to him that wasn't exactly cheerful, pointed the pen at the wall, and said, "Change color." The room responded with two medium-pitched tones, the second higher than the first. The chomile display flashed repeatedly. "Now what?" she grumbled.

"Look at the display. It wants you to make a choice."

The display was showing primary colors and the word *none*.

He suggested, "Pick a color."

She chose blue. Now the display showed a multitude of different shades of blue with the word *test* at the top of the display. She smiled. He was glad to see the smile. She touched a light shade of blue. Immediately the wall around the washroom changed to that shade of blue. Now the display showed the title "Accept?" and the words *yes* and *no* below it. She touched *no*. The wall again turned white, and the display returned to the multitude of blues. "Now this I like," She said enthusiastically. "But how does this help me locate my door?"

"Say the word *cancel*."

"Cancel," said Holon obediently. Immediately, the chomile stopped flashing and the display went blank.

"Point at the wall again and say, 'Change color.'"

She pointed at the wall and said, "Change color."

Again, the two tones were heard and the display flashed. Again, the primary colors and the word *none* were displayed.

"This time, touch the word *none*," said Agap.

She smiled. He could tell that she had it now. She touched *none*. Immediately, the wall became clear. The entire washroom could now be seen through the wall.

"This is really drus. I've never seen through walls before!" she exclaimed.

"Glad you like it." He really meant that.

"Axi. So I think I'm getting the hang of it now. I can point and create a door."

The room started buzzing again.

She sighed. "How do I turn the chomile off for a while?"

He smiled slightly. "Say, 'Hide the chomile.'"

"Hide the chomile, *please!*" she exclaimed with a special emphasis on the please. The chomile disappeared. "Now, as I was saying, I can point to create a door." She paused as if waiting for the buzz sound again, but it didn't sound. "Will the chomile ask me about the door?"

He nodded.

"Axi. Then the furniture can be created in much the same way, I assume."

Again, he nodded.

"So, axi! I think I can do this on my own now. I can always call you if I run into trouble. Do the rooms have commterms?" she asked.

"You didn't bring a commterm?" he asked in a surprised tone.

"No. I don't own a mobile commterm. I always used the commterm that was in my house or my office," she said worriedly.

He smiled, holding back a laugh. It was sort of ironic that a communications specialist didn't carry a mobile commterm. He then said, "The rooms don't come with a real commterm, but you can create a sim commterm. It will work the same as a real commterm. Only you don't have to punch in commterm codes or hit buttons. Just tell the commterm who you want to call, and it will connect you. Think of it as having your own personal operator." He started for the door, and then stopped. "I'll stop by around eight parzes to pick you up for dinner, if you can wait to eat until then. The team meeting starts at nine parzes, so that should give us plenty of time to eat. That will give you a couple of parzes to finish your room and get ready since it's only twelve spens after the sixth parz now."

Holon nodded acceptance.

He went to the door and grabbed his bags. He couldn't resist one last poke of fun. "Maybe by then you will have your washroom properly hidden."

A passing couple peered curiously at him as they walked by the room.

He felt his face flush. After he watched them get into the lift he said, "I'm sorry, Holu. I didn't know anyone was in the hall."

He could tell that Holon didn't know whether to laugh at him or to bat him across the head, but she finally said, "I'll see you at eight parzes, Agapu."

Agap said, "Axi. Then at eight parzes." he then left the room, and the door closed behind him.

He had become so flustered that he turned down the hall to the right from the room. It was only after he saw the burgundy ninety-eight door and the black lift door that he realized his mistake. So, he made an about face and headed toward his room. He was thinking about embarrassing Holon. It was accidental, sure, but he should have been more careful. He did apologize though, so that should keep his conscience toward Thaoi clear. But that didn't make him feel any better. As he passed by Holon's door he thought, *There it is, room eighty-one, the scene of the crime.* He passed by her door and a blank burgundy door and then came to room seventy-seven. The blank door told everyone that passed by that room seventy-seven was a double room.

He was a bit embarrassed by the fact that he had a double room, but council members were expected to have enough room to entertain company properly. He pressed the alert button. A voice of a woman said, "There is currently no one occupying this room. Please state your full name." Agap thought, *Oh, that's very cute, guys, a woman's voice for a man's room and a man's voice for a woman's room. I can't leave my team alone for long without them creating some sort of mischief.* He responded, "Agap Jost Margon Virdod."

The voice responded, "I'm sorry. I do not recognize that name. Please repeat."

He sighed. He had only been a council member for a little over three months. He had forgotten that his full name was only one name now. "Agapoi," he said in a semi-disgusted tone.

The door opened.

He entered the room and threw his bags down on the floor. He stood and looked at the room for a moment. The room did seem awfully long. It might make a decent speedball court if he didn't put up any walls or have any appliances, fixtures, or plumbing fixtures in the way. There were also boxes in the way, quite a few boxes in fact. Then he reconsidered. *Maybe the room is not too big after all.* He had managed to gather quite a collection of books. Looking at the boxes, he suddenly felt very tired.

He said, "Show me the chomile." The chomile appeared.

He took the pen in hand and pointed at the floor in front of the first window. "Create bed."

The two tones sounded.

He turned to the chomile panel and touched the first bed he saw. A bed appeared, complete with sheets and blanket. Everything on the bed was white.

He pointed to the floor close to the bed. "Create stand."

Two tones sounded. He touched the panel without looking. A stand, all white, appeared. Agap pointed to the top of the stand.

"Create alarm clock."

Two tones sounded.

He sighed and touched the display. An alarm clock appeared, all white, except for the display, which was green.

"Hide the chomile. I'm going to take a nap."

The chomile disappeared.

Agap set the alarm display for 7:00 and climbed in bed. He was asleep before he could think of anything else.

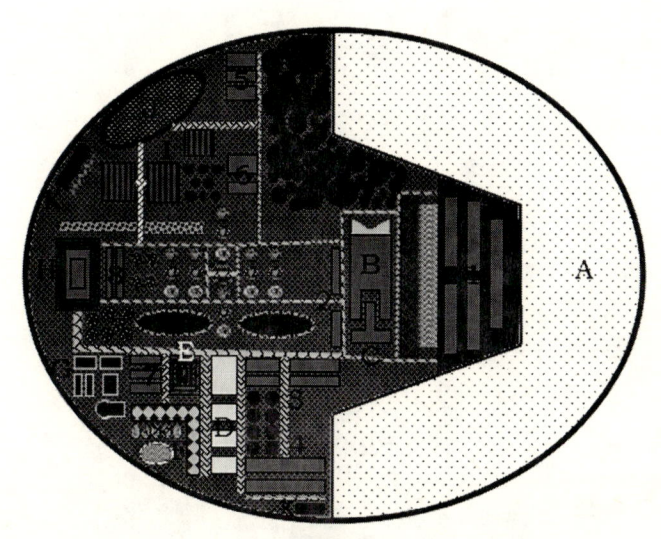

Bojoa
Legend
Numbers are Commercial Sector Numbers

A--Agrodynes
B--Living Complex
C--VIP Living Complex
D--Technology Complex
E--Adminstration Complex
F--Entertainment Complex
G--Athletic Fields
H--Recreational Complex
I--Manufacturing Complex
J--Mining Dome
K--Waste Disposal Units

3

A Slow Start

He was sitting on a bench in the gardens of Bojoa going over his notes from his first day's work. It was still early in the evening so he felt he had time. His notes showed only one real event and that was his fault.

He bent forward and fingered the scar on the right side of his neck. He couldn't remember the last time that he was spotted while working. It wasn't the subject that spotted him, but his companion. He would have to be careful when the subject was with her. She was either very observant or she got lucky. Either way it was a close call. He had stayed to the shadows of the trees so that his dark clothing would blend in, but he must have gotten careless. At least, he was sure that the subject never saw him.

Other than that, the day had been routine, even boring. The subject had left the sub, accompanied by an unidentified woman. It was the woman's first time here. He knew that because of the way she reacted to the new things that she saw. They laid on the beach, they walked in the arbor, and they went into the living complex. Nothing special to report there. It was a slow start to this assignment.

The alert on his comm sounded. He pulled it out and saw that the contact was his current employer. "I am here," he said.

The voice of his employer said, "Did you manage to board the sub that the subject took?"

"I did. I rode with the baggage. He is in a domed city called Bojoa. It appears to be underwater," he said.

"Underwater?" asked the voice incredulously.

"Yes, but I don't know where. I could see nothing from the cargo hold," he said routinely. Then he added, "He had a woman with him."

The voice replied, "This is unexpected. What did she look like?"

"She was Cirrian, of course," he began. "She was about a det shorter than the subject with a slender build. She had long hair with a touch of red highlights, and she was wearing a blue jumpsuit."

"That sounds like it might be the woman that was seen with the subject occasionally in Cirri City and Zaria," said the voice.

"It appeared that the woman was more than an acquaintance," he said. "How close was the subject watched previously?"

"Not closely," said the voice. "I want you to watch him closely though."

He ignored that last comment. He always watched his subjects closely. "The subject exhibited great familiarity with this woman. They were on the beach together and walked arm in arm in the arbor," he commented.

"I want to know more about this woman," said the voice. "Did you get close enough to hear what they were saying to each other?"

"No I couldn't risk it," he said. "The woman is observant. I will plant some listening devices in discreet locations once I learn the subject's routine."

"She didn't see you, did she?" asked the voice with concern.

"She caught a glimpse of me," he admitted. "But, that was all. The subject never saw me."

"Be careful," warned the voice, "she might be looking for you in the future."

"Don't tell me my business," he replied curtly. "She will dismiss me as her imagination. I will make sure of it."

"How are you going to do that?" asked the voice.

"That's none of your concern, let's just say that technology can make people see things. Don't make contact with me again until early tomorrow morning. I will be watching for the subject near his quarters and I won't be able to talk," he said forcefully. "And don't use your commterm again. Once is more than enough. Get an unregistered comm, like I have. We certainly don't need to be seeing each other's face anyway. Until you get the comm, leave a message for me at the living complex's lobby counter."

"What name should I leave the message under," asked the voice.

"Leave it under *Ketesku*," he said.

"*Ketesku?* Doesn't that mean *spy* in the old tongue?" asked the voice.

"Yes, fortunately counter clerks don't know that," he said and ended the communication.

His employer paid well, but he took too many chances. Registered comms carry a contact history should someone become interested. He didn't know what his employer was thinking by using a commterm. There are two signals to track with those, a video and an audio signal. Audio only signals are far more discreet. He should know, discretion was his life.

⁂

Agap awoke when he heard what sounded like a cricket, a very loud cricket somewhere in the room. He sat up suddenly, too suddenly, the spinning, all-white room made him wonder if he was upright or not. After a tic or two, the feeling subsided and Agap could see the room clearly. The sound seemed to be coming from the table beside him. He looked and saw the alarm clock and then realized that the sound was coming from the clock. He should have looked closer at the type of alarm he chose instead of just picking the first thing he saw. The sound of that alarm was confusing when first waking up. He reached over and turned off the alarm. He checked the clock for the time, and it read 7:00. As he looked, the display changed to 7:01. He must not have awakened right away with the alarm.

He stood up, trying to decide what he should do first. Should he set up his room or take a shower first? Maybe he should unpack his clothes. *Well, I can't do that yet. There's no dresser,* he thought. He glanced at the clock. It read 7:02. Apparently, he still wasn't awake yet since a spen went by before he could decide what he needed to do.

He decided to set up his room or at least create a dresser. "Show me the chomile," he said.

The chomile appeared. He stepped over to the chomile, took the pointing pen from the side of the chomile, went back over to the bed, and sat down. He pointed the pen at the floor near the wall by the bed.

"Create dresser," he said.

Two tones sounded. He sighed when he realized that he had to get up. He had forgotten that he had to choose a dresser

A Slow Start

style. He glanced at the clock. Another spen had passed. He got up and went over to the chomile. The panel displayed the title, "How many drawers?" Under it, there were choices for numbers one through thirty. *Who would need thirty drawers in a dresser? Does anyone make a thirty-drawer dresser?* he thought. He thought that someone might make a thirty-drawer dresser. *But what would a twenty-nine-drawer dresser even look like?* He pressed the button for five drawers. Now the title displayed was, "How tall?" The options were eight and one-half dets, nine dets, nine and a quarter dets, nine and one-half dets, ten dets, ten and one-half dets, and eleven dets. He looked at the options. He stood about eleven dets tall, eleven and a half dets to be exact. Did he want a dresser that stood nearly as tall as he did? He probably didn't. Most dressers were in the nine-det range. He decided to touch the nine and one-half dets option. Now the title was, "Choose style." *Finally,* Agap thought, *the last choice.* He looked at the panel. There were a lot of styles to choose from, about thirty of them. He chose one that had handles that would allow him to open the drawer palm up. The dresser appeared. It was all white. He opened and closed the drawers. The handles seemed convenient to him. That was one thing he did love about the chomile. It didn't ask you to name the style you wanted; it showed it to you. The images of the style would get bigger when your hand paused over the style. The dresser he had created would do fine. It appeared to be just about the right height for convenience. So, that job was done.

 The clock read 7:05. It took two spens for the dresser, and nothing is colored yet. This might take longer than he thought. At least he had a dresser created, but it really did need color.

 He pointed the pen at the dresser and said, "Change color."

 Two tones sounded. The panel showed pictures of his

dresser with different wood tones and other colors. He chose what he thought might be a wood tone of chirrud wood. He liked the deep reddish color. Instantly, the dresser was the color of a deep reddish wood with silver handles. Maybe the handles would be better in lotan. The deep yellow metal might look rather nice with the darker wood. Agap glanced at the clock. It read 7:05, but the display changed to six spens after during his glance. He was wasting time. *Who cares what the dresser looks like right now?* he asked himself. He could always change it whenever he wanted. Silver handles would do for now.

He looked around his room. It had two washroom areas, one of them right in the middle of the room, without any walls. That looked rather strange. There was only one cooking area that needed to be walled. He decided he at least needed to set up some walls around the washrooms.

He pointed to the wall where the windows were located and said, "Create wall."

A loud buzz sounded. He moved over to the place where he had pointed and looked back across the room. The wall he requested would have gone through the middle of the washroom.

That was silly. What was I thinking? he asked himself. He pointed to the wall again and this time said, "Create washroom wall."

This time, a wall was created, not exactly where he was pointing but where it needed to be in order to go perfectly from the wall to the back of the washroom and around it.

He pointed to the wall he just created and said, "Change color."

The two tones sounded, and he walked over to the chomile panel and chose the *none* button. The walls were now see-through.

He confirmed his choice and then pointed to the part of the washroom wall that faced his bed and said, "Create door."

Two tones sounded. Agap turned back to the chomile and chose the door style. The door appeared. Of course, it was white. Agap proceeded to color the door the chirrud tone and to color the walls a light green. No. He decided to make them a medium blue.

"Hide the chomile," he said. The chomile hid itself. He checked the clock and saw that only a couple of spens had passed since his last check. Good. He still had ninety-two spens before he had to be at Holon's door.

He ignored the fact that the other washroom still had no walls. At least no one could see it from the front door now. He did like the room much better in blue, but the bed stand and clock really stuck out since they were still all white. There would be time to deal with that later. He grabbed his suitcases and began to put his clothes in the dresser. To his dismay, he had more clothes than he had room in his dresser. It then occurred to him that he could have created a closet. There was no time to worry about that now. He threw his suitcases on the bed and grabbed a change of underclothes and some grooming aids, and then he headed to the washroom.

The washroom's inside walls were still all white. Agap thought that that was just as well since the washroom fixtures were white. The fixtures were real, not bands of solidified energy, so their color could not be changed with the chomile. He reasoned that a bit of color would be brought into the washroom when he unpacked his accessories. The washroom wasn't fancy at all, nor that spacious; but it allowed a person to do what must be done in a washroom. He guessed that the room was about nineteen or twenty dets long and about fifteen dets wide. It had the basic amenities: a personal waste disposal, or PWD as some dubbed it; a sink; an air jet shower; and a tub. The ceiling over the washroom areas and the cooking areas had lighting built-in, so he didn't need any other lighting for the washroom unless he wanted some over the mirror. Just then, it hit him that there was something missing: a mirror. This stood to reason since the wall had just been made. He was beginning to think that maybe having everyone set up their own rooms might need to be rethought. The setup process may be a bit more time consuming than the team had anticipated.

The chomile will be a good thing to bring up in tonight's team meeting, Agap thought as he exited the washroom and tossed his things on the bed.

"Show me the chomile," he said to the air.

The chomile appeared. Agap grabbed the pen and went back into the washroom. As he looked at the sink, he decided it needed a cabinet around the sink. He pointed to the sink and said, "Create cabinet."

Two tones sounded. He grumbled to himself that maybe the choice menu might not be as great of an idea as he thought. As he exited the washroom again, he thought that maybe making the chomile panel portable, like the pen, instead of part of the wall would be a good idea. Someone really should have thought of that, but the team was so pressed for time to get the system up and running that no one took the time to properly demo the thing. He made his cabinet choices and went back into the washroom. A white vanity was now around the sink. That would do for now, but he really did need a mirror.

He pointed at the wall above the sink and said, "Create mirror."

Two tones sounded. Agap went back to the panel and made his choice, a mirror without a frame, just big enough to see his face, shoulders, and midsection. He would finally be able to finish getting ready now.

"Hide the chomile."

A loud buzz filled the room.

He realized he was still holding the pen. He replaced the pen on the chomile and said, "Hide the chomile."

The chomile disappeared.

Clock read 7:11. Axi. There was still plenty of time to get ready. He went into the washroom and promptly came back out when he realized that his underclothes and grooming aids were still on the bed. He picked up his things and went back into the washroom.

As he hurried to get ready, his thoughts once again drifted to the mysterious all-council session called for the next day. Just what could have happened to necessitate this meeting, and how could it be that no one knew what had happened? It certainly was a mystery.

4
THE FIRST ENCOUNTER

Holon sighed and sat down in the chair she had just created. She had spent the better part of two parzes setting up her room, and she still wasn't quite finished. Agapu had made it seem like fun; but truthfully, she would rather have had the room, whatever the color, whatever the style, ready for her when she arrived. Then she could have spent some time resting instead of pointing and choosing and choosing some more. Setting up wasn't too bad at first. She could stay by the panel to get a lot of the things created. She set up walls for her washroom, bedroom, and cooking room; and then she had to create things inside those walls. It was great having exercise, but she'd rather the exercise not be a constant movement to a room and then back to the panel. If each one of her trips was a marble, she thought she'd have a large jar full of marbles by now. Still, as she looked around the main room where she was sitting, she did have to admit that she did like the living space that she had created. It had a nice, comfortable feel to it, not too casual, not too elegant. She still had to do some little things in the bedroom, and she hadn't set up her dining area by the cooking room just yet; but that could wait. Agap probably had his room set up by now and would wonder why she hadn't finished yet.

When the thought of Agapu crossed her mind, she had to smile. He was very successful, very talented, and very attractive. She thought herself fortunate that he, as great a figure as he would be, no, as he was, wanted to share his life with her.

Agapu was indeed already a great figure. She could remember the first time she had seen him. He was about to give a commencement address at the College of Communications at Cirri City. It was the commencement ceremony for her graduating class. He was quite a figure even then. She was twenty-five then. That would have made Agapu...let's see...forty. He was all decked out in robes and honorary decorations. He looked splendid. The robe was dark blue and served a great contrast to all the gold, silver, and red chords, ribbons, and medals that adorned the robe. His trousers matched his robe perfectly. His white, high-collared sark with maroon neck wrap made for a perfect blend of color near his perfectly proportioned face. His pale skin was without blemish, and his yellow-white hair was cut to perfection. He was dashing. The only flaw was his left shoe. The shoes were elegant enough, black with small, gold buckles across the top of the shoe; but there was a small, yet visible, white scuffmark on the top of the left shoe, near the toe. As she had watched him, he must have tried to use the back of the right leg of his trousers to wipe away the scuff at least a half dozen times to no avail. She laughed at the thought of him glancing down at the shoe in disgust several times while watching the ceremonies.

She remembered the college president's introduction of him, then known as Agap Jost Virdod. The list of accomplishments that he had compiled was staggering back then. The president must have taken five spens just to list them. And with every item that was listed, Agapu grew more uncomfortable. You could clearly see his white face turn red. Then the red color in his face was gone, as if by magic, when he stood up to speak. It was as if he had commanded his skin to return to normal and it instantly obeyed.

As great of an impression that the first sight of Agapu had been for her, the one that really impressed her was the night he first spoke to her about two years ago. It was at the communications and technology seminar. The seminar was her first speaking engagement in Cirri City, and Agap Jost Margon Virdod was the keynote speaker for the seminar's technology community. By happy happenstance, she was to precede Agapu in that day's schedule. He had come in with an entourage of associates, whom she later learned to call "Agap's team." The schedule had been modified that day to include a previously unscheduled session, and he had arrived early, just as the speaker in front of her had finished. Through error and some assumption, no one informed him of the schedule change. When the speaker finished, he made his way on to the stage at the same time she was arriving on the stage. Not being one to waste time, he went straight to the chair to the right of the podium, meant for the next speaker while the host of the seminar made the introduction. Of course, she had recognized him immediately and yielded without hesitation. But as Thaoi had planned, he saw her retreat off the stage. When the host stood up to announce the next speaker, she noticed that the host had quickly put the top card on the podium and was ready to read from the next card. That's when Agapu did it. He interrupted the host and strode to the podium. She would never forget what he said.

The First Encounter

First, he said to the host, "Forgive me, honorable host. May I have the honor of introducing our next speaker?" The host was, of course, caught off-guard; but what was he to say to someone like Agap? He graciously acquiesced and pointed to the card on the podium. He picked up the card, glanced at it, and put it face down on the podium. He looked at her and made a slight gesture with his head toward the chair to the right of the podium. She was rather surprised and, quite frankly, terrified, but managed to make it to the chair without incident. Once she was seated, he continued. "Our next speaker graduated at the top of her class from the Communications College of Cirri City. She has since been involved in five projects on the cutting edge of her field. She is imminently qualified in three communications disciplines and is recognized as a rising star in her field. She has just been awarded a third name for her pioneering work in the field of visual satellite communications. As I understand it, she has been able to reduce the lag time of this type of communication to microtics. Please give a warm welcome to our esteemed colleague, Holon Tapienus Arkita."

She recalled how startled she was by the mention of her third name. Her name was not yet published by the nomenclature committee, although she had been informed. It was at that point that she realized that Agapu had noticed her sometime in the past. Later, she learned that the academic dean of her college had mentioned something about her to him and pointed her out before the graduation ceremony.

Then, when she had come up to speak, Agapu whispered in her ear to meet with him after he had finished his speech. She nodded to him, and she remembered the smile crossed his face when she did. It was all academic after that. He proposed to her about a year and a half later and became her Agapu.

She glanced at her watch. It was time to start thinking about getting ready for Agapu's arrival. He would, no doubt, be punctual. She smiled again, thinking of his obvious embarrassment earlier as he was leaving. Knowing him, he was probably just embarrassed about embarrassing her. She did not even see the people that passed him in the hall, so she was not really embarrassed by the remark. She did adore how Agapu was always so concerned about her feelings.

His faithful adherence to the way of conscience was the thing she most admired about him. His love for Thaoi was clear. Thaoi had taught him to love as no man could learn to love on his own. There was no doubt that he loved her more than any mortal had ever loved her. She knew that she was indeed fortunate to be his Holu. She could only hope that she could one day learn to love as Agapu loved.

5
Faces

All she could see was a fine white mist, but she knew it was a place that welcomed her. It was an old friend that she had seen many times before. She found relaxation for her mind and body here. The mist caressed her as if she were its child. She felt that she belonged to the mist and the mist belonged to her.

Many delights waited patiently for her here. She would forget them when she was away, but she knew them well when she returned. In the mist, she could bound and play as if she were a little girl again and her body never tired. She had known love, joy and contentment in this place of serenity. She settled herself effortlessly into the mist waiting for the delights that she knew so well to come to her.

She waited expectantly for what seemed like forever, but none of the delights that had welcomed her here before came to her. Her expectation turned toward anxiety. Her mind became disquieted, and the muscles in her body twitched. She tried to turn her mind toward serenity again, but her mind would not be comforted. She became aware of the tensions that she knew in other places creeping into the mist and the mist turned from white to grey.

She had known many tensions in other places, and she wondered which of them was about to visit her. The grey mist that now surrounded her started to pulsate. She knew what the pulses meant. A tension had overpowered her mind and was about to manifest itself in the mist.

The mist became a window into another place and another time. Gradually, the pulses faded with the mist and she saw images, blurred and indistinct at first, but then the images became increasingly clearer.

Her muscles twitched as the mist transformed into a scene that was familiar from elsewhere. She was in a hallway which she knew should be white but the hallway walls took on a grayish tone as did most the people that she passed in the hall. Everyone in the hall was wearing lab coats that also should have been white. The hallway was long, she walked and walked never coming to its end.

Her mind recognized the people that she passed in the hall, but they didn't seem to know she was there. As she watched the people pass by, she noticed that some of them looked peculiar to her. It wasn't their clothing, as everyone was wearing the lab coats and the expected clothing underneath. It wasn't the way they walked. They all walked with a familiar gait. The difference was in their expressions. Some of the people had expressions of purpose. Some of them had expressions of humor. Some of them had a bored expression on their faces. None of these seemed peculiar to her. It was those that had no expression at all that stood out from the others.

Then one of the expressionless people looked directly at her. She felt her muscles tighten noticeably. The eyes of the person were dark and had no pupils; or the pupil had swallowed the eyes' irises. She couldn't decide which it was. But this she did know. The eyes were an empty void. It was as if there was no one behind the eyes.

Suddenly, she found herself surrounded by a multitude of people whose eyes were empty. All of the eyes stared at her. She felt she was losing herself in their stare. The feeling terrified her. She closed her eyes, but it didn't help. She started to run with her eyes closed, but she could still feel the empty eyes draining her very soul away. She opened her eyes and saw only a speck of light in the distance ahead of her. She ran as fast as she could and when she was close enough, she lunged at the small glimmer of light.

Now there were flickers of light around her. The flickers turned into pulses. The pulses then stopped and she realized that she was in a grey mist. The mist lightened and became white. She was back in the white mist.

Her muscles that were tired from running relaxed, her mind became calm. Again, all was well.

But as she spent time in the mist, she realized that the delights had again betrayed her. They were not coming to fill the whiteness, because the mist around her was dimming into grey once again. Again the pulses came and again the pulses gave way to a slow developing image.

She did not want to know what images were going to develop so she chose to see darkness. As she held her eyes tightly shut she became aware of noises. That was strange because she never before recalled noises in this place. She recalled only voices reaching her ears in this place before. The noises were faint and she couldn't identify them. The noises made her feel uneasy, but she felt herself walking toward them despite her discomfort.

A BEACON OF HOPE

As she walked, the noises became louder, until it became apparent and that the noises were crashes and bangs. A particularly loud crash made her open her eyes. She saw a window in front of her. It was close and she should have been able to see through it, but she could see nothing. The noises persisted and even grew louder. She could no longer help herself. She walked to the window put her face close to it. A chair hurtled toward her face. It hit the window with such force that she felt the window vibrate, but it did not break. After the chair fell to the floor on the other side of the window, she saw people.

They were people that she knew. They were running toward her. They came to the window and started pounding on it. She wanted to help them but felt powerless to do so. The people all were frantic with fear.

She looked behind the people that were at the window and saw creatures that she also knew. The creatures looked like men and women, but she knew they were not what they seemed to be. These creatures were chasing people around the room, tossing heavy furniture aside as if the furniture was made of foam. The people were running and screaming, but she could not hear their screams. She only saw the screams. When a creature caught one of the people, it tore the person apart as if they were paper. She then realized that the floor was covered in blood. It was the blood of the people that were torn asunder.

She was horrified yet couldn't look away. It was as if the horror beckoned her gaze and kept her spellbound. She then became aware of a huge creature that was not in the room, yet she could see his silhouette. The creature seemed to be looking directly at her. Her pulse quickened as the thought of this creature seeing her was more horrifying than the scene she witnessed in the room behind the window. She stepped back from the window, but she still saw the huge creature looking at her.

The creature then pointed to the window in front of her. She looked as the people that were pounding on the window were pulled away one by one by the creatures in the room. The faces of these people stared at her as they were plucked apart by the fearsome creatures. The faces looked at her even after the bodies of the people were scattered in pieces about the room. She knew that she would remember these faces even when she left for another place. These faces would haunt her very soul.

She closed her eyes to try to block out the faces, but the huge creature greeted her in the darkness. She felt the creature reaching toward her. She felt the creature grab her throat and pull her up to his dark face. She couldn't move. She couldn't breathe. She couldn't resist as the creature said, "Look into my eyes." She felt her soul being drawn into the creature. She was losing herself and becoming something else. She screamed as she realized that she was going into nothingness and tried one last effort to free herself from the creatures grasp.

Her body hit the floor with a thud. She then became aware of pain. The pain came from her bottom, but it was minor. She opened her eyes and she saw her quarters. The sight of her bedroom made the memories of the mist fade into obscurity. She knew that she had just had a horrific dream, but the details soon faded. The more she tried to remember, the faster the memories fled. But, she knew that she had had that nightmare before. She knew because of the faces. The terrified faces staring at her still remained strongly in her mind. The faces were from her past. They were from many years ago when she was a much younger woman. She was approaching middle age now. Then, she was more of a girl then a woman.

She was sitting on the floor by her bed. She had often found herself out of her bed when she had that nightmare. She felt a bit out of breath as if she had held her breath for a period of time. She took deep breaths until the desire for air dissipated.

She wondered what time it was, so she turned to see the clock that was on her nightstand above her. It was nearly time to get up. The pain in her hinder parts made getting up a chore, but she managed to slowly come to her feet. She turned off the alarm that was about to go off and walked over to the vanity and turned on the light.

The light, blinded her at first, but soon she could see her reflection in the mirror. She flicked the ends of her short red hair as she thought of the faces that continually haunted her. Those people died so long ago, but it seemed like it was just yesterday to her.

Her eyes looked bloodshot. The redness made her grey eyes look old. She must not have gotten much real rest last night. Nightmares were a common thing for her ever since the day she saw those people die. She couldn't remember that much about that day, but she remembered those faces. Those faces never seemed to go away for long.

She had bought a book by Lidar Tombun. The book told of his famous relaxation exercise. The exercise was reported to give a person a restful sleep if one performed it close to their bedtime. She decided that she would give it a try this evening.

Laysa wouldn't approve since the exercise involved what she would call dangerous spirit guides, but the book portrayed them as mentors that assisted each individual mind to find its own quiet place. It seemed harmless, besides Laysa didn't have to know.

She took one last look at her bloodshot eyes. Laysa was a good friend, but she could be kind of old fashioned. It was time to try something a little more cutting edge. It was time to banish the nightmares and get a good night's sleep.

6
An Out-of-building Experience

The clock read 7:97. It was nearly time to meet Holon. Agap looked about his still-mostly-unfinished room. At least he had chosen colors for the bed and stand and had replaced that annoying clock with one that had a decent alarm sound. He also was creative with the tile flooring, creating a very nice tile for the washroom and cooking areas. He had also created a mostly blue rug that had a few other colors subtly mixed into the fabric. He thought it looked quite nice. He also created a rather long bookcase that dominated the main area, although he hadn't actually taken the time to put his books on it yet. Of course, he created a nice, comfortable chair so he would have a place to read his books. There was a lot yet to do, but he was satisfied with the room so far.

He went to the washroom mirror to check his hair and outfit. He had chosen a medium blue dinner jacket. Holon liked him in blue.

Once he saw that everything seemed to be in place, he headed out the door and down the hall. He arrived at Holon's door and checked his watch. It was 7:99:61. He supposed that being less than half a spen early was not bad, so he pushed the alert button. He didn't have long to wait. Holon walked out the door and greeted him with a hug. The smell of flower blossoms greeted Agap. The scent seemed to make the hug that much more pleasurable. Then Agap looked at Holon with concern in his heart.

"You know there is an answer button you could have used to find out who was at the door," chided Agap.

"Oh, don't be silly. I knew it was you. You're always on time."

Agap smiled. He didn't know if he was actually *always* exactly on time, but he accepted the compliment.

He noticed that Holon looked past him for a tic. "Look, there!" she shouted suddenly pointing in the hallway behind him.

He snapped his head around quickly, but he didn't see anything. He looked back at Holon who had a puzzled look on her face. "What am I supposed to see?" he asked as he turned back toward her.

She looked behind him again. Her forehead creased with doubt as she shook her head slowly. "I thought I saw—" She cut off abruptly. She then took a deep breath and said, "I guess I was mistaken." She tried to sound nonchalant, but she didn't pull it off very well.

"What did you think you saw?" he asked.

Holon hesitated answering.

He started to become troubled for her, so he said softly, "It's axi, Holu. Tell me what you thought you saw."

She pressed her lips together and gave a half shrug of her shoulders. "It's silly," she said finally.

"But, I like silly," he said trying to coax her.

"I thought I saw the same man that I saw in the arbor

standing in the hall behind you," she blurted. Then she stood looking toward the bottom of her door with her arms crossed.

There was an awkward silence. He wanted to reassure her, but he couldn't think of how right away.

"See, I told you it was silly," said Holon, breaking the silence. She was still looking down at the base of her door.

"No, it's not silly," he said hoping that he would know what to say next. "You're in a new place. You're going to be working on a new team. You had a scare this afternoon. It's only natural that your mind might bring back the image that frightened you. You've had a lot to take in today."

Holon smiled a small smile and said, "You're probably right. She turned to face him and her smile grew larger. "The chomile didn't help with my stress level either," she said in an almost accusing tone.

That was more like the Holon that he knew. "Step back, and let me take a look at you," he said with what he just knew was a silly smile on his face.

Holon was wearing a bluish green dress. He was not very good at the names of colors and wasn't exactly sure how to name this color, but it was quite pretty. The dress had rather short, loose-fitting sleeves that were intricately laced in white and that same bluish green. That lacing was also apparent around the neck, the waist and the bottom of the dress. Below the bust, the dress hung loosely, coming just to the top of Holon's shoes. Holon had worn her reddish-blonde hair up tonight with seven braids of hair hanging down the side and back of her head. As always, she was a vision.

"You're as stunning as ever, my dear," he said with a slight bow.

Holu actually blushed slightly as she gave a quick giggle.

She then gave him a gentle shove. "Let's go, before someone real sees you bowing to me," she said lightly.

As they walked toward the lift, he noticed that she seemed taller tonight. Her eyes reached about to his upper lip. He looked more closely at her shoes. The shoes were a green color, very close to the color of the dress, and they had a small, lacey bow in a darker green on top. The heels of the shoes were narrow and were six or maybe seven bits tall. Holon didn't usually wear heels that high; but it was her first night in the dome, and she probably wanted to look especially elegant. She had accomplished that indeed. She seemed to float along as she walked.

They came to the lift, and Agap pressed the call button. Holon looked at him, and he couldn't help but smile. Her smile grew wider in response to his smile. He must look like a smiling idiot when he was with her, but he couldn't help it. The lift door came open, and they stepped inside.

Within the confines of the lift, Holon's scent was intensified. Holon always wore just a hint of a flowery perfume. He didn't know what kind it was, but it certainly smelled good on her. Agap shook himself from her scent. She was now looking curiously at him.

"What did you want for dinner tonight?" he asked, having recovered from his daze. He put his right hand above the lift panel in readiness.

"You choose. I don't have anything in particular in mind."

"Would some Northern Cargagru cuisine be axi?"

"That sounds perfect." She smiled and squeezed his left arm.

He paused for a moment. "I believe there is a Cargagru restaurant in commercial sector eight," he said as he punched in the code ComSec8 and hit the green button. The translift began to move up; then to the right; and then, when the lift started to move forward, there was a slight bump, and the sil-

An Out-of-Building Experience

ver sides were raised into the top of the lift, leaving clear walls all around. The lights inside the lift had turned off as well. They were out of the living complex, moving toward some commercial buildings at a height of nearly five hundred dets—495.7 dets to be exact—from the floor of the dome. Agap didn't know why the exact height of the junction leaving the LC stuck in his mind, but it did.

The look on Holon's face was one of surprise at first, and then an expression of wonder came across her face. After a moment, she said, "I didn't realize the lift could go outside the building. Oh my. Look at that garden! It's all lit up with colored lights. From this height, you can see the patterned shapes of the walkways and flower beds. How high are we, Agapu?"

"About five fets." He had rounded off the measurement for the sake of simplicity.

"Are we flying?" she asked, looking all around for what supported the lift.

"No. We are suspended on a pair of iri wires. Iri allows us to create thin but very strong wires. These two wires can support as much weight as a ten-bit-thick pirru cable," he said, stretching his first finger and thumb about to their limit to illustrate the diameter.

"I can't see the wires." She was looking intently upward.

"You'll be able to see the wires between the junction and the translift tube when we descend far enough. It's hard to make out the wires against the dome, even when the dome is simulating sunlight. And the dome is simulating moonlight right now," he said as the translift began to descend.

As she looked up she said, "Oh. I see," as the translift reached the junction and a slight bump was felt.

At that point, the sides of the lift started to come back down from the hiding place at the top of the lift and the lights turned back on inside the lift.

"The wires really are thin. I wouldn't have thought that they could support a lift box as well as passengers."

"Yes. Iri lets us do some wonderful things," he said with a hint of excitement in his voice. The possibilities of iri always excited him. They seemed endless.

The lift stopped, and the doors opened. In front of them stood a line of shops and restaurants. They exited the lift, and he led Holon to the left.

"I believe that Gultirru's Restaurant serves excellent Northern Cargagru cuisine," he said, pointing to the restaurant building about six buildings down.

As they walked toward the restaurant, Holon remarked, "I must say that I am impressed, Agapu. You seem to have created a complete mini city down here. It has everything Cirri City has and more."

"Why, thank you, Holu. I am glad you approve," he said sincerely, not sarcastically.

They had come to the restaurant, and he held the door for her.

As Holon walked by, she smiled and said, "Now, about that chomile thing..."

He could only smile. He imagined this dinner conversation might prove to be quite spirited. He followed her into the restaurant, nodding as she talked; and he loved every tic of it.

7

The Team

Yotux was a petite young woman who was well liked by all who knew her. She had a way of brightening people's lives by her presence. Her effervescence of spirit shined forth through her lively blue eyes. Her willingness to assist others in any way she could was unmatched by anyone else on the team. But it was her attention to detail and motivational talent that caused Agapoi to promote her to assistant team lead fifteen years ago. Until that time, Agapoi had no assistant team lead.

At Yotux's request, Agapoi's team was assembled in the team meeting area. The meeting area consisted of desks complete with dataterms. The desks faced a large desk called the speaking desk, which had its own term embedded in the top of the desk so that the speaker could view it without it being in the sightline of the team members. Behind the speaking desk was a wall of large, glass windows, interrupted only by a windowed door in the center of the wall. On the other side of the windows was the large tech lab, which housed a wide array of devices used to monitor and test technical systems, design technologies, and create test devices for new or existing technologies. To one side of the desks and speaking desk was Agapoi's office. It was a large room with a large desk, several guest chairs, an entertainment area, and a connecting washroom. A large window allowed Agapoi to see into the meeting room from his desk. The office could be accessed by two solid wood doors. One door was to the left of the window, which was adjacent to the guest chairs in front of the large desk in the office, while the other door was to the right of the window and opened into the entertainment area of the office. To the other side of the desks and speaking desk in the meeting area were rows of dataterms that could display an array of data types. Behind the desks was a refreshment area where a variety of food and beverages were available for the team. In addition, there were café-style tables and chairs in the refreshment area.

Yotux was looking forward to seeing Agapoi in person again. He had contacted her and the rest of the team often during his absence, but it just wasn't' the same as him being here. She felt a closeness to him despite his absence of over three months. The years she had worked closely with him brought a feeling of great familiarity. It wasn't that their relationship was personal, but she held out hope that one day it might become personal. She didn't think that any two people could be closer on a professional level than they were.

Agapoi had just been appointed as the newest member of the technology council. She thought the appointment was well-deserved even though he was still a young man. The last time that she saw him he was known simply as Agap. Her biggest concern was to try to make sure that she remembered to use his new honorific name. So she was trying to think of him as Agapoi in her mind.

The team sat and stood around the tables and chairs of the refreshment area, except for Supeb, who was sitting at his meeting desk, reading from a nona and jotting down notes. Supeb was not a tall man, but he had broad shoulders. Like all Cirrians, he had a shade of blonde hair, his being a darker blonde. Like all of Agapoi's team he was younger than Agapoi, but he acted as if he were in his middle years. He had sharp, gray eyes that seemed to look through the nona instead of at it. He was a serious person who didn't like to engage in a lot of needless chatter.

The polar opposite of Supeb was Eutay. He was a gregarious young man that saw humor in life. It wasn't that he was always joking. Agapoi wouldn't have a team member that didn't have a serious side. But he tried to find humor where he could. When there was a lull in conversation, he could generally be counted on to try to fill the void. There was such a lull now as the team waited for Agapoi. She could see that his mind was searching for something to say. Finally he said, "There is something very ironic about the new showers that we have here in Bojoa."

No one responded immediately to Eutay's foray into light conversation, so she felt obliged to respond. "How's that?" she asked.

"Well, think about it," he said. "The shower doesn't use water, and what is all over and around us?"

She smiled and said, "Water." She noticed that she was joined in the answer by Opsil. Opsil was just out of college. At age twenty-seven, he was the youngest member of Agapoi's young team.

Eutay's attempt at conversation failed however, as nothing ensued from his remark. The team members stared at their drinks and played with their food. No one was really in a talkative mood. The pending all-council meeting in Bojoa weighed heavily on everyone's mind right now. The mood could best be described as reflective. She noticed that Eutay made his way into the restroom since no one took up any conversation.

A couple of spens of silence passed. She was beginning to wonder if no one would talk until Agapoi arrived.

"Twenty-two more spens until Agapoi arrives with our new team member," Kowtsom announced suddenly. Kowtsom was standing between the desks and the tables. She was of an average height for a Cirrian woman and had medium blonde hair with soft, bluish gray eyes. Apparently she had had enough of the silence. That wasn't surprising since she loved to talk, especially about other people.

The announcement made everyone look up at the clock. The display read 8:78. Indeed, it was twenty-two spens until nine parzes.

Supeb glanced up from his work. "I guess I should wrap this up then. Agapoi is going to want to cover a lot of ground."

Kowtsom smiled. "But with whom. I saw him with a woman earlier today. She was a very attractive woman at that. They were heading to the LC lobby. I waved, but Agapoi seemed to have his attention on the lady."

She tried to ignore that remark, but Kowtsom did have a knack of knowing things about people that others didn't. Her heart sunk just a little to picture Agapoi socializing with a woman.

"Maybe that was our new team member," said Phunex at a volume that was a bit louder that most people speak conversationally. The team members supposed she had a hearing problem that caused her to speak loudly, although none of them had any other evidence to suggest it. She was a taller woman with a stocky frame. Her hair was nearly white; and she had green eyes, which were not that common in Cirri.

Phunex did have a point. No one knew whom Agapoi was bringing in, not even her. All she knew was the new member was a communications specialist. She hoped that that was all that Kowtsom had seen—if indeed, she truly saw what she thought she saw.

"Are you guys talking about our new team member? Agapoi hasn't said much about who it would be. Does someone know something?" questioned Eutay, who had just returned to the area. His dark blue eyes darted about the team, hoping for a reply.

"Naw. We don't know anything," Phunex said still rather loudly. "Kowtsom just said she saw Agapoi with someone earlier. It could have been anyone, even someone Agapoi met on the sub. He never said he was traveling in with the newbie anyway."

Axopen piped in, "How about it, Kowtsom? Did you see if they went into the translift together?" Axopen fancied himself an amateur investigator at times. He seemed to enjoy separating fact from fiction, especially if it made him look superior to someone else. He was above average in height. He used a heavy hair product to hold his darker blonde hair in place, which made his hair look even darker. The gel in his hair also made his hair do some humorous things at times. He could almost be mistaken for an Ispra because of the gel if not for his pale Cirrian complexion.

"Unfortunately, no. There were too many people milling about the LC to get close. I didn't even see if they went into the LC together," admitted Kowtsom.

"So, there is no evidence that this woman is anything more than an acquaintance," Axopen said, trying to sound like a judge.

"Ah, come on, Axopen. You're always taking the fun out of everything," complained Kowtsom.

Kowtsom was right. Axopen could be a killjoy at times, but this time he had actually brightened her mood. "Personally, I don't care who comes with him. Agapoi hasn't been here in nearly four months. I for one am not too afraid to admit that I miss him," she said.

"Kowtsom says that you have a thing for Agapoi, Yotux," teased Opsil.

Opsil reminded her of a child by the way he teased. He had the face of a child. He even wore his golden colored hair longer, as if he were a child. Cirrian males traditionally cut their hair shorter when they passed adolescence. To top it off his eyes twinkled with the energy of a child. So, she addressed him as if they both were children. "Oh, come on, Opsil. Even you should know better than to believe everything Kowtsom says." She felt bad as soon as she said it. She didn't want her jab at Kowtsom to be the last thing she said so she added, "I like working with Agapoi, nothing more."

It was very unlike her to say anything disparaging to anyone. She felt the eyes of the rest of the team resting upon her. She wished that she could have her words back, but it was too late now for that. Her face became hot with shame. She bowed her head toward the floor to hide her red face, but she feared that the redness of her skin would show though her bright blonde hair. Her emotions had got the better of her. She held no animosity toward Opsil or Kowtsom, but she didn't know how to tell them that at the moment.

Supeb of all people came to her rescue by saying, "The whole team has missed him. He is the head of our team. And I am looking forward to seeing him too. Maybe he can shed some light on this mysterious meeting Odanoi has called. Think of it. All the councils have come here for a meeting. Here, not Cirri City. Something's going on," Supeb said earnestly.

"Leave it to you to state the obvious," Eutay said. "We know. Some of us just choose not to dwell on such things all the time."

Suddenly, Phunex stood up. The rest of the team looked at her. Then she said in a surprisingly subdued voice, "Hey, what time is it?"

Supeb said, "8:80. Why?"

"I just saw the security light at the lobby entrance go green. Agapoi must... I don't believe it." Her voice became uncharacteristically soft at the last. She stood motionless, with her mouth open.

Everyone stood up and looked in the direction Phunex was looking. The reaction was unanimous. Everyone had varying degrees of open mouths. They all saw something that they had no clue they would see. They saw Agapoi, twenty spens early, which was unusual; but that is not what caused the open mouths. Agapoi was walking into the far side of the lab, holding hands with a woman, a very elegantly dressed, very attractive woman.

The woman was dressed in an old style formal dress in a beautiful shade of turquoise. The dress didn't gather at the waist, but flowed freely off the bust line. It had puffy medium length sleeves and the dress was laced with white intertwined with turquoise patterns. As soon as she saw the dress, her heart sank into the pit of her stomach. There was only one reason that a young woman would wear an old style formal dress. It announced that she was no longer available to men. The woman was someone's intended, and she wanted everyone on the team to know it.

She drifted toward the back of the room so that she was out of Agapoi's direct line of sight. She was fighting off tears of disappointment. If she lost the battle with her tears, she would rather not be front and center.

As Agap approached, he at first was puzzled at the surprised expressions each member of his team had on their faces;

A BEACON OF HOPE

but then he realized that Holon and he were holding hands. It was accidental, but at least now he didn't have to wait for the right moment to tell his team about her. The holding of hands gave away the fact that they were an item. There was an awkward silence building as they approached and then stopped in front of the gaping faces.

"I know it's been a while since you have seen me in person, but do I look that differently?" Agap blurted, breaking the silence.

The team members became aware of their expression, and most changed their expression to a grin—except Eutay, whose expression was more of a smirk; but no one said anything. So Agap figured he might as well get the introductions out of the way.

"Team, I would like to introduce our newest team member. Everyone say hello to Holon Tapienus Arkita."

Some team members muttered a hello. Some just nodded their heads. Each was expecting more to the introduction, so he continued, "Holon is also my intended."

That revelation started an overwhelming frenzy of exclamations and questions.

"Intended? I didn't even know you were seeing anyone!"

"Who is she?"

"How did you meet?"

"How did we not know?"

"Why didn't you tell us?"

That last question was the one that stuck.

One by one, much of the team echoed, "Why didn't you tell us?"

"I like to keep my personal life and my professional life separate," he offered.

"It doesn't appear you will be able to live by that principle anymore, does it?" That comment came from Eutay.

99

"No. I guess you're right. Holon is a part of my life and will officially be a part of our team on Diotiri," he replied.

"Diotiri? So she's not a member of the team yet?" bellowed Phunex.

"No. Her contract begins the first day of next week," he answered. Although he didn't understand what difference that would make.

Phunex seemed to grow louder as she spoke again. "Then why are you calling her Holon? If she's not a team member yet and she is your intended, shouldn't you be calling her Holu?"

"Yes, Agapoi. She is your intended," said Kowtsom, "You should be using Holu."

The rest of the team nodded in agreement, except Yotux who was standing toward the back of the room who seemed quite interested in checking the ends of her shoulder length hair at the moment. When she saw him look at her, she blushed and nodded her agreement.

He thought about telling the team that he only used the more formal name of Holon because this was a professional setting whether she was a team member or not. Yet, given the atmosphere, he thought better of it and just agreed. "Yes. Tonight, her name is Holu."

The team seemed to approve, Yotux even had a slight smile on her face now, though it looked as though she might cry.

He began to wonder if something was troubling Yotux, but all thoughts of Yotux left his mind when he looked toward Holon. She looked extremely upset. He bent and whispered in her ear, "Are you well?"

The question only seemed to agitate her more. "May I speak privately with you?" she said firmly. She didn't speak loudly, but it was loud enough to be heard by those standing around them.

"Umm. Excuse us for a moment, team. Uh. We'll be right back," Agap stammered as he turned to the door of his office with Holon.

Whispers immediately began within the team, though Yotux quietly stood away from the rest of the group.

He opened the office door for Holon, and she went inside and he followed. Once the door was closed he asked, "What's wrong?" Holon didn't answer him, and her face was turning red. She was as angry as he had ever seen her. They were standing in front of the large window that faced out to the meeting area. He could see his team looking at them, so he moved between Holon and the window and turned to her so that all his team could see was his back. "You think I should have told the team about you, don't you?" he quickly said before she could open her mouth.

Holon shook her head. "Agapu," she began. She was obviously trying to repress the anger in her voice, but it came through clearly. He was glad that she used the endearment form of his name. It gave him hope. "It's not that you didn't tell them about us," she began slowly, but she was just getting warmed up. "I respect the fact that you wanted to keep your personal life personal. But you didn't tell *me* that you didn't tell them. You let me stroll into that room"—Holon pointed emphatically through the window behind Agap—"holding your hand, wearing *this dress,* knowing full well that it would shock the team to death. I have to *work* with those people, Agapu. I didn't want their first impression of me to be improper." Tears were welling up in her eyes.

Her words made him feel ashamed. He hadn't considered that she was expecting to be introduced as his intended first and foremost. The dress was beautiful, but he didn't know it

THE TEAM

carried any special meaning to her. At the moment, he felt like the stupidest man in Kosundo.

She wasn't done either. Her voice became shaky with tears as she said, "Then, when you introduced me, you introduced me as a new team member? A team member first, not your intended? Then you use my formal name to introduce me? Why, you built a splendid first impression of me, didn't you?" She was red, as red as a fully bloomed oiksith. She was utterly furious with him and he couldn't say that he blamed her.

But the most terrible thing for him was that he had made Holon cry. He had never intended to make her cry. He said softly, "Holu, I am so sorry. I never intended to make you appear to be anything but an accomplished communications technician." He tried to put his hand on her arm, but she turned away from him. He retracted his hand and continued to plead with her. "I perceived the occasion wrongly. I was thinking professional decorum when I should have been thinking about holding you up in the best light possible. I was wrong. Do you forgive me?" He had stooped down nearly on his knees in front of her.

Holon turned back toward him. Her face was still red and wet with tears, but her eyes had lost their fury. She looked tenderly at him and said, "Get up, Agapu. They can see us."

He sheepishly rose to his feet.

"I am no longer angry." Tears were still flowing down her face, but she pointed to her tears and said, "These tears are to my shame. I know, Agapu—I know you wouldn't have done anything to belittle me intentionally. It is I who should be sorry."

He shook his head and started to object, but she looked him in his eyes and put a finger up to his mouth. "I am sorry for doubting you, Agapu. I assumed the worst about you. I should never have done that. You do not deserve that. Please accept my apology. It was wrong of me to shame you in front of your team." She then smiled at him. Her smile made it seem as though everything was again all right in his world.

He smiled back with what must have been one of his goofy smiles because Holon broke out in laughter. Agap held Holon—he would think of her as Holu, especially tonight—close to him.

"Agapu, they are still watching," Holu said softly through her tears.

"Let them watch, Holu. Let them watch," he said. He had decided that he would never again put his ridiculous professionalism before his beloved Holu.

They held their embrace for a few more moments, and then he asked, "Are you ready to be introduced properly?"

"Yes, Agapu. I do believe that I am," said Holu with a teary smile. "Just let me make myself presentable." She then turned and hurried into his office washroom. She reemerged shortly without the tears or even red eyes. He wondered how she was able to look like she hadn't cried so quickly. "I am ready for my introduction now," she said.

With those words said, he took Holu by the hand and opened the office door. The team watched with various expressions on their faces as he strode toward them.

He said robustly, "Team, I would like to reintroduce this lovely lady to you. This wonderful person is my intended, Holu. Holu, I would like you to meet the team." It was only then that Agap noticed that his team had varying degrees of teary eyes themselves—well, all except Axopen, who was pretending to be totally bored, and Supeb, who seemed to be genuinely bored.

He started at the team member standing closest to him. "Holu, this is Kowtsom. She is the person to see to get the scoop on the latest happenings in the dome." He paused and smiled at Kowtsom. She bared her teeth in return. She was never fond of him teasing her about her penchant for gossip, although it was always in good fun. She liked to talk, but there was never anything malicious in her gossip. "She is also the foremost expert on technology metals," he added hoping the compliment would take away any edge that was perceived by his teasing.

It must have worked because Kowtsom smiled broadly and nodded her head in greeting to Holu.

Next was Eutay. "Holu, this is Eutay. You should see him when you need a laugh to relieve some stress." Eutay gave him a roll of his eyes for that introduction. Then he added, "He is also pretty good with energy technology."

"At your service," Eutay said as he made his nod.

Then there was Axopen. "This is Axopen, Holu. He is brilliant even by his own admission." Axopen grunted at Agap and then nodded to Holu. "He is also the man I have entrusted with transporter beam research."

Supeb was next. "This is Supeb. You will have to work on him to get him to smile." Supeb forced a smile at Holu, just to show he could smile. "Supeb is our lead designer."

Opsil nodded to Holon before the introduction was made. "This is Opsil, Holu. He is very eager in everything he does, I suppose," he began. "He's the youngest member of our team and shows great promise. He has a bit to learn about life, but he is a very gifted designer. He assists Supeb."

Opsil nodded again with a childish grin on his face.

Holu couldn't help but chuckle a little, but Agap didn't know if Opsil noticed.

He then came to Phunex. "This is Phunex, Holu. You

won't have to worry about knowing what is on her mind. She has a way of letting you know." Phunex nodded but gave him a crossways look afterwards. "Phunex is our manufacturing specialist. Give her any design, and she'll get it done for you."

Phunex smiled broadly until Agap added coyly, "We think it's because of her great people skills."

The rest of the team got a chuckle out of that comment. Phunex just gave him another look, a prolonged one this time. He thought she might even stick out her tongue.

"And, finally, this is Yotux. She keeps the team functioning while I am away and does a splendid job at it. I guess you could say that she is my right hand man," he said lightly.

Yotux seemed to cringe a moment before nodding to Holu formally.

"Of course, she is definitely a woman. I just meant to say that she is indispensable to my team," he said hurriedly. Apparently, his attempt to take his foot out his mouth failed with Yotux as the look on her face only darkened. He attempted to patch up his mess by saying, "She is the alternate team lead. When I am out of communication with the group, she is in charge. She has degrees in twenty-five technology disciplines. She is also the person who designed the translift software." She also designed the chomile software and interfaces; but given Holu's experience today and the unfortunate timing of his humor toward Yotux, he thought it might be best not to mention that right now.

He turned to the entire team to finish the introduction. "Holu is also our new team member. She will be in charge of communications for the dome. She is eminently qualified, which is what first attracted me to her. Of course, her appearance didn't dissuade me any either."

A few team members gave a hint of a chuckle. He glanced at Holu to make sure she was still smiling after that comment. Thankfully, she was smiling.

He finished up by saying, "Holu brings a vast array of communication technology experiences with her. She is the person who designed our deepwater communications array. She finished this array before our dome was set in place. It is her work that allows you to communicate with your friends and loved ones outside the dome, not to mention allowing you to receive your favorite PT programs. Please welcome Holu to our team."

The team responded with fist salutes and a rousing set of "Hum-harri's," followed by a nicely timed foot stomp.

Holu blushed at the appreciation showed. A short acceptance of the appreciation would be expected. She cleared her throat. Her voice had barely recovered from her recent emotions but he thought she managed admirably. She said with a relatively clear voice, "Thank you, team. It is an honor to be able to work with such esteemed and friendly people. I believe our work here will be of great importance to Cirri and to Kosundo as a whole. May our minds be one as we endeavor to fulfill all that our country demands of us, to the glory of Thaoi."

Everyone repeated in unison, "To the glory of Thaoi, may we be found faithful." Then everyone except Agap sat down. Holu had to be pointed to the correct desk but still made it to her seat before the entire team put their seats in order and sat down at their desks.

The desks were arranged in a two-row semicircle, with the second-row desks filling the spaces between the first-row desks. There was an empty desk in the center of the first row that Agap used when he was in lab session with his team. But this was a meeting session, so he took his place behind the speaking desk, which was literally the size of a desk but set up for standing. There were also controls for a video presentation on the speaking desk, but that was not needed for this meeting.

He found the folder for tonight's meeting on the desk. He had faith that Yotux would have it there, as he had asked. "I know that I have not allowed you the privilege of celebrating our upcoming union with us. I do apologize for that oversight. You all have been a large part of my life, some of you for over twenty years. Yotux, you have been with me since my first team commission in Zaria." As he looked Yotux's way he noticed that she was on the brink of tears. She must have missed him during his long absence. They had become close, professionally over the years. He then looked at the rest of his team and continued. "The rest of you, with the exception of Opsil, were with me in Cirri City, and, Opsil, you were added to the team at the beginning of our current project here in Bojoa nearly three years ago now. I now understand how wrong it was of me to keep you from sharing in our joy. Therefore, we will have a celebration of tryst for just our team on eKureaki morning at 3:50. I will make the arrangements to reserve the small party room in the Kumphus Restaurant. Holu and I ask that no gifts be brought and we want you to leave your credit monitors at home. The party is as much our tribute to you as a celebration for us."

That brought an openhanded salute from the team, though Yotux's salute seemed less enthusiastic than the rest of the team's. Yotux seemed especially emotional tonight. It was good that he was going to be with the team in Bojoa now. It appeared that she needed a break from the responsibility that his absence had brought upon her.

He smiled at the rest of the team's smiles. They deserved it, and he wished he could do more for them. The Kumphus was the best restaurant in the dome. He just wished he could have found a way to make the celebration on a workday to reward the team more. But it was uncertain what Odanoi's meeting would mean for his team. They would need to have the week clear in case anything was asked of them.

He continued. "Bojoa is just now beginning formal operations. Much will be expected of our team. Phrunoi himself appointed our team to this post. It is indeed a great honor. But with this honor comes great responsibility. We must prepare ourselves for what might lie ahead. We will be expected to provide the best progressive technologies to assist Cirri for years to come. That is why we were selected. That is why we are here. May Thaoi be glorified."

The response was a hearty, "To the glory of Thaoi, may we be found faithful."

"Tomorrow at four parzes, we will be expected to attend the all-council meeting, which will bring all Cirri councils into the same room for the first time since the invasion of the Doetoran continent by O'ONaso some two thousand years ago. It is also the first all-council meeting ever to be held without the council of nine sitting in the council center. None of us will really understand the significance of this until tomorrow, if then. Nevertheless, make no mistake. Tomorrow's meeting will be a historic gathering. Pray that it be a blessed gathering."

Everyone responded reverently, "Thaoi grant it so. May Thaoi be praised."

"I will sit in my place with the technology council. You will sit, in honor, just behind us."

This surprised most of the team, except Yotux who already knew about the honor. The team gave a resounding, "May Thaoi find us faithful," if not quite in unison.

"But that is tomorrow. Today, we discuss how to make improvements for the sake of those who live in and visit

Bojoa." He couldn't help but smile when he saw the first item Yotux had listed. It had the sign "5+" beside it, meaning it had highest priority and probably the most complaints. He cleared the smile from his face before he spoke. "The first item on our list is the chomile system." He heard grunts and groans among his team—grunts signifying knowing agreement, groans for all the work that they knew would have to be done.

Agap read the complaints about the chomile aloud. As he read the complaints to the team, he thought he heard Holu's voice echo each one of them. Dinner had reverberated with chorus of the shortcomings of the chomile. Of course, he was imagining the echoes now; but as he glanced at Holu, he saw that she was basking in the utter enjoyment of being absolutely right. He would never hear the end of this. He was sure. But he found that he really didn't care.

As he continued to read the complaints and gather suggestions from his team, he came to realize that he was with the people he loved, doing what he loved. He had nearly forgotten the feeling, but Holu had put his mind right. He didn't have to be Agapoi here. No matter what his team called him out of respect, he was now with friends; he was Agap again.

But even now, he could not get the thought of tomorrow's meeting out of his mind completely. He couldn't help but think that everything could change tomorrow. Exactly how, he didn't know; but he was sure that tomorrow might change his life and the lives of those around him.

The meeting moved on quickly and was over in just a few spens. He took Holu home, went to his unfinished room, and readied himself for bed. The clock read 9:98. In just a couple of spens, it would be tomorrow. There were only four parzes until the meeting. Somehow, the feeling of curiosity that surrounded the meeting just this morning was replaced with a feeling of dread. *What was going to be announced in such an odd fashion?*

He set the alarm and climbed into bed. As he lay there, thinking, he caught a chill and pulled the covers up to cover his shoulders. His mind knew that the temperature of the room hadn't changed; but his soul felt something had changed, and the chill it brought felt measurable. The clock read 10:00. Tomorrow was here. What changes it would bring, he could not know; but he did know that there was nothing to be done about it now. With that thought, Agap closed his eyes and wished for sleep.

8

THE AWAKENING

Neaotomo began to wake. He opened his eyes, but everything appeared dark. He took a moment to focus his eyes. There. He could make out a few familiar things in the room. He could see his desk and chair, but they appeared strangely positioned to him. He glanced about the room. He saw the door, but it seemed to be sideways. He turned his head and felt his head skim over a hard surface. As he turned his head, he saw his dresser and his bed. He began to realize that he was on the floor. He tried to move his arms, but they would not move. Neither would his legs. All he could do was turn his head.

He tried to think of why he was lying on the floor, but his mind was fuzzy. It was as if a fog filled his mind. All his thoughts were a jumble. One thought kept floating in his mind, but it wouldn't stay long enough to be understood really, although it seemed an urgent thought. Instinctively, he cleared his mind of all his jumbled thoughts. That was it. His mind was clear now—no jumbled thoughts, no thoughts at all. He let his mind relax, thinking of nothing. There. The thought was there. He could see the thought like a package that could not be opened. He again cleared his mind. The thought receded. He knew he needed more time, so he commanded his mind to sleep. He again fell to a dreamless slumber.

Again, he woke. He opened his eyes; and again, all he saw was darkness. He did not try to focus his eyes this time. The thought was there again. He could almost grasp it. But he knew it was pointless to try to capture the thought just yet. The jumble would just return. Instead, he closed his eyes and again cleared his mind. He could do this instinctively. It was a method of concentration he had mastered long ago—at least he felt it was long ago. Again, his mind stood blank, completely relaxed. He stayed that way for what seemed like a long time to him. Now, let the thought come. Only one thought filled his mind. It was open now. "Gas! Must sleep, deep sleep; deep, deep sleep..." So strong was the memory that he had cried those words aloud.

He opened his eyes. Now he remembered. There was gas, poisonous gas all around him, yet there was no gas now. He now realized that he had put himself in a deep sleep, a type of hibernal state, a state where his bodily functions slowed to almost nothing, a state of near death but not death. He did that to avoid inhaling the poison. But how long did he hibernate? He did not know. He had never put himself under so deep before, so he really did not know when his mind would wake him again. He theorized that it could have been a very long time indeed. His mind would probably wake when his body was nearly running out of energy, but that could be a long time at the drastically reduced metabolic rate. The reduced rate of his bodily functions would cause no heartbeat to be detected, no brain activity to be detected; it would appear as though he was dead.

"Food." That thought came unbidden, but it was a necessary thought. Yes. Food would be necessary, but first he knew he must be able to move. He again cleared his mind. This time, he commanded the thought of moving his arm. The thought came, *Move!* His arm responded with a jerk. Good. Now the other arm. His other arm jerked back to life. Now the legs. Yes. His legs moved also. *Now sit up.* His body responded.

He again focused his eyes. His chair still looked out of place. It had fallen to the floor. He realized that he must have grabbed at the chair when he was falling to the floor. He focused again until he could see his desk clearly. Food was underneath the desk in a compartment that he had built into the desk while the lights were out in his room. He remembered that he hid dehydrated vacuum packs of food in the compartment when he sensed that his creators and keepers had grown wary, even fearful of him.

He commanded his body, and he managed a minute crawl to reach the bottom of the desk. He could not believe how tired that made him. He must be nearly out of energy. He hoped he had enough energy to open the compartment and the food pack. There would be a few sealed bottles of water in the compartment too. He reached for the compartment latch. The latch was not obvious, nor easy to open; but he knew where the latch was and the way it had to be grasped to open it. There. The compartment was open. He reached inside and bumped a bottle. The bottle fell onto the floor. It was one of the bottles of water he had stowed away. Beside it should be the food packs. Yes. He felt one of them. Now where is the knife? He thought that he might need it to open the food pack if he was in dire need of food. Yes. It was taped to the top of the compartment. He pulled the knife loose but failed to grasp it. It fell to the floor with a clank. He ignored the knife for the moment and reached for a food pack. He managed to grasp one and pull it out to the floor.

He could not support himself with his other arm any longer. He collapsed to the floor. It was a strange feeling, this feeling of weakness. He had never felt it before. He lay for a moment, face down on the floor. Then he felt for the knife. There it was. He managed to hold his head up slightly. Yes. There was the food pack and, next to it, the water. He managed to grasp the knife in his left hand and reached for the food pack with his right hand. His hand could not reach the pack. He dropped his head. He knew that he must reach the food pack or die.

He cleared his mind and concentrated on his feet. There must be enough energy in his body to move him forward a couple of bits. He pushed with his feet. His body slid forward the smallest tad, but his right hand felt the food pack. Now to have enough energy to raise his head so he could see to cut the bag. He managed a small movement of the head upward to see the bag. He shakily brought the knife toward the bag. The edge of the knife clipped the corner of the bag, and it was open. He put some powder in his mouth.

He realized that he had very little water in his body. Now he needed to get the water bottle with his left hand. It would be sealed, but it would open with just the smallest squeeze of the cap in the right place. He dropped his head. He could not expend the energy to hold it up any longer. He must feel for the water bottle, with his left hand; but the knife was still in his left hand. He commanded the hand to let go, and it did. The knife hit the floor with a small tinkle. He was breathing hard now, and he smiled. It was another new experience. His body was nearly exhausted. He flailed with his left hand. It hit the bottle, and the bottle rolled away a couple of bits.

He heard laughter come from his mind. All this planning and he was going to die because he packed away a round bottle instead of a rectangular one. Then his mind stopped laughing as he felt the bottle come back and hit his hand. The bottle had hit the knife and rolled back.

He raised his fingers and felt the top of the bottle. It was the top, but he needed to find the push valve that would open the bottle. He didn't have any energy to waste. He felt around the top until he found what he believed was the right place, and he used his last ounce of energy to squeeze the bottle. The bottle popped open. Water rushed out and hit his face. He opened his mouth and stuck out his tongue. Moisture met his tongue. Then he felt it, the most exquisite feeling he could remember. The food powder formed a paste when the water hit his tongue. He swallowed the small morsel of food and the water and then stuck out his tongue again. More water and a little more food powder. He continued in this fashion until no more water or food could be felt hitting his tongue. Now he must sleep. Sleep to repair the body, let the little bit of food digest to give him enough energy to find more. Without hesitation, Neaotomo fell asleep.

9
THE CIRRIAN AGENT

Tryllos impatiently waited, pacing back and forth, making his blue royal robes ripple about his legs and feet. Where was Temeos? There was news, strange news from his Cirrian agent. Tryllos's lips automatically formed a sneer when thinking about the Cirrian agent. He did not like him at all. He considered him a traitor to his country; but his information had always proved valuable, so he knew he had to use him. His pacing continued. What is taking so long? He was sent for ten spens ago. Tryllos hated waiting, but it seemed that everyone was always keeping him waiting. No one ever moved fast enough for him. He knew that people thought him impatient, but he was the emperor after all. He came from a long line of emperors. Emperors should not be kept waiting. Still, it would not do to let Temeos see him anxious. Temeos already believed that he was paranoid. No. It would not do at all to let Temeos see him anxious.

He stopped pacing and looked in the wall mirror of his office. His brown, wavy hair looked to be in order. He then strode to his desk and sat down. He would show Temeos that he was not at all anxious. After all, what was there to worry about? Nothing at all. That's what. With that, Tryllos pretended to look through the papers on his desk. *Eleven spens now. Where is Temeos?*

As if Tryllos's last thought summoned him, Temeos was announced by the office page. Finally, he was here.

"Well, send him in," he said impatiently to the waiting page.

The page bowed and left the room. As he was leaving, Temeos entered the room, a bit out of breath. He was dressed in the customary, high-collared, black director's uniform. His red and gold medals that displayed prominently on his right chest were the only interruption to the black. Temeos was a tall man with broad shoulders. His dark hair and dark brown eyes stood in stark contrast to his pale skin.

"Sorry to keep you waiting, Your Imperial Highness. I was in the middle of a training session when your summons reached me, and I did not wish to offend you with my appearance, so I took the time to freshen myself and change my clothes before coming into your presence," said Temeos rather matter-of-factly.

Temeos knew him well. Yes, he would have been offended by training attire and profuse perspiration. He supposed that he would have to accept Temeos's explanation, so he nodded to the chair in front of the desk. Temeos promptly sat in the indicated chair.

"I have received word from our Cirrian traitor of a high council meeting to be held in Cirri the day after tomorrow." He paused and looked at Temeos to try to read whether he might have heard about the announcement. Temeos, as usual, gave no indication one way or another, so he continued. "It appears that the meeting may not be held in the Cirri council center." Temeos raised his eyebrows slightly. "The traitor did not seem to know where the meeting was going to be held, but Odanoi boarded a submarine shortly after announcing the meeting. What are your thoughts?"

"The submarine could be a rouse or a coincidence. However, if the meeting is not to be in Cirri City, perhaps the Cirrians have uncovered some sensitive information that they mean to keep private. Since our spy only gets information from the technology sector, his information about the high council might be misleading," surmised Temeos.

"That may be, Temeos. However, the traitor also told me that the last message he received from the technology council was from a different broadcasting room, one that he did not recognize. When he asked when the council acquired a new broadcasting room, they only said, 'Very recently.' No elaboration was given, though the traitor tried to get the council operator to elaborate. He was told that this location was classified but, in time, he would be told about the location. Do you suppose the Cirrians are on to him?"

"I don't believe so, but the mysteriousness surrounding the location of the technology council is intriguing." Temeos saw that his answer did not satisfy him, so he added, "Cirrians take security very seriously. If they suspected anything, they would have replaced him by now."

"I see," he said thoughtfully. "You might be right. The traitor didn't seem to be concerned, but he believed that the announcement of a high council meeting and the subsequent departure of Odanoi combined with the mystery location of the technology council to be significant."

"These facts may be significant, my lord, but to what end? Did your spy have any further information regarding these events?"

"No, he did not," he snarled disgustedly. "Temeos, tell the Cirrian trade council that the Doetoran empire has become ... annoyed ... with its current technology advisors and would like to have them recalled immediately."

"My lord!" said Temeos incredulously.

"We have given this traitor enough money. I believe that his services are no longer required. We have what we need from him anyway. Our Avengers are nearly complete. Soon, Kosundo will no longer look on the Doetoran Empire as its stepstool. Don't just stand there with your mouth open. Do as I command. We shall show them ... when the time is right." A wicked smile crossed his face when he thought of the Avengers.

"Yes, my lord," said Temeos, bowing his way out of his presence.

10
Aide to the Lord Director

Abin, Temeos's aide, was seated in the hall, waiting for Temeos to finish his audience with the emperor. Upon seeing Temeos emerge from the room, he rose to his feet.

"My lord director," he stated with the formality that befit Temeos's position perfectly. Abin had been his aide for over forty years. He had picked him as an aide as he was graduating upper school.

He strode down the hall, stopped alongside his aide and said, "You have always been a loyal aide, Abin. I knew that you would be the moment I laid my eyes upon you."

"Many thanks, my lord," Abin said formally.

"What I am going to say next to you I say because I care for your safety." For the first time that he could remember, Abin's expression changed, if only slightly. For Abin, that slight change was tantamount to shock in anyone else. He continued in a very soft voice. "I fear that the emperor has lost his..." He paused, searching for the right words, "...sense of reality. I do not know who he is anymore. Should the worse happen, I want... no, I order you to flee to the countryside on foot, taking nothing that can be considered to be technology with you."

Abin shuffled his feet. That shuffling of the feet for Abin was like running away screaming for anyone else.

"I am being deadly serious. I mean what I say. You've been present with me everywhere and know nearly everything I know. You know what I am talking about. The emperor is determined to use them, whether or not the neural link security has been completed. The emperor refuses to listen even when he is more lucid than he seems to be today. Abin, these things are dangerous! Even if we can control them, they have no place in civilized society." His voice had become a bit louder than he had wished toward the end. He quickly looked up and down the hall to see if someone might have overheard. Seeing no one, he whispered to Abin, "Promise me."

"I promise, my lord," Abin said in a bit of a stammer.

"No, Abin. Do not promise me as an aide. I treasure you as I would a son. Promise me as my friend." He tried to put an urgent quality in his voice as he spoke.

Abin turned to face him and grasped his right arm about the elbow with his right hand.

He returned the grasp.

"I am honored that you think to call me your friend. I will honor your wishes as a friend," vowed his aide.

They held the grasp silently for a moment, and then Abin looked at him earnestly and asked, "Will I be seeing you if the worst happens?"

He was deadly quiet for a moment. Then he gave a slight smile. "No, friend. You will not see me. My place is by my emperor, especially should the worst occur."

Abin nodded his head knowingly. The two stayed in the embrace of friendship for a moment longer.

Then Abin resumed his role, turned his side toward him, and said, "Will there be anything else, my lord?"

He shook his head and began walking with Abin toward the large front door of the palace. Then he stopped. "There is one more thing, Abin," he said suddenly. Then he paused, fighting himself over whether he should continue or not.

"My lord?" Abin said, more anxious than formal this time.

"I feel a need to send you on an errand," he began and then paused again.

"Where would my lord require me to go?"

"Any place that neither I nor my staff know anything about." He paused and looked around to see if anyone was near. "But I think it best if you put some distance between yourself and the capital. I wish you to leave Manku City discreetly this weekend when you are not on duty. Remember what to do should the worst happen."

Abin did not answer, but nodded.

"There is still one thing more," he said as he pulled a plain, white envelope out of his coat pocket. "Take this," he said softly as he began to hand the envelope to Abin. But he did not let go when Abin took hold of it. When Abin's eyes met his, he said, "This envelope contains important information that you should know. However, you must not know it now. The information is...dangerous. Promise me that you will keep this envelope safe and show it to no one." He stared directly into Abin's eyes as he spoke.

"I promise, my lord Temeos," said Abin earnestly.

Being satisfied that Abin understood, he let go of the envelope.

Abin quickly put the envelope into his inside vest pocket.

He leaned toward Abin and spoke softly. "You may open the envelope on Diotiri morning, not before. Make sure you are alone and someplace safe when you open it. Things are going to happen soon, Abin, for the good or the bad. You will know when you hear of it. Do you understand?"

Abin nodded solemnly.

He smiled and fit his imperial ehri cap on his head, signifying he was ready to leave the imperial palace.

"Your transport stands ready, my lord. Shall I make ready your way?" said Abin formally.

He nodded.

"It is my pleasure to serve, my lord," Abin stated formally.

He thought he saw a slight smile on his aide's face as Abin walked in front of him.

"It has always been my pleasure to have you in my service, Abin."

Abin paused. This time, there definitely was a smile and perhaps a slight blush. He then continued out to ready the escort.

He smiled to himself. Abin was worth the world to him. Abin had always been the only one he knew he could confide in without question, without fear. He realized, just now, that Abin was the only true friend he had in all of Kosundo. He wished he could tell Abin the whole truth, but he needed to keep that truth to himself for now. It was not safe for Abin to know yet. He had to know that his plan had support first. He could be told then. He would be sorry to see him go, but it seemed the only way for now. Temeos had fulfilled what his conscience had demanded. He was now ready for whatever Thaoi willed.

11

THE GREAT ONE

Nenavis was in a foul mood. He had tried to maneuver behind the scenes to achieve a world that was ripe for his dominance. But he was being outmaneuvered. Something always happened to thwart his plans. He had seen this before, and he knew who had to be ruining his plans. It had to be the Other One. He would prevail though, first in this world and then in all the other worlds that he had been banished to and then banished from in the past. There had been five of them. He would prevail then in any other world that would become the domain of men. After he became the supreme being of all the worlds, he would have power. The Other One had been holding an advantage for eons, but it was an unfair advantage. He held the advantage only because the Other One was first. If he had been first, then he would hold the advantage, not the Other One. Even now, the Other One was cheating him, making it difficult to maneuver. He hated the Other One and all men who associated with the Other One. And his hatred was getting worse and worse with each passing world. He would be victorious in this sixth world of men. The Other One would not prevail this time.

"My D'Yavoly, give me a report on the affairs of Kosundo," he snarled.

"Your plans for Doetora are bearing fruit, great one," hissed Vrasku.

"There is small fruit perhaps, Vrasku, but not a full harvest. When will I have the emperor's mind completely?" he snapped.

"Soon, great one. Soon. His mind has been vexed for some time now, ever since his dealings with you," crowed Vrasku.

"And what of Grasso?" he demanded.

"Dricho is nearly ours," growled Ubmenchek. "The leaders and the people alike rely on their science. There is no thought of anyone but themselves in their minds and certainly not in their souls. They reach out to us, unaware. They will be little resistance to your plans here."

"Excellent, Ubmenchek. Let us hope that your boastful spirit has not caused you to exaggerate," he warned his underling.

"O'ONaso is also ready," boasted Pupyten. "Their hearts are set on pleasure. There is no room for thoughts of sacrifice. There will be no heroes."

"No heroes. It seems I have heard that before from you, Pupyten. There were to be no heroes in our last world either. Do you see me ruling there? No. We were banished by not one but thousands of heroes with help from the Other One. Think before you make that boast to me." The thought of losing to the Other One always made him angry, particularly when he thought of a time when the Other One had thoroughly bested him.

"Forgive me, great one," said a cringing Pupyten. "But there will not be thousands in this country," he offered.

"It only takes one who will stand for others to join. Remember this, and do not take anyone for granted," roared Nenavis.

Damun hesitated, seeing his mood, but then decided to dare to mutter, "The leadership of Schwinn is deceiving their people, my master. They intend to house tools of evil to silence their enemies. These could be of use, my master. And does that show they're falling from faith, to have leaders capable of such deception?"

"Indeed, Damun. This is more like it. Who else has some tangible evidence of the demise of conscience in Kosundo?" he demanded.

Svirap decided to speak this time. "O great and mighty one, I have a piece of news from the place where science is worshipped in Dricho. I have heard it from my connections about the abominations that had been crafted."

"This is old news, Svirap," he growled.

"Ah, but, my master, there is something new." Svirap hesitated and then continued quickly when he caught his angry look. "One of the abominations might still exist. A sound was heard that sounded like a voice from within the sealed rooms."

"A sound, Svirap? You tell me of a noise? It could be vermin or even the ice cracking. Nothing could survive in those sealed rooms. It would have run out of air long ago," he scoffed. "Does anyone there consider there to be a chance of anything living being in those rooms?"

"No, Your Excellency," admitted Svirap, "but they are just mortal, and they do not trust their senses, especially when their senses are heightened by our presence. I heard this sound while visiting in their world. It was not ice cracking or even vermin. *I* heard it, my master."

He considered the words of Svirap.

While he thought, Purhit conjectured, "Perhaps, my master, the sound was distorted before reaching Svirap's borrowed ears. This is probably nothing more than the hopefulness of Svirap's mind since he could not deliver in Dricho when the time was more opportune."

"Perhaps," considered Nenavis. "But Svirap's words ring unusually true." He turned and sounded a large cymbal, which echoed in the Labile Mist where the D'Yavoly resided and elsewhere. "I shall call in a new D'Yavoly to explore Svirap's claims. If there be any truth to the claims, my plans may yet bear fruit quickly," he said. He knew that Svirap could lie as well as any of his D'Yavoly, but Svirap was shrewd. He didn't believe that Svirap would take this risk unless he was very sure.

The D'Yavoly were immediately curious who would be called and murmured among themselves. Their curiosity was satisfied as Zlux answered his call. Zlux had come with him as an original D'Yavoly to the first world, but he began to think too much of himself and he banished Zlux in the third world. Since that time, Zlux had resided outside the realm of the Labile Mist. He had resided in the abyss for ages, where he could do nothing but wait.

"My master, it has been a long time. How many worlds have passed?"

"You have missed two worlds of men, Zlux. Be careful, lest you miss this one too," he growled.

"How can I be of service to my master?" Zlux responded with a slight sneer in his voice.

"I have decided that there is a use for your talents, Zlux. But be warned. If you again think to tell others of a plan other than the one I give you, you will not return from the abyss another time," he said with a full sneer on his lips.

"I will not fail you, great one," said Zlux in a low, almost humble voice.

"You will go to the icy land of Dricho, to a place where men worship their knowledge and spy for me within our contacts. You are looking for a man who is not a man but is an abomination of man's imagination. You will know him if he arrives, for you will see him but will not be able to feel him. This creature can be used to bring me from the Labile Mist, to reside fully in the world of Kosundo. Once I am fully in Kosundo, I will be able to use hapless men to bring legions of my followers into Kosundo, this sixth world of men." He paused while sizing up Zlux before continuing. "Do not inform anyone but me when you have found him. By this, you can prove yourself to me. Remember, Zlux, I will know if you betray my wishes," he warned. "Now go."

With that command, Zlux was off to Dricho to find a contact, a contact who wouldn't mind if he visited for a while, maybe a long while.

"Svirap, if you are right about this abomination, you will become my second until the return of Sarditu," he declared.

Svirap raised his head proudly. Then he growled, "But if you are wrong, you will take the place of Zlux in the abyss."

With those words, Svirap lowered his head and slunk a short distance away from him.

He smiled. He loved to watch his D'Yavoly squirm. *Soon, all of Kosundo will squirm*, he thought triumphantly. *Yes. If Svirap is right, the abomination will want revenge. I will be able to give him that and more ... for a price!*

Nenavis's smile became a laugh, an eerie, sick laugh, a laugh that could shake the foundations of Kosundo. He looked at Svirap with his lowered head. "I think you will suffer much if you are wrong," he said casually.

Svirap prostrated himself on the ground, not daring to look up or to say a word.

His mood had improved. Now he just might have a way to outmaneuver the Other One. Then he would rule Kosundo absolutely...whatever part of Kosundo survived anyway. Nenavis laughed and laughed as he had not laughed before during his time on the sixth world of men.

12

A Voice Heard

Degmer Medchad looked at the door of the pressure lock. On the other side of the pressure lock, through two security doors, were the sealed labs. Degmer had worked as an intern in those labs. She knew what they contained. The scientists who worked in that lab were all dead. Most died with their creations. Some died later, but all were dead. All of their creations were dead too. At least that is what she used to believe.

A week ago, when Degmer had been doing relaxation exercises in her quarters just a few dets away, she had heard something. Relaxation exercises were catching on in Dricho, having been brought to Dricho by people who had recently visited Calisla. She had learned how to perform the exercises from a book that she had purchased for her nona. The exercises helped people cope with problems. Sometimes people even found solutions for their problems while doing the exercises. She was looking to rid herself of the faces that haunted her. Faces that she had seen while working in the sealed labs as a young intern.

She had begun her exercise session, doing the usual steps. First, she cleared her mind. Second, she opened up herself. This was when she made herself an open book to the universe—at least that is how it was termed by the author of the book. She sort of thought of it as sending out party invitations to the whole world; you never knew who would show up. Third, when a guide was encountered, she made her introduction. Once a successful introduction was achieved, she became one with her guide.

It was when she felt at one with the guide that she heard it. The first word was clear: "Gas!" It was practically shouted. There were other words, she was sure; but she could not make them out. It was strange, but the words did not come from her mind as she had heard before while doing the exercise. These words were audible and had a direction to them. The words seemed to come from the direction of the hallway. It seemed so urgent that the words had shocked her. She immediately had lost her concentration and, consequently, her guide. She had run into the hall outside her room. The hall was long. If someone had spoken outside her room, she should still be able to see them. That is when she saw the door to the pressure lock and wondered. She dismissed the thought immediately at that time, but now she was wondering again. *Could she have heard a voice from the sealed labs?* Degmer was startled out of her thoughts by a voice.

"There you are, Degmer. What are you doing just standing in the hall?" said Laysa. When Laysa saw her jump, she added, "Oh. I didn't mean to startle you. What were you thinking about?"

Laysa was a friend of hers, a good friend. She was a slender woman with light brown hair and brown eyes. Like all Drichonian women, including herself, Laysa's hair was cut short, just covering her ears. Laysa's skin was a bit darker than hers was, but only slightly. They both were of Ispra descent. She contributed Laysa's darker color to the sun that Laysa managed to get during her summer sabbaticals. Apparently, Laysa was blessed with skin that kept a tan's copper tone better than Degmer's skin did. Today, Laysa was wearing a loose-fitting green blouse and brown, casual slacks that came down to her mid-calf. It was a normal look for her. She dressed casually on most occasions.

"Nothin' much," she answered absently. Then she turned to her friend. "What brings you out here?" she asked.

"You do, silly. I came over to see you. I thought maybe we could visit for a while since we are both off-duty today."

She smiled. "Yes. I would like that. I could use the company today."

She turned into her room, and Laysa followed.

"You looked deep in thought as I approached. What were you thinking about?" asked Laysa.

When Degmer made eye contact with her, Laysa raised her left eyebrow to try to coax an answer. "You would think me foolish, Laysa. What I was thinking could not be so." At least she hoped it could not be so. As she spoke, she flicked her short, dark red hair about her right ear with her fingers. She had this habit when she felt uneasy. When she realized she was flicking her hair, she stopped abruptly.

"How could I ever think you foolish, Degmer?" Laysa said with a laugh in her voice.

She cracked a slight smile, and then it vanished. "All too easily, I am afraid." She offered Laysa a seat as she shut the room's door.

When Laysa sat down, her look became serious. "Degmer," she began, "I have worked with you for over twenty years. In that time, I have never thought you to be a foolish person. Perhaps you have had a foolish thought or did a foolish thing occasionally, but who hasn't. I will not think you a foolish person no matter what you were thinking." Laysa wore a reassuring smile now.

"Before I tell you what I was thinking, let me tell you what I heard," she began. She flicked her hair for a moment and then continued, "I distinctly heard a voice shout the word *gas* and then the voice trailed off, saying something that I could not understand."

Laysa was now looking at her curiously.

"I did not hear the voice in my head. It was a male voice, and it sounded familiar to me."

"So, you heard someone say, 'Gas?'" Laysa looked puzzled. "What does this have to do with what you were thinking about?"

"Let me finish, and you will see," she said impatiently. She hated to be interrupted while telling a story.

Laysa held up both hands in a gesture of surrender.

"I heard the voice while I was here in my quarters. It sounded distant yet distinct. It came from outside of my room from that direction." She pointed to the door.

Laysa started to say something, but she held up her hand to stop her from talking.

"I ran into the hall to see who might have been there, but I saw no one."

"Perhaps you heard someone down the hall and they turned the corner before you came out into the hall," Laysa offered.

She shook her head. "No. I am sure of the direction. If someone was speaking in the hall, it would have to have been in front of my door. No one could have covered enough distance to get around either corner in the hall before I got to the door. Besides, the floor in the hall is covered in tile. I didn't hear any footsteps."

Laysa looked thoughtful, as if she was trying to puzzle out where she was going with her thinking.

"Do you remember what I told you of my internship?"

Laysa looked a bit troubled now. "I remember that you said you didn't want to talk about it."

She nodded. "With good reason, Laysa. I am the only person who has firsthand knowledge of the project that was in the sealed labs. That is because I am the only person still living that worked in there. I told the authorities what I witnessed there when they questioned me, as did all of us who got out. They retrieved the logs and saw the aftermath. You know that they ordered the labs to be sealed, sealed forever."

Laysa nodded. Her thoughtful expression turned to one of anticipation.

"I have not spoken of this to anyone, Laysa. It brings back terrible memories. The logs were also restricted. Only the very top administration of the lab can access them. I am not permitted to go into much detail, Laysa, but there are a few things that I can tell you."

Laysa leaned forward in her chair.

She continued. "We had a special genetics project, Laysa. I work in genetics now, and I interned in genetics."

Laysa crinkled her brow in doubt of why she had told her something so obvious.

"I mention that to draw a comparison. We experiment with the human genome in hopes of finding genetic cures for diseases. The project in the sealed room was called origin genetics. We try to slightly manipulate an existing genome. Origin genetics tried to create a different new genome while producing an organism that retained the humanoid form. They succeeded."

Laysa's mouth was open in incredulity. "They created a different species of human?"

"They created monsters, Laysa," she said emphatically. "They looked human, but they weren't. The last of them was powerful, too powerful. He was about to lead a revolt. People were being manipulated. I was lucky. I was stationed outside the main lab area, and I had limited contact with the test subjects, as they called them. But that last one, called Neaotomo, he was cunning. You didn't have to be in direct contact with him to know that. He took control of people, Laysa. He took control, and people were helpless to fight him." She trailed off. She was thinking of that day again, so long ago and yet parts of it were so vivid in her memory.

"If he was so powerful, how did you escape?" asked Laysa.

"There was a failsafe," she said. "Once it was discovered that over half of the project staff were under Neaotomo's control, someone decided to use the failsafe. There was a deadly gas, a neurotoxin. The outside lab was evacuated, and the whole lab complex was flooded with the gas. At the time, the terms set up on the wall by the airlock in the hall outside were active. Each of the terms showed a different portion of the lab complex. Laysa, we evacuated the lab and watched in that hallway," she said pointing to the hall outside her door, "as the gas killed everything, humans and test subjects alike. It was horrible. Not all of the humans inside of the lab were being controlled. They were killed just the same as the others, just as horribly." Tears filled her eyes as she thought of the scene. She wiped her eyes with the sleeve of her blouse, flicked her hair a couple of times, and then continued. "Neaotomo died too quickly. He was one of the first to collapse and stop moving. He should have been the last. He was strong, Laysa, so strong." Then she said it. "It was his voice I heard, Laysa. It was Neaotomo. I am sure of it."

Laysa looked shocked as she sat and stared in her direction. Finally, she sputtered, "How...how could it...how could he? No. You must have imagined it, Degmer. I mean, it couldn't be. You couldn't have heard anything from the sealed labs anyway."

"It was him," she affirmed confidently. She wasn't sure if she should tell Laysa about the exercises. Laysa had some old fashioned notions about her. Still, if she was going to convince her, she felt she had no choice. "Laysa, I haven't told you about this because I know how you feel about it. It was last week when I heard the voice, as I was doing relaxation exercises."

Laysa stared blankly. After a while, she spoke only a word: "Degmer?"

"It is true. The exercises really do help, Laysa."

Laysa still had a blank expression.

"I believe I was able to hear the voice because when you find your guide, your senses are heightened. I really believe I heard Neaotomo inside the lab."

"I have heard that said about the heightened senses," said Laysa very deliberately. "I have also heard it said that the exercises cloud your conscience," she finished at a faster rate.

"Oh, come on, Laysa. This is modern times. It is time to put some of our relics behind us," she blurted. She knew that her words had come out harshly, but Laysa was part of a dying breed in Dricho. She should wake up and join modern Kosundo.

Laysa put her head down, rubbed her forehead, and sighed.

"I never claimed to be part of the faithful." She wiggled two of her fingers about as if signifying a quote upon saying the last four words. It was she that sighed now. She had shocked Laysa more than she had intended. She regretted it, but there it was out now. Nothing could take it back. "About Neaotomo. I don't know how he could have survived, but I believe he did," she said hoping to bring the conversation back to Neaotomo.

Laysa nodded. "I am sorry, Degmer. I didn't mean to doubt your word," she said soberly, "but it does sound unbelievable. It's been over seventy years since the lab was sealed." Laysa rubbed her forehead again. She sighed still again and said, "If you say that you heard him, then I believe you."

She nodded and smiled. Laysa was trying to keep a clear conscience even now. It was admirable, even if it was archaic. Having established her reason, she decided to tell Laysa her decision. "I intend to speak to Beltram. I want to check the lab. I will tell him that our project could use some of the equipment that is in the sealed labs."

"You would lie to Beltram, Degmer?" asked Laysa, still sounding shocked.

"It's not a lie, Laysa. We really could use some of that equipment. I just won't tell him everything. I will ask to accompany the move team to pick out the equipment. I have clearance from the origin genetics project, so it would be protocol for me to accompany them anyway," she explained.

"Do you think going in there is wise?" asked Laysa in a warning tone.

"I have to know, Laysa. If Neaotomo were alive, he would have to be very weak anyway. Plus, what if he found a way out on his own? He is very clever, that one. Wouldn't it be better if we get to him before he gets to us?" She was very impressed with her own quick use of logic, but Laysa still looked doubtful.

After a moment, Laysa sighed and answered, "I can see there is no stopping you. But if you go, I go. I am the co-head of the project."

She smiled. "Agreed. I will see Beltram tomorrow." She offered a hug of friendship to Laysa.

Laysa smiled and rose to embrace her.

"It will be fine, you'll see," she said. As she spoke the words, she wondered who needed the encouragement more, Laysa or her.

Zlux smiled as he observed from his shadowy place in the Labile Mist. That red-haired human sounded convincing. She will make a nice place to visit. She will want to relax at the end of this day. She will give a blank invitation, and that will be his opportunity to visit. He just knew it.

"I think I will pay her an extended visit tonight, just in the background, nothing blatant," he mused. "After all, I don't want to alter her plans, not yet anyway."

Then Zlux slunk down in the mist. He just had to wait. There would be opportunity here. He decided that he would pass the time by dreaming of the number of people who would come under Nenavis's power through this Neaotomo. Perhaps there will be a way for him to get in on the action himself. He smiled as he imagined the destruction and chaos. Such thoughts made him smile broadly. *Should the redhead be correct, Nenavis will be very pleased,* his thoughts interjected. With that, he resumed his dreams of destruction; and the smile on his face grew larger and larger.

13

THE
ALL-COUNCIL MEETING

It was the fifth of Setmi, the day appointed for the all-council meeting. Agap had awakened early. As was his custom, he had read a passage from the Levra. This morning's passage had been about the importance of keeping your conscience clear before Thaoi. There were several passages in the Levra that dealt with that subject, but this one also included several warnings about an unclear conscience affecting a person's strength of faith. Guarding one's faith was often overlooked in these modern times. It was certainly something that he felt he could learn to do better. Sometimes, he thought that Kosundo's reliance on technology lessened their ability to have the faith that they should. He wondered if Odanoi was truly a man of faith. He didn't know Odanoi personally, so he had no way of knowing.

He put the Levra on the table next to him and pulled himself out of his thoughts. He had already cleaned, dressed, and groomed himself. He had even worked with the chomile briefly. He had colored his clock and nightstand. He created floor coverings for the main space, washroom, and cooking area. He had even created a couple more pieces of furniture—a couch, which he placed in front of the chomile, and a table bedside it. He had not unpacked most of his things yet, including his books.

At this moment, he was sitting in the comfortable chair that he had created yesterday, waiting for the proper time to go pick up Holu. The clock read 3:70. He still had ten spens before it was time to go. As a member of the technology council, he should be there slightly early; but he didn't want to be there too early. After all, the meeting didn't start until 4:00. He really did hate being too early. He also hated being late. He guessed he was known for being on time, and that is how he liked to be known. He didn't want to appear overly eager, and he definitely did not want to appear to be slothful or uncaring.

The chair was nice. It was covered in soft leather—well, simulated leather any way. But he did remember that it tended to leave creases in his clothes if he sat too long, so he decided to get up. He paced back and forth for a bit and then decided to check his clothes in the washroom mirror.

He checked the front of his dark brown dress jacket and trousers as he walked into the washroom. No evidence of wrinkling there. That was a relief. The last thing he needed today was to mess up his only pressed council suit. All council members wore the same dark brown suit. All council members also wore white sarks with a golden yellow neck scarf. He checked out his neck scarf. It seemed properly wrapped and tucked in the neck of his sark. He then made sure that his council medal was properly centered on the right breast of his jacket. The medal was rectangular, about 4 bits long and about a bit tall. Each council medal had three colored rectangles in continuous order on the face of the gold medal. His medal had the colors silver, white, and blue from left to right on the medal.

These were the technology council colors. Of course, other councils had other color combinations; and the chair of each council had an elongated brown rectangle under the three colors. He turned to see the back of his suit again and this time saw a slight crease in the pants where he had sat on them. It didn't appear to be too bad though. He tugged on his trousers to stretch out the fabric. The crease seemed to be unnoticeable in the mirror now. So He went back into the main room.

He glanced at his watch. It read 3:71. There were still nine spens until it was time to leave. He thought about putting a box of books on the shelf, but he quickly dismissed that idea because of his suit. He could put a few more furnishings in the room, but he didn't really feel like bothering with that right now. He was pacing again, he noticed. It seemed like he couldn't wait for things without pacing. He glanced at his watch. Only a spen had passed.

This is ridiculous, he thought disgustedly. *I don't want to go early, but I don't want to do anything either.* But most of all, he didn't want to think about the meeting. He concentrated on pacing for a few more tics. He then decided that he might as well go and pick up Holu. It was a bit earlier than he had told her. Maybe she wouldn't be ready yet. He looked at his watch again. The display hadn't changed. He could call, but he never asked her if she created her commterm yet. *Did Yotux design the chomile to create a default commterm if a call came in regardless of whether the occupant created one?* he asked himself. But he didn't know the answer. He would have to make it a point to ask Yotux that question. He noticed that he was pacing faster now. He decided that he'd better just go. He was liable to work up a sweat at this rate. He was certain he didn't want to be known as the smelly councilperson. He grabbed his dark brown portfolio case and headed for the door.

In a few tics, he was at Holu's door. He looked at his watch and sighed. It read 3:73. . He was seven spens early, which was noticeably early, especially for him. But he may as well push the alert button to see if Holu was ready. He pushed the alert button and waited.

Holu answered using the answer button. "Yes?"

"It's me," he said. Immediately, the door opened. Holu was standing on the other side of the door. She seemed shorter than usual, but the fragrance of flower blossoms greeted him just the same as always.

Holu greeted him with a hug. "You're early. I guess there's a first time for everything," she said as she retreated into the room.

He stepped into the room as the door closed behind him. He felt a flush of panic because the door closed. It was not proper in his estimation to be alone in a woman's apartment. Of course, Holu was his intended. Perhaps that was acceptable, but he wasn't really sure. Someone ought to write a manual about what is proper and what is not. Until he came to Bojoa, he had never been in Holu's residence and she had never been in his. They had always met in public. They accompanied each other a lot in the last couple of months, but they always met in public—mainly due to the timing of their meetings.

Holu had gone into her bedroom, so he was busily looking at the furnishings in her main room. From the looks of it, Holu had her room just about finished already. He wondered if he would ever get his completely done.

"I hadn't put on my shoes yet, Agapu."

Holu's voice was behind him. He turned toward the voice, and there was Holu. She definitely was taller again, and she looked radiant. Her face was like that of the ongiloi described in the Levra. It was perfect. She wore a brilliant smile. Her hair was piled up on top of her head. Somehow, not having her hair surrounding her head made her perfect face seem even more perfect. She wore a yellow dress—not bright yellow. It was a darker yellow and was made from a shiny fabric. The dress had medium blue trim and a medium blue slash and a dark green slash across the front. She wore a delicate gold chain from which dangled a brilliant, greenish blue gem stone cut in a shape resembling a triangle with curved sides. She wore a shimmering medium blue belt around her waist and carried a very small medium blue handbag. The dress flowed to the tops of her shoes that were also medium blue.

"Well, how do I look?" she asked after a brief moment.

"Absolutely wonderful," was what he heard come out of his mouth. That was true, but it didn't seem to do her justice. As she approached, he could see that her shoes had thin high heels, about the same height as she had worn last night.

"Well, I'm ready," she said with a quick breath thrown into the pause.

That breath made him feel, well, excited. As Holu moved past him and went to the door, he noticed that the dress that Holu was wearing exposed her back to just below her shoulder blades. He had never seen any part of Holu's bare back before. He noticed that his heart was beating faster, so he took a deep breath and followed her out the door.

"Nervous about the meeting, Agapu?" asked Holu with a smile on her face.

"Not right now," he said. He could feel that silly smile spreading across his face again. They had arrived at the lift door and were now standing in front of it. He couldn't take his eyes off of Holu. Finally, he realized that Holu was waiting for him to push the call button for the translift; so he pushed it. "Right now, something else is occupying my thoughts," he said after he pushed the button.

"Really? What else could possibly be occupying your thoughts right now?" Holu asked coyly. She was clearly playing with him.

The lift door opened, and they stepped inside.

He thought about escalating the frivolity, but he really wasn't in a frivolous mood. "You are," he said and turned to punch in the junction code for the recreation complex viewing room, where the meeting was to be held. Codes had been provided to all the guests invited to the room, but he didn't need the reference. He punched in RCVIEW and hit the green button. The translift delayed for just a moment to perform a security bio scan before it sprang into motion. The extra security was because of the meeting in the destination room. As he turned back to face Holu, she jumped into his arms and they embraced. As he responded with his embrace, his right hand found the bare skin on Holu's back. He felt a rush of excitement, and his heartbeat quickened. He felt Holu's embrace tighten, and he reciprocated. He then became aware that his left hand was on the small of Holu's back. He felt another rush, and he held Holu closer. He felt as if he couldn't hold her tight enough. Then he felt a bump; and the translift emerged from the living complex, raising its silver sides. He reluctantly released his embrace, as did Holu. They settled now for holding hands.

Wishing to take his mind off of the embrace he just shared with Holu, he looked below the lift and saw the gardens approaching below. "We will be passing directly over the gardens on our way to the recreation complex," he said in an effort to redirect the focus of the moment.

"Oh how drus, Agapu! The gardens are even more beautiful in the daylight! The colors of the flowers are absolutely stunning!" Holu leaned on his shoulder, her view transfixed down at the gardens.

He nearly corrected Holu since it wasn't really daylight that was shining overheard, but he quickly thought better of it. It looked like daylight. Daylight was actually a good description of the light in the dome during daytime parzes. Besides, he was enjoying the feeling of Holu leaning against him.

"It seems we are going higher," noticed Holu.

"We are. The lift is rising to meet the top of the recreation building. We will be at about seven and a half fets high by the time we reach the building." He looked up at the building that seemed to be approaching.

Holu's eyes followed his to the building, and she straightened slightly and shook her head.

"What's wrong, Holu? Are you afraid of heights?" he asked.

"No. Nothing's wrong. I just can't get over how buildings so large can be constructed under so much water. Just a little bit ago, no one would ever have imagined building anything this deep under the sea, especially not a whole city with such huge buildings," declared Holu.

"Yes. A lot has changed since that first vein of iri was found on Cysor Mountain," he said, sounding a little far away. He remembered that day as if it was yesterday; but it was fifteen years ago, in reality. The discovery had earned him his fourth name.

"Reliving the past, Agapu?" asked Holu, looking into his eyes.

He broke a smile. "I suppose that I was, Holu."

Just then, the lift gave a bump as it arrived at the recreation complex. He glanced at his watch. It read 3:78. "I guess we are arriving just a bit early," he said.

Holu took his arm to be escorted into the viewing room.

The All-Council Meeting

Then she gave his arm a squeeze and said, "It's axi, Agapu. I imagine most people will be here earlier than normal."

The doors of the lift opened.

His stomach knotted as he looked out on the view room, already filled with people. In this room, history was going to be made today. All the council members would be in one room. The high council would be sitting in session outside of the Cirri City council center for the first time since the center was built. A common citizen would be speaking at the all-council meeting for the first time in history. Then there was the announcement that Odanoi had promised.

He led Holu into the large, well-lit room from the middle of three translift doors spread out around the back of the room. The podium that was set up at the front of the room was the first thing that caught his eye as he exited the middle door. The stage was built low—only about a det from the floor—so that a person needed only to step up normally to mount the stage without the necessity of stairs. On the stage behind the podium, there were ten seats set up for the nine high council members, including Odanoi and the special guest of the meeting: Jahnu Vija. Behind the stage was the middle of the three front wall migoterms. There were also two migoterms spaced out on the side walls. News and entertainment generally showed on these giant screens, but they were all black and silent now. He searched the crowd for familiar faces. He saw plenty of faces he knew. He immediately picked out seven members of the technology council off to his left. To the right, he saw a few members of the trade council. As he scanned the room further, he spotted no less than thirty other men wearing the dark brown council suits with the golden yellow neck scarves. Holu was right. Many people were here early. He did not see Odanoi yet. He would be hard to miss since he would be wearing the formal headdress of the high council chair called the Kepasrun. He did not really expect to see Odanoi since the speaker for the meeting traditionally arrives just on time.

As they made their way down the aisle to the left of the center section of seats, he was spotted by Phrunoi, the chair of the technology council. "Agapoi, good to see you again," he said heartily. Phrunoi was dressed as he was, with the exception of his council medal, which displayed the brown elongated rectangle at the bottom that indicated his position as chair. Being the chair of the council also meant that Phrunoi was a member of the high council.

"It is good to be seen," he said, giving a slight bow. He brought Holu forward and said to Holu, "Holon, this is High Council Member Phrunoi, my council chair," Holu set her gaze to the floor and lowered herself slightly by crossing her feet and bending her knees to acknowledge Phrunoi's position. To Phrunoi, he said, "I am pleased to present Holon Tapienus Arkita. She is my newest team member and, more importantly, my intended."

Phrunoi showed only a little surprise as he took Holu's hand. "It is my sincere pleasure to meet you, Holon. I hope you don't take me too forward, but I must say that you are a vision, my dear." Then he kissed her hand and released it. He turned to Agap. "I say, my boy, how did you ever manage to keep her a secret?" Phrunoi waved his right hand to stop a reply. "It doesn't matter in the least, Agapoi. I am happy for you both. May Thaoi shine his blessings on your lives."

"May the blessings of Thaoi shine on you," he replied.

"I hate to bring up business right now, but what progress has your team made on the transport array since the last council meeting? The whole council is watching this project with great interest," asked Phrunoi.

He looked at Holu standing by him and said to her, "Would you like me to escort you to your seat? This question may take a little while to answer."

"Oh no, Agapoi. I am just as curious as the honorable Phrunoi seems to be. Do continue your conversation. I would like to hear your answer."

He smiled and then turned to Phrunoi. "As I recall, at our last meeting, I explained how we were using the array to mine iri here in Bojoa. By the way, Phrunoi, what do you think of our little settlement?"

"It is astounding what you've been able to do down here, my boy. I must say that I am very impressed. The mere fact that there can be a dome of this size at a depth of twelve hundred and fifty sunds is amazing. And you can build a large passenger submarine that can dive at these depths. I didn't even hear any stress on the hull. It's magnificent! That's what it is!" Phrunoi said in an enthusiastic but dignified manner. Phrunoi was born and raised in the northwestern coast of Cirri, where a touch of the unique Jontu way of speaking had integrated the culture and warped into its own unique way of speaking, so he took "my boy" as a term of fondness, not a sleight.

"As always, your generous praise is appreciated, but it was the discovery of iri that made Bojoa and the performance of the hulls possible. No great feat of engineering was required, just a little ingenuity. And most of the ingenuity originated from within my team, not from me personally," he admitted.

"You are always too willing to sell yourself short, my boy. An admirable trait, to be sure, but I believe you lack clarity about your own accomplishments. Was it not you who discovered iri? Was it not you who first discovered its splendid qualities? Was it not you who came up with the technical data that allowed the idea of the hulls and the dome? Shall I continue?" said Phrunoi, obviously ready to continue.

"No, no. As always, you make your point well. I bow to your wisdom," he said, giving a slight dip to his head.

"Now, about that transport array?" Phrunoi's inflection went upward, indicating a question.

He glanced at his watch. There was still enough time to give a bit of detail before everyone would have to find their seats at ten spens till four parzes. It was customary at all meetings for the guests to sit before the introductory music could be played. The introductory music was a medley of high orchestra pieces of the speakers choosing, generally lasting about ten spens. "Our team has made a good deal of progress with the array since the council's last briefing. We have resolved the issue of re-materialization contamination by refining the containment beam as the transport energy travels through a solid or liquid media. The material retrieved is now the material that the matter exciter beam was programmed to retrieve. The accuracy has reached a hundred percent."

Phrunoi looked impressed. "How did your team accomplish the refinement?"

"We did it by lessening the gap between energy streams in the containment perimeter. We were able to reduce the gaps as close to zero as is possible according to the law of energy field proximity. As you know, if the energy fields make contact, the beams will lose their integrity and the energized matter will be lost to chaos, resulting in a rather large explosion," he explained.

"But how are you able to manage the fields with such precision? The slightest fluctuation in energy intensity or direction would be disastrous," asked Phrunoi.

The All-Council Meeting

"We are now producing the power with a new generator we call the millennium generator. We call it that because it could theoretically generate a perfectly consistent stream of power for a thousand years. We tested the generator thoroughly and found absolutely no power spikes or ebbs in power output. This was made possible by iri. An alloy of iri, silver, and copper yields the perfect conducting material. Absolutely no variation in energy conduction exists in this alloy. The perfect energy insulator exists in an alloy of iri, carbon, and zinc. This alloy is soft and completely malleable but will not conduct any energy of any sort, including heat energy, and remains completely inert unless it comes into contact with pure iri. Then it combusts. Since inside circuitry is not likely ever to be in contact with pure iri, we now use these same alloys in all of the transport devices, making energy precision absolutely certain."

Phrunoi smiled and shook his head slightly. "Well, it seems you have found another use for iri. I wonder what else you will discover about it next, Agapoi."

"That is hard to say," he said, but then he noticed that a small crowd had gathered in the aisle, listening to the conversation he was having with Phrunoi.

Part of the crowd was technology council members, some were part of his team, some were other people he recognized, and some were people he did not recognize at all. The circle of onlookers had left a respectful distance around the two of them; but some were crowding Holu, and she was starting to look a bit harried by their presence in the aisle and in the nearby rows of seats. She was probably thinking that she should have taken him up on his offer to escort her to her seat about now. He made eye contact with Holu. The harried look was replaced with a completely serene look. He knew that the quick change in look meant that she didn't want to interrupt his conversation for her sake, so he continued.

"Iri is so unusual. It defies prediction. The only certainty seems to be that the percent ratio of iri in a compound or alloy is always a multiple of seven. Firocryl, the compound that composes the outside dome, is twenty-one percent iri, and the alloy that coats the exterior of the subs is fourteen percent iri. Pure iri defies manipulation unless you heat it slowly. It then melts just a little above the boiling point of water. Heat it quickly or try to pound it or cut it or do anything else with it and it remains untouched. But once it is melted, it combines with just about anything."

Phrunoi looked a bit puzzled. "Say you throw purified iri into a vat of boiling iron. The iri would not melt?"

He shook his head to indicate that it would not.

"You can't scratch it with a diamond?"

He again shook his head.

"That is completely unbelievable."

He smiled. "I cannot count the number of times that iri has made me say that during the last fifteen years. But I am afraid I am a bit off my course. I was supposed to be updating you on the transport array."

"That is quite all right. Iri seems to be a fascinating subject of its own. How much does manufacturing know about iri?" asked Phrunoi.

"Only what our team has told them, which is enough to get our devices manufactured. No one else has experimented with iri. In point of fact, no one else believed us when we published our results ten years ago. As a result, my team alone actively researches and designs with iri. Given the skepticism we received, we wanted to show what could be done with iri

THE ALL-COUNCIL MEETING

before I openly commented on it further to the council," he said with a shrug.

"A prudent decision, Agapoi. I can see why you have progressed so quickly. I will be looking forward to our next formal meeting. Can we expect a full report then?" asked Phrunoi.

"It would be my honor," he said formally.

"Good. I would hear more now, but the time is approaching that the council of nine should be seated, and I have a quick matter to attend to before then." Phrunoi shifted his attention to Holu. "And I must say it has been a real pleasure to make your acquaintance, my dear. I think that you have ruined me for other beautiful things, as I will always have to compare them to your beauty."

With that rather poetic statement hanging in the air, Phrunoi was off toward the right side of the room. He looked at Holu. She was blushing noticeably. He assumed it was because of the flowery compliment that Phrunoi had bestowed on her. After Phrunoi had left the aisle, the people who were entertaining themselves listening in on the conversation began to disperse, each giving Agap a polite nod before turning their attention to other things. It somewhat amused him to see how crowds developed around council chairs when they were in public. He noticed that his team was on their way to the seats reserved for them and were completely ignoring him. They were instead exchanging grins with each other as they passed by.

He glanced at his watch. It read 3:87. The music would begin in three spens. It was time to move to their seats. It was considered impolite to be standing when the music began. It was considered outright rude to talk after the music started. At an oration meeting such as this was to be, the music was intended to set the tone for what would be heard during the meeting. The custom was that the music should set the opposite tone but directly reinforce the topic. Nevertheless, music is a subjective art, so the message of the music was often not fully understood until the oration was complete and, quite often, not even then by some. He was not exactly sure what music he would hear, but it would be a sign of what would come.

He led Holu to the second row of the section on their right, the section directly in front of the podium. The technology council and his team had seats of secondary honor to the seats on the stage for this morning's meeting. The room had been set up with nine sections of chairs making an arch in front of the rounded stage front. In each front row, there were eleven seats for the eleven council members on each of the nine councils who were not going to be sitting on stage. The number of chairs grew progressively with each succeeding row of each section. Due to the room being rectangular, the sections on each end had the fewest rows while the section in the middle had the most rows. By the time they arrived at Holu's row, the rest of his team had found their seats. The two end seats on both sides of the row had been sealed closed so that no one could sit in them. This left eight open seats for his eight team members. Holu's seat was as close to directly behind his as could be managed since each successive row had one more seat than the row in front of it. Since his seat was the middle seat, Holu's seat was one of the two middle seats on the second row. There were three team members between Holu and her seat: Kowtsom, Phunex, and Yotux. Supeb, Axopen, Opsil, and Eutay were seated on the other side of Holu's seat. Agap remembered that Supeb beamed when he learned that he would be sitting next to Holu. He had hoped it was because Supeb believed that Agap trusted him the most. Maybe he should have put Yotux between the boys on the team and Holu. No. Supeb could be trusted. Besides, he would be sort of sitting between Holu and Supeb anyway.

"I believe this is your row, young lady," he said in his best impression of a theater usher.

"Why, thank you, sir. Could you shine your light down the aisle for me?" Holu answered, trying her best to follow through with the hoax he had perpetrated.

Holu was always very quick to react to his attempts at wit. It was just another trait that endeared her to him. Once he saw Holu take her seat, he gave her one last smile and went to his seat in front of her.

He glanced at his watch. It now read 3:88. A couple more spens and the music would start. A random thought about how long the oration might take passed through his mind. He answered the thought with, *Not more than a parz, I suppose.* He then scolded himself for having such an improper thought. After all, the length of the oration had nothing to do with the importance or value of it. It may be a short oration for all he knew. He just knew that it had to be something unusual given the circumstances.

The row for the technology council was empty before he sat down, but now it was filling up fast. Lezumanoi sat down to his right and Radoi sat down immediately afterward to his left. As he glanced down the row, he thought that Mageloi's seat was the only empty seat in the row now. The high council seats were filling up now as well. This was the first time he had ever seen any of the high council members in person, except for Phrunoi; but he only saw him in person for the first time yesterday on the sub. He didn't speak to him then, but he had seen him. Except for the high council, councils rarely met in person simply because the members rarely lived in the same city. The lower council positions were not full-time positions, as the high council positions were.

He passed the time until the music started by trying to remember all of the names on the council of nine, as the high council was sometimes called. Let's see. On the end, to his left, was Timoi of the manufacturing council. Next to him was Pholoi of the trade council. Then it was Pulamoi of the judicial council, then Gietroi of the health and safety council. The next two chairs were empty. Those were the speakers' chairs, Odanoi and Jahnu Vija. After the empty chairs came Phrunoi, and then Dikugoi of the legislative council, Merchoi of the urban council, and Agrutoi of the rural council. Odanoi was from the business and agricultural council. Jahnu Vija was not from any council. He did not know anything about him except his unusual name.

Now it was 3:89. He looked at Mageloi's seat. It was still empty. Mageloi had better hurry. He wouldn't want to be guilty of insulting Odanoi. Agap could not see the rows behind him, and he certainly wasn't going to turn around to look; but they felt as if they were now occupied by the fact that he couldn't hear voices anymore. He reasoned that whoever was not sitting would be sitting soon.

Just then, he had the feeling that someone's eyes were staring at his back. He thought that it might be Holu. He pictured her eyes looking at him and smiled.

There was a stirring down his row. It was Mageloi sitting down. He glanced at his watch. It still showed 3:89. Mageloi had cut it close this time. He had only attended a few council meetings, but Mageloi's hologram was usually among the last holograms to appear in the few that he had attended.

He looked at the stage and saw the section arrangements in his peripheral vision. The arrangement of the sections in relation to the stage reminded him of a Levra proclamation service. Every community, including Bojoa—he hoped—would have an occasional service where a scholar of the Levra would bring a discourse on a passage from the Levra. The services were called when one of the local Levra scholars felt that a certain discourse was needed or thought that a worship service was in order. Some discourses exhorted a clear conscience before Thaoi. Some discourses spoke of Thaoi himself. Some discourses warned of the dangers of certain philosophies. Some discourses espoused the virtues of faith in Thaoi's promises. Some were just for a service of worship toward Thaoi. Sometimes they were held once a month, sometimes three times within a week. Most services had good attendance unless the service was held when most of the community was working. Even then, some would come during their work shift if their boss could spare them. They would then go back to work afterward. Services were generally held with a similar stage and seating arrangement as the viewing room was arranged now. It had been this way since the beginning of Cirri as far as he knew.

His watch now read 3:91. His musings took longer than he had been aware. Still, there was no music; but that was not totally unexpected. A speaker was given ten spens for music, but it did not mean that all of the time had to be used.

Then he heard it. The music had begun. Agap recognized the tune right away. It was "Mwo Egeput Cirri," a patriotic Cirrian march. He reasoned that the oration was to be familiar and informative or at least pragmatic in nature. He felt let down in a way. Apparently, he had built up this occasion far too much in his mind. He did enjoy this tune though, and he let his mind focus on the music.

However, the march did not last very long. The music soon bridged to a quiet melody that was unfamiliar to him. Apparently, it was unfamiliar to others because he heard a gasp or two in the crowd; but no one dared talk or even whisper. Those gasps followed by silence matched the mood being conveyed through the tune. It was a haunting tune, nearly sad. He didn't know what to make of it. He reasoned that this music conveyed that the message would be unexpected and emotional or perhaps contemplative.

Odanoi and Jahnu Vija were not yet seated. Their absence was typical for a meeting that was going to be an oratory-style meeting. There was no reason for them to listen to the music that they had arranged to be played. He wondered if the shortness of the march had any particular meaning. He realized that a headache could be the reward for his current analysis of every beat of the music, but he could not help himself. He thought that the music might be implying an order in the delivery of the oration. He also wondered if the timing of their appearance on stage would be significant. *This is how people get headaches from the introductory music,* he thought to himself.

The hauntingly sad melody was still playing. He was having a hard time focusing just on the beauty of the music this time. He was full of anticipation and dread at the same time. He wished he could see Holu. Her face was all he needed to quell his anxiety. He pictured her face in his mind. But what would her expression be? Would it be concern or confidence? She had a way of giving him confidence just by being with him, regardless of what her face was conveying. Still, the same music played. He feared that the melody might haunt his dreams after today.

It was exactly 3:97:77 when the music stopped. It just stopped. He noticed the time to the tic because the three sevens at the end caught his eye. Neither speaker had yet taken their seats. Still, everything was still. More gasps were heard, followed by stillness, eerie stillness. Was this a technical problem? Surely if it was, the speakers would make an appearance to dispel any alarm. Yet there was only quiet—no chaos, and no noise. Notwithstanding, alarm was building in the quiet. As tic after tic passed, the anxiety in the room increased.

Then, a chord, a discordant chord was heard. He checked his watch. It was 3:98:47—exactly seventy tics of silence. Another chord and then another sounded—not at certain intervals but randomly, with apparently no purpose. The chords sounded like … chaos. There was no other word to describe them.

A figure was seen walking on the stage. He was a man of slight build and not very tall. He wore brown clothes, but his clothes were nothing like the pristine suits that the men seated on the stage wore. His clothes were the clothes of an everyday worker, a laborer. His sark was uncovered—no jacket, no vest, not even an outer closing shirt. The sark was plain brown—pressed and clean, but plain. His trousers were of a heavy material, not meant for dress. They were meant for labor.

The sark was a Cirri custom meant to remind Cirrians of their humble roots. Everyone wore one; but the modern practice was to dress it up in public, embroider it, partially cover it—do anything to make the sark look like something it was not. This man must be Jahnu Vija. He made no effort to cover his humble sark. He was now seated just to the left of the podium as the audience viewed it. As expected, he was to be the secondary speaker.

The chords had become a bit more frequent now and a little bit louder. They seemed to be headed for a crescendo. As the chords continued to build and build, he glanced at his watch to see when they would stop. The noise of the chords was beginning to become unbearable. The time was 3:99:87, and the chords stopped. The chords played for exactly one hundred forty tics. He didn't think that the number seven's prominence in the timing of the chords could have been an accident. In their place, a single clear tone of a bell sounded. It was quickly overlapped by a lower but harmonious tone of a bell. Both tones died out at precisely 4:00:00.

Agap thought that his eyes had been focused on the podium; but he was apparently not actually looking at the podium until now because there stood Odanoi, in his full council suit, and on his head was the kepasrun. The kepasrun had a large, billowing center with two tall fins on either side of the center. The color of the headdress was dark brown with gold trim. His gray hair and full beard seemed to fit his attire perfectly.

Odanoi stood, looking at the gathering. All present at the meeting were influential members of Cirri society. He was tempted to exclude Jahnu Vija from that description, but he was one of the people on the stage and in a speaker's place of honor. If he was not influential before tonight, he certainly would be afterward. Jahnu Vija looked out of place, but something told him that he was not. No. Jahnu Vija belonged where he was.

Still, Odanoi did not speak. He stood behind the podium, scanning the faces of the audience as if trying to memorize them. The already-hushed crowd began to become even more hushed than Agap had thought possible.

Finally, Odanoi uttered his first words. "I would like to start my remarks today by answering a question. No, there was not any technical malfunction with the music. And yes, it really was intended to sound that way." Odanoi's face remained stoic as he spoke.

One or two chuckles were heard in various sections; but they soon vanished, as Odanoi stood motionless and sober behind the podium. Odanoi continued to stand motionless for a time. The quiet was deafening and nearly horrifying.

Odanoi finally continued. "This meeting will be conducted in the oratory format. No questions will be entertained by our guest speaker, Jahnu Vija. Nor will I entertain questions. Once the meeting is over, I will be escorting Jahnu Vija to his quarters in the guest building. The high council will also depart immediately to their quarters. Please do not attempt to contact us after the meeting. We ask that we be left in solitude. We will contact the high council once we have made ourselves ready to entertain discussion."

The silence of the gathering seemed to grow louder. The request for solitude from Odanoi was quite unusual, but not without precedent. He recalled that Cirri history recorded this same request from the high council chair about two thousand years ago, when wars abounded in Kosundo. On that occasion, the chair used the time of solitude to discuss the crisis that Kosundo was facing with Levra scholars and to devote time to meditation before Thaoi. The chair's name was Yarukoi. He was the author of the last book of the Levra: Malluntekas.

Odanoi continued. "It is customary to start a council meeting with a passage from the Levra, but I am deferring that honor to our guest speaker, Jahnu Vija."

This was something new. He did not know of another time when the reading of the Levra was deferred to a guest speaker. It was considered a very high honor to read the Levra in a council meeting and had always been reserved for a member of council. The silence around him was roaring.

"This honor is bestowed on Jahnu Vija because Jahnu is a very special man. He has proven to me that he is a man whose conscience is clear before Thaoi. Until recently, his occupation had been that of a maintenance supervisor. And he has humbly dressed in that role today. He has since been appointed as the Levra scholar to the high council chair. He does not have any credentials from a Cirri university or college that would merit this appointment. What he does have is a mandate from Thaoi."

The quiet was gone. There were murmurs scattered throughout the audience. He was stunned both from what Odanoi had just said and by the murmurs from the audience.

Odanoi raised his hand, and the quiet returned. "I understand the confusion that is here in this gathering, so I do not take the small interruption as an insult. Your consciences may remain clear toward me. Thaoi has seen fit to use me as the proof of the mandate that Jahnu has received. My meditations in the Levra were accompanied by an impression of a voice for seven consecutive nights, the last coming one week ago. That voice told me to expect a visit from a man with a name after the old custom. Other distinguishing details were given to me about this man as well. As some of you may have suspected, Jahnu was named after the old custom. The other details will remain between Jahnu and me."

He thought he saw a trace of a smile on Odanoi's face, but it was gone before he could be sure he saw it.

"Jahnu came to see me on that seventh night. His coming coincided exactly with the conclusion of my impression on that night. That night, Jahnu Vija revealed to me his mandate from Thaoi." Odanoi glanced back at Jahnu.

"Jahnu is a special man because of his mandate. He is not thoroughly acquainted with the seating honors for speakers, however. You see, I am here only to introduce Jahnu. He is our main speaker. Please honor Jahnu Vija by rising as he approaches the podium."

Jahnu stood, and the audience stood with him. As Odanoi passed, Odanoi offered a partially clenched right fist to Jahnu. Jahnu responded by grasping Odanoi's curled fingers with his fingers. The action was completed with both men pulling the other toward him until their shoulders nearly touched and eye contact was made. The stance was held for about two tics.

The All-Council Meeting

This act was known as grasping fists and was a common way to greet a friend among men in Cirri. Once the men released each other, Odanoi continued to the seat that Jahnu had been occupying and Jahnu continued to the podium. When Jahnu reached the podium, the audience sat down.

He noticed that Jahnu didn't have a Levra when he came toward the podium. This surprised him since Odanoi had said that he was going to start with a reading. Jahnu took a deep breath and started in a somewhat quivering voice. "I will be quoting from the book of Malluntekas to start my oration. This is the passage from Malluntekas that is often referred to as the prophecy of the soulless." Jahnu then began to quote the entire passage from memory. His voice was quite steady as he quoted.

"'The time will come when the works of men will wax great. Barriers of old will be broken down. The heavens will feel the presence of man. The depths will be his abode. Men will think to be the creator, but his work will be empty, waiting to be filled with evil. Only the faithful will remain.'

"'The time will come when men will think that his work can surpass the work of Thaoi. They will be swallowed by their own work and bring death and destruction to the whole of Kosundo. It is Thaoi that gives life, but men, through pride, will think of the one as a work of their own hands. Thaoi is the only giver of life. Man will only make abominations from the life that Thaoi created. For the one who is not a full man will have no soul, and he will hate the ones that took his soul and made him an abomination. His being will yearn for that it does not have and will seek to take captive the souls of men. His hate will cause him to destroy the body of those who will not give their souls to him. Only the faithful will remain.'

"'Beware the soulless. They will offer gifts, but the gifts are not true, for they have a great price. Because the time will come when men will give their souls to the will of the one who is not a full man and the destroyer will laugh. Beware then the soulless. They are destroyers of souls. Only the faithful will remain.'

"'The time will come when the one who hates will bring destruction. All men will come to fear his works, though few will see the one. The soulless one will demand the will of the proud, and the proud will give it for a gift. Nevertheless, this will not satisfy the one, and his hatred will increase until he will seek to dominate the souls of all who dwell on Kosundo. Then will he know the destroyer. Only the faithful will remain.'

"'He who hath understanding, listen and take heed. When the destroyer comes, he will cause man to war with man. Man will not be given rest from war save for a season, and then will the soulless be unleashed by the destroyer, for the one will be vanquished by the destroyer. Then the works of men will be turned against man, and the destroyer will destroy men's souls. This is the beginning of sorrows. Only the faithful will remain.'

"'Nevertheless, Thaoi is faithful. He will raise up a prophet and will appoint a faithful servant who will understand Thaoi's great gift, which is the way of salvation from the destroyer. Heed the words of the prophet, for in the latter days, Thaoi will save a remnant to himself. Only the faithful will remain.'"

Jahnu had quoted the passage with great conviction in his voice. That conviction brought Agap's full focus on Jahnu's words. As Jahnu continued his oration, a sound of authority entered his voice; and he delivered the oration very deliberately. It almost seemed as if he was pausing after each word. Or maybe that was just how he perceived what he heard.

The All-Council Meeting

"I did not choose this passage to begin my oration," were the first words uttered by Jahnu. "Thaoi left no choice in it for me. It is my mandate to be the messenger of Thaoi.

"On the night spoken of by the honorable Odanoi, it was my mandate to deliver a message that I had received in a visitation from a shining apparition who identified himself as Mechial, high ongiloi of our Lord Thaoi. Since the night the ongiloi appeared to me, I have been receiving the impressions from a voice much like Odanoi described today. These impressions have given me the basis for my oration today.

"This room contains the most influential persons in Cirri today. You have been gathered here at the request of the high council chair, Odanoi. It was I who asked Odanoi to have you gathered together to hear the oration that Thaoi has mandated of me today. The voice that has impressed my mind has identified itself to me as *Phunu tu Thaoi*. As this room is filled with highly learned individuals and many Cirrian names have origins that spring from the old tongue, I am certain that you recognize that name as Odanoi did. It is an old tongue phrase meaning the *Voice of Thaoi*. I was told to assemble you today by the Voice of Thaoi.

"It has been two thousand years since the last visitation was made by Thaoi. Malluntekas was written because of the visitation received by Yarukoi. I have not been instructed to write anything of that I have been told, only to proclaim it as I have heard it. Thaoi has blessed me since the visitation with an ability to remember each word of the Levra as well as each word uttered by the apparition and each word impressed to me by the Voice of Thaoi. This is His gift to me and a sign to you of my visitation and mandate. None of you knew me before tonight; but the people who did know me before the visitation are also proof of this sign of the mandate given to me, as I was not known for my ability to memorize before the visitation.

"The Voice of Thaoi sends His greeting to all in attendance who have strived to keep a clear conscience and are faithful to the things they have learned from the Levra. To you, He says these words: 'Your strivings are a testimony of your faith in Thaoi. Love Thaoi as He has loved you and your faith will stand the test. Your faith will be rewarded in this life or the next.'

"Those who received His greeting now bear the sign of remembrance for these words. These words will not leave your memory. Share these words with those people who will hear them. They are words of good tidings from Thaoi. One of you before me who received His greeting will be given five perfect words from the Voice of Thaoi. I was not told the words or given your identity. The words will be revealed to you at the time appointed by Thaoi.

"Not all in attendance here were given His greeting. At this time, some will have already forgotten the words of His greeting. If you are among the ones who have forgotten His greeting, the Voice of Thaoi sends you His warning. To you, He says these words: 'You have said the words of faith, but no faith has been found in you. Do not deceive yourself. Your conscience is clouded. You will fall prey to your pride if your ways are not mended. Seek Thaoi now, while he can be found. If you have no faith in this life, you will not see the next life. There is no life without Thaoi. There is only death.'

"All in attendance now bear the sign of remembrance for the words of His warning. Share these words if you are faithful. Heed these words if faith was not found in you. Thaoi will grant the sign of remembrance for the words of His greeting to all who seek Him. Forsake your pride and strive to clear your conscience before Thaoi and men. This will stand as a testimony of your faith before Thaoi.

"Thaoi has chosen to let you hear His words. This is a great honor. This honor is bestowed on you to honor the faith of your fathers. Do not fear these words or take these words lightly. Thaoi has given you the responsibility to use the words of this oratory wisely.

This place of wonder would not exist had Thaoi not willed it so. It is not by chance that you are here today. It is not by chance that the wonder of Bojoa was completed at this time. This place will be needed to be a beacon of hope for all of Kosundo. A large responsibility has fallen to each person seated in this room today. You will be given choices in the days that lie ahead.

"A crisis will face all of Kosundo in seven days' time. As I stated before, the passage that I quoted for you today was not my choice. The fulfillment of this prophecy is upon us. What we do here must be done with a clear conscience. We must not just pretend any longer to have the faith of our fathers. That faith must gather strength and become resolved or Kosundo will perish and our lives and the lives of all in Kosundo will be forfeit.

"Hear now the message of my visitation. The time has come. The father of the soulless is among the people of Kosundo. Only the faithful will remain.

"This is not a dream. We are in the latter days. The destroyer has been with us since the time of the last visitation two thousand years ago. Now the time of the prophecy of the soulless has arrived.

"This prophecy is not metaphoric, as we had thought through our ignorance. The prophecy is literal. The phrase we have adopted as a banner of our spirituality, 'Only the faithful will remain,' is more than a spiritual teaching. It is a literal warning. When the times of the soulless play out before us, only the faithful will remain. According to the prophecy, only a remnant will remain. The full meaning to that has not been revealed, but it is sure that a remnant is not all. Not all of the faithful of Kosundo will remain, but we will be given choices as events unfold. Just what effect our choices will have has not been revealed, but our choices will make a difference for many.

"Before we dismiss the meeting, I would like to quote two other passages from the Levra that give further insight on our responsibility during the times of the soulless.

"The first is from the book of Sonaydasa: 'A clear conscience before Thaoi requires a man to clear his conscience before man. A man cannot keep a clear conscience if he refuses to help those who cannot help themselves. Help as you can when you are able. This is part of the way to life.'

"The second is from the book of Alpida: 'Thaoi gives gifts, as he will, and the great gift he will bestow to a people apart. The great gift is the way of salvation.'

"We are the 'people apart.' What we do will make a difference.

"Thank you for your attention today. You may now stand."

The audience stood as one. Jahnu went to stand in front of the empty seat. Once Jahnu reached his seat, Odanoi went to the podium.

"May Thaoi be glorified," proclaimed Odanoi to signify that the meeting was about to be adjourned.

The unison response was, "To the glory of Thaoi, may we be found faithful."

Somehow, that ritual chant seemed to mean more to Agap than before the meeting.

The All-Council Meeting

That was it. The meeting was adjourned. The high council and Jahnu walked off the stage and back to the lift doors. Everyone in the audience watched in silence, until the last of the high council disappeared into a lift. No one had spoken. It seemed that no one dared to speak.

The time was 4:21:21 to the tic, according to the clock above the lift when the last high council member left the room. He wouldn't be surprised if the official transcript of the meeting showed that it ended at exactly 4:21:00. It just seemed that it would fit. The Levra placed a special emphasis on the number seven. It was the number of completion and prophecy. Twenty-one was a multiple of seven—seven times three. Three was the number of Thaoi in the Levra. The timing of the introductory music certainly had emphasized the number seven as well. He knew that he was just engaging in speculation, but it did seem to fit. Probably no one else really noticed the timing, but he had always paid close attention to time. Even to him, the whole meeting seemed surreal. It seemed that no time had passed, and yet it seemed that time had advanced to another era during the meeting.

He had heard many Levra proclamations, but none had been like this one. Jahnu Vija had spoken with a confidence and an authority that he had never before heard among Levra scholars. That authority had him testing his memory to check if he remembered the greeting of the Voice of Thaoi. *Your strivings are a testimony of your faith in Thaoi. Love Thaoi as He has loved you, and your faith will stand the test. Your faith will be rewarded in this life or the next.* He remembered, but somehow he knew that he remembered before he actually mentally recited the greeting. He also remembered His warning. Both seemed to be more at the forefront of his mind than any other memory. It seemed that he had to get past the memories of

His greeting and His warning before he could access the rest of his memories. They did not exactly get in the way of his other memories; they just seemed always to be on his mind. He could still remember other things without distraction; but once his concentration on the other thoughts waned, those two memories were there.

Then there was that mysterious reference to five perfect words. Jahnu had described the recipient of five perfect words as "one of you before me who received His greeting." At least that is what he thought the words were. It was strange. It seemed he could not be as sure about his other memories as he was about the greeting and the warning they received today, yet he seemed to be sure about his memory of the recipient; he was just more certain about the greeting and warning. It was astonishing how those two memories stood out. But the description of the recipient did rule out some people. It ruled out the high council as being recipients of the words. They were all seated behind Jahnu. He then wondered if the "before me" was more specific than it seemed. No. He didn't say, "directly before me." He just said, "before me." A person could come to too many false conclusions by reading too much into what had been said.

It was now clear why the meeting was held in person and even, to some extent, why it was held in Bojoa. The message that Jahnu delivered was meant for the people who were invited to the meeting only. And here, in Bojoa, the meeting could be kept from the news. It was simple enough since the dome was not yet made public. Simply do not invite any newspersons to Bojoa. Still, we were exhorted to spread the two greetings to other people; but nothing was said about spreading the message of the prophecy. It seemed that we were to keep to the prophecy to ourselves for now.

The All-Council Meeting

Then there was the message of the visitation. Jahnu had said, "The father of the soulless is among the people of Kosundo." He knew the Levra pretty well himself. He could not recall the name father of the soulless ever mentioned in the Levra. It certainly wasn't in the prophecy of the soulless that was quoted in the meeting, but it tickled his memory. He had heard or read that name somewhere before, but he couldn't think where or when.

Just then, he realized he had bumped into someone. It was Radoi. Agap did always tend to pace when he was thinking. He must have started to pace. Radoi seemed to be awakened out of a trance and took a moment to realize he had been bumped.

"I am terribly sorry, Radoi. That was careless of me," he said in a hushed voice that somehow still seemed too loud.

"No. That's axi, Agapoi. The oration was very... unusual," was what came softly out of Radoi's mouth; but he thought it had more meaning.

"Yes, it was," was all he managed to say.

Radoi nodded his head and headed toward the aisle.

The accidental bump and subsequent conversation seemed to stir the people around them from their thoughts. Soon, there was a stirring throughout the room. Low voices could be heard scattered across the room, but only scattered and sporadic.

He turned to find Holu. She had been saying something softly to Yotux. The conversation didn't last long, and Yotux filed out of the row behind the two other girls on the team. Holu caught his gaze and smiled as she saw him. She then followed Yotux out of the row. Agap went to the beginning of the aisle to meet her.

When Holu was close enough, she asked in a very soft voice, "Have you ever had a meeting like this before?" She seemed shaken.

He would have to reassure her, but he thought he might need reassuring himself.

"It's not every meeting that announces the beginning of a new period of time." He had attempted a light comment and had failed miserably in his attempt. There was no way of talking of the oration casually. "I am sorry, Holu," he said softly. "I am afraid that I don't know how to react to what was said. It was delivered so simply, so directly, yet so forcefully..." His voice trailed off. He seemed to be at a loss for words.

"I understand. I feel the same way, I believe. It is as if a thousand things are hammering at my mind only to have them come back to those two thoughts."

Holu cut off abruptly, but she had said enough. She was right; she had described it perfectly. The most important parts of the oration were the greeting and the warning. That was what the introductory music was telling us. Don't worry over what was to happen in Kosundo, not yet anyway. The important thing is to make sure of your own faith. He had assurance now that his faith pleased Thaoi. So did Holu. This was an occasion to rejoice. Hard times were coming, sure; but for now, Thaoi had let them know where they stood with Him through that wonderful oration.

A broad smile crossed his face. "You are an absolute genius!" he exclaimed softly.

Holu looked at him, obviously not understanding the epiphany that he had just had. He grabbed Holu and hugged her like he had never hugged her before. As he let her go, Holu's look of puzzlement bordered on a look of apprehension.

"Don't worry, Holu. I am not mad. You have unlocked the meaning of the whole oratory. I will explain on the way to lunch. Suddenly, I feel very much like eating something."

Holu gave him a slight smile and held out her arm. The crowd had already thinned considerably, and they seemed to be the only ones not already at the lift doors. It would dawn on many of the others in the crowd eventually. They were not as fortunate to have a genius for an intended, so it just might take them a while longer. By the time they walked back to the middle lift door, there was no one waiting. He pressed the call button rather enthusiastically. He knew that he had that silly grin on his face again, and he was glad.

As they entered the lift, he began telling Holu what she had discovered. Before they reached the restaurant, they were both sharing in laughter. The mood all around them seemed subdued, but nothing could dampen the joy they shared at that moment. They were given assurance that Thaoi was pleased. All was well today, no matter what tomorrow may bring.

There were those who found the joy that Agap had found later that day, but others struggled with the message delivered by Jahnu. Their minds were filled with fear about the foretelling of the soulless and did not allow the message of His blessing to give them joy that night. Many of these would find that joy at a later time, but not that day.

Still others found the joy that Agap had found by clearing their conscience before Thaoi and men. They made things right with those they had wronged and with those to whom they bore ill will. The cloud had been lifted, and they found a joy that they had never experienced before. This stood as a testimony for them and others of their newfound faith.

There were those who left the meeting in despair. His warning was all that rang in their ears, and the pride because of position or accomplishment haunted them. They were reluctant to humble themselves to admit that they had no real commitment to Thaoi. These thoughts clouded the conscience further; and no joy was found for them—only the despair and fear of the prophecy that Jahnu revealed.

Only one left that meeting that day without a change in his soul. He was not impressed by the message of Jahnu, and he would not be impressed if the Voice of Thaoi himself was to have spoken. He was annoyed that he was sent a message only last night that he was to board a sub in less than a parz. He was annoyed that he had known nothing of this underwater dome. But most of all, he was annoyed at a message he had received this morning. A message from the trade council had said that he was no longer to be one of Cirri's technology advisors to Doetora. It seemed that the emperor found no use for his information anymore. He liked the lifestyle that the credits from that arrangement had given him and was not at all happy to have lost that source of income.

That was the emperor's loss because there was a treasure of information to be had here at Bojoa, a place that he didn't even know existed until his *Ketesku* informed him of it. He had paid his *Ketesku* well to report on that upstart councilman. The councils were wise to keep Bojoa from him until now; but Odanoi was foolish to have brought him here, nearly as foolish as that Jahnu had sounded today. He would have to find a way to stay in Bojoa. He thought that perhaps the great one would like to have someone here, in this place. That fool, Jahnu, had called Bojoa "this place of wonder" and a "beacon of hope." He imagined that he would be rewarded well for information about Bojoa. That thought brought an eerie

The All-Council Meeting

smile to his face. He would contact Purhit tonight to see if he thought the great one would have interest. He believed he would have a great interest. With the right information, the great one could smash this "beacon of hope" into a million pieces. Still, he would have to be careful. He did not want to have Bojoa smashed before he made good his escape.

14
BOOKSHELF HISTORY

It was now nearly seven. Six ninety-two was the time according to the clock in the room. Agap sat in the chair he had created last night with a stack of books at his feet. He had tried to create a chair that resembled the chair he had back in Zaria. This one was close. The chomile had actually allowed him to create a chair that had the feel of being used. The simulation of the used feeling was really quite good. Yotux had done a nice job with the software for the chomile. Next week, the team would work on some improvements to it, including making it mobile and also making the wall-making routines a bit less command-driven and a bit more menu-driven and therefore less complicated. There were other little improvements, like having the input for color included before the chomile actually made something. It seemed that was another popular complaint, and it seemed that Holu had been right about that too.

He was munching on some snacks he had purchased on his way home. It wasn't quite suppertime just yet, but Holu was going out with Yotux this evening for what Holon had termed, "Some shopping and some girl talk." Whatever the "girl talk" involved, he was not exactly sure; but he thought that his name just might come up somehow. Yotux was also taking Holu to supper. So he decided that he would dine in tonight. The snacks where not that nutritious. That was true. But they were tasty and filling. Plus relaxing, reading, and snacking just seemed to go together extremely well. A lot of people liked viewing programs on their personal terms, or PT's as they were called, but he didn't really see the appeal of just watching other people do stuff. Unless it was a sporting event—especially speedball—or news, he rarely watched PT programming. However, most people seemed to be avid viewers. He much preferred a good book to the PT. Books were around for millennia before PTs and all the other entertainment devices, after all. Books were around before anything that could be considered a modern technology was around. Now he wondered if Kosundoans could get along without modern technology. It was integrated everywhere now.

Even Calisla's remote resort villages relied on technology to bring tourists to the villages. He had been to Calisla with his parents about twenty years ago. His parents wanted to see what it would be like to live without technology for a time. They thought the experience would be good for him too. It was quite an experience. The villages were cut out of the tropical forest on the island. It was hot; and being from Cirri, he was not used to such heat. Calisla was situated right above the equator. Actually, the southern tip of Calisla sat right on the equator. The nights were kind of drus though. It cooled down, and the stars were magnificent. The nights in remote places in Cirri were generally too cold to do much stargazing. *Both moons were visible that night,* he remembered. The closer one, Kliste, was in its waning quarter; and the other moon, Mekry, was nearly full. Still, Kliste dominated the sky. Mekry looked like a small pebble next to a slice of tropical fruit. That was to be expected. Kliste was much larger than Mekry in addition to being closer. The point was that the moons, combined with all the stars, made for a spectacular sight. The quarters in the village were nice; but without any modern conveniences, it really wasn't someplace most people would like to stay for more than a couple of weeks. He thought that the week that he and his parents stayed were long enough. Even there, his parents could bring their mobile comms, although comms had now been replaced by commterms. Now, one could not only talk to anyone anywhere but one could also see anyone anywhere if they desired. Holu had a great deal to do with perfecting the innovation that enabled small personal commterms to be practical both technologically and economically. More to the point, even in the remote villages of Calisla, his parents had access to technology through their comms—not only communication capability; but most comms and commterms usually have other technologies built into them like navigation, Kosundo networking, amusements, plus a myriad of other things. So even in Calisla, people were generally not without lots of technology at their fingertips. Although he seemed to remember that one resort chain did not allow comms of any sort to be kept during visits now. It was a new one, but he couldn't remember the name of the chain at the moment.

Of course, there were modern cities in Calisla as well. There, sparkling resorts of all types were huge consumers of Cirri technology. Many of these resorts catered to the elite of Kosundo society and treated anyone who could afford it like they were royalty. He supposed that resorts or other tourism enterprises provided nearly everyone's livelihood in Calisla in one way or another.

He reached down to his right and grabbed a handful of elongated, airy blue things from a bag with the name "Sweet Puffs" on it. The product was true to its name; it was sweet and certainly puffy. They were pretty good, but they made him thirsty. So he grabbed the bottle of water that was sitting on his left and took a big swig.

He then reached in front of him to see what books were there. He had just opened one of the book boxes, truly meaning to put them away. But that chair looked so inviting and the snacks were calling to him, so he just put the armful of books in front of the chair, grabbed some snacks, and decided to relax a bit. The first book he picked up was titled, *A Complete History of Technology*. This was one of his old school books. He wasn't really interested in reading it again right now, but it did conjure up some facts that he had committed to memory back then in his mind. *The first wheeled vehicle to be powered by grain alcohol was invented in Nurd in* 2118 *MENS by Dann Eotu. The first flying transport was invented in O'ONaso in* 2174 *MENS by Fliag Flech.* Fliag Flech was a catchy sort of name, he thought. He also remembered, *The first complete mass transit system was invented in Magelus in* 2167 *MENS by Mese Trens.* Mese Trens was an appropriately named person to have invented mass transit, to be sure. He still remembered more firsts. *The first geothermal generator was pioneered in Cirri in* 2158 *MENS by Tharmutoi. The first successful fission reactor was created in Dricho in* 2207 *MENS by Broch Eosain. The first fission of non-radioactive heavy metals was successful in Cirri in* 3151 *MENS by Stetharoi. The first stable fusion reaction was produced in* 3874 *MENS in Cirri by Kulloi.* He guessed that the next thing to add to the energy production list was the millennium generator in 4510 by his team. He was afraid history might record that it was by Agapoi. He had discovered the reaction between iri and helium and came up with a basic idea, but his team did the rest. They deserved most of the credit, not him. But history was often not fair to the people who did the actual work. It tended to reward the thinkers. That was unfortunate, in his opinion. Perhaps the whole invention of the millennium generator was unfortunate. *If we didn't have that, we wouldn't have had the power for the chomile.* He chuckled to himself. *Then again, if the generator didn't exist, neither would the dome, the transporter, or any number of things that are now possible because of the generator.* He put that book aside.

The next book was titled, *Doetora: The Continent of Secrets*. Well, the title was true enough. Ever since Doetora broke off trade with the Jontu after the Great War, they had completely isolated themselves, only accepting trade and a few advisors from Cirri. The emperor, Nekash, had effectively wrested all control from the Edvukaat, the body that once shared power with the emperor. Since that time, the emperors became more paranoid with each succession. The current emperor, Tryllos, was especially paranoid. Some in the Cirri trade council feared the emperor might be losing his rationality all together. He sighed and thought, *Now that is a nice, comfortable thought for a person who is trying to relax.* Anyway, the empire's isolation made it well behind other countries in technology. That is why a technology advisor was appointed to Doetora about twenty years ago. He heard on the news while eating lunch with Holu that the emperor decided to terminate the technical advisor agreement with Cirri just yesterday. That was the trade council's affair, but it was unexpected as far as he knew. Still, since it involved a technology advisor, he probably had a communication waiting on his commterm, which he hadn't looked at all day. The sudden dismissal of the advisors was another sign that the emperor was not acting rationally, unless there was an offence committed by an advisor. However, he had not been notified of one if an offence did occur. His commterm would have given him an urgent message warning light and three tones would have sounded repeatedly had such a message been sent. He thought that that was enough thinking about Doetora for now, so he put that book down and picked up the next book on the pile.

The next book was entitled, *A Study of Gratonin and the Rise of the Grassoan Empire*. He had obviously opened the box containing a portion of the history section of his collection. Gratonin was the name of the largest and most influential country in Kosundo before the breaking. Gratonin, through conquest after the breaking, established the Grassoan empire that covered the whole continent of Grasso. That was probably where the book would stop its history, but the story didn't stop there. The Grassoan empire lasted until 1569 MENS, when revolution separated first Dricho and then the rest of the current countries on the continent except for O'ONaso, which was the modern-day Gratonin. O'ONaso, still dreaming of empire, attacked Doetora in 2520, starting the Great War, which lasted for centuries. Although O'ONaso was eventually expelled from Doetora, the war led to a loose federation of nations on the Grasso continent. Ironically, through the losing war effort, O'ONaso had gained great influence in Grasso as the lead nation of the federation. Only Calisla was not part of the Grasso Federation. The island separated itself from the federation six hundred years ago, when it successfully seceded from Nurd. Calisla never went to war after its independence, so it joined Cirri as the only two countries that had never gone to war. He was familiar with the history of Gratonin and had already read several books on it, so he placed that book aside for another time. He just wanted something that would be an interesting, relaxing read for this evening.

He grabbed some more Sweet Puffs from his right. They seemed to be hard to resist. As he munched, he picked up the next book from the stack in front of him.

The book was titled, *A Study of the History of Agriculture in Nurd*. Well, he didn't know much about agriculture. That was true. But he wasn't sure he wanted to read about that this evening. Nurd only had a handful of settlements that could be called cities, but it was a country that had a lot of farmland and a lot of herd animals. There were giant herds of koh, a main source of meat; herds of towrus—the females were a great source of milk, the males were a bit dangerous though—; herds of schef, which were good for meat, and their long, hairy coats made excellent cloth. There were also herds of cattle. Cows were a good milk giver, and the bulls provided excellent meat. There were herds of pfards once used extensively for transportation. Now they were mainly used for entertainment, although ranches still utilized them, he understood. There were herds of schwain that produced many types of meat ranging from breakfast meat to dinner meat. He could list more, but that last one made him hungry. Funny how snacks never seemed to satisfy your appetite until you had gorged yourself on them. He put that book aside.

Another book, *The Ships of the Cargagru*, looked interesting. He opened the book and leafed through the pages. It had a lot of pictures of wooden and more modern ships produced during the history of Cargagru. He found one ship in particular quite interesting. It was a wooden ship called a scharar. It had tall masts with billowing sails and a very sleek hull. It looked like it would cut through the water as fast as the wind would carry it. The scharar was made from a lighter-colored wood. The lighter color could be seen on the part of the ship that would be far above the water line. A clear coat of some sort of sealer was probably used there. The bottom part of the ship was black. Obviously, a different, more durable sealer was used there. But that two-toned color of the ship made the ship look even faster in the picture. The Cargagru were master shipbuilders. In fact, a lot of Cirri ships were manufactured in Cargagru. He sat and looked through the book for quite some time. The descriptions of the ships and the manner of producing them were intriguing. After a while, he put the book to the side and reached for the next one.

The book was *Minnunglindor, Then and Now*. The corners of his mouth rose slightly. "Now there is an appropriate title for a book," he thought. If ever a country's culture had drastically changed, it was Minninglindor's culture. A thousand years ago, Minnunglindor had a very conservative, even ritualistic culture developed from a couple thousand years of blending of separate tribal cultures. The culture back then was rigid and formal. The people held to many strict social practices, some of which even forbade a man and woman to touch in public. Now, there is not a culture in Kosundo that is looser in it morals than Minnunglindor. There are now open brothels, illicit clubs, and many more forms of debauchery available for the asking in all the major cities of the country. Yet, he knew that many of the smaller villages of the country retained at least part of the former culture. Most rural Lindors, as people from Minnunglindor were called, never ventured into the cities unless they absolutely needed to be there. It was quite a change that took place over the years. A lot of it was brought on by all the wars that precipitated from the Great War. Minnunglindor had several major naval bases, and the sailors would be looking for a way to blow off steam. The coastal cities started to oblige them, making some fast cash. The wars stretched out so long that it soon just became of way of life in the major cities. His slight grin faded as he thought how sad that was. He wouldn't be surprised if the coming crisis started in Minnunglindor. Then again, Dricho may be a possibility as well, with their fascination with dubious science. Still again, Schwinn would also be a definite possibility. That country is also known to have aggressive intentions with their study of science. Then he thought about reasons why nearly every place in Kosundo might be the place for the crisis to start. The only places he ruled out in his mind were Nurd and Calisla and, of course, Cirri. Nurd was ruled out because of their non-aggressive attitudes and work ethic, and Calisla was ruled out because nearly everyone there was just trying to make people from other countries happy. Cirri had received a blessing from Thaoi but also a warning. Surely, the fact that Thaoi had given the message about the soulless deliberately to Cirri and given encouragement for Cirrians to assist indicated that the soulless would originate elsewhere. He was mostly sure about that anyway.

He put the book down and stood up. He had promised himself that he would not think about the soulless tonight. He was supposed to be giving himself the night and weekend off from such thoughts. Yet, here came the thoughts, unbidden—well, sort of unbidden. He should have just stuck to putting books on his shelves. Oh well. No use second-guessing himself. He could have just as easily come by these thoughts by putting these books on the shelf. Maybe he should go visit someone from the team, like Axopen or Eutay—well, not Eutay by himself anyway. Eutay with someone else is fine, but Eutay by himself could be a little more than he wanted to handle right now. No. He'd be best off just to clean up the mess by the chair and start putting his books away. It was still early, only 7:45, about time to eat supper if he was eating a formal supper this evening.

He gathered up his bag of Sweet Puffs and bottle of water and started for the cooking area when he saw that he had not yet created any walls or cupboards for the area yet. There was a place for a sink but no sink yet either. He guessed that Yotux must have figured that different people might want a different type of sink in the cooking area. He elongated a sigh and put the puffs and bottle of water on the stove—at least a stove was already there—and went back to get the books near the chair.

The book on top of the pile in front of the chair was a history about the Jontu. *It figures. That's about the only country I haven't thought about too much tonight,* he thought partially aloud. "The Jontu are a good-natured folk, and they are good trade partners, so why not think on them?" He chuckled as he found himself talking fully aloud now. Then, to himself, he thought, *They are our main trade partners ever since the Big War ended.* The Jontu Etirraze, as the country was now known, was a nation forged of four former island countries: Magelus, which was the largest island in Kosundo; Dydome, which was composed of two small islands; and then Vostraw and Lignut. Lignut was a small island whose southernmost point was about the same latitude as Zaria, his hometown. However, Lignut benefitted from a northern current on its west coast that made the island much more temperate than Zaria.

He stooped down, picked up the pile of books, and began to arrange them on the shelves. He had seven main categories of books, which is why he had created the long bookcase with seven shelves. He had books that were categorized as fiction, biography, history, spirituality, philosophy, science, and technical. He didn't have the same amount of books in each category, so he figured he would put the category that had the most books on the bottom shelf and the one with the least amount of books on the top shelf. There was no doubt that he had more books about history than anything else, so he put these books on the bottom shelf.

Agap continued to place books on his shelves throughout that evening. Some titles brought him pleasant thoughts, but most seem to draw him to the prophecy of the soulless and the message that he had heard that day. One book in particular stirred a memory he had puzzled over this morning in the meeting. It was simply entitled, *Thoughts: The Memoirs of Yaruko*i. He opened the book and searched its pages for a mention of the soulless. He soon found it. It was Yarukoi that had used the term, "the father of the soulless." It was a term that he applied to the "one who is not a man" from the Levra. He quickly read the surrounding context. He concluded that whoever planted that thought into Yarukoi's mind might have also planted the thought into Jahnu's mind. *Perhaps Jahnu and Yarukoi had something in common: the Voice of Thaoi*, he thought. Of course, Jahnu could have been influenced by reading Yarukoi's writings; but he didn't think so. This book written by Yarukoi was rare. He thought that he might have one of the only remaining copies in existence, if not *the* last one. He thought that it wasn't likely that a maintenance supervisor would have access to such a book. He concluded that it was much more likely that Jahnu had just been given a message by the same person that gave Yarukoi messages two thousand years ago: the Voice of Thaoi.

He brought himself out of his thoughts to realize that he hadn't even placed all the history books on the shelves yet. He looked at all the boxes. He really must stop thinking about every book title he placed on a shelf. He then determined only to look at the title for placement purposes. It worked, for the most part; and he made much better time placing the books after that.

When he finally finished placing all the books in all the boxes, it was late—9:75, twenty-five spens till midnight. He wished now that he had had something substantive for supper. The puffs and water were still there, but he decided that he had had enough puffs for the night. He wanted to try to get some sleep tonight more than he wanted to satisfy his hunger anyway. Tomorrow was eKureaki, the weekend. He didn't have to be up early, but somehow he thought he might be up early anyway. He just hoped that this night brought him some decent sleep so he could bring this day, the fifth of Setmi, quickly to an end.

So, he began to get himself ready for bed. Tomorrow would be a fun occasion. He would try to think about tomorrow tonight. That thought should provide some pleasant sleep so long as thoughts of other tomorrows didn't creep in to steal the pleasantness of tonight's tomorrow.

15
Confronting the Unknown

Holon sat, looking at her plate. Yotux had called the dish that was on her plate cereci. There were six of them in a circle on her plate. She glanced over at Yotux, who was busily eating her cereci. Yotux was using a long utensil that she had called a tong, which had an elongated hole at one end in tandem with a sharp, curved end. She had used the tong to pick up one of the six cereci with one hand and was using a strange kind of two-pronged fork to tear meat from the cereci with the other hand. The cereci were situated in what looked to her to be a shell. She looked at the shell. It looked a lot like a snail's shell. She thought she might get sick. Cereci were snails. She looked doubtfully at Yotux as she had now finished the meat of the snail and now was using bread to sop up the juices that were still in the shell. Yotux certainly seemed to be enjoying her meal, but she wasn't too sure about it. Maybe it would help to think of the dish as cereci instead of snails. She looked down at her plate at the six shells. The aroma from her plate was appetizing, so she took the funny-looking tongs in her left hand as Yotux had done. Yotux seemed to have the point of the shell fit into the hole in the end of the tong, and she was securing it with the other end of the tong. She attempted to get the shell into the end of the tong with the elongated hole, but with the shell resting on her plate, she wasn't sure how to get the shell into the hole without touching it.

"Use the pointy end to press down on the front of the shell so that the tip of the shell lifts off your plate like this," said Yotux while demonstrating the maneuver to her. "Never ate cereci before?"

"Is it that obvious?" she asked.

"Between the look on your face and your trouble with the tongs, yes, it is sort of obvious. But everyone has to do everything for the first time sometime," said Yotux in a reassuring tone.

"These are snails?" she asked rather timidly.

"Yes. Did you want something else instead?" offered Yotux with a concerned look on her face.

"No, no, no." she said quickly and then added, "It is good to try new things...and not to let your preconceptions rule you."

"Bumvoce!" exclaimed Yotux. "Everyone should have such an attitude toward new things. You and I are going to mesh splendidly on the team, I believe."

She smiled at the encouragement; but inside, she was still wishing that she had taken up Yotux on the offer to reorder. She used the sharp end of the tong to lift the end of the shell as Yotux has demonstrated. Sure enough, the shell fit into the elongated hole, so she picked up the shell and then picked up the odd-looking fork. She found that the fork fit nicely into the small shell. She delicately tore some of the meat out of the shell, drew a quick breath, and put the meat into her mouth. It tasted pretty good. The spices that had been used in preparing the dish blended nicely with the meat, although the meat was a bit rubbery. She would have to get used to the texture; but all in all, it wasn't bad. Around the meat in the shell was a spicy, buttery sauce, which added flavor. She smiled at Yotux to indicate that she liked the dish.

"You like it then?" asked Yotux. "Good. I should have thought to ask if you had tried cereci before I suggested it. I've eaten it most of my life, so it doesn't always occur to me to ask. Some people just can't get by the fact that they're eating snails. But I don't even really think of them as snails any more than most people would think of basted corni as koh."

"Yes, I like it. And it does help to think of the dish as cereci rather than snails. Although I will admit I thought I might get sick when I realized what it was," she admitted.

"You must try the bread in the sauce. It is really delicious," Yotux said in that encouraging tone.

She had to admit that the bread dipped in the sauce was great. Soon, both women had finished all of the cereci.

"Would you care for any dessert tonight, ladies?" asked the waiter as he picked up the empty dishes.

Yotux looked at her in a way that asked for an answer. She shook her head no, so Yotux said, "No, but thank you very much. It was a fine dinner."

The waiter smiled, nodded, and went off to his other tables.

As she looked at the waiter, she could have sworn that she saw a man wearing a dark hooded running suit. He was watching her. She looked at Yotux. She wanted to ask her if she saw the man, but when she looked back in the direction of the man, he was gone. That was the third time she thought that she was the same man. "Have you ever seen a man watching you here in Bojoa?" she asked trying her best to sound relaxed.

"No, but I've seen plenty of men watching you," said Yotux lightly.

She gave a slight smile to Yotux and then looked down at her plate.

Yotux leaned forward across the table and asked softly, "Have you seen something out of the ordinary?"

She really didn't want to let Yotux know that she might be imagining a hooded figure, so she said, "I just had the feeling that I was being watched a couple of times."

"It's the price of your looks," said Yotux a bit more seriously.

She smiled at the compliment more openly this time. Yotux obviously didn't know what she was talking about. She decided to try to exit out of the subject gracefully. "I suppose you're right. I'm just letting my imagination get the better of me," she said.

"Well, you have had quite a few changes in your life. You have every right to feel a bit skittish," said Yotux.

She smiled and said, "That sounded like something Agapu might say."

"So, exactly when did you meet Agapoi?" asked Yotux with a grin.

She returned the grin. She was surprised that Yotux had waited so long to ask that question. They had been to six different shops. They both had the bags to prove it lying under the table. They had finished their meal with the exception of the beverage, which tonight was a brew of hurtale leaves called che, her favorite drink. Che tasted fruity yet minty and very smooth. It was just as good cold as hot, but they were drinking it hot. "I first saw him seventeen years ago, but I feel like I've known him forever."

Yotux's grin increased, and then she started giggling. She started giggling too because that did come out sort of melodramatically.

"But, seriously," she continued, "it took fifteen years for Agapu to actually speak to me. The first time I saw him, he was speaking at my college graduation. It was at my first speaking engagement that he actually spoke to me. I believe you were there, Yotux."

Yotux looked puzzled. "That was the first time he talked to you, when he whispered something in your ear? But he introduced you as if he knew you."

"I am a bit surprised that you remember that. Do you want to know what he said?" she asked.

Yotux nodded eagerly.

"No. I shouldn't. Agapu ... might have considered that private," she said teasingly.

"Oooo! Sounds juicy!" said Yotux enthusiastically.

She smiled and shook her head to indicate that she wasn't going to tell.

"Oh, come on, Holon! Pretend like we're sisters. I have a feeling that we will become just like sisters soon anyway. Let it out of there," Yotux said, pointing to Holon's mouth.

"Oh axi, Yotux. You seem like a good sort of girl," she said with a giggle. "He said,"—she paused for effect and to let herself stop giggling—"'I have thrown you off on your first public speech. Allow me to make it up to you by taking you out to lunch after I speak.' All I could do was nod. Then he gave me that big, wonderful smile of his ... " She trailed off.

"I never would have guessed that Agapoi was a romantic. He's always been so businesslike around us. Did you know that last night was the first time he really showed us his personal side? I don't know how he is able to channel himself into one mode or another like that."

She answered with a sigh. "I've gotten to know Agapu pretty well, but I guess I am not as familiar with Agapoi as you are, Yotux. What is he like as a boss?"

"Oh, he's been the perfect boss recently," said Yotux. "He hasn't been here." Yotux tried to keep a straight face, but first a grin crept across her face. Then Holon started to giggle, which made Yotux break into a downright laugh, with Holon joining in heartily.

When they finally regained their composure, Yotux said, "No. Really, he is a great boss. He can be demanding, but it's just because he demands so much out of himself. Our team has accomplished astonishing things, especially since Agapoi's discovery of iri. I believe that you will like the challenge, Holon. And I am going to love to watch Agapoi try to separate personal and business lives so perfectly now." Yotux sounded as if she were half-challenging Agapoi and half in awe of him.

"I know Agapu mentioned something about how long the team has been together, but he didn't mention details in years. How long has the current team been together, Yotux?"

Yotux thought for a moment and then said, "Opsil replaced Psawton as assistant designer about three years ago. That you might know. Other than that, we've all been with Agap for at least twelve years. I've been with him for twenty-two years, since his first team started in Zaria. Agap was then thirty-five years old, the minimum age to run a team of his own. He had just been given his third name: Jost. Sorry. I've called Agapoi 'Agap' for so long that 'Agap' still slips out now and again."

"No need to apologize to me, Yotux. I'm the one that has trouble saying Agapoi instead of Agapu. So Agapoi had his third name when he was thirty-five? The nomenclature committee doesn't give out names before a person's thirty-fifth birthday. Do you know why he was given his third name?"

Yotux had a quizzical look on her face.

She thought her look must be because she didn't know about Agap's third name, so she explained, "Every time I asked him about his third name, he would just make light and say things like, 'The nomenclature committee got me mixed up with someone important,' or, 'My parents wrote the committee so often that they gave me another name to stop the onslaught of letters.' I could have looked him up on the Kosundo network I guess, but I never had."

"I guess that shouldn't surprise me too much," began Yotux. "Agapoi hates to admit that he is somebody important or has done something important. He can play as if it was no big accomplishment to discover iri, but the reason for his first name cannot be accounted to his luck, only to his intellect. The reason he was given his first name on his thirty-fifth birthday was that he wrote a paper on a new theory for his college thesis. The new theory was his original theory. It is the theory that made the mining transporters possible. In his paper, he proved his theory mathematically and rationally. His theory was the theory of controlled particle disintegration. He was twenty-two when he wrote his paper. His theory is now a law in physics."

She smiled. "You seem to know Agapoi rather well, Yotux. I suspected it was something that he wouldn't be able to attribute to anyone else or else he would have told me. He would have had to take the praise for the theory. Yes, I believe you are right. He is always free to admit that he received his fourth name for discovering iri but was always so elusive about the reason for the third name. It's almost as if he is embarrassed about being gifted." She paused for a moment. She really didn't want to ask this question, but she felt she must. She had a hard time maintaining eye contact with Yotux as she began,

"I noticed the expression on your face the night I was introduced to the team." She glanced at Yotux whose eyes darted down to look at the table. She made herself look directly at Yotux as she continued, "About your feelings toward Agapoi. Have they always been professional?"

Yotux showed obvious discomfort with the question. She fidgeted in her seat as if her seat had become a rock.

It was an awkward question. She wished that she could take it back, but since she knew that was impossible, she hastily added, "I am not accusing you of anything, Yotux. But you are young, young enough to be interested in someone Agap's age, and very attractive. Haven't you ever thought about you and Agapoi having a personal relationship? It would be only natural. You obviously know him very well. How could you not be attracted to him?"

That question had changed the mood of the evening. Yotux took some time before she spoke. When she finally did speak, she didn't look at her. "I would not be a normal female if I was not attracted to Agapoi." She paused as if she were trying to decide what to say next. Yotux's eyes only glanced at her as she said, "I had fantasized, in the past, about taking his last name, yes." Yotux then fixed her eyes on her as she continued, "But fantasies were all that those feelings ever were. Agapoi respects me, and I respect him. He knows me fairly well, and it is part of my job to know him very well. There was a time that I wished our relationship could have been more than professional. But there was never anything personal in Agapoi's relationship with me. It is and always has been a professional relationship. I will admit that seeing you with Agapoi was difficult because I always held out that glimmer of hope. Now that the hope is gone, I will no longer hope, and you will not need fear about Agapoi's feelings for me. He had twenty-two years to choose me, but he didn't. He chose you. I am disappointed, yet relieved. I can now get on with finding someone else. As you say, I am still young, only fifty-one. Agapoi is yours, Holon. I am not a threat now, nor will I be a threat in the future."

She felt tears come into her eyes, and now, she felt ashamed that she had asked the question. She averted her eyes from Yotux.

Yotux leaned forward on her seat and spoke softly, "My heart is happy for you. You are a very lucky woman indeed. I am the richer for knowing Agapoi, and I believe I am the richer for knowing you. I believe Agapoi made a wise choice, as he always seems to do, in choosing you. You're a bright, vibrant young woman. You earned your third name already at forty. I have not earned a third name yet. You are a magnificent example of womanhood, Holon. Agapoi deserves to have someone like you."

The tears that were formed in her eyes earlier began to stream down her cheeks. "You shame me, Yotux. You are a better woman than I."

Yotux picked up an unused napkin and gave it to her. She dabbed at her checks as Yotux smiled and said, "Nonsense, Holon. It is only right that you make sure of Agapoi. You are his intended. I certainly would if I were in your place. I am sure you would be just as I am if our places were reversed." Yotux's voice was calm and reassuring.

Holon was in a full-blown cry now. She tried to talk through her tears. "You...are a...wonderful person, Yotux. Agapoi was...wise...to pick you...as his assistant." She wiped her tears with the napkin, took a deep breath, and continued. "I am a better person for knowing you, and I truly mean that."

"What was said needed to be said, Holon. You have nothing to be ashamed about. Now that it has been said, we can get on with getting to know each other better. My role is to make sure that I help Agapoi be the leader he needs to be. Your role is to help Agapu be the best man that he can be. Agreed?"

"Agreed, Yotux," she said trying to smile. She took a deep breath as she tried to stop her tears. The tears did begin to dwindle. She then gave her best smile to Yotux and said, "I think we will make a marvelous team."

"I'm sure of it. Agap needs the both of us. Let's just be sure not to let him down," said Yotux as she touched her hand.

She nodded. She was very delighted to have spent time with Yotux this evening. This turned out to be a very good day after all. She now understood what she must do clearer than ever thanks to Yotux. She must give Agapu all the love and support that she could muster. Trying days were going to come shortly. She knew that. But now she knew that she wouldn't have to look after Agapu alone. She and Yotux became a team tonight. Together, they would ensure that Agapoi would lead well and that Agapu would retain his humanity no matter what the soulless had in store for them.

16
The D'Yavoly Reports

Nenavis sat restlessly on his makeshift throne in the Labile Mist. Two of his D'Yavoly were due to report soon. He was eager to find out what information his top-level operatives might have concerning the assignments they were given. Both reported that they had news. It had better be good news for their sakes. The Other One had had the upper hand for too long in this sixth world. He needed a break, something that would turn the tide in his favor. Perhaps the news that these two had was the break that he needed. Then he wouldn't have to be sitting here on this sorry excuse for a chair in this infernal mist. He would have any throne of his choosing once he had a means to escape to the physical world of Kosundo and didn't have to exist in this spiritual halfway house.

Just then, Zlux came into his presence. His appearance was slightly faded. He had the look of one partially in a host. "My master, I have news concerning the abomination named Neaotomo," Zlux said with excitement in his voice.

He allowed his countenance to show a small measure of pleasure at that statement. "You have seen him?"

Zlux's enthusiasm waned considerably. "No, my master," he said with downcast eyes, but he hastily added, "But I have obtained access to a human woman called Degmer. She refers to the name Neaotomo when she speaks and thinks of the voice that she and Svirap heard a week ago. She seems very sure, my master."

He once again showed contempt in his countenance. "You have access to a feeble human? How is this woman so convinced of the identity of the voice?" Nenavis was now manifesting himself in an ominous manner over the head of Zlux.

"My master, oh great one, she had foreknowledge of this abomination," cried a cowering Zlux.

"Foreknowledge you say? How did she know the abomination?" he demanded.

"She worked in the sealed lab, my master," pleaded Zlux.

He considered Zlux's report. This was important information, but he dared not let Zlux know of the importance. Zlux was not yet to be trusted; but ironically, he could not trust any other of his D'Yavoly with this assignment. They all knew too much about the abominations. It was best to let Zlux have first contact with Neaotomo, if he truly had survived. It was only as the humans gassed and sealed the lab of the abominations that he had truly understood what could be accomplished through this attempt by humanity to recreate itself. Svirap had pushed the envelope in directing the minds of key human instruments, but he did not keep him informed closely enough. *If only Svirap had given his information to me earlier, the whole of Kosundo could have already been mine,* he thought. The thought irritated him, just the emotion he wished to show to Zlux right now. He conveyed his irritation to his countenance. "And how are you going confirm this information?" he growled.

"I had planned to extend my visit with the woman. She plans to enter the lab tomorrow. She seems to think she has the ability to persuade the authorities to let her and some others into the sealed labs tomorrow. I can make my observations through her," said Zlux is his usual hissing manner.

He smiled a nasty smile. "That is an excellent idea, Zlux. But only visit—."

He was cut off in mid-sentence by the arrival announcement of Purhit. "My master, I have news from Cirri."

"You're early, Purhit. Can you not sense when I am in audience? Do you need training as a tormented spirit again?" he bellowed.

Zlux looked with a gleeful look.

He rounded on him, "As for you, Zlux, you are not to fully control the human. Only I can give you that permission. Is that understood?"

Zlux resumed his cringing posture, "Only too well, my master."

"Good. Then be gone to watch over your human. You can think what she thinks, hear what she hears, feel what she feels, and even make subtle suggestions, but you will not take her fully," Nenavis commanded in a roar.

"It will be as you say, my master," said Zlux, and then he was gone.

He turned to Purhit. "I hope you have something worthwhile to tell me. It was very careless of you to interrupt me."

"I believe the information I have will be very valuable, my master," said a groveling Purhit.

"Did you get this information from one of your few contacts in Cirri?" he growled.

"It is not an easy place to gain contacts, my master. You know that the Other One has sway in this place," protested Purhit.

"And many think that is because of your sloth, Purhit," he retorted.

"I have been diligent, my master. My underlings have been kept busy, but that book is read widely there. This you know, my master," said an unexpectedly bold Purhit.

He actually softened his countenance, but only by a hair. "I do know this, Purhit. Now, tell me your news before I grow tired of your insolence."

"The Other One is calling for the end, my master," began Purhit.

His attention heightened at those words.

Purhit continued. "There was a meeting held in a secret location today. Apparently, the whole of the Cirri councils were in one place, attending this meeting. In this meeting, a human called Jahnu Vija presented a message on the prophecy of the soulless. He declared that he had a visitation where he was given this message: 'The time has come, and the father of the soulless is among the people of Kosundo. Only the faithful will remain.' This man further called the location of the meeting 'a beacon of hope.'"

He was intrigued. The father of the soulless was not a name that was used in connection with the prophecy of the soulless. This was a new name, yet it seemed ageless to him. "Tell me, Purhit, did your contact give a time for this visitation?" he asked.

"Yes, my master. It was given one week ago to this day."

Could it be? he wondered to himself. He then spoke to Purhit. "This may indeed be as you say, Purhit. Did your contact reveal where this meeting was held?"

"No, my master, he did not. He indicated that he only heard of the meeting secondhand and was not privy to its location," said Purhit.

He rubbed his chin and looked directly into Purhit's gaze, "And what do your feelings tell you about this contact, Purhit?"

Purhit stared blankly back into his eyes. "The contact was not entirely forthcoming, my master. He might know more than he tells," said Purhit dramatically.

He diverted his gaze, and Purhit drew an elongated breath.

"You have done well, Purhit. I believe the information that your contact withheld was the location of the meeting. He may have done this because he is afraid of reprisals against this location. Search out your contact again. Tell him that he has done well and will be rewarded. Let him know that you suspect that he is withholding something, but be subtle. Don't threaten him in any way. Just let him think that you may know something that you do not. Oftentimes, this bears fruit in the weaker humans. Eventually, you might have to take him by force. Contacts are valuable, so do not take him until you are sure he is isolated from any other of your contacts. While you are not dealing with this contact, search out other contacts you have established and see if they know anything concerning this contact's whereabouts. Again be subtle, Purhit."

"As you command, my master," said Purhit before vanishing into the mist.

The news couldn't have been better. Zlux may well find his vehicle to the real world tomorrow. Unless he missed his guess, Zlux may be in for a bit of a surprise when he finds this Neaotomo. Neaotomo was to the physical world what he was to the Labile Mist, except the physical world didn't know it yet. But he believed that the world would know it soon enough. Zlux would find out tomorrow. That thought humored him almost to the point of real laughter. That is something that he had not experienced for what seemed like an eternity. Just as always, however, he found that humor could not quite reach him. The only thing that stirred his laughter was the suffering he would inflict on the real world. This world was rightfully his, after all. He could do what he pleased with this world's creatures, no matter what interference the Other One may offer. Anyway, it would be good news indeed if Zlux was not able to leave the woman tomorrow. That would mean that Neaotomo lives and is as powerful and crafty as ever.

He was not one to give out credit too publicly, but he had to admit that neither the possible discovery of Neaotomo nor the control of the simpleminded fool would have been possible without the teaching of Lidar Tombun to many lost souls in Kosundo. Of course, this master teacher of the relaxation technique was controlled by Sarditu, one of his most trusted D'Yavoly. It was Sarditu that had prepared this sixth world for his appearance over two thousand years ago. For thousands of years, Sarditu and his minions had been the only influence representing him on Kosundo. He had to hand it to Sarditu. His method was flawless. Control a well-known master teacher and add a little bit extra, just enough to let those poor lost human souls find their spiritual guides, which just happened to be his D'Yavoly and their underlings. This deception was wrapped in the guise of a relaxation technique taught by a master teacher in Calisla, which is a place where multitudes flock to find a bit of relaxation.

Once it was verified that Neaotomo lived, he would pay a visit to that weak-minded fool in Doetora. It would then be time to spring his surprise, a nasty yet wonderful surprise, on the people of Kosundo. Appearing physically in the sixth world of men was indeed appropriate. The Other One symbolized men with the number six, and now he thought it deliciously ironic that he would appear as a man in the sixth world of men. He could almost hear the screaming of the humans now. Then he could laugh, and laugh he would.

17
CELEBRATION OF TRYST

> Pride will keep many from the ways of their fathers after the destroyer comes. Men will think their ways to be wiser than the ways of their fathers. The latter days will reveal the foolishness of man's pride; and his way will lead him to the destroyer, who will devour all who trust in their pride. Know this. The beginning of sorrows for Kosundo is come, when men yield their wills to the one who is not a man. Yet a remnant will follow the ways of their fathers. The hope of the remnant lies in the great gift of Thaoi and the faithful servant. Only the faithful will remain.

Agap was meditating on what he had just read from the Levra. He was reading from the book of Sonaydasa, which was one of the latter books of the Levra. It was his custom to meditate on a passage each day. This morning, his reading pattern took him to this passage. He had long thought, as most scholars did, that the great gift of Thaoi mentioned in the Levra was a clear conscience. There were some scholars who believed that the great gift of Thaoi was something more tangible. He did not spend several parzes a day in the griphas, as did Levra scholars; but given the recent happenings, his view on a lot of things was being altered. *Perhaps the minority has a point here. Perhaps the great gift is something more than a clear conscience.*

One thing was certain. This passage did accurately assess the current state of Kosundo. People in many countries were forsaking the ways of their fathers. Most scholars agreed that the destroyer came to Kosundo a couple thousand years ago. One of the signs of the destroyer was war, according to the Levra. The Great War began two thousand years ago, and many wars stemming from that war had been waged since. The past hundred years have been an era of peace, but it was not a settled peace. There was still a threat of war breaking out at any moment, between any of the three military powers in Kosundo. Since the breakout of war, the faithfulness to Thaoi in Kosundo had waned considerably.

A lot of griphas in the last section of the Levra refer to the latter days and the prophecy of the soulless. There are even passages that deal with the latter days in other sections of the Levra. The latter days are always described in the Levra as a time of great hardness; a time of faithlessness, when men will trust in themselves more than in Thaoi; a time of sorrow. Such times were upon Kosundo. The Cirrian way of life was the only way of life in Kosundo that still held to the three main tenants of faith that the Levra espouses: "Strive to keep a clear conscience before Thaoi and man, asking forgiveness when transgressions are committed against Thaoi or man; believe that Thaoi will vanquish the destroyer through his greatest gift; and submit to Thaoi's will, not your will or the will of man." Yet, even so, he could not help but wonder how many under the sound of Jahnu's voice yesterday could not remember the blessing that was imparted.

All of the early writings that were preserved by scribes from before the breaking mention Thaoi regularly. Thaoi seemed pre-eminent in the thoughts of all the writers, and it was implied that the whole of Kosundo society thought that way then. He had noticed a steady decline in the prominence of Thaoi in later historical writings. Present-day writings, even in Cirri, mention Thaoi only if the subject matter dictates it. No more did writing mention Thaoi as though he was an essential part of living itself.

He broke from his meditation to check the clock. It was time to start getting ready. It was the end day of the week, eKureaki, the sixth of Setmi; and it was to be a day of celebration. The celebration of tryst for Holu and him would start at 3:50. He had told Holu that he would pick her up at 3:45 so that they would arrive close to the appointed parz. It was considered an ill portent of the future of a union if the two intendeds were not the last to arrive to the celebration. He had confidence that his team would arrive at least five spens before time.

He looked through his clothes, looking for something appropriate. The celebration was to last the whole day. He should wear something casual but not plain. Both he and Holu would be expected to be wearing bright colors, but not yellow. It would be bad luck to wear yellow at a tryst celebration, or so it was said. Yellow was the color reserved for the union, a yellow neckwrap for him as the cuma and a yellow dress for Holu as the ecayta. Yellow had been the color of choice for unions to symbolize the vibrancy of the union—the brighter the yellow, the more vibrant the union. Intendeds tried to get the brightest yellow material they could find to make their union neckwraps and dresses. But that was for the union. The celebration of tryst called for any bright color except yellow.

He found a rather bright green, short-sleeved sark that was trimmed in white on the neck and sleeves. He was a conservative dresser, so the selection of bright colors in his wardrobe was limited. The green sark would do, but the trousers that he saw were all dark. He had thought he had a pair of white trousers somewhere. He had worn them once for his appearance in a civil trial as a witness. Witnesses at trial in Cirri were to wear a plain white sark and white trousers. It was a custom to remind witnesses that only truthful words should be spoken at the trial. He found them tucked in the bottom of a box that he had not yet unpacked. The trousers were a bit creased, but he could create a misting closet to take out the wrinkles.

He said, "Show me the chomile."

Immediately, the chomile was visible. He kneeled on the seat of the couch he had so cleverly placed in front of the chomile. He grabbed the pointing pen and pointed to the wall nearest his bed.

"Create misting closet."

He heard two tones. The chomiles showed several styles. He chose a full-sized one with a door that looked like his washroom door. The chomile created what looked like a white door in the wall. He pointed to the door and said, "Change color." He would be glad when Yotux modified the chomile choices to include color before creating. He chose a chirrud-colored door like the washroom door. The door changed colors.

He went over to the door and pulled the handle straight out. The misting closet opened by extending from the wall. The closet came fully ready, with hangers and hooks. He took a hanger off the center rod and placed his trousers on it. He looked at his sark and decided that it could use a quick freshening up as well; and so he took a second hanger off the rod and hung his sark over the top of the hanger using the neck hole to keep the sark in place on the hanger. Inside the door was a single green button. He pushed it. The closet closed back into the wall. After just a few tics, the closet opened again. His trousers and sark were now wrinkle-free and looked as if they had just been laundered. He thought that the misting closet was the best invention ever for a bachelor. It was certainly quicker and did a much better job than he could have ever done with the old, hand-held, hot misting devices that he had used before the misting closet was invented. He looked at the misting closet and considered making a regular storage closet and then thought better of it. He didn't have time to put any clothes in it right now anyway. He took the sark and the trousers and placed them neatly on his bed as the misting closet closed itself.

    He grabbed some undergarments from his dresser and headed for the washroom. He glanced at the clock. Good. He still had time to shower and shave if he hurried. He hurriedly shaved and cleaned his teeth and then jumped in the air jet shower. He donned his shower goggles and turned on the shower. The air jet shower, also called just an air shower or even just a shower, first sprayed a light mist of chemicals; so the goggles were necessary to protect his eyes. After the shower disinfected with the mist, it dried a person off with fragranced jets of air. Once out of the shower, he put on the usual washroom essentials, dressed in his undergarments, and headed to his bed to put on his clothes. Once he put his sark and trousers on, he found some white socks and his white casual shoes and put them on. He then stopped by his dresser where he had laid his watch and put his watch on his wrist. By the time he had finished dressing and grooming his hair, it was 3:42, just about time to go.

He made a quick detour to the washroom mirror to take a look at himself. He thought that the attire was suitable. The green sark with his white trousers looked like a bright outfit—as far as the mirror would allow him to see his trousers anyway. So, Agap strode toward the door.

Once Agap got to Holu's door, he glanced at his watch. It read 3:44:29. Agap then pushed the alert button. The door opened almost instantly, and Holu walked out. She was wearing a casual dress that was white with bright pink, red, violet, blue, and green designs on it. The designs were disjointed, square outlines with spirals inside them. Each of the squares and spirals alternated with different colors. The dress was sleeveless, and the hem came just below the bottom of Holu's knees. Holu wore her reddish blonde hair down today. It was straighter than normal for Holu, flowing to the middle of her back; and she wore a white, bar shaped hairpiece toward the top of her head. She wore sheer, flesh-colored coverings on her legs and feet. Her white shoes were flat and showed her toes and a good bit of her foot through the straps that made up the top of the shoes.

"Good morning, my intended." Holu exuded enthusiasm. "That's a very nice green, Agapu," she said as she fingered his sark sleeve. "I believe this is the first time I've seen you in green. It fits you well. And those pants are certainly bright." Holu said, shading her eyes as if his pants were blinding them.

"And your dress is quite colorful. How did you manage to find a dress with so many colors without yellow in it?" he asked.

"Actually, Yotux found it last night," confessed Holu as they turned down the hall toward the translift. "We both thought it would be perfect for the celebration today."

"How did you and Yotux get along?" he asked.

"We enjoyed the evening very much. I found out how wonderful a person Yotux really is last night. You were quite fortunate to find her," said Holu, still bubbling enthusiasm.

They had reached the lift now, and he pressed the call button. "You're right there, Holu. I doubt that we would have accomplished nearly as much as a team without her. I've often wondered why she has not found an intended yet. She would certainly make a great soza for some lucky guy," he remarked.

The lift door had opened, and they were stepping inside. He busied himself with typing in the code, ComSec1, to name the junction that would take them to commercial sector one, where the Kumphus Restaurant was located.

Holon hid an amused smile as she heard Agapu's remark about Yotux. He was completely oblivious to the fact that Yotux had longed for him to make her his intended. Yotux was right. Agapu had never considered Yotux as a possible mate. Holon thought that was probably due to Agapu's penchant to keep his personal and professional lives separate. It certainly wasn't because Yotux was unattractive or had character flaws. She considered herself lucky that she wasn't part of Agap's team before now. If she and Yotux had changed roles, she would probably be the one left vainly waiting instead of Yotux.

"I'm glad you two girls got along well. You're both important to me. You have been my personal savior in many ways, more that I think you know. Yotux is a very important part of my professional life. She is one in a million as an assistant. Besides, you and Yotux will be working with each other closely on the team," he said rather candidly.

Holon noticed that the lift had stopped. "Is there a problem with the translift, Agapu?" she asked.

He shook his head. "It most likely just stopped for a busy junction." Before he had finished, the lift had begun to move again. "See. Everything is fine. The lift had to cut through the heart of the living complex since it had to leave the building on the other side. Commercial sector one is on the other side of the sub bay." As he spoke, the lift emerged from the building.

As the lift's sides went up, they could see the beach and the sub bay. Just on the other side of the sub bay, there were several lines of small buildings. The buildings were the buildings that made up commercial sector one. The elegant building in the middle of the first row was the Kumphus Restaurant. This restaurant was considered to be the most elegant restaurant in Bojoa. As were all the merchants in Bojoa, the owner of the Kumphus was invited to come to the dome by the technology and manufacturing councils. They could do business here as long as they kept the fact that they owned a business in an underwater dome secret. Cirrians were known throughout Kosundo for being people of their word; so when an owner gave his word to the councils, it was his bond and he would most likely be unable to do business again in Cirri if that bond was broken. In the case of the owner of the Kumphus, the invitation was extended personally by Phrunoi, the technology council chair. This gave the Kumphus special notoriety by default. But the restaurant lived up to the hype. It was a special place to eat and was very popular already in Bojoa. He was sure that the only way he was able to book a room for the day, especially on such short notice, was that fact that he was a technology council member. Being a council member did have its perks.

The lift started to descend to the junction. After the lift settled into the junction, the doors of the lift opened. The lift junction marked "ComSec1" was directly in front of the Kumphus. They exited the lift and went toward the restaurant.

"This place looks expensive, Agapu. Are you sure you can afford it?" said Holu, only half-teasing.

He chuckled. "Credits won't be a problem, Holu. The challenge is going to be shedding the extra weight after today. They have excellent food here."

"Don't even bring that up. You'll spoil the whole day," replied Holu, feigning indignance.

He smiled, although he couldn't imagine Holu having any difficulties with weight. She always looked perfect. He, on the other hand, was known to gain a few libs from time to time; and then he had to do some extra time in the recreation building to lose them again.

They had arrived at the door, so he opened the door for Holu and they went inside. They were greeted by a man in black and white. He wore a white sark with a black neckwrap, a black suit jacket, and black trousers. His shoes and socks were also black. He was the princampre of the restaurant, and he was waiting to escort them to their private room.

"Good morning, sir," he said to Agap. Then, turning to Holu, he said, "Good morning, miss." He then faced them both and said, "It is my pleasure today to take you to our best private room, the Prusthat."

He recognized that the name of the room was old tongue meaning special. He bowed formally and then turned to lead them to the room. The princampre lead them to a set of doors made of a light-colored wood and opened the doors for the couple.

Inside, the team was assembled around a large, rectangular table draped in a white cloth. There were two chairs open, one at each end of the table, that were reserved for the two intendeds. The large rectangular table was not the only table in the room. There were also two round tables covered in a blue felt material. Behind these tables were a variety of table games that would be sure to occupy some of the day's time. There was also a square table draped in a bright, multicolored cloth. The cloth had a multitude of colors but no yellow in it. That was the gift table. As requested, there were no wrapped gifts on the table; but there was a single nona on the table.

The top half of the walls in the room were painted a beige color with three rather wide stripes at the very top of the walls. The top and bottom stripes were a medium brown with a gold-colored stripe in the middle. The bottom part of the walls had the same light wood as the double doors of the room. There were lotan sconces lining the room just above the wood. A large chandelier styled like the sconces was the centerpiece of the room. The carpeting of the room was very plush and made of tan, white, and brown threads piled in odd-shaped patterns throughout.

As he viewed the room, he decided the room was well named. It was a special room. He looked over at Holu, who was taking in the room as well. Her eyes were drawn directly to the massive chandelier. Then she saw the two empty chairs at opposite ends of the table, and she gave him a sad glance. He understood the emotion, but it was the traditional table arrangement for the celebration. Holu might be a little sadder when she realized why there were two gaming tables. He led Holu to the nearest end of the table and helped her to her seat. He then went to the other end of the table and sat down.

To his immediate right was Supeb. He had on a rather raucous red sark with orange starburst patterns and trim that made him look twice. To his immediate left was Axopen. Axopen was wearing a vivid blue sark with bright green trim. Going further down his right, he saw Eutay attired in a bright purple sark with the alternating colors of blue and red and white as trim. Then there was Kowtsom in a bright pink, short-sleeved dress that had solid red trim. After Kowtsom sat

Yotux. She wore a very bright red, sleeveless dress with small, white and orange dots on it. Then, of course, was Holu at the other end of the table. On Holu's immediate right sat Phunex, in a solid bright green, long-sleeved blouse. Then there was an empty chair. But in the next chair sat Opsil, who had on a white sark that had red and orange patterns throughout. Everyone was looking at him. He just realized why. Since he was the prospective cuma, it was up to him to greet everyone so that the celebration could start.

He stood back up and said, "Thank you for coming to our celebration of tryst. We are honored by your presence."

Then all eyes went to Holu.

Holon stood up and said, "May this celebration be filled with the joy of all our tomorrows and lift our spirits to better serve Tháoi."

Then everyone stood up and said, "Blessed be Thaoi for the goodness He gives. May He bless this union with love and joy."

With that, everyone sat down; and the servers entered the room and started to serve the traditional breakfast of the celebration: strips of fried koh, eggs, and biscuits.

"So, Agapoi, when are you and Holon going to be joined? I don't recall hearing a date," asked Supeb.

"We had planned it for the last day of the Week of Remembrance," he answered.

Eutay piped up, "Aren't you the sly one! That way you'll only have an anniversary once every twenty years."

Everyone laughed at that, except for Holu.

He noticed that she was giving an accusing look right at him, as if he had just made that comment. So he hastened to add, "We thought by having the union during the Week of Remembrance, it would be easier for our guests to come since no one works during that week. I hadn't really thought of when we were going to celebrate our anniversary, perhaps on the first day of Ducim," he suggested, looking directly at Holu.

Holu broke a slight smile to indicate her pleasure at that answer. *For the sake of paradise! She can already order me about without saying a word,* he mused to himself.

After that opening foray into conversation, the room erupted with talking. He and Holu were served first, so he just listened while he ate. He heard conversations about what the team agenda would be tomorrow. There were speculations that the chomile would be the first item. They were right about that. So far, there was no word from Odanoi or Jahnu. He didn't expect there would be until sometime tomorrow or maybe not until Treti, if they felt they needed another day to meditate. There were conversations going on among the women folk about how Holu thought she would be able to handle having her intended for a boss. There were other conversations about other trivial things of life, like the lack of weather inside the dome, the comfort of their quarters, and how their favorite sports team was doing; and there was even a philosophical question about the merits of the sport of speedball over the sport of line goal. Personally, he liked speedball much better. It had continuous action, and it was very fast paced. The chases of the scrum in line goal were fun, but the players had to reset themselves after every scrum—a lot of dead time in his opinion.

He had just eaten his last bit of koh when Axopen quieted the room by asking him, "What do you think might happen next Diotiri?"

He had wished to avoid that subject today. But he knew it would have to be faced sooner or later. The day Axopen mentioned was the seventh day after yesterday's meeting, the twelfth of Setmi. It was the day that Jahnu had predicted that a crisis would occur involving all of Kosundo. He felt the silence of the room. It was beckoning him to answer, although he really didn't wish to. A simple, "No one can be sure," would not be acceptable for his team. This was his team. He had always tried to let them know what he knew. But what did he know? He couldn't be sure of the answer to this question; but he could tell them what he thought, based on his understanding of the prophecy. He looked around and saw everyone looking at him, waiting to hear his answer. Understandably, that day was on everyone's mind. He decided that it would be best to address this question privately with his team, so he asked the nearest waiter if the wait staff could wait outside the room. Once they left and shut the door, He stood up. He decided to start with a proviso.

"I can only tell you what I understand of the prophecy of the soulless. I cannot guarantee what I say as being accurate, nor can I give you as much detail as I would like—not because I am holding back from you, but because I can only draw generalizations from the prophecy." He paused, waiting to see if the team wished him to continue.

"We all would like to hear what you think, Agapoi." That was Yotux.

"Axi then, but I want you to promise that this subject will not be brought up after we have this discussion. This is a day of celebration."

Everybody nodded in agreement.

"Very well. I will give my opinion of what sort of things might happen next Diotiri and how it might affect us here. After I give my opinion, we will open up the topic for discussion." He drew a deep breath before he began. "One thing that we know for a fact from Jahnu's message is that the father of the soulless is now in Kosundo. Since the main prophecy does not call the first of the soulless the father of the soulless but rather the 'one who is not a man,' I deduce that the first of the soulless was created some time ago. I deduce this not from the Levra but from something that Yarukoi wrote in his personal memoirs. I had read Yarukoi's memoirs about one month ago. Last night, when I was putting my books on my shelves, I saw his book, and I was reminded about what Yarukoi had said. He said that he had a vision that the one who is not a man will attempt a rebellion before he is known. His rebellion will be quelled but the one will survive. I can quote what Yarukoi said about the surviving one: 'After many years, the surviving one will then create an army of the soulless and the soulless will call him *father*. The father of the soulless will become the destroyer of men.' According to the memoirs of Yarukoi, the one becomes the father of the soulless and the father of the soulless will become the destroyer. Since we are being given the warning about the father of the soulless now, I believe that the father of the soulless either has created an army or is about to. Since we can see no evidence of a soulless army in Kosundo right now, I would say that the father of the soulless is about to start his army.

"So this is what will happen? The soulless will begin to gather an army?" Phunex asked.

He looked at her and said, "Next Diotiri? No. I don't think so." He readjusted his gaze to take in the whole team. "The army of the soulless may have already begun, but there appears to be more to the prophecy than just the soulless. I may be reading too much into the words used in the prophecy, but at the beginning of the prophecy, it talks about man's work. The word *work* is always single here. The word *work* seems to refer to the 'one who is not a man'. The result of this singular work is the one, or, in other words, the father of the soulless. Toward the end of the prophecy, however, there is a reference to the *works*, plural, *of man*. I believe I can quote it. 'Then will the soulless be unleashed by the destroyer, for the one will be vanquished by the destroyer. Then the works of man will be turned against man, and the destroyer will destroy men's souls. Only the faithful will remain.' These *works* could be referring to the soulless or the army of the soulless, except the army of the soulless are not the works of man. They are the works of the father of the soulless. I believe that the works of man will be turned against man on the twelfth of Setmi. I don't know what works, though weapons of war can be considered works, but I am not sure it will be war in the conventional sense. The prophecy almost makes it seem that the works themselves will turn against man. It is hard to know exactly how that will happen. No matter what happens, I believe that Bojoa will not be affected on that day because we are to be a beacon of hope."

His team was dumbfounded. They expected that Agap might have some political insight into possible reasons that there may be a crisis on the twelfth. They did not expect an analysis that would shame a Levra scholar.

Finally, Supeb spoke. "You are talking about things, like technology, turning on man? How could that even be possible? And you think that men are responsible for creating the father of the soulless? I have great respect for you, Agapoi, but how could any of this be true?"

Agap looked down for a moment to gather his thoughts before speaking. "I don't know exactly how it could be true, Supeb. But you heard Jahnu, and Jahnu has Odanoi's blessing. The prophecy of the soulless is literal. If the prophecy is literal, how can any other conclusion be reached?"

"Who is Jahnu? Where did he come from? He doesn't dress like a Levra scholar. How are we supposed to take him seriously?" protested a bewildered Kowtsom.

"He said he was a maintenance supervisor," quipped Eutay.

"Yes, that is what he said he did for a living," said Agap. "But that is not what he is. I know that none of us has come to terms with this whole thing that was thrown at us yesterday. But all of you heard him speak. All of you heard the signs that he gave. Who among you cannot quote the warning given without a moment's hesitation? That was a sign. Is it natural to remember something of that length without giving it thought after hearing it just once? Or is it supernatural?"

"I for one cannot forget either of the two signs that Jahnu gave. They are there in the front of my mind, yet they are not in the way of other thoughts. I have never experienced anything like it, and it doesn't seem to be going to fade away anytime soon," said Holon rather forcefully.

"So is it with me," said Yotux.

"I thought I was going crazy. Yes, those signs are like a neon light in my skull," said Eutay.

"Yes. I have experienced the same," said Kowtsom reluctantly. "I cannot deny that what he said rang true. I just cannot get my head around it."

"I am glad that you are plagued with this wonderful condition. It means that you have had your faith confirmed. Isn't it a marvelous thing?" said Agap rather enthusiastically.

Kowtsom broke into a smile, as did others. Even if that thought had entered into all their minds before, it was nice have the thought refreshed. The team was silent, apparently thinking to themselves for what seemed like quite a while.

Finally, Axopen broke the silence. "Very well. I accept that the prophecy must be taken literally. So if someone has done this blasphemy, who could it be? Nothing close to this has been reported in the news media, so it would have to be a place where the government or scientific foundations are good at being clandestine."

"It could be Doetora," offered Opsil.

"No, I don't think they have the necessary knowledge to actually create an artificial man," said Supeb.

"The Levra says that the one is the work of man, but it does not say that man created him. It says that man's work made him into an abomination. It is likely that this was done with some sort of manipulative genetics, quite possibly mixing of animal genes with human genes or some other method that made this creature an abomination before Thaoi," said Agap. "I do agree that Doetora would not have the science to do this though."

"You are correct. Only Thaoi can create life. Forgive my error, Agapoi," said Supeb.

"It was only a misstatement. I merely wanted to avoid the thinking that man could create life. Thank you for your input, Supeb," said Agap.

Yotux, wanting to get the discussion moving again, said, "If not Doetora, then who? Certainly not the Jontu. They have always showed a great deal of candor in their dealings. It would seem out of character for them."

"Agreed," said Eutay. "We can rule out Calisla too. They are only interested in pleasing tourists. How about O'ONaso?"

"No. It doesn't fit. O'ONaso already thinks they are superior to all other nations. Why would they be looking to mess with their genome?" retorted Phunex.

"Cargagru is out. They have expelled scientists who even thought of playing with genetics," said Axopen.

"That leaves Nurd, Minnunglindor, Dricho, and Schwinn. Nurd has experimented with breeding plants and animals," offered Kowtsom.

"But they haven't spliced genes or anything. They've only tried crossbreeding," said Holon.

"True," said Yotux. "And I think that Minnunglindor is not a good candidate. They still have a large population in the countryside that can control votes. Their government has been conservative. It is only the local city governments that have fallen into corruption. They seem only interested in making a quick credit. They would never have the patience to commit to long-term research."

"Well done, team," said Agap. "You have narrowed the field down to two prime suspects: Schwinn and Dricho. It is known that both have dappled with genetics. Schwinn has the government that could be capable of such a thing, and Dricho has private companies that are rich enough to invest large sums into such research. Manipulating the human genome is against the law in Dricho now, but I believe that is a recent law. I'd say it is anyone's guess between those two."

"One in the North and one in the South. Why couldn't they have been neighboring countries?" complained Eutay. "At least then we would know what part of Kosundo to watch."

"You know, I know of someone who runs a project that could help in locating unusual thought waves. I wonder if he still has that probe design he was working on," wondered Agap aloud.

"You don't mean Noso, do you? Isn't he sort of a quack?" asked Phunex much louder than necessary.

"I don't know, Phunex. I admire him," said Axopen. "He has some radical ideas to be sure, but he is a visionary. I follow you, Agapoi. His TWR could possibly uncover any thought waves that are radically different from the normal human. Certainly, the soulless would have to have different thought-wave patterns than a human. At least it would seem logical."

"Yes. I see your point," said Supeb to Axopen. To no one in particular, he said, "Where is his project located?"

"Skapsu," said Yotux. "Before Bojoa, it was the only Cirri city built below sea level. I hear they have large lifts just to ferry vehicles down into the cavern where the city is built."

"Yes. It was the perfect place for Noso to develop his TWR. There is lead in the rock there. Noso's team built several chambers below the city to test the TWR," explained Agap.

"Are you going to invite Noso to Bojoa?" asked Opsil.

"I will have to run that one past the council, but I believe it would be a good idea," said Agap.

"That's all well and good," said Kowtsom, "but how about the twelfth of Setmi? Is there anyone with a bright idea on how to stop whatever will happen from happening?"

"I don't think we could even if we knew exactly what was to happen, Kowtsom," said Holon. "It was prophesied in the Levra and confirmed by the Voice of Thaoi. It *is* going to happen. All we can do is to react to it the best we can when it does happen."

"We don't even have a clue where it may occur. Even if Noso has a working prototype for a TWR probe, we couldn't be in a position to use it for several weeks. It would have to be approved by several councils. Even if we had the probe up tomorrow, we might find the soulless. But there is no guarantee that finding the soulless would find the origin of the crisis. As much as I hate to admit it, there is absolutely nothing we can do to prevent the crisis. Holon is right," said Agap ruefully.

Agap and his team were not used to being in a position of helplessness, but that is exactly where they were now. They sat there somberly for a few moments.

Eventually, Yotux said, "Agapoi, perhaps we should get on with the celebration. It will be lunch time before we play any of those wonderful games over there."

"Yes, of course," he said. "Opsil, would you invite the wait staff back in to take care of the breakfast dishes?"

He sat down as Opsil went to the door. Soon, they were playing Quick Paddle, Tower of Trouble, Short Table Ball, and many other games. The girls played at one table, and the guys played at the other. Holu would be happy to find that they would combine game tables after lunch. He also was glad of that. It was hard to be in the same room with Holu without being beside her.

She handled that session with the team very well, he thought. She was going to be a valuable member of his team as well as the love of his life. But he already had assumed she would do well. If he hadn't, intended or not, he would not have made the invitation for her to join his team.

The rest of the celebration would go on without another mention of the twelfth, just as the team promised. It was a happy celebration. Agap could only hope that they would be able to have other celebrations that were as happy as this one. Only Thaoi knew that for sure.

18

The Road-weary Inn

Temeos looked around the empty street in front of the Road-weary Inn. The street was always empty in this neighborhood on eKureaki morning. He was dressed in nondescript clothing: a plain, tan shirt with brown pants. Over them, he wore a plain, brown coat. He was going to meet with nine Suvatens this morning. A Suvaten was a member of the Edvukaat, a ruling body that used to wield much more clout than it now did. They chose this inn because it was not frequented often during the day and especially not on weekend mornings. As expected, very few people were in or around the Road-weary Inn this morning.

He knew that he was taking a chance in meeting with the nine Suvatens outside of a normal session, and he didn't want many people to be around to see. The less eyes the better as far as he was concerned. The emperor would consider it suspicious if he knew he was meeting with Edvukaat members out of session. Of course, the emperor thought that nearly everything to be suspicious these days.

He wanted to be sure that none of the Suvatens were followed, so he was keeping watch from across the street. So far, he saw six members of the Edvukaat enter the inn. Inside so far were Dikurzk, Cemyoz, Dizkuh, Andryo, Nurmen, and Stivan. Duvary was strutting down the street now. He was dressed in ordinary clothes as well, though his were blue. He hoped that that strut wouldn't draw undue attention. Appearing around the corner was another Suvaten, Shipunke. He was sneaking down the street, pausing at alleys and then darting across. He wished they would all just walk like normal people. Normal walking would draw less attention than the strutting or sneaking. At least he didn't see anyone following any of them. That left Pitar. Pitar was a fine man, but he did have a bit of a problem with punctuality. He glanced at his watch. It read 3:09. He had asked them to gather at 3:10. If Pitar didn't show soon, he would have to go in to make sure that some of the more nervous of the group didn't decide to use his lateness as an excuse to leave. Just as he was about to cross the street, he saw Pitar half-running toward the inn. He looked up and down the street. He saw no one.

The inn was located in the old part of Manku City, where the streets were wide. He remembered seeing old pictures of these streets. Back then, the streets were filled with wheeled vehicles that were powered by grain alcohol. Now, only an occasional battery-powered vehicle would traverse the streets. Otherwise, the streets were the pedestrian's domain. Mass transit now moved people from here to there. Hardly anyone owned a vehicle of their own. He supposed that was for the best. Overtrack was the mass transit of choice in Kosundo now, whether it ran on the ground, above the ground, or under the ground. Most of the Suvatens had emerged from the underground overtrack station down the street. A couple lived close enough to walk from their homes. He took a last look to be sure that there was no one and then crossed the street and entered the inn.

The Suvatens were all assembled around a large table in the back of the inn when he entered. He carefully surveyed the room. There was a polished wooden bar off to the right rear of the room. There were no stools there at the bar. It was a standing bar. A door that seemed to lead to the kitchen was located on the right wall near the bar. All of the tables were covered in dark green tablecloths. There were dozens of small, round tables in the front and middle of the room. The back left of the room had four large tables capable of seating about a dozen people. The Suvatens were sitting at the table closest to the left rear corner. The lighting was poorest there, which was all the better. No other customers were in the inn at this time, and a serving girl was the only other person he saw in the room.

As he approached the table, Pitar, a giant balding man, rose to greet him.

"It's about time you showed up. We thought maybe you changed your mind."

He, being a tall man himself, was able to look Pitar in the eye and nearly said Pitar's name; but caught himself and instead said, "You are one to talk, my friend, since you have only just arrived yourself."

"Ahh. We thought you might be watching somewhere," said Stivan, a tired-looking man who was otherwise average in almost every way.

"Just watching out for everyone's wellbeing," he said flatly.

"That is very considerate of you, but I believe we can look

after ourselves," said Shipunke. He was a thin Mugmi man who resembled a large rodent. He had beady eyes and his two front teeth were larger than normal.

He really didn't like Shipunke too much; but he was here at the invitation of Pitar, so he was worth tolerating. "One can never be too careful," he said.

Cemyoz, a graying man who looked distinguished even in ordinary clothes, stood up for a moment and said, "Come. Sit down, my friend. We have much to discuss over breakfast this morning." Then he sat down.

He and Pitar joined him in sitting. He sat at the end of the table that faced the kitchen door.

"Tell the young lady what you would like. The rest of us have already ordered," said Cemyoz impatiently.

The serving girl, dressed in the traditional black and white, came up to him and said, "Your order, sir?"

"I'll have schwain roast and potatoes with gravy," he said.

"Anything to drink, sir?" asked the girl.

"Just water. Thank you," he said.

The girl scurried off to the kitchen to give the orders to the cook and ready their beverages.

"Schwain roast and gravy. Now that sounds like a hearty breakfast," said Dizkuh, a younger-looking man.

"Breakfast is an important meal, my friend," he answered.

Cemyoz looked around the room to make sure they were alone. After he was satisfied, he said, "Axi, my Lord Director Temeos. We are here, although I am certain we should not be. Tell us what it is you wish to discuss with us that could not be discussed in open session.

He looked Cemyoz in the eyes. "Emperor Tryllos," was all the he said.

It was enough. Every eye in the room now went to him, so he continued.

"We must declare a no-confidence vote in the Edvukaat. Tryllos must be stopped."

Now faces started to turn white. A silence like death filled the room. No one spoke for what seemed like many spens.

Finally, Cemyoz fastened his eyes on him and spoke softly yet firmly. "You are mad, Temeos. There has never been a successful no-confidence vote. It would be a death warrant for anyone who proposed it."

"Cemyoz, I realize that proposing a no-confidence vote is risky. But that is the only real power the Edvukaat has left. You say that I am mad. Perhaps I am. But if I am mad, Tryllos is a thousand times more so. He would put all of Kosundo at risk because of his paranoia. No. It is more than paranoia. He seems tormented within himself. He is not capable of rational thought any longer," he blurted a bit louder than he had intended.

"The Edvukaat is aware of some of Tryllos's idiosyncrasies, Lord Temeos. But what do you mean that he is putting all of Kosundo at risk?" asked Cemyoz just above a whisper.

Just then, the serving girl emerged from the kitchen with their drinks.

"I will explain shortly," he said softly. Then he continued in a loud, jovial tone. "And that is why you should never go on a date without seeing her first." He broke out into as genuine a laugh as he could muster.

The others did the same.

As the girl served the drinks, various impromptu conversations about women started—one about what to look for in a woman, one about what to avoid in a woman, and one about the merits of avoiding women altogether. When the girl disappeared again into the kitchen, all conversation stopped.

He continued softly. "As most of you already know, the emperor has a number of informants around Kosundo."

Most of the men nodded.

"The information that the emperor has most coveted from these informants is information about their countries' technology, particularly technology that can assist the emperor in a project that he has kept secret from all but a few people. He calls it the Avenger project. He has the best technology scientists in Doetora secluded away, working on the project."

Andryo, a short, plump man, interrupted him with a question. "How long has this project been in existence?"

"To my knowledge, it has existed for five years, maybe longer," he answered.

"How could this have been kept secret for over five years?" demanded Duvary, a large man who was the seventh man in his family's history to become a Suvaten. He tended to carry himself like an aristocrat.

"Very easily," he replied. "The emperor took all the people who are working on the project by force and saw to it that everyone who knew anyone working on the project met an untimely accidental demise."

"You knew of this and did nothing?" scolded Dikurzk, a thin, wiry man.

"There was nothing I could do without finding myself in a death trap," he retorted. "There is no paper trail or recordings of these atrocities. I only know of them by rumor myself. The only evidence I have are words I have recorded. The emperor spoke them to me when I asked him about working the project workers such long shifts. He said, 'The workers no longer have anything or anyone else to concern themselves with, so they do not mind working long hours.' At best, it would still be my word against the emperor's, and I'm sure the emperor would have been able to find someone who would refute my word for a price," he explained. "I did get one worker to nod when I asked if people that he knew were dead," he added, "but that is the only information that I was able to get from any of the workers. Tryllos has them intimidated."

Cemyoz put his hands up, palms out, in front of him. "Fellow Suvatens, you all know the peril anyone faces in matters concerning the emperor. We all have stories of injustice and oppression of our own. Please remember that the lord director is now coming forward with this information at great personal risk. We do not need to assign blame to anyone in this room for what the person did or did not do in the past. Let us focus on the issue at hand to see if we can afford the risk of opposing the emperor on this occasion." Cemyoz put down his hands and said to him. "I am sorry for the interruptions, my Lord Director. I can see that the serving girl is readying plates in the kitchen. We will let you continue unimpeded once the serving girl has delivered the food. I will speak to her so that we will be allowed a few spens of private time once she has finished her delivery duties." Cemyoz had pulled out his credit monitor, indicating that he was going to let credits do the persuading. A few of the Suvatens raised an eyebrow; but everyone knew, since Cirri was given administration duties of the credit system because of their neutral status, that even the emperor could not monitor credit accounts without a Cirrian business council hearing.

After the serving girl delivered what she had in her hands, Cemyoz waved her over, whispered something in her ear, and handed her two printouts from his credit monitor. Her eyes grew wide as she nodded her head to whatever she was being told; then she went off to the kitchen smiling. She made several more trips to the kitchen and back, serving food and refilling drinks. Once she was finished, she gave Cemyoz a huge smile, went to the front door of the inn, turned on the closed sign, and retreated to the kitchen. He supposed that they wouldn't see her again this visit.

Cemyoz nodded to him and said, "I don't believe she will be coming out again for a while. You may now explain what this project is and what evidence you have to convince our colleagues in the Edvukaat to sustain a no-confidence vote against the emperor."

He rose to his feet, cleared his throat, and continued softly. "First, permit me to explain myself. As lord director, it is my duty to execute the commands of the emperor. He has never issued a command to me that was illegal. He has always gone to other sources for actions that do not coincide with the laws of Doetora. He is a troubled man, but he is also very clever. I do have evidence of what I will tell you today. Some are documents, and some are surveillance images that I was able to put away in a safe place. However, I will not produce this evidence unless a unanimous consensus can be reached by all Suvatens present here today. If you can agree that action needs to be taken, I will hand over the evidence during an open session of the Edvukaat. If not, I will destroy the evidence and make plans to stop the emperor myself. I take risk in making that statement. My life is now in your hands. But such is my resolve and my personal belief that what the emperor plans is an imminent threat to all of Kosundo, including Doetora. I would not be here otherwise." He paused to take a drink of water, and whispers developed among the Suvatens.

He put down his cup and stared at the faces of the gathering. He checked the kitchen door to be sure no one was peering through the window. The window was clear. The faces looked expectant. He knew that after he told what he had to tell, there would be no going back; he would no longer control his own fate. Finally, he continued.

"I will try to be brief to allow you time to ask questions after I am finished. I wish I could afford the luxury of allowing you time to consider the matter for a day or two, but I do not have the luxury of time. I must know if you will be taking action in the Edvukaat before we leave this place because if you do not, I will have to set other plans in motion. You, gentlemen, are the only legal resource that I have. The other plans will cause me great pain and disgrace, but such will be the cost of being able to live with myself."

Suddenly, he felt a cold chill creeping down his back. He shook off the feeling and continued. "Before I tell you what the Avenger project is, let me tell you why the emperor calls it by that name. His stated goal for this project is to avenge Doetora. The reason that Doetora needs avenged has eluded me, as the emperor will not entertain that discussion. The important thing to consider about the goal of the project is not the reason for the vengeance but rather who the targets of his vengeance will be. The emperor defines the targets of his vengeance as anyone who opposes the empire. As most of you know, the emperor views himself as the empire. So the target of the Avenger project is anyone who opposes Emperor Tryllos. Right now, that could include anyone sitting in this room."

He paused to let that point sink in before proceeding to his next point. The Suvatens were silent, all eyes glued on him, so he continued.

"The Avenger project itself has morphed over the years as new technology was stolen from other countries and incorporated into the project. I did not take the project too seriously at first. But then, about two years ago, an informant retrieved the schematics for a revolutionary new targeting beam. It was not clear what the beam had been designed to do, but rough tests on a prototype made from these schematics revealed what the beam could do. The beam can be programmed to isolate and excite any type of matter or energy patterns. The prototype was programmed to target a magnetic pulse field that displays a particular pattern. I will illustrate how that can be done. I have a commterm in my pocket." He reached into his pocket and pulled out his commterm. He then turned on the device. "This little pocket device radiates a magnetic pulse field. So does every other item with circuitry, whether it be solid circuitry, liquid circuitry, gas circuitry, or plasma circuitry. This commterm uses gas circuitry, I am told, but it radiates a very similar field as this credit monitor." He produced his credit monitor, turned it on, and held it side by side with his commterm. "The credit monitor has solid circuitry, I am told." He placed both devices down by his plate. He then produced a third device that look something like a commterm but had two short, round appendages on each side of the term that extended slightly below the main body of the device. "The project scientists call this device a magnetometer. It uses a very weak detection beam that allows the device to show a graphical representation of magnetic pulse fields. I do not know all the science involved with this device, but I was shown how to use it. I will take a reading of the magnetic pulse fields of the two devices in front of me. I will first separate the devices on the table so that it is clear that I am taking two separate readings." He picked up his commterm and put it in front of Cemyoz and then picked up his credit monitor and put it in front of Pitar. He then proceeded to take a reading from both devices, first the commterm and then the credit monitor. He then hit the appropriate buttons to display the results side by side. The only discernable difference in the two graphs was that one was slightly larger than the other one was. Both three-dimensional graphs resembled a thin bar with triangular ends. He showed this to each of the Suvatens. "Notice that the shapes of these two graphs are remarkably alike. The only difference is the size of the graphs. The size difference is because the commterm uses much more energy when turned on than does the credit monitor. But the patterns of magnetic pulse fields are virtually identical."

"That may be true, Lord Temeos, but how do we know that this device will register any other pattern than the one that we now see?" asked Nurmen in his usual cynical tone. Nurmen had closely set eyes and a nose that resembled the nose that children might place on a snowman.

He knew that question was likely to be asked, and a pompous creature like Nurmen was certainly a likely person to have asked it. "That is a good question, Sir Nurmen. Would you like to help me measure a different type of magnetic pulse field?" he said, purposely putting Nurmen on the spot.

"Er...ah, yes, I suppose so. What do I have to do?" asked Nurmen.

"Not a thing. Just let me use the magnetometer to measure your magnetic pulse pattern," he said casually.

"My magnetic pulse pattern? I never knew I had one. Yes. By all means, measure away," said Numen.

He pointed the magnetometer at Nurmen and pushed the button to display the pattern. "Here you go, Sir Nurmen. This is your magnetic pulse pattern." He showed Nurmen the term display and then the rest of the Suvatens in turn. The display showed an oblong, circular graph.

"Well, that certainly does look different than the patterns for the devices. I guess that means I am not a piece of technology," Nurmen said, trying to be witty.

"That is exactly my point," he said. "Humans do not have the same magnetic pulse pattern as do pieces of technology. The prototype is set to detect the magnetic pulse fields that surround technology, particularly any technology that has circuitry. As you can tell by my little demonstration, this is clearly possible with this type of detection device."

"But how can a detection device possibly pose a risk to all of Kosundo?" asked a weary-looking Stivan.

"I cannot explain how, Sir Stivan, but I can show you. I loaded a few video clips of tests that were run with the prototype device. I was told that the beams produced by this prototype are only slightly more powerful than the beams produced by the device that I used. The main difference is that the prototype uses five beams that work in concert as opposed to the two beams that my device uses. You will see that the prototype is not much bigger than the device that I used as you watch the clips on my commterm. I will start playing the clips and pass around my commterm." He opened the file on the commterm where the test clips were stored, and the commterm started to show the clips. He passed his commterm first to Cemyoz.

Cemyoz's face grew very somber as he watched the clips. After a few moments, Cemyoz shook his head slowly and passed the commterm to Dikurzk to his left. This same type of reaction continued around the table until everyone had viewed the clips.

Pitar, who was the last Suvaten to view the clip, handed the commterm back to him. "That *is* incredible," was all that he said. But Temeos could see sweat developing on his balding head, a sure sign of the tension that he held within him.

He reached inside his trouser pocket and pulled out a card with notes jotted on it. He glanced at the card and then began again. "This video just shows a small prototype. The actual beam devices are going to be housed in several small flying platforms that the emperor has dubbed the Avengers. These Avengers will fly in formations made up of five aircrafts. These formations will duplicate the five-beam pattern of the small prototype. The Avengers can use their beam only when they fly below the thick, ionized ozone layers that surround Kosundo. That means that their operating ceiling is about an altitude of six point five stets. The Avengers can target anything within their horizon that gives the beam an effect range of two hundred and twenty-eight stets. They are capable of targeting up to one thousand different targets per tic. That translates to one hundred thousand targets per spen. The flying platforms can hover so the Avengers can sit outside of a target's weapon range and create the destruction that you witnessed on the video."

"This is nearly unbelievable!" exclaimed Dizkuh, a burly Miera man with a broad nose. The look of surprise made his nostrils flare. Once his nostrils were back to normal he said in a calmer voice, "Really, I suppose I should say that I do not want to believe it. The reprisals that Doetora would suffer for using these Avengers would be devastating."

He nodded. "And I have not even told you the worst of it."

The room grew deathly still once again as he paused.

"The Avengers are to be controlled by a very experimental means. It is something that is called a thought wave processor. It is so new that no security is yet available to protect this device from being compromised. This processor is to be connected to the emperor's brain so that he can control the Avengers himself. He will be able to identify targets and track the progress of the Avengers through several overlay maps. And as I said before, the emperor is not in full control of his faculties. When last I saw the emperor, he was pushing to deploy the Avengers in about a week."

The leader of the group of Suvatens present was Cemyoz, so he turned to Cemyoz and asked, "What do you think, Cemyoz? Is this beam device, along with the delivery platform and the Avengers, enough of a threat to validate my claim that they put Kosundo at risk?"

Cemyoz's face was still very solemn as he looked at him. He responded to the questions posed to him by standing up. Temeos took that as a cue to sit down, so he sat. Cemyoz cleared his throat and started by saying, "I believe everyone in this room is surprised by what we have heard and seen here today, with the exception of the lord director, of course. I know that each one of you has questions right now. I know I do. But I think that you will have to agree that this information casts a different light on matters concerning the emperor. I encourage each of you to compare any risk that we may have to take to the utter destruction of Kosundo both in other lands as well as in our own land of Doetora. I am willing to state before the Suvatens present that I believe that the use of these Avengers by the emperor will initiate a terrible response by any country or federation that is attacked. I can foresee a Kosundo, including Doetora, lying in ruins. These Avengers would unleash the kind of destruction that no war, including the Great War, has ever caused.

"I have stated my opinion, but still I have questions, as I am sure do the rest of my colleagues. I ask that my colleagues send their questions to my commterm so that we may question the lord director in an efficient matter. After all, I did not pay enough credits to keep the inn closed all day."

That last comment brought a few halfhearted laughs and brought a slight smile to Cemyoz's face, which quickly vanished as he started to speak again.

"Lord Director, would you be willing to take the floor again and answer a few questions as you are able?"

He nodded and stood as Cemyoz sat back down. It took a few tics; but soon, he could hear Cemyoz's commterm make a sort of chirping sound that he presumed were questions for him. He directed his attention toward Cemyoz, who was busy looking through the messages coming into his commterm, so he decided to make a qualifying statement about his knowledge of the Avenger project. "Sirs, I am glad to answer any question that you may have, but I am not a scientist, so my answers will reflect my best understanding of the project and may be deficient technically. I will, however, answer your questions to the best of my ability and knowledge."

Cemyoz now was ready and answered, "We all understand that you may not be prepared to answer a lot of technical questions, Lord Temeos. But I believe you will find our questions to be of a more general nature, so be at ease. Is there any other question that someone has not sent to me yet? If so, please indicate this by raising a hand." No hands were raised. "All right then. I believe that I can now begin. Many of the questions are repeated by several persons, so I will read the ones that seem to be more numerous first. The first question is, 'How many Avengers have been built?'"

He nodded slightly as he began. "That is an excellent question and one that needed posing. Currently, three full squadrons are completed. In addition to the fifteen Avengers that make up the completed squadrons, four other Avengers also have been completed. There are currently seven other Avengers that are under construction—of which I am aware. The emperor had wanted to have seven squadrons, but he is growing impatient. I believe he may very well have five full squadrons within the week." He looked around the room to see if the answer was satisfactory.

No one indicated that it was not.

Cemyoz asked the next question. "Do you have a sense of who the emperor plans to attack first?"

"In his more lucid moments, he talks about attacking Schwinn first because he suspects them of having some terrible chemical weapons stockpiled. However, he also has spoken of attacking a western port city in Doetora first. The one he has spoken most often about is Anark City. His rationale, if it can be called that, is that unleashing the Avengers on Doetoran soil first might help conceal the origin of the Avengers."

This answer brought many murmurs from the gathering.

Cemyoz held up his hands, and the gathering fell silent. "That is quite a revelation, Lord Temeos. Which location does the emperor speak of with the most frequency?"

"Recently, he has spoken of beginning his attack in Doetora, as he has become less rational and more … I believe *maniacal* is the word that best fits."

Again, murmurs arose.

"That is most disturbing," said Cemyoz, "but there are a few more questions that need an answer." Cemyoz read the next question. "Describe the Avengers, what they look like, how fast they can go, and any weakness that you may know about them."

He thought for a moment on how best to answer and then said, "I have seen the Avengers up close on the ground a few times, and I have personally seen a squadron flying once. The craft is a sphere perhaps ten dets in diameter," he said while holding his arms wide apart to estimate the distance. "It is light, weighing perhaps fifty libs. I've seen two men pick one up and put it on a bench without struggling. It is silver in color. It appears like a metal ball in flight. When it is preparing to use the beam, a single, long rod extends out of the front of the craft. The rod tapers to nearly a point. This rod is used to discharge the beam." He paused to remember what other details he knew and then continued. "I do not know exactly how fast the Avenger can fly, but it is very agile and appears to fly at a high rate of speed. When they fly together, they fly in a formation that is referred to as the dotted diamond. Four of the Avengers make up the points of the diamond, and the last avenger flies in the middle. As for weaknesses, I am told that the Avengers have to fly in a dotted diamond formation to make the beam most effective. If the formation loses one of the Avengers, they will fly in a dotted triangle formation, which reduces the effectiveness of the beam. The beam will not be at all effective if there are less than four Avengers in formation. That being said, the only thing that limits the range of the beam is the curvature of Kosundo. Given the ability of the beam to self-target and the range and effectiveness of the beam when the Avengers fly in the dotted diamond formation or even the dotted triangle formation, I cannot see how anything could get close enough to the Avengers without being targeted and destroyed before being in range to fire. Missiles would be ineffective because they could easily be targeted and destroyed before getting close to the formation, and energy weapons are limited just as the beam is by the curvature of Kosundo. The Avengers would sense these as priority targets and eliminate them before the Avengers could be targeted. Satellite weapons might have stood a chance, but satellite weapons have been banned for a millennium. The only real weakness is a double-edged sword. It is the thought wave control interface. If someone could gain access to that interface, the Avengers could be stopped, but they could also be redirected to other targets." Again, he looked around the room for indication that more needed to be said. There was no indication, so he looked toward Cemyoz.

"I believe there are only two more questions that are worthy to be asked," said Cemyoz, "and the first is, 'What powers the Avengers?'"

"There is a small generator inside each Avenger. I am told it can produce enough power for an Avenger to operate continuously for five years. This generator needs only to be refueled that often."

"Well, there goes the idea of a limited reign of terror, should these things be unleashed," said Cemyoz. "Very well. Here is the last question. 'You have said that the Avengers are programmed to target the magnetic pulse field generated by circuited devices. Would turning off the device prevent the Avenger from targeting the device?'"

He anticipated this question, and it was a good one. He quickly answered, "Yes, but perhaps no. Many devices retain energy for hibernation operations, such as an internal clock. Others retain energy in a capacitor to enable a quicker startup. Many devices still draw power when not on if they are still connected to a power source. Still others cannot be turned off quickly, such as fission and fusion reactors or even electronic watches. Therefore, the answer is yes if the device is truly disconnected from a power source and retains no energy. But the answer is no for most devices. I am told that the detection ability of the five-beam array is far more sensitive than the two-beam device that I used today. Kosundo's integration of technology into every facet of life has left it quite vulnerable to the Avengers."

Cemyoz stood up and said, "Thank you, Lord Temeos. Now, if you will excuse us for a few spens, we will discuss what we feel can be done." Cemyoz was pointing to a round table at the front of the room as he spoke to him.

He picked up his devices and his food and drink and made his way to the specified table. He figured he might as well eat what he ordered, even though it had gotten a bit cold. Once he reached the table, the Suvatens began to talk softly amongst themselves. This went on for a few spens with the talk sounding quite spirited at times. All he could do was wait.

Finally, Cemyoz waved him back over to the large table. He couldn't tell from his face or the faces of the other Suvatens what had been decided, if anything. Once he was seated, Cemyoz spoke to him.

"Lord Temeos, we have decided that action is needed."

His hopes rose.

Then Cemyoz continued. "However, there is one thing that is preventing us from being able to take the action of declaring a no-confidence vote."

This made his heart sink.

"The emperor has eliminated all of his heirs, and he never had any children of his own. Normally, this would not be an obstacle, since the lord director, you, could assume the role of emperor. However, you cannot be named to this role if you testify or provide evidence against the emperor."

His hopes rose a little again. He understood this problem before he scheduled this meeting; but he knew something the Suvatens did not know, so he immediately spoke. "Is that the only obstacle stopping your action?" he asked.

Cemyoz looked a bit bewildered but nodded.

That nod made his heart light. He smiled and said, "Then I have information that you should know. Tryllos doesn't know it, but he has a living heir. And I have the papers to prove it." He was relieved that he did not have to act illegally against the emperor, but the Suvatens were shocked. As he told them how he came to know about the heir, their disbelief dissipated and the Suvatens came to understand. It was now possible for them to sponsor a no-confidence vote.

Cemyoz indicated that he would send out a general message to the rest of the Suvatens to convene this week as a session because having all twenty Suvatens present was necessary for the vote to be taken. And so the matter was decided, although the outcome could not be entirely sure.

Still, Temeos was relieved that the matter would ultimately be out of his hands. He only prayed that his actions today would prevent the slaughter of untold millions, possibly billions of people. Only time would tell now.

19

THE SEALED LABS

Degmer felt more nervous than she had in all her hundred years. She was on her way to Beltram's office. Beltram was the site administrator for the Dricho Genetics Foundation Complex and, as such, had the authority to grant her access into the sealed labs. She could not get what she believed was the voice of Neaotomo out of her mind. She could only hope that if he did survive, he was still very weak. She tried to clear her mind last night with the relaxation technique, but the thoughts of Neaotomo entered her mind even after she had contacted her spiritual guide. It was funny, but it seemed that she still had the sensation of heightened senses that she experienced while doing the relaxation exercises even now, though she had bid the guide farewell last night before going to sleep. Accompanying her was her friend, Laysa. Degmer was still considered young, not quite middle-aged; but Laysa was much younger than she was. Although she wasn't sure of her exact age, she thought Laysa was fiftyish.

It was eKureaki, the weekend day in Kosundo; so the two girls passed many empty offices on their way to Beltram's office. The halls in this part of the complex were a light green color decorated with a border just above her head level. She was of average height for a Drichoan woman. The border had a white background with dark green designs in the center that were spaced about a det or so apart. She thought they were much preferable to the plain white walls that existed in the laboratory part of the complex. Somehow, the contrast of the green walls with the white border background seemed to be much greater today to her. The green designs seemed much more vivid then she had remembered them. She had remarked about the walls to Laysa earlier, but Laysa didn't seem to think the walls were any different from the last time that she had seen them.

As they approached the office of the site administrator, they noticed that the door to the reception area was open. Upon entering the reception area, they noticed that the administrator's secretary was not in, which was not unexpected since this was the weekend. The door to Beltram's office was standing open, so the girls walked in. Beltram Chaf was reclining in his big leather desk chair with his commterm in hand when the girls first entered but quickly sat up straight when he saw the girls. Beltram was a tall and stout man.

He said, "I'll see you then. I've got to go now," and ended his conversation on the commterm, placing it on his desk.

Degmer distinctly heard a female voice say, "Okay. See you then, sweetie," come from the commterm; but it wasn't the voice of Beltram's soza. She knew Beltram's soza.

As they walked farther into the room, Beltram was taking an earpiece out of his ear, as if he was listening to the person he was talking to through it. If that was the case, she couldn't have heard a response from across the room so clearly. She shrugged off the thought and walked to meet Beltram. He was dressed casually in a light blue, short-sleeved, pullover shirt, which didn't seem to match his formal office.

"Good morning, ladies," he said cheerfully, gesturing with his hand for them to take a seat. Beltram was of Mugmi descent, having skin that was a tone darker than Laysa's tanned skin; and he had vivid green eyes. Beltram's hair was brown, and it was cut in the short Drichonian style that sort of looked like the barber put a bowl over his head to cut his hair. All Drichonian men cut their hair that way, as did the women. The only difference between men's and women's hairstyles in Dricho was that the men wore their hair above the ear, while the women wore it below the ear. Well, there was one other difference. The woman usually made their hair curl in toward the face at the bottom. The women called the hairstyle a bob cut.

Degmer actually envied Beltram's skin color and wondered what she would look like with that tone of skin. It was good that Beltram was in a good mood, even though she had sent a message to him only last night asking for permission to enter the sealed labs to retrieve some equipment for her project. Whenever someone mentioned the sealed lab, people tended to get a bit paranoid; but Beltram had merely requested her to come to his office at 3:20 this morning in his response.

The two women said, "Good morning," almost in unison.

Beltram started the conversation with a casual question. "So, why aren't you two young ladies off enjoying yourselves today instead of coming down to try to get permission to go into an old laboratory to fetch some equipment?"

"There are a couple pieces of equipment that we could really use on our project, Beltram. The sooner we can get them, the quicker our project can be completed," she explained.

"What pieces of equipment are we talking about, Degmer?" asked Beltram.

"There is a genome splicer that can render much more detailed forecasts than our current one and also a small computer drive that has some notes that would be very valuable to our project. The notes I am looking for only exist on this drive, and they do not have anything to do with the origin genetics project. You can have a technician come and delete all the notes that deal with the origin genetics project if you wish. I, for one, want nothing to do with those notes," she said.

"That is very reassuring, Degmer. Do you feel the same way, Laysa?" asked Beltram.

She hoped that Laysa would back her up in her assertion. She could end the whole idea of getting into the sealed lab with the wrong answer or even a hint of hesitation.

Laysa took only a quick glance at her before saying, "Oh, I want nothing to do with any notes about the project that was located in the sealed lab. I take Degmer's word that there are useful notes on the drive, and the genome splicer could be very useful."

That was a better answer than she had hoped. She believed that Laysa really did trust her judgment, although she was slightly doubtful of her own judgment on the matter.

"Axi. Your request sounds reasonable. It's not like anything is going to jump out of the lab if we open it briefly," Beltram said with a laugh.

Her eyes met Laysa's eyes for a moment, and then each forced a slight laugh.

"Of course not. The lab has been sealed for seventy years. Nothing will jump out," she said a little less casually than she would have liked.

"I will have a security team remove the equipment you require tomorrow. You will have to accompany them, of course. I doubt they would know one piece of equipment from another," said Beltram, and he started to get up.

Something in her told her that she could not wait until tomorrow, and something else did not want the presence of a security team, so she stopped Beltram from rising by quickly saying, "A moment more of your time, if you please, Beltram."

Beltram let himself sit back down and said, "There is something more, Degmer?"

"Not more really," she began. "I just hoped it would be possible to get the equipment today. Time is really working against us."

Laysa looked at her as though she was wondering why she was pushing for entry today. She ignored her.

"Today?" said Beltram. "It's eKureaki. There is only a skeleton security staff on duty today. There wouldn't be any spare security personnel to go with you, and I can't allow you to go into that area alone. It's not that I don't trust you. That area has been deemed a sensitive area by the company."

She felt like she must persuade Beltram to let her in the lab today, although she was not sure why. She decided to try to coax Beltram. "We would only need one security person, Beltram. There are only two light pieces of equipment, and it wouldn't take long at all to get the equipment out of the lab. Not only that, both pieces are in the outer lab. We wouldn't have to go into the inner labs."

Now Laysa was beginning to look uncomfortable. She ignored that as well.

"That may be so, Degmer, but the company policy is explicit when it comes to access to sensitive areas. A minimum of two security personnel must be present when a sensitive area is entered," said Beltram, who seemed to be getting impatient to leave.

She calculated that she only had one chance to get into the lab today: a little subtle blackmail. She decided that she would use what she heard when she came into the office. "I am sorry to trouble you on eKureaki with my request, Beltram. I know you must be in a hurry to spend time with your family."

Beltram flinched slightly when she mentioned his family, but she was not sure she would have normally noticed it since it was extremely slight.

"Well, now that you mention it, I do have another engagement this morning. I will assign a security team to you first thing in the morning, Degmer. I promise."

She got up, and Laysa followed suit. Laysa started toward the door, but she didn't. She felt compelled to get into the sealed lab today, not that it made any rational sense to her; but something seemed to be driving her. Instead of following Laysa toward the door, she walked toward Beltram's desk and said, "Does your soza know about her?" She nodded toward the commterm on Beltram's desk.

She was not sure who was more shocked, Beltram, Laysa, or her. She really didn't know why she said that. She just seemed to be compelled to do so. Laysa stopped in her tracks, looking as if she didn't know her. Beltram just looked guilty, his eyes cast downward.

After a moment, Beltram leaned back into his chair and looked at her. "You are very perceptive, Degmer. How did you know?"

She was just getting over the shock of her own actions. She couldn't very well say that she heard another woman call him sweetie through his earphone. She thought for a moment, and then it hit her. "You were awfully quick to schedule a meeting for this morning. A meeting with an insistent scientist would be a great excuse to get away for a while. I suppose that you told your soza that this could be a long meeting. I never insisted on meeting today in my message, as evidenced by the fact that you were surprised that I wanted access to the lab today."

By now, Laysa had timidly walked up beside her. She looked as though she could faint at any moment.

"Hmm. I see," said Beltram. "I knew you were intelligent, but I never figured you for a blackmailer, Degmer, especially over something as trivial as a couple pieces of equipment. What is the real reason that you want in that lab?"

She hesitated. Part of her wanted to tell Beltram the truth, but another part of her screamed at her not to tell Beltram anything about what she had heard.

"She can't shake the thought that one of the test subjects survived. She just wants to go into the lab to confirm that they are all dead so she can sleep at night," said Laysa.

Laysa had told the truth as her mind would let her understand what she had told her. Degmer was relieved. She couldn't have thought of a lie that sounded more convincing. Laysa's words had an element of truth in it. She could capitalize on this. She tried to look ashamed as she cast her gaze to the floor before she spoke.

"I know it is a silly thought, Beltram. But I really do feel as if I may go crazy if I don't prove to myself once and for all that all of the test subjects are all dead. I just can't sleep at night. Please, Beltram." She had tried to sound pitiful. That often seemed to work on men.

Beltram scratched his head. "What put the thought in your head that a test subject might be alive in a lab that has been sealed off for seventy years?"

She had stretched Laysa's truth in her first answer. Now she was prepared to lie, no matter what Laysa might think. "It is hard to explain. They could get into your head, especially one of them. The research team called him Neaotomo. He got into mine. Somehow, I believe he inserted a latent memory into my mind, a memory that only recently is causing this feeling to stay with me. I just really need to make sure that they are all dead. It won't take but a moment. It would really mean a lot to me." She hoped that she hadn't put on too thick of an act.

Laysa was looking at her doubtfully again.

"I have the access code to unseal the lab, Degmer; but the lab doors will not open after it is unsealed without at least two security personnel. I am not sure that they will be inclined to commit two people on a weekend just to let you sleep better tonight," said Beltram apologetically.

She knew she had won Beltram's sympathy now. She leaned forward on the desk just enough to let her loosely fitting top hang just a bit and said, "There must be a way. Please. I must know," she said with what she hoped was the proper mixture of pleading and passion.

Laysa now was past doubtful. Now she looked shocked again.

Beltram was not paying any attention to Laysa at the moment, not with her top hanging loosely in front of him. He thought for a moment and then turned to his computing term. "There may be a way that we can pop down to the lab for a quick look," he said as he brought up a personnel search screen. "We had to let go several people from security recently. Knowing our inefficient personnel department, their records might still be in the system. Their supervisor's handed me their IDs last week. I am to destroy them in the presence of a company executive. They didn't send an exec down last week, so I still have the IDs," he explained. He then turned to a locked drawer in his desk, unlocked it, pulled out the IDs, and put them near his computing term. He then began to search for the names of the female personnel that had been recently terminated. He found the first two names that were on the IDs. The files listed employee information and included a copy of the employee's thumbprint. Beltram clicked on the each thumbprint and selected print to film. A machine was heard in the reception area. Beltram put the two IDs into his shirt pocket and locked the rest back in his drawer. Beltram got up and went toward the door. He then turned and said, "Are you two girls coming?" which prompted the women to nearly trip over each other when they started for the door together.

Laysa gave her a disapproving look, but she said nothing. As they reached the reception area, Beltram was pulling two pieces of adhesive film out of a small device.

He turned around and said, "Hold out your right thumbs." He then took off a backing and applied a piece of film to the two women's thumbs. He said to her, "You now have Janica Thosbiti's thumb print. And then he turned to Laysa and said, "You now have the thumbprint of Rossett Doynun." He handed them the respective IDs and said, "Use these IDs and thumbprints to open the door after I enter the code. It should fool the system. We keep those thumbprints so that we can provide them to the authorities should the need ever arise. I guess that means that criminal tracking info has just provided us a way to commit a criminal act, at least as far as the company is concerned. Kind of ironic, isn't it?" The question was rhetorical. As they started out the door and down the hallway, Beltram said, "Now, remember, just a quick stroll around the labs. Don't touch anything. I should warn you girls that you are likely to see a few skeletons in there. According to the records, the labs were sealed without claiming any of the bodies. Somebody really wanted that lab sealed fast."

20
A Means of Escape

Neaotomo was running out of air. He had tried to conserve air by going into light hibernation, but it was no use. Soon, the air would be too foul to breathe. He guessed he had maybe a day's air left. He had scoured the lab complex for a way out, but there was none. Perhaps if he had his full strength back he might have been able to get to the outside lab, but there was an air lock between him and freedom, and he had no way of negotiating it without powering the airlock. Even at his full strength, he wouldn't have been able to get out.

He could see the lab without too much difficulty during the day. His eyes could adjust to very low light. A little light came through a long tube in the ceiling in the main lab area during the day. The rest of the complex was dark, but that little bit of light was all that he needed to be able to see. He had noticed when he moved around the lab during the day that his creators had perished, along with some of his keepers. His fellow test subjects, as the creators called them, had all perished as well. He had seen their remains and knew their skeletal features well enough to recognize them, even in their present state. Judging from their state of decomposition, he estimated that he had been asleep for at least fifty years. Beyond that, it was difficult to tell. It was cold in the lab but not really cold enough to affect decomposition that much, but the labs were kept sterile and that limited the amount of bacteria in the air. Still, there was warmth that emanated from below the complex that encouraged the body's own bacteria to multiply. He guessed the warmth was from a geological anomaly of some sort that produced heat. He had studied about those, and it seemed plausible. Whatever it was it kept the lab warm enough so that his body didn't freeze.

The keepers who had been in the outside lab had escaped. At least he could see no evidence of them through the impenetrable windows that separated the inner labs from the outside lab. They had shut off all power from the complex. It looked as though they had sealed his fate by doing so, no matter his superior abilities and cunning. He had thought of every contingency except the possibility of no one coming in to claim the bodies. He had expected that the jostling of being carried out of the labs would revive him. But no one ever came to claim the dead. They had abandoned them just as they had the lab. He had to admit that that was very clever of the survivors. He hadn't anticipated that.

Since no one had come back to the lab in so many years, it was probable that no one would come back. The lab had probably been forgotten by now. It seemed that he was only faced with the decision of when to die. He could go into a deep hibernation. That may give him a couple of years to live, but he would likely die in hibernation. He could conserve air by frequent light hibernation, but that would reduce his waking parzes. That left the choice of staying awake, which would use up the air in less than a day. None of the choices seemed too appealing to him, but his survival instinct was strong. He decided that he would put himself into a deep hibernation in a few moments.

First, he would write a note. Someone would eventually stumble on the lab. He thought he should give whoever found his corpse a little message. He could still be the subject of controversy in death even if he never did gain the notoriety that he wanted in life.

He had already found a writing stick and some paper, so he wandered to a desk in the main lab where the light was best. He knew how he wanted to begin the note, so he jotted down the first few words.

> I am the last surviving member of a species that was callously cut off by an inferior species called humanity.

Yes, that line should create some controversy amongst humans, his inferior creators. It was not that he didn't find humans fascinating. They did have something that he did not possess, although he really didn't know exactly what that was. He encountered it every time he probed into their consciousness. It was just that their bodies were inferior. They were prone to disease, succumbed to injury easily, and were weak. They tended to use very little of their mental abilities as well. It was as if part of their brains were walled off.

He was thinking about adding a couple of lines to his note when the lights in the lab suddenly turned on. He blinked. He had not seen light this bright in quite some time, and it took his eyes a moment to adjust. He could not believe it. If the lights were on, then the power was restored. That would mean that the air was being renewed again. That also meant that there would be someone entering the airlock soon. He put down the writing stick and went to the door that led to the outer lab. He could see the airlock indicator from there. As he looked, the indicator light went from red to green. Someone had just entered the airlock. He had no way of knowing who was coming or how many, so he thought it would be prudent to hide himself.

Whoever it was would come into the outer lab first. He needed to find a place where he could see them but they could not see him when they first entered. That would give him a chance to know what he would be facing. It then occurred to him that all he had to do was to go into the adjacent lab on the opposite side of the main lab and turn off the lights. This would conceal him quite nicely from human eyes. He quickly moved to the lab opposite the outer lab door and turned off the lights. Then he crouched down and waited for the airlock to open.

He could feel the freshened air circulating now. It seemed to clear his mind as he breathed it in. He watched the airlock. The light was still green, but the door had not opened yet. That could mean that there were many humans coming. On the other hand, it could just be that the airlock door would not open until the air in the labs was better circulated. Human lungs did not have the ability to filter out oxygen as well as his did, so it would seem reasonable that the airlock would prevent humans from entering an environment with such little oxygen.

He felt anxious as he waited to see who would enter through the airlock. Anxiousness was another new emotion for him. He decided that he did not altogether like the feeling. It made him feel unsure yet sort of exhilarated. It was a strange combination of emotions. If armed men came through the airlock, he would have to hide. They probably were not looking for him, whoever they were, so no need to risk a confrontation. Yet if he hid, he would not be able to gain freedom from the lab; and it was hard to know if anyone else would enter the lab again after this. He hoped that whoever entered would not be armed. That would give him a distinct advantage. He could risk contact then.

He saw the handle on the airlock move. The door opened, and in walked a large male and two females, one taller and more slender, but her muscles looked well toned; and the other was of average build for a female. The man's skin was darker than the two women's skin. He thought that he might be of Mugmi descent, a human euphemism for a crossbred human. The two women looked to be of Ispra descent by the looks of their lightly toned skin. One of the women had brown hair, and the other one had red hair. He could not see their faces clearly yet, but the one with the red hair did look familiar. He watched the airlock as the door closed. The light had turned red. He would have to see if it turned green again before deciding what to do. There might be more humans coming. He would just observe for now.

The humans had moved to a part of the outer lab that he could not see from his position. His eyes went to the main lab to look for a concealed vantage point with a better angle. Instead, his eyes caught the table where his one-lined message was still laying in plain view, should anyone enter the inner lab. He thought about going to get the message, but his body was rather large. He may very well be spotted, and then his hand would be forced. He would have to make his move before anyone entered the inner lab. He glanced at the airlock. The light was still red. It appeared as though there were only going to be the three of them. That was good. If worst came to worst, he could easily overpower them, even though he wasn't in peak condition.

He was just going to move into the main lab when the redhead peered into the room through the door. He did know her. He believed her name was Degmer. As she moved her head, he became sure. It was Degmer. She was referred to as an intern back when she worked in the very lab that she was in now. She looked older now, though he wouldn't call her old. She still looked to be young, just not as young. Then the brown-haired woman looked into the main lab through the door. She looked younger than Degmer. She probably wasn't born yet when Degmer worked in the lab. The two were joined by the man. He looked to be older than Degmer but not by much. He certainly wasn't old, like some of his creators were. The younger woman was pointing to the table where the message lay. He thought that he must act before they saw the message. That message would ruin his chance of using these humans to get himself free of the lab. It would make them fearful and that would cause complications. He decided to reach out with his mind to Degmer.

Degmer, help me, he thought. Degmer didn't respond to him with her mind, but he saw confusion on her face. She had heard him. *Can you hear me, Degmer?* he thought. This time there was a response.

I can hear you.

Degmer had walked away from the door; and the others were looking back, probably at her.

I need your help, he thought.

This time the response was a question. *Who are you?*

He could not risk telling her, for he was unsure how she would react. She had never had any direct contact with him before. They had only seen each other through the windows and doors. He knew her name through interaction with the others. He was sure that she would know his name by the same method. His name could have shock value and send her racing for the airlock. This is the last thing he wanted to have happen. He would have to soften her up a little first. Human women tended to be emotional, so maybe he could play on her softer emotions. He sent this message: *I can sense your presence but I can't tell where you are. Are you in the lab? I don't know what happened. I can't see anything.* He hoped that pretending he was somewhat incapacitated would give her confidence and cause her to start caring about the voice.

He sensed other conversations going on within Degmer. She was probably talking to her companions. He was only trying to read thoughts plainly sent to him. He figured that anything too invasive would scare Degmer off. Finally, a thought was directed to him.

Are you hurt?

He smiled. He felt now that his messages were having the desired effect. He sent, *I don't know. I might be. I feel very weak.*

Again, there was a delay. Her mind was being occupied by something else to be sure. Then he received, *Do you want me to come to you? Are you in the inner labs?*

He seized on that response and sent a weak, *Yes.*

There was an immediate response. *I have people with me who don't know about you. I may have to find a way to come back alone.*

Erith, he thought to himself. He couldn't let her go. He had to put more urgency into her mind. He thought for a moment and then sent, *I don't know how much longer I can survive. Please help.*

The people I am with wouldn't understand. They could make it impossible for me to help you. I must find a way to draw them away, was the next message.

He thought it was time to put a thought in Degmer's mind. *There are tranquilizer sticks in the main lab.*

There was a long delay this time. Degmer's mind was now jumbled. It seemed that it was arguing against itself, literally. He had not sensed this amount of disharmony in a human's mind before. It was odd. Finally, a response came.

I am coming.

He sat back, away from the door, as the door to the outer lab opened. His breath caught just slightly when Degmer burst into the lab and walked directly to the message on the table, read it, and wadded it up. "It's nothing but a to-do note someone was writing," she said. She was covering for him. She glanced around the lab as if looking for something and then walked toward the medical cabinet to her right. The brown-haired woman followed, with the man bringing up the rear. Degmer tossed the wadded paper into the waste receptacle near the cabinet.

The brown-haired woman said, "I don't care if it's just a to-do list. It was someone's last words." She headed toward the waste receptacle where Degmer had thrown the paper, with the man following close behind.

As the brown-haired woman sorted through the trash in the receptacle, Degmer was opening the medical cabinet. As the brown-haired woman was retrieving the wadded paper, Degmer had placed three medical sticks into her pants pocket and left her hand inside the pocket. As the brown haired woman was smoothing and reading the paper, Degmer moved toward her.

"Hey, this isn't a—."

That was all that the brown-haired woman had managed to say. Degmer had stuck a medical stick into her neck. The brown-haired woman lost a grip on the paper and started to fall. Degmer caught her and asked the man for assistance. As the man reached to assist, she let the brown-haired woman fall the rest of the way to the floor and stuck another medical stick into the man's neck. He immediately started to fall to the floor. She managed to soften his fall and then turned to the woman who was lying beside the man.

"I'm sorry, Laysa, but there's something I have to do," she said to the brown-haired woman, although it was obvious that the woman couldn't hear her at the moment.

The humans lost consciousness quickly. It appeared that Degmer had taken the type of tranquilizer sticks that were used on the test subjects, as he and the others like him were called. The sticks didn't work quite so quickly on him, but they were potent. He supposed that the humans would survive. She didn't seem overly concerned about her companions, so perhaps she had some experience with the tranquilizers.

He was still hiding in the darkness of the adjacent lab. He felt comfortable that he could not be seen, and he was breathing very lightly so not to be heard. He wanted to make mental contact with Degmer before facing her, since she obviously meant that third tranquilizer stick for him. To his surprise, she threw open the door and lunged at him with the tranquilizer stick. He managed to catch her wrist with his left hand just before the stick made contact with his neck.

As he continued to hold her wrist, she continued to try to make contact with his neck. Then she said in a strained voice, "I see you are not blind or hurt, Neaotomo."

"No, but then I didn't realize that your version of helping me would be a stick in the neck with this," he said in an even voice, his eyes gesturing with his head to the medical stick in her hand. "Just out of curiosity, what were you going to do if you succeeded in getting this thing into my neck?"

She stopped straining, "I am not quite sure. I guess I was just trying to buy a little time."

He took the stick from her with his right hand and put it in his trouser pocket. "How did you know where I was?" he asked.

She was looking at the ground and nervously rubbing her wrist. "I heard your breathing."

"That is not possible. Humans do not possess that kind of ability to hear. I was breathing quietly. Why do you lie?" he said disgustedly.

"I am not lying," she said, looking him defiantly in the face. "I heard you breathing when I entered the lab. There was a small catch in your breathing when I burst through the door. It caught my attention. After I sedated Beltram and Laysa, I focused on trying to hear your breathing. It didn't sound like the breathing of someone hurt or in pain, so I decided to try to surprise you. I believe I did surprise you, but you were too quick and strong for me."

He remembered the catch in his breathing when she had suddenly come into the lab, but it was barely audible. He was having a hard time understanding how she could hear as well as he could hear. "How is that you can hear such insignificant noises?" he asked, looking at her with more intensity now.

She looked away from him as she answered, "I am not sure. My senses are often heightened when I do my relaxation exercise. I did the exercise last night." She looked at him as she finished, "I still seem to have heightened senses now. The smell of this place sickens me."

He considered what she had just told him. He walked past her, into the main lab, where the two humans lay. As he entered the room, he could hear the humans breathing. They were just unconscious. He heard Degmer following him. He stopped and looked back at her, over his shoulder. "What noise do you hear in the distance in that direction?" pointing in the direction he had been walking.

She smiled coyly, "You can't decide, so you're testing me. I didn't think it was possible to make Neaotomo indecisive."

"Yes, I am testing you. I cannot understand how what you have told me can be true, yet your words so far have been accurate. To be sure, I am testing you. It is the only logical course of action given the circumstance. What do you hear?" he said. He was growing impatient.

Degmer's smile diminished slightly as she paused to listen. Before long she said, "I hear the sound of the main exhaust fan outside the facility. That seems to be the most distant sound I can hear."

He nodded. "That too is what I hear." She was not only right about the noise, but also the smell. It did smell of death in the labs despite the number of years that had passed since those bodies had ceased functioning. The smell lingered in the air. It still smelled as if the bodies were in middle stages of decomposition to him. The smell was sickening.

However, the fact that she could hear and smell as he could did not explain how she came by these heightened senses as she had described them. The reference to relaxation exercises did not help much. He would have to find out what she does when she does these exercises. He asked, "What are the steps involved in doing this relaxation exercise?"

"Before I answer still another question, when do I get the opportunity to ask you a question?" she said rather bravely.

He restrained a smile. He really did like this human's spirit. He turned to face her and said, "Of course. It is only fair that I answer a question for you first. What is it?"

"How did you survive? How did you survive the gas, and how did you survive these seventy years?" asked Degmer.

He shrugged and said, "I knew of the humans' paranoia concerning me. I was prepared. I sensed the gas coming while it was still in the air vents. I put myself into a deep sleep, near death really. In this state, my breathing was so slow that the gas dissipated before I inhaled enough to hurt me. I had put some sealed water and dried food packets in a compartment under my desk. I nearly died before I could get to them when I awoke. But the food and water has sustained me for the time I have been awake." He had lost his awareness while in thought for a moment while answering the question. Degmer had moved a little closer to him in that moment. He looked her in the eyes and said, "Now that I've answered your question, what are the steps involved in doing this relaxation exercise that you mentioned?'

She shrugged her shoulders, imitating him, and said, "There is really not much to it. You first clear your mind," she said, moving even closer to him. "Then you open up your mind." She was close enough now that she touched his forehead with her left hand and bumped against him when she did. "Then you wait for a guide to sh … agh … uhg … "

He had noticed her right hand going for the tranquilizer in his trouser pocket, and he stopped her by grabbing her by the throat and suspending her in front of him. She really did look ridiculous, with her eyes bulging, her mouth wide open, and her legs kicking violently. He did have to credit her for her persistence, but he questioned her sanity. Why would she continue to try to fight against him? It made no logical sense. Even if she succeeded, she had no logical course of action by her own admission. He waited until her legs had nearly stopped flailing and her face began to swell slightly. He did not want to let her die when he needed to ask her more questions. He just wanted to teach her a lesson, so he let her go; and she fell to the floor with a thud.

Degmer struggled to fill her lungs, rolled on her side on the floor, and brought her knees up close to her stomach. He knelt in front of her and said, "You said *guide*. Did you mean a spiritual guide?"

She nodded her head while she was still struggling to take a breath.

He straightened himself into a sitting position. He did not know anything about the spirit world, if it truly existed. He had never really seen any evidence of it. Of course, all he had ever experienced was life in these labs; and spirits were not part of his education, although he had heard some of the humans refer to them from time to time. From what he heard, the head spirit went by the name of Thaoi; but there seemed to be some difference of opinion about the existence of spirits among humans.

Degmer was still gasping, trying to breathe. She was holding onto her throat as if to make sure it was still there. "Come now, Degmer. I did no permanent damage. You really must stop trying to fight against me. There really is no use. The next time, I might lose my temper and really damage you. I have no desire to do that. Like I told you, I need your help."

Degmer tried to talk, but all that came out was a few coughs.

"You have to relax your throat muscles. I'm afraid my hold on you put those muscles into a bit of a panic. Just relax and breathe deeply and concentrate on relaxing those muscles," he said in his best soothing voice.

Degmer rolled to her back and closed her eyes while trying to breathe deeply. He could not help but admire the female form. It really was a thing of beauty. She was not quite as well-toned as her friend, Laysa; but she still had rather pleasing curves. The male form had its own beauty, but that beauty was more of strength and structure. The female flowing curves seemed more pleasing to him.

"How can I ... help you?" she asked in a raspy voice.

"See. I told you that no permanent damage was done," he said. "You can help me get out of here. All I really want from you is my freedom."

"I don't think ... that I should do that," she managed.

"You know, I think I've decided that I like you, Degmer. You've got more courage than any human that I've encountered so far. But be reasonable. What's to stop me from reaching down and ripping your throat out and trying my luck with one of your friends over there?"

She closed her eyes again. "I don't believe you would kill me for not helping you. It wouldn't be in your best interest." She was beginning to sound a bit more normal now, but she still struggled speaking.

"And why is that?" he asked.

She opened her eyes, glared at him, and said in a breathy voice, "Because you don't terrify me. You scare me, make me tremble, but I am not frozen with fear. People who never have encountered the likes of you would be too terrified to act even if they wanted to. Intimidation wouldn't work. You'd have to win their trust, and that would take a lot of time. You don't have that kind of time. You say that all you want is your freedom. I believe that you want your freedom all right, but that is not all you want. You want to make a name for yourself, and you would do anything to do it, no matter who you would hurt," she said defiantly.

He could tell that despite her defiant words, she came to this lab to find him. Somehow, she knew he was alive. "So tell me, Degmer. What brought you to the lab today?" he asked.

"I heard you ... about a week ago. I heard you scream, 'Gas!' and then I heard you say something in a normal tone, although I couldn't make out the words. I heard you after my hearing was enhanced during one of my relaxation sessions. At first, I dismissed it. But your voice stayed in my mind. I came here to find out if you were truly alive," she ended quickly.

"All right. I believe you. But that doesn't answer why you came with only two humans and no weapons. It would appear that your friends had no real expectation of finding me alive or you would have been more candid with them when I contacted you," he said.

Degmer closed her eyes again. "I cannot answer that question. I don't know the answer. It's as if part of me wanted to believe you were dead and the other part hoped you were alive. I told half-truths to get Beltram to let me in to the lab today. I withheld information to get Laysa to feel pity for me. She came because she thought seeing that you were dead would clear my mind. Yet, I knew you were alive deep down inside. Part of me hoped to find you helpless so that I could finish you off. Part of me hoped to find you as you are for what purpose I am not sure."

He smiled, "You sound like a confused young woman, Degmer. You know what I think?"

She opened her eyes again and looked at him.

"I think I know why you still have enhanced senses." She looked at him curiously. "But I cannot be sure unless you let me probe your mind."

She looked at him accusingly.

He put up his hands and said, "Only probe, nothing more. I could do that without asking if I wished to. I am trying to be gentlemanly."

She sighed.

He could tell that a war was being waged within her mind. He would probe her mind regardless what she answered. There was nothing she could do to prevent it at this close distance. But he was curious what the outcome of the war would be.

Finally, she said, "Go ahead and probe, but only probe."

He admired her feistiness. If he was right, she just proved that she was still the stronger in her own mind. He leaned over her and looked her in the eyes. "Look directly at my eyes. It helps the probe go more smoothly. I promise that that is all that I will do," he said in a reassuring voice. Degmer looked into his eyes. He looked past her eyes and probed her mind. He could feel her presence, strong and defiant. There was a barrier between him and what he liked to call the hidden place, but the barrier was not steady; it rippled. He could also feel another presence. It was in her mind but had not made itself part of her mind. He located the part of her mind where the other presence was strongest. He imagined a strong metal cage and placed it over the other presence in her mind. Degmer shivered as he put the cage in place. He then closed his eyes and broke off the probe.

He opened his eyes and then noticed bruising on Degmer's neck. She was breathing heavily, sweating, and still stared where he had positioned his eyes. He concentrated on the bruises. Soon, the bruises disappeared. He then said, "How do you feel now, Degmer? Less confused?"

She tilted her head to look toward him. "That depends. Did you break your word?" she demanded.

"I probed your mind and found another presence. I sealed the presence off from your mind. I didn't suppose that you would hold that against me," he said casually.

"A presence?" She looked shocked.

"Yes. I suppose it was your spirit guide still hanging

around. It must have found a nice place to roost in there," he said, pointing to her head. "Do you still have those enhanced senses?"

Degmer sat up and became intense and still. "No, I don't. The air doesn't smell so bad, and I can't hear anything outside this room. My neck isn't sore either." She sounded relieved but slightly puzzled.

"All right then. I have helped you. Now it is your turn to help me."

She looked at him with dread in her eyes.

"Oh, Degmer. Do not be so dramatic. I am not going to ask for much. You made most of what I will ask for necessary by your actions. First, you will need to contact anyone who knows your friends here and make up a story to explain their absence. I doubt your friends will be waking up today. I will find a nice, comfy bed for both of them. Do not worry. Then you will need to do some work with the access panel on the airlock. It registered three people going in. You will have to make sure it registers three people going out and then disable the link from the airlock panel to the main computer. It can be done in such a way as to not trigger an alert. The last one is for me and your friends. You will need to make the lab appear as if it was sealed again without actually sealing it. This will keep the company from becoming suspicious."

She had an incredulous look on her face.

"Come now, Degmer. The knowledge that I have about the company systems should not come as a surprise to you. You are aware that I was in the minds of many influential people of this company. I remember the information I gained there."

Her look changed to one of realization.

He smiled and said, "I will tell you exactly how you can do all this. I will stay here for the time you are doing these things to take care of your friends. You will come back tomorrow and spend the day with us. Be sure to make all your excuses."

"And if I refuse to cooperate?" she asked quietly.

He kept a cheery voice. "Oh, let us not talk about silly things. You are not going to refuse to do such simple things for me. After all, I just rescued you from whatever that presence is in your mind. You are going to do these things out of gratitude. Correct?"

Degmer nodded slowly. Neaotomo continued to explain to Degmer what she needed to do. As he did, he thought of how he would enjoy getting out of this lab. But he would have to be patient. Take one step at a time. That was always the best way.

21

Triumvirates

Jahnu and Odanoi had spent the night in prayer, seeking wisdom from Thaoi. Jahnu had gone to bed very early this morning and had awakened just after noon—5:03, to be exact. Odanoi had awoke just before him and had ordered breakfast. They were staying in the guest building, which was located behind the living complex. It was like a large hotel. The quarters came fully furnished, including a small kitchen area. They really hadn't used the kitchen area. Instead, they ordered meals from the main kitchen. Today, they ordered a simple meal of eggs and koh for breakfast.

The two of them had eaten breakfast and were still at the breakfast table, talking about what might happen in six days time and how to best prepare Cirri for it. Jahnu was trying to explain to Odanoi that when the Voice of Thaoi impressed his mind, he could sense more than just words.

"It's as if the Voice of Thaoi imparts moods with the words, as if His spirit is speaking to my spirit. Well, *moods* isn't exactly the right word." He paused to think for a moment. "For example, when I received the warning about the twelfth of Setmi, the words were, 'A crisis will face Kosundo in seven days time.' But I received an impression of a great fear, people wandering in the wilderness and destruction, a lot of destruction."

"Like a war?" asked Odanoi.

"Yes and no. My impression was more like of something that was previously unknown, and Kosundo has certainly known war before," he answered.

"Well, I don't know, Jahnu. You experienced the impression, but can't it be said that anyone who is caught in the path of war has really experienced something unknown to them before?" argued Odanoi.

"Yes, but this seemed different. The fear here is a fear of something that is literally unknown. *Inexplicable* might be a better word for it," he offered.

"Then this might tie back in with the soulless," said Odanoi.

"In a way, perhaps. But it didn't seem as though it was directly linked to the soulless," he interrupted.

Odanoi got up from the table and said, "Let's move into the main area and sit in the chairs there. My old bones can't take too much more of these wooden chairs. Besides, I feel that this line of thought is not really leading us anywhere."

He nodded and got up as well. They walked into the main room. The chairs there were made of a soft leather material and were quite soft. They were the type of chairs that a person could sit in for a long time.

Once they were settled in the chairs, Odanoi said, "Were you going to call a Levra proclamation this week?"

He sighed, "If Thaoi wills it. I have no plans unless I am told to hold one by the Voice of Thaoi. I might hold a worship session next eKureaki. I believe it would be appropriate to gather the faithful in song and prayer considering what the next Diotiri may bring."

Odanoi nodded. "Yes. That sounds like a good idea. I believe I could use the spiritual support as much as anybody else."

He nodded and said, "Me too."

Odanoi picked up the Levra that he kept on the table by the chair where he was sitting. "It is too bad that Thaoi did not grant me the sign of remembrance for the Levra like he has given to you. When one gets to be over two hundred and seventy years old, one could use the help remembering. I think my memory on the prophecy of the soulless might need refreshing while we talk. It will just take a moment for me to turn to it." Odanoi opened the Levra and found the place in Malluntekas that contained the prophecy of the soulless.

He smiled. His memory was not as good as Odanoi's before he had been given the sign of remembrance. Now he could remember any passage in the Levra that he had read, and he had read the entire Levra several times. It was almost as if he could remember several copies of the Levra, although each one said the same thing. They all had slight variations in print or mars on the pages. He could actually see the pages of the Levra in his mind, as if his mind was reading it.

"What you said about the upcoming crisis caused me to think of a line from the prophecy, although it was vague in my mind," said Odanoi. "Here it is: 'Then the works of men will be turned against man, and the destroyer will destroy men's souls.' I had always heard that the 'works of man' were the soulless. But look how the prophecy begins. 'The time will come when the works of men will wax great.' The next phrase talks about how man has a presence in the skies and lives in the depths. These are works that do not appear to be related to the soulless. There are four uses of the singular word *work* in the prophecy. All of them relate directly to the 'one,' or, in other words, the first of the soulless."

He rehearsed the lines in his head and then answered. "Yes, you are correct. So you are thinking that the works of men that will be turned against man does not refer to the soulless but to other works. Yes. That makes sense. In fact, it could not make sense that the works of men refer to the soulless because we now know that the father of the soulless is not a man. The father of the soulless is the 'one' of the prophecy."

Odanoi's head was swimming after that explanation. He hated when Jahnu did that. It made him dizzy. But after he thought about what Jahnu had said, he asked, "So what are these other works?"

Jahnu shrugged his shoulders and said, "Something that will strike fear into men's hearts. That is all I can say with certainty."

He frowned. "We must be missing something, Jahnu. There has to be more. I need something more substantial to tell the people of Cirri. Anything that is announced will also be picked up by all the major news agencies throughout Kosundo. What am I to tell them? Watch out for something to happen that you've never seen before?"

"I understand your frustration, Odanoi," said Jahnu compassionately. "But how am I to tell you something that I have not yet been told? I believe you should just announce what you know."

"What do I know? I am not certain of it, Jahnu," he lamented.

"You know that a visitation has been received and announced. You know that we have entered the age of the soulless. You know that a crisis of unknown origin will occur on the twelfth of Setmi," offered Jahnu.

He forced a weak smile. After more than a week of prayer and meditation, they knew three things, none of which gave them a clear course of action. "That's not much, is it?" he said to the air in front of him.

"Well, you also know that the prophet of the end times spoken of in the Levra has been revealed. You know that you are the prophet's advocate and council, 'the one who must be told,'" offered Jahnu.

"Only you and I know of my role, Jahnu. I think that maybe it is supposed to be that way. But you are right. You are the prophet. Perhaps the announcement should be handled in a similar way as the meeting," he said.

"Perhaps, but I have not yet been told to reveal myself to all people, just to the people that we invited to the meeting. When must the announcement be made?" asked Jahnu.

"Nothing has to be announced to the people until two days before it is to take place, according to the old Cirrian law. But traditionally, we have made announcements a week ahead when we can," he answered.

"Perhaps we cannot follow tradition but only the law in this case, Odanoi. Perhaps we will know more by Paraskevi," offered Jahnu.

"Yes. I might be getting ahead of Thaoi. Thank you for your wisdom, Jahnu. We will wait until then to see if more will be revealed." He sighed and began to rise from his chair, but Jahnu stopped him with a question.

"It's hard not to be the one in control for you, isn't it?" asked Jahnu.

"Yes. I suppose it is. I suppose that that might be the hardest thing about this whole thing for me," he admitted as he settled back in his chair again.

"There is one more thing I wish for you to consider before we conclude our talk and go off privately," said Jahnu.

He indicated that he was listening.

"There is a triumvirate of evil at play in the last days.

There is the unknown works, the father of the soulless, and the destroyer. They will work in concert. This much is sure."

He nodded that he understood.

"Did you also consider that there is a triumvirate of good as well?"

He scratched his beard. "No, Jahnu, I hadn't really considered it. I know that you are the prophet and I am the one who must be told, as mentioned in the book of Sonaydasa. Who else is part of the good triumvirate?"

"It is a person that has been overlooked by Levra scholars who have studied the prophecy of the soulless simply because this person has been overlooked as a generalization. The reference to this person is not emphasized. I believe now it is because he will work without formal recognition. This person is called only 'a faithful servant.'" Jahnu paused.

He decided to wait for Jahnu to make a further point.

"I believe that this faithful servant might hold many answers that even he is unaware that he has."

He considered the possiblity and then asked, "How do we find this person?"

Jahnu smiled and said, "I believe this person would have been invited to the meeting by the voice of Thaoi. But I don't believe that we will find him." Jahnu stopped without further explanation.

He was perplexed by the sudden end to Jahnu's thought. He started to ask a question. "Then how will he—?" Then he too stopped short. "We will not find him because he will find us," he declared with a satisfied smile.

Jahnu nodded.

When he saw the nod, he went into the washroom to ready himself for the day that was already half over.

Once Odanoi left, Jahnu sat still in his chair and wondered.

He wondered what would happen on next Diotiri to be sure. But he also wondered what might be happening today, including what the faithful servant might be doing today as well as when he might meet him. He also wondered if he would know him when they did meet. But most of all, he wondered if this person would be the one who would actually stem the tide of evil. *If Odanoi and he were destined to play the role of watchmen, could the faithful servant be the person who would general the forces of good?*

22

A Perfect Reflection

> The prophet and the one who must be told will give Thaoi's greeting to a blessed people in the latter days. Then will they spread Thaoi's greeting to the people of Kosundo so that the ways of their fathers might be known again.

Agap's reading this morning was from the book of Sonaydasa, found in the latter books of the Levra. He thought about recent events when he read the passage. No one had said it publicly yet, but he realized that Jahnu may very well be the prophet of this passage. If that was true, the "one who must be told" would be Odanoi; and the people at the meeting, including him, were the "blessed people." That thought made a chill go up his spine. It was one thing to read the Levra. It was another thing to think that you had become a part of the fulfillment of Levra prophecy.

He got out of his comfortable chair and put the Levra back in its place on his long bookcase. It was the first day of the week, Diotiri, and it was a workday. He looked at a calendar he had posted on the side of the bookcase. Today was the seventh of Setmi. A week from today would be the twelfth of Setmi, a day that Jahnu had said would present a crisis for Kosundo. He wondered if the crisis was avoidable or inevitable. If the crisis was inevitable, then why the warning? But if it were not inevitable, then Jahnu's prophecy would be wrong. It was all very confusing, and it was too early in the morning to be thinking about such things.

He wished right now that he had bought a few groceries on his way home from the celebration yesterday. He felt hungry, very hungry. He supposed he would have to order some breakfast after he got to work.

He did manage to make cupboards for the kitchen area last night. He had also made a dining table and chairs. Both had a wood color that matched his dresser and doors, chirrud wood. He supposed that he could be a bit more original, but he liked the dark wood tone. Maybe one day he would tire of it; but for now, chirrud was his wood tone of choice.

The team started work at three parzes. It was 2:45 now. He had plenty of time to shower and dress. There was no hurry. But a breakfast would be nice. Maybe he could call Holu and ask her if she wanted to go find some breakfast this morning. *No,* he thought. *She might not be awake yet. Then again, she is a woman, and women do seem to take longer to get ready than men do, so she may very well be up. But unless she has been awake for some time, she might not have the time to get ready in time to eat.* He had told her that he was going to pick her up at 2:90. Maybe that would be enough time to get something to go. That was it. He would ask her if she wanted to stop to get something to take with them. Then again, she might have stocked her cupboards and might have already eaten this morning. *Erith! I can't seem to think straight this morning,* he thought. He guessed that he would just stick to the original plan to order something after he got to the office.

Today was to be Holu's first day working with the team. He stopped in his thoughts to correct himself. He had to remember that she was Holon while at work. It wouldn't do for him to call her Holu at work, so he would think of her as Holon when thinking about work. *Well, it might work,* he thought.

There was not much going on with communications on the team right now, so he decided to have Holon help Yotux with the reprogramming of the chomile interface. Everybody on the team had to work a cross-discipline at some point, so she might as well begin by doing a cross-discipline project right away. Besides, she was a gifted programmer in communications. She'd just have to learn different coding routines and she'd be off and running. He was sure. Yotux would be a good teacher.

Just then, his commterm signaled that he had an incoming call. He had set the incoming signal differently for each person that called him often. This signal was a lively yet beautiful tune. It was the signal for a call from Holon ... er, Holu. *Erith, having my intended on my team is going to be confusing,* he thought. He had laid his commterm on his dresser, so he hurried to his dresser to answer. He was still dressed in his robe; but his robe covered him decently, so he answered with the video on. "I am here," he said, using the customary greeting to answer a call after he hit the orange answer key on his commterm. As he spoke, an image of the top half of Holu became visible on his screen. She too was dressed in her robe, which was equally as modest as his robe. Her hair looked windblown though, so it looked like she already had her shower.

"Good morning, Agapu. I knew you'd be up. Would you mind going out for breakfast this morning? I never got out to do any food shopping just yet," said Holu all in one breath.

"Oh, not at all. That sounds like a great idea. I didn't do any shopping myself. When will you be ready?" he asked.

"I can be ready within a quarter parz. Will we have enough time if you pick me up at 2:70?" asked Holu.

"As long as we don't get a slow waitress, we should be able to squeeze in breakfast and still make it on time," he answered. "We can always leave before we finish if we have to."

"Axi then. I'll be ready by then. Love you, Agapu," said Holu.

"Love you too," he said, and he ended the call.

I guess that answers the question about who is more afraid to take chances in our relationship, he thought, *It's me.* He smiled at that thought. He certainly wasn't overly timid in his professional life. Holu just mattered more to him than his professional life, and he always tried very hard not to offend Holu—maybe too hard. Maybe he needed to loosen up a bit.

He hurried to take a shower and get himself ready. He dressed in a dark blue sark and light grey trousers. He decided to use a blue and red neck scarf. There was no need to wear a jacket for work, although he did occasionally, especially if he was meeting with someone from outside the team that day. But this day would be spent entirely with the team. They had plenty to do just to make sure that the chomile was updated and that the mining transport device was monitored, plus any research they could sneak in. Every day was a busy day, it seemed. He couldn't count how many times he and some or all of his team put in extra parzes just to meet a deadline. The day was scheduled to begin at 3:00 and end at 6:50, but it was not unusual to work until 9:00 on certain days.

After he was ready, he checked his watch. It said 2:68. He grumbled to himself that he must have daydreamed in the shower again and headed out the door and down the hallway to Holu's door. He pushed the triangle-shaped alert button and waited for Holu to answer or come out. It took just a moment this time; but soon, Holu hopped out of the room, still putting on a tan, flat-heeled shoe as the hall filled with her scent.

"Sorry. I wasn't quite ready. I must have zoned out while combing my hair," said Holu hurriedly.

He smiled. It seems that Holu and he did have a good bit in common. "Not to worry. I was a bit early," he said.

Holu gave him a smile and a hug, and then they turned toward the translift. He hit the triangle-shaped call button, and the lift door opened. He punched in CommSec3 since that was the nearest commercial sector to the technology complex. They were silent as the lift moved up and then sideways. Holu had worn a solid, light tan blouse with dark green pants along with her tan shoes. Her hair was drawn to the side today and gathered on the right side of the back of her head in one long, flowing strand. The front of her hair was combed to the right so that it came diagonally down the right side of her face, just above her right eyebrow. Just then, she ran her fingers under the front of her hair and pushed it up slightly. When the lift broke out of the top of the living complex into the dome's version of sunlight, the red highlights in her hair seemed to radiate as she peered out upon the scenery of the dome. Agap still had a hard time believing that this beautiful woman actually wanted to be his soza. He would be very glad when he could call her soza and she could call him sozo. That would be something special. For some reason, he suddenly pictured Holu in bed, waiting for him, without anything on except a smile.

"You're embarrassing me looking at me like that, Agapu," said Holu shyly.

"I'm sorry. I didn't know I was staring at you in any particular way," he apologized.

Holu brought herself closer to him and whispered, "You were looking at me like my father used to look at my mother before he took her to bed."

He felt a mighty rush of warmth flow across his face. He quickly looked down. "Was I?" was all he managed to say.

Holu started giggling and leaned against the side of the lift for support. This certainly wasn't what he had in mind when he thought he needed to loosen up. He turned from Holu and looked outside the lift, trying to regain his composure. He was sure his face was a brighter red than the giggling Holu's face was right now. The lift was starting to descend. He thought of the green mountainsides that he roamed in the summers of his youth near Zaria and the feeling that he had while running across one of the mountain meadows. He felt his face cool. He looked back at Holu, who was still giggling.

When Holu caught his gaze, she stopped giggling and said in a tone of wonder, "How do you do that?" Apparently, the thoughts of his youth had worked; and his face was now its normal color. Her face was quickly returning to its normal color as well.

"I just focus my thoughts on something else. It seems to have worked for you as well. Your face is not red anymore either," he said. "I guess you caught me that time. Sorry if I made you feel uncomfortable."

"I wouldn't say that I felt uncomfortable," said Holu with a shy smile. As she spoke, the lift door opened, and she put her arm in his so that he could lead her out of the lift.

They walked out of the lift to the right. Then he stopped. He had just realized that he didn't know any of the restaurants in this sector. He turned to Holu and said, "Do you feel adventurous this morning?"

"It depends. Maybe," she said cautiously.

"How about we try breakfast at the first restaurant that we come to going this direction," he said.

"Axi. Any particular reason?" she asked.

"I've never actually been to this sector after the businesses moved in until right now," he admitted. "Any restaurant will do when you haven't got a clue," he said, trying to sound like a Cirrian proverb.

Holu giggled and snuggled against his arm. They walked a short distance when they saw a restaurant called The Old House. They looked at each other, smiled, and walked toward the door of the restaurant. He opened the door, and she walked inside with him following close behind. The restaurant delivered on its name. All the tables and chairs had a rustic look to them, as did the walls and counters. It reminded Agap of a freshly cleaned agrodyne barn, minus the animals and straw.

A waitress soon appeared and escorted them to a seat by the front window. She handed them a menu and asked for their drinks. They both ordered milk—cow milk, not molare milk. Soon, the waitress came back with two rather large glasses of nicely cold milk. She then took their breakfast orders. He was pleasantly surprised to see that the restaurant offered gelinhe eggs as well as chicken eggs. Gelinhe eggs were larger than a chicken egg and had a larger concentration of yolk. Gelinhe were indigenous to northern Grasso, particularly Nurd; and not every restaurant was able to get them in Cirri, even though Nurd exported vast quantities of Gelinhe eggs. Nurd exported vast quantities of food of all sorts. It was known as the breadbasket of Kosundo. However, Gelinhe eggs were in high demand; and even Nurd couldn't supply these eggs to everyone who wanted them. He ordered the gelinhe eggs and some schwain strips. Holu ordered three flat cakes with pratesbeges syrup. He raised an eyebrow at the pratesbeges syrup. It certainly tasted fantastic, but it tended to stain your teeth black. Holu noticed the look and triumphantly raised a toothbrush above the table after the waitress left. He got a chuckle out of that, as did she.

The conversation of the meal started with their union week and the union day ceremony, then transferred to the food, and finally ended with him asking Holu about the prospect of working on the chomile programming.

"Are you kidding? It's a chance to program for new technology. I am really looking forward to it," was the start of her answer. She continued talking about the chomile and the team and ended up talking about Yotux. She ended by saying, "That's why I am so glad to be working with Yotux. I'm going to have to talk with you about her one day."

That left him wondering what person she had just been talking about for the last couple of spens. He couldn't remember her rattling on like that before. He attributed it to nerves.

He glanced at his watch. It was 2:92. "Looks like we better get moving or you might be late for your first day of work," he said as he waved over the waitress.

Holu looked at her watch, and her eyes grew large.

"Don't worry. We don't have to catch an overtrack or climb any stairs. We'll make it," he said, patting Holu's hand overdramatically.

She rolled her eyes and shook her head. The waitress came over and scanned his credit monitor. Then they headed out the door and to the lift junction. He pressed the call button, and the lift door opened. He punched in the junction code TC07MAIN for the main lab on the seventh floor, where his team was based. The lift started gently upward, gaining speed as it moved. Holu was looking out of the front of the lift. He looked in that direction and saw the technology complex coming up. The technology building was coated in a material that resembled white marble, and it gleamed in the artificial sunlight that had grown more intense now. The dome was designed to try to mimic times of the day by gradually increasing the light intensity in the morning and decreasing it in the evening. Like all the clocks in Bojoa, the lighting system was synchronized with Cirri City time.

"Drus! The technology building certainly looks more magnificent in the sunlight. It gleams like a palace," said a beaming Holu, not bothering to hide her excitement.

He smiled at her, and she beamed a smile back.

Then something became apparent to him, so he said, "You may want to use that toothbrush that you were so proud of before we ate."

"Oh, did the syrup stain my teeth?" asked a suddenly self-conscious Holu.

"Just a bit. Don't worry. It's hardly noticeable. There's a private washroom off my office that you can use. I'm sure you will be able to remove the stain without a problem," he said.

The knowledge that her teeth were stained reduced Holu's beam a fraction. She replaced her toothy smile with a closed-lip smile. The lift walls descended as the lift approached the technology complex, and a slight bump signaled that it had entered into junction tube. The lift went down and then went laterally. Soon, the lift stopped and the door opened.

It was 2:97 according to the clock in the lab. Holon greeted Axopen and Eutay, who were sitting at their meeting desks, with a nod and a closed-lip smile as she scurried to his office to find the washroom. He made his way to the speaking desk and found the day's assignments that Yotux had laid out for him. Yotux and all the other team members were drinking che and cefa in the refreshment area. He continued to scan over some notes about chomile programming that Yotux had made. When Holon emerged from his office, he looked at his watch. It was 3:00:12. It was past time to get started.

"Good morning, team," said Agap robustly.

The team members responded with various tones of a good-morning greeting as they ambled to their desks.

"I have today's assignments," he said.

The team waited expectantly. All of them wanted free research time, but it wasn't always possible to give them any during the day. *Well, one team member wouldn't be disappointed today,* he thought as he began down the list.

"Yotux and Holon, you have chomile programming scheduled all day."

"That sounds like a hoot," commented Eutay.

He ignored him and continued. "Axopen, you're working with Supeb and Opsil on a possible design structure for a long-distance mass transport device today. Basically, you'll tell them what you want, and they'll tell you what is possible."

That remark brought a couple of snickers.

"Eutay, you need to hammer out the details of your energy waste disposal unit this morning so that manufacturing can get started on it. We will need it on some systems within the month I understand."

Eutay nodded.

"This afternoon, you will need to get some serious work done on a smaller version of the millennium generator for the transporter. None of Axopen's transporter tests can start without it. Phunex, you will help out Yotux and Holon with the chomile programming."

Phunex grunted.

"I know it's not exciting to do the programming grunt

work for them, but it will speed things up considerably." He feigned stepping away from his desk.

Kowtsom called out, "Hey, what about me? Aren't I still a member of your team, Agapoi?"

He smiled. "Oh, Kowtsom, did I forget you? Let's see ... ah, you won't like this," he said as if commiserating with Kowtsom. He then said, "You have free iri research today."

"Hoohoo! That's drus!" said Kowtsom excitedly while giving an openhanded salute. Then, in the spirit that he had shown, she added, trying to sound discouraged, "I mean, I will try to struggle through the day, Agapoi." She ruined any chance of feigning discouragement by getting up and nearly running to her metallurgy station in the lab.

The other team members got up to get to their work areas as well. He heard Phunex mumble something like, "Some people have all the luck," as she went over to Eutay's work area to see how much longer it would be until the waste disposal designs were ready for manufacturing. He decided that he would go talk to Yotux and Holu ... er, Holon, *her name is Holon at work,* first to see how they might split the chomile programming.

They saw him approach, and Yotux said, "Coming over to check on us so soon, Agapoi?"

He shook his head. "Not really to check up. I'm just curious to see how the work will be split up among you two and how long you believe it will take to make the changes."

"Well," began Yotux, "I will need to work on implementing and programming the new mobile panel interface. I suspect that will take the better part of three days. That will leave everything else to Holon, with a little help from Phunex from time to time. Holon will need to rewrite the main menu command structure to have the choice of color be a prerequisite for creation. Once the main structure is complete, she and Phunex will have to direct each item module to reference the new command structure." She looked at him briefly before continuing, "This change can be made very quickly, but there are over ten thousand item modules in the chomile program. That's a lot of grunt work. Then Holon will get to tackle the wall programming. She will need to make several subroutines that will do the many tasks that it will take to simplify the process for the end users. The program already includes the washroom and kitchen area subroutines, so she can study those for the commands necessary to make the other auto-subroutines. She can base the pointing subroutines on the existing pointing subroutines. She just needs to make this subroutine end the wall instead of begin it. I would guess Holon's tasks may take three or four days, depending on how much Phunex is available to help."

"Do you think that all the testing can be done by the end of Paraskevi? I would really like the work on the chomile to be done this week. Only Thaoi knows what next week will bring," he said with a sound of urgency in his voice.

Yotux looked a little surprised. Then she said, "I can start testing once I finish with the mobile module, Agapoi. That may allow us to complete testing on Paraskevi."

He nodded. "Axi. Do your best to see that this project is off the schedule before next week." He turned and headed for his office. Agap knew that Yotux would do her best, but he really wanted both her and Holon available next week. In fact, he wanted the whole team to be available next week. Next week held unknown secrets. He never was comfortable with not knowing something. He guessed that was why he always worked so hard to know everything he could about the work his team was doing. He never was one to like professional surprises. But the way he felt about next week was more than just not knowing something professionally. It was as if he had a personal responsibility to do something about something that hadn't happened yet. He just wanted all the mundane things out of the way before next week right now. He thought he might give the rest of the team research time on things that would enable his team to make a real difference in Kosundo. One of those things was the development of a long-distance application for the transport beam. He already had two of his best thinkers on the project. He hoped that they could make some headway this week.

After he entered his office, he checked his messages. There was nothing of an urgent nature there. He decided that he would best be served by catching up on his own grunt work that he had not been able to get through during his absence from his team. Grunt work was what he called the administrative details that he had to do. Nobody really liked grunt work, but it had to be done. He decided he would spend the day doing this so that he could help with more interesting things the rest of the week. The first items on his dataterm were receipt and requisition forms. He groaned to himself when he saw how many he needed to go through. Then he took a deep breath and started on the first item. It was a receipt form for cefa. He had to smile at that. His first administrative act after getting back would be to make sure that the delivery of a refreshment item was inventoried and debited to the team's account. *It certainly is thrilling to be a team lead sometimes,* he thought. Then he shook his head and got to work.

Yotux turned to Holon after Agap left and said, "Did he seem rather uptight to you just then?"

Holon sighed. "He's got a lot on his mind right now. I believe that he really does feel that the fate of Kosundo will rest with him and his team. He may be at least partially right.

What he has told me about his thoughts on it makes sense. He will be fine once next week gets here. He's just not very good in dealing with the unknown. It bothers him not to know. I think he feels like he is helpless to prepare for the unknown. But that won't stop him from trying to prepare for it anyway." she smiled at that thought. He would try to prepare and probably at least partially succeed in his preparation. His insights had always amazed her.

Yotux leaned toward her and said, "Well, if part of his way to prepare for next week is to get this chomile thing off the schedule, I guess we'd better get to it."

She nodded. Yotux then showed her what to look for in the programming and what needed to be done. She had never seen some of the terminology that related to the chomile's functions, but the programming language was familiar. She felt confident that she could do it without much trouble. She was relieved. She didn't want to be the one who slowed the progress of getting the chomile work done. More importantly, she didn't want to disappoint Agapu—make that Agapoi—in her first assignment with his team.

Over at one of the transporter workstations, Axopen and Supeb were discussing a way to overcome the problem of pattern identification when attempting indirect mass transports. Opsil, being the assistant designer, was listening intently.

"There has got to be something wrong in the design somewhere, Supeb. In theory, the beam ought to be able to determine an infinite number of pattern variations. All it is doing is scanning and copying," said Axopen. Axopen was put in charge of the transporter technology, and this problem was annoying him a bit. It ought not to be happening. The last test design of the transporter array was a miserable failure. They had arranged a number of items together and tried transporting them to another transport workstation. Everything looked good as the items disintegrated. The patterns seemed to be recognized by the disintegrating station; but when the reintegrating station received the energy and data streams, all the matter was reintegrated randomly. Some of the items reintegrated intact but inside of other items, while other items were lost completely, reforming instead into a blend of the original items.

Supeb had suggested that there might be a limit to the pattern recognition ability of the beam itself, but Axopen was insisting that the beam was fine. It was getting them nowhere with the problem.

It was then that he made a suggestion. "Maybe you're both right and you're both wrong," he said.

Axopen and Supeb stopped arguing and looked at him incredulously. He had never really spoken up like this before.

"What is it you are thinking, Opsil?" asked Supeb.

He was shocked himself that he had said something but recovered to say, "Well, there might be a design flaw because of a limitation of the beam itself. I mean, the beam seems fine when it goes into the receiver, but when it is transmitted to the other receiver, it seems to be degraded."

Axopen thought for a moment at that statement. Then his eyes grew wide. "Like clones," was all he said.

However, Supeb picked up on the idea. "Yes, that could be it," said Supeb excitedly.

"Thank you, Opsil," said Axopen, and he was off to his personal workstation.

"Yes. That was a very good catch," said Supeb. "Now let's get to work then." He turned toward the designer's workstation.

He was a bit puzzled. As he followed Supeb, he asked timidly, "To work on what?"

Supeb stopped and looked at him. "To work on what?

Why, it was your idea, Opsil. We shouldn't try to capture and retransmit the beam. We should just monitor the flow and deflect the beam to the reintegrating receiver," said Supeb.

"Oh. Yes. Of course," he said quietly. He hadn't actually thought that far yet. He was young and working with the best technology team in Cirri. He thought that it was drus that he could even hint at an idea that other team members hadn't thought of yet.

As they arrived at the design station, he thought of another question. "How do we know what material to use to reflect the beam?"

Supeb smiled. "We don't. But that's not our problem. That problem is Axopen's. Our problem is to design a way for the data stream to reach the second transport device before or at the same time that the beam arrives. We will have to trust Axopen to work out the materials." Supeb paused for a moment and then asked him "How would you get a data burst transmission that travels at about one hundred and sixty thousand stets per tic to arrive at the same time or before a transport beam, which travels at exactly one million stets per tic?"

He thought for only a tic or two and then said, "The data burst would either have to be given a shorter route or a head start. It would be easier to give the data burst a head start design wise."

"I was thinking along the same lines. In this case, the transport beam is the detection beam, however. How do we get a data burst a head start when it needs the transport beam to create the data?" Supeb said the question rather quietly and slowly, as if thinking to himself.

He was not sure if Supeb really was asking him the question, but he thought he might have an answer. He said, "Supeb, didn't Axopen's notes on the transport device say that the beam was first used as a detection beam only?"

Supeb smiled. "Yes, it did, Opsil. I believe you may have hit on the answer again. We would need to use two beam array nozzles instead of one. One would be a low-powered array just to detect the matter pattern, and the other a high-powered beam to disintegrate the matter into energy. Let's see. It would take just a few hundredths of a tic to process the detection of the beam into the matter stream, just a shade over three-tenths of a tic for the data burst to get five-sixths of the way to a destination that is halfway around Kosundo, counting time to a satellite and back to the ground. It won't matter if the data burst is a fraction of a tic earlier than the transport beam as long as the receiver is programmed to wait for transport beam input. I think we'll be all right with about a .31 tic delay between the two arrays. Do you concur?"

He would have needed a moment to run some of those numbers. He knew that Supeb had been working with satellite computations for a few decades; but he couldn't be sure, so he said, "If you are sure of the numbers, Supeb."

"Don't worry, Opsil. We will run the numbers before we put anything into the design specs, but I wouldn't be surprised if I am pretty close with my estimate," said Supeb candidly.

He wouldn't be surprised either. Supeb was quick with mathematics. "So, do we have enough information to get started?" he asked.

"To get started, yes. But we will need some information from Axopen, like the kind of reflectors to use and the energy output for the low-powered array. We can fill those details in as they become available. Let's go ahead and get started on a design for our two-headed monster," said Supeb rather enthusiastically.

He nodded; and before long, they were both headlong into discussing and drawing up designs on their dataterms. Axopen still would need to approve the concept; but it was very likely that he would approve, so he was confident that they were not wasting their time. In fact, they might just have saved a lot of time in the end since it would probably take a few designs to get even the rudimentary simulations to work as they wanted.

By this time, Axopen was asking Kowtsom if she had run any formal tests on the reflective qualities of iri. Kowtsom was in the middle of testing an iri-silver alloy and was not very pleased to be interrupted.

"I know it's your free research time Kowtsom, but this could be important for making long-distance transport of multiple items a reality," said Axopen.

Kowtsom sighed. She knew that Agapoi had Axopen's research high on his agenda. "Axi. What did you need to know about reflection?"

Axopen looked relieved. "Thank you, Kowtsom. I need to know the intensity a reflected energy beam would retain as a percentage. I know that a polished silver surface typically reflects at ninety-seven percent intensity and a mirrored glass surface at about ninety-six percent intensity. Iri has many unusual properties. I just wondered if the reflection waves of an energy beam off of polished iri would be closer to one hundred percent than silver would be."

"We're talking pure polished iri?" asked Kowtsom.

"Well, I don't know," he admitted. "I had hoped that you would try pure iri and then maybe an iri-silver alloy."

"Today is your lucky day. I remember running reflection intensity tests on pure iri," said Kowtsom. She walked over to her dataterm and hit a few buttons. Before long, she turn backed to Axopen and said, "Iri reflected ninety-five point eight percent of a fifteen-thousand-phusen light beam. It reflected ninety-seven point four percent of the energy of a twenty-thousand-domen energy beam. That's higher than one would expect for a yellow metal."

"That's good, a little better than silver's reflection efficiency, but not what I was hoping. What about the iri-silver alloy?" asked Axopen.

"That's the alloy I am currently researching, so, again, you are in luck. I haven't yet set up for a reflection yield test. If you're in a hurry, you can help me set it up," suggested Kowtsom.

He was only too glad to oblige. He was hoping to find a reflective surface for the transporter that was at least ninety-eight percent efficient.

"If anything can be told from the color, the alloy shows promise," said Kowtsom. She walked over to a tall, rectangular machine. Kowtsom had nicknamed the machine the metal mixer, though in truth it did more than just mix metals. Through a glass, a sample bucket could be seen inside the machine. "This is what the molten iri-silver alloy looks like."

He walked over to peer into the bucket. The molten alloy was brilliantly white. "What does it look like when it solidifies?" he asked.

"I don't know yet," she said, "I just was able to get the two metals to mix. Iri is the only substance that I know that needs a particular ratio with another substance before it will mix. It seems to create a chemical bond with the other substance when it mixes, but it will not bond or even mix with the other substance until a perfect ratio exists in the mixture for the bond. The ratio of iri is always a multiple of seven, no matter what combination of other substances are introduced into the mixture. This particular mixture is fourteen percent iri."

He smiled knowingly. "Yes. I remember that little quirk about iri from my study of the iri compounds. At least it makes it simple to adjust the mixture ratio."

She nodded as she searched a large drawer in a metal cabinet near the small furnace. She emerged with a small mold. The mold had a short, rectangular section at the top. It then had a small, rod-shaped section at the bottom that extended from the center of the rectangular section. "This is the mold for the reflecting plate I use for all the reflection efficiency tests that I run. The rod will lock into place in the testing chamber." She held the mold so that the bottom of the mold was resting inside a mechanical hand that extended out the side of the machine. She then hit a series of three control buttons, and the hand grasped the mold and retracted inside the machine. The top opening of the mold then appeared inside the metal mixer below the sample bucket. After she pushed a few more buttons as well as some numbers on a key pad, the bucket tipped until the molten alloy was pouring into the mold. The bucket stopped pouring once the mold was filled. Then the mold was lowered into the machine, and a door covered the opening. A few moments later, a clank was heard. Kowtsom went to a covered chute on the other side of the machine and took out a freshly polished reflection plate that had just been poured and cooled from the molten iri-silver alloy. The color of the plate was still a brilliant white. She turned to him and said, "The color is still white." She then announced, "It's time to set up the test."

A few dets from the metal mixer was another machine that Kowtsom dubbed the energy machine. It was used to measure the energy intensity and speed of particles. It could be set to create and emit multiple kinds of energy and then measure the intensity of the energy as it hit a measuring panel. The machine stood only about ten dets off the floor, but it was about twenty fets long and ten fets wide. As the two walked over to the machine, Kowtsom handed him the freshly made reflection plate.

"If you will do the honors of inserting and calibrating the reflection plate, I will program in a couple of tests, one for light and one for energy reflection efficiency. I understand that light is a component of your transport beam."

He nodded. He moved the release lever that was located in the middle of the energy machine down, and the machine split open to allow a person to walk to the middle of the machine. At the middle of the machine was a programming panel, and beside it was a movable socket where the reflection plate could be inserted. He inserted the plate. It fit perfectly in the socket and locked into place. He programmed the reflection plate to reflect at a forty-five-degree angle. When he locked in the angle, the socket turned slightly, moving the plate. A sound of an electric motor was heard inside the machine as the computer in the machine adjusted to the measuring panel, which was to receive the reflected beam, to the proper position.

Meanwhile, Kowtsom was programming the standard test beams: a light beam with an intensity of fifteen thousand phusens, and then an energy beam at twenty thousand domens. The standard test would send the beams a distance of twenty fets through a vacuum measuring the intensity of the beam when it reached a measuring panel. Each beam would be measured twice, once without reflecting the beam and once after the beam was reflected.

He walked outside the machine and returned the release lever to its original position. The energy machine closed and a sound like wind rushing outward was heard. The machine had created testing tunnels where the beam would travel and then created a vacuum in those tunnels. A large light display near the top left of the energy machine turned from red to green and then started to flash.

"Looks like we're ready to roll," said Kowtsom enthusiastically. She then pushed the triangular button that was located beside the flashing light. The flashing green light turned into a steady amber light. A few tics later, the steady amber light turned into a flashing red light. Four numbers displayed at the top right of the machine, one under the next number. The first number was 14999.9999968, the second number was 14999.9999967, the third number was 19999.9999997, and the fourth number was 199999.9999997.

Both Kowtsom and Axopen stared at the display in disbelief. "No way," was all that Kowtsom managed. She pushed a button near the display, and the screen flashed two numbers, one above the other. The first number was .999999999993, and the second was 1.00000000000.

"Axopen, I think you may have found the compound you need to reflect your transporter beam," she said, looking as if she still didn't believe the data she was seeing.

He rubbed his chin. "That display does indicate what I think it indicates, correct?"

"Well, I can't be sure exactly what you are thinking, but the display does indicate a reflection efficiency of nearly one hundred percent for light and a full one hundred percent efficiency for a standard energy pulse," said Kowtsom rather flatly given the circumstance.

He scratched his head, making some of his greased hair stick up. "Is there a chance of a system error?"

"There is nothing to indicate an error," said Kowtsom, scanning the other displays on the machine. She suddenly had a smirk on her face when she looked at him.

"What's with the smirk?" he asked.

"Nothing," she said, but her smirk persisted as she looked back at the display. "The system does download a complete log of every test to its memory card. I'll check it out. But right now, it looks like a good test." Kowtsom stepped to the side of the machine; pushed a button; and retrieved a thin, small, clear card from the machine. "I'll go run the data right now, Axopen. I'll let you know if the system detected any error. The system will have a visual of the test as well so the test can be verified visually. Right now, I believe we might have found the perfect reflection surface." That smirk reemerged on her face as she looked at him again.

He ignored it this time and nodded. "Send a copy of the test visual if you would. Thank you, Kowtsom." He stood looking at the display for a couple more moments before turning toward the design station.

When he arrived, he saw both Supeb and Opsil working on a design concept that incorporated a reflected transport beam and two beam nozzles. "What's with the two nozzles?" he asked.

Supeb turned his head, looked at Axopen and said, "We needed to give the data burst a head start. This concept will allow a low-powered beam to feed data for the data burst while enabling a delayed high-powered transmission for the actual transport. This way the transport beam will not have to be interrupted. It will cause a point .309 tic delay in disintegration of the target. It will also give us twice the light show. Of course, the second will be much brighter than the first," said Supeb lightly. He noticed part of Axopen's hair standing straight up and gave a slight smile.

"The data transfer only takes about six hundredths of a tic. Couldn't the same thing be accomplished with one beam?" asked Axopen.

He shrugged his shoulders. "Yes, it could. But a two-nozzle design will be a safer design. We can put safety cutoffs in the low-powered nozzle to protect against a dual transport beam in case of an unexpected power spike. A dual beam could feed against itself and destroy the transport array and the target. The cutoff would prevent both nozzles from discharging."

"Can't a cutoff be incorporated into the single-nozzle design?" asked Axopen.

"Not for a power surge. The single-nozzle circuitry would have to be built to withstand large amounts of current because of the amount of power needed to create a transport beam. A power surge during the data beam phase could result in two transport pulses being initiated. The second nozzle will be designed with a less robust circuitry. The circuitry itself would cut the power to the array, triggering a system shutdown. The array would produce no beams instead of two powerful beams," he explained patiently.

Axopen nodded. "You know, of course, that a millennium generator is the most stable power source that has ever been developed."

He nodded but said, "Anything made by man can malfunction, Axopen. I believe in designing for safety even if the danger is slight. Besides, I think that the two-nozzle design is sort of striking."

Axopen actually laughed. "I am sure that any space beings passing by will revel in the beauty of your design." Axopen then continued in an excited tone for him. "Unless Kowtsom finds something that she doesn't expect, we will be using her new iri-silver alloy for the reflection plates. It is the perfect reflecting surface. Kowtsom's own words."

Opsil chimed in, "I wonder what name Kowtsom will give her alloy. I hope she doesn't just call it the reflecting alloy."

Axopen and Supeb looked at each other and then burst into laughter. It was the first time he had ever seen Supeb laugh, and he was heartily laughing at the moment. He wished he had a recording term turned on to capture the event. He didn't, so a memory of it would have to do. It looked like they just might be on the brink of making long-distance mass transport work. It would take some time to finish the new design and manufacture a prototype to test; but within a few months, it may very well be ready for manufacturing to construct the real thing. Agapoi was pushing for a breakthrough in long-distance mass transport, and he would no doubt continue to push to get the prototype up and running.

He felt a great deal of satisfaction and maybe even joy that they had finally accomplished the feat. Agapoi seemed to know that it was possible, although he had his doubts. Axopen and Supeb certainly seemed happy. He thought Agapoi would be happy as well. Axopen would probably be the one to tell Agapoi, but he was sure Supeb would insist on being present as well. *They might even invite me along,* he thought. *And I would be glad to go. Maybe I will even tell Axopen about his hair before he goes to see Agapoi. Then again, maybe I won't.*

23
Civility

It was Diotiri morning. Temeos was standing in front of the emperor's desk, trying to puzzle out what he was seeing in the emperor. Tryllos was always in a notoriously bad mood on the first morning of the week, yet Tryllos seemed to be in a very good mood indeed. He had smiled at him when he had come to deliver his daily reports, which was a rarity in its own right. Now Tryllos was talking to him about the weather. Tryllos had never tried to have small talk with him before. He wasn't quite sure what to make of it.

Then Tryllos asked, "How was your weekend?"

His heart skipped a beat. Was Tryllos truly just making small talk now, or was the small talk just a ploy Tryllos was using to lead up to asking him about the weekend? He couldn't be sure. He answered as nonchalantly as he could.

"It was a good day. It seems that weekends always go by much too quickly."

Tryllos smiled. It was an honest smile, one that he had not seen Tryllos wear in years. He even thought he saw a sparkle in Tryllos's green eyes.

"Perhaps we can arrange to have the day repeat itself just for you," Tryllos said with a laugh.

He smiled. It seemed as if Tryllos was a different person today. For quite a while, Tryllos had been acting more and more paranoid, more and more maniacal. He could not help but wonder what had caused the change in Tryllos's demeanor. "One day out of five is fine for a weekend, my lord. There is no need to trouble yourself."

"It would be no trouble, Temeos. How long have you been my lord director? I seem to remember you came to your post shortly after my father died," asked Tryllos.

He stiffened into a formal stance and said, "It has been my privilege to serve my lord for these past eighty-two years."

Tryllos rose from behind his desk, positioned himself in front of him, and then leaned back on his desk. "How many times have you and I eaten supper together, Temeos? Not at an official banquet, just you and I having supper together."

He shifted his eyes to meet Tryllos's eyes. "I do not recall ever eating supper with my lord."

"I believe we should remedy that, Temeos." Tryllos righted himself and began walking in a circle around him with his hands behind his back. "You have been a mentor and a confidant for me during all these years. You have done everything that I have asked of you, even when I knew that you did not agree or even approve. The only thing that I have done especially for you all these years was to never ask you to deal with my more unsavory business."

"I am truly grateful for the kindness and respect that you have shown to me, my lord emperor," he said formally.

Tryllos stopped slightly in front of him on his left. He moved his head to meet Tryllos's gaze. "It is true that I have respect for you, Temeos. My motives for not involving you in my less admirable but necessary activities are not entirely for your benefit, however. I did it so that you can remain above reproach, so that you can better serve me in my more official endeavors. I also did it merely because I believed that there were some things that you would refuse to do for me. You are a far too valuable public servant and friend to risk a confrontation that would ultimately lead to your disgrace."

He was slightly taken back by the fact that Tryllos called him his friend. He had never heard Tryllos call anyone his friend before. "You truly honor me as lord director and as a person. My words are insufficient to express my gratitude."

"No, no, Temeos. It is I who am grateful," said Tryllos. Tryllos bowed his head slightly and said, "Would you do me the honor of being my guest tonight at the palace? I will have an exquisite meal prepared in your honor. It is but a small gesture to show my appreciation for your many years of service." Tryllos raised his head, awaiting his response.

His mind was in a quandary. Should he believe that the emperor had suddenly regained his senses and was now making a sincere effort to reach out to him? Or was there an ulterior motive in Tryllos's offer? He knew that Cemyoz was going to call a full session for tomorrow. He was to speak at that session and offer his proof of Tryllos's instability and lack of good judgment. Did Tryllos know this? Was this a ploy so that Tryllos could get him out of the way quietly? He could not be sure. He spoke slowly, choosing his words carefully.

"I am honored that you would extend such a gracious invitation, my lord Tryllos. Could this offer be extended on another evening?"

Tryllos looked disappointed but not angry, "My zeal to make up for lost time has led me to be overeager. My apologies. I should have thought that you might have plans. Given your dashing looks, it may very well be with a female. Of course, Temeos, the supper can be moved to another evening. Which evening would best suit your schedule?"

He was again surprised. Even if the offer was genuine, he expected some pouting from Tryllos. Tryllos had not acted this civilly for quite a long time. He decided to accept Tryllos's offer for this evening. Perhaps Tryllos was beginning to recover from whatever mental malady had inflicted his mind. He would need to know before going through with his testimony tomorrow.

He bowed deeply to Tryllos and answered softly, "I am sorry that I had answered clumsily, my lord emperor. I was not asking you to move this evening's engagement. I was merely stating my desire to dine together on some other evening as well. I am honored to accept your gracious invitation."

Tryllos put his hand on his shoulder and pushed him up gently to signal that he wished for him to rise and look at him. As he met the emperor's gaze, Tryllos said, "You do not know how happy you have just made me, my friend. I will see you this evening at half past the seventh parz." Tryllos returned to his desk and started to work on some paperwork.

It seemed to him that he was being dismissed, but he had not yet discussed his reports. Tryllos always wanted an explanation. He cleared his throat and asked, "Am I dismissed then, my lord?"

Tryllos looked up and smiled, "Yes, Temeos. You may go."

He started to move toward the door and then stopped and said, "You have not heard my explanations about the reports."

"No explanation is needed, Temeos. I can ask you tomorrow if I run into anything unexpected."

He nodded and continued out the door. As he strode down the hall, he thought about Tryllos's apparent lucidity. Could it be real? Could Tryllos have regained a measure of his sanity over the weekend? Perhaps he would find out tonight. Given his present situation, he *must* find out tonight.

24
To Tell or Not to Tell

It was Diotiri morning, and Shipunke was seated on an overtrack, wrestling within himself. Cemyoz was going to make a general call for tomorrow's full session. As the organizer of the session, Cemyoz was also bound by Doetoran law to inform each of the other nineteen Suvatens of the purpose of the session personally before the session was held. The law did not specify who was to inform them, only that they be informed. The law also did not say how long before the session that this needed to be completed, but it was certain that a full session could not be held without every Suvaten being informed of the purpose of the meeting. In the case of this session, informing the wrong Suvatens too soon would be disastrous for Cemyoz, Temeos, and perhaps several other Suvatens as well. He knew of six Suvatens that should not be told until the last possible moment. They were purchased long ago by Tryllos, and they would not hesitate to inform the emperor of the session. Tryllos could then move against the organizers of the meeting to squelch any possibility of a no-confidence vote. He was wrestling whether or not to let Cemyoz know what he knew.

If he had not attended yesterday's meeting at the Roadweary Inn, he would have most certainly informed the emperor when informed of the purpose of the full session. He would also have been the seventh vote against the no-confidence motion, but not because the emperor was bribing him. He was not. He would have told the emperor simply because he believed it would have been the right thing to do. He was loyal to the emperor because of his family's history with the imperial family. Like the other emperors before, Tryllos had shown nothing but kindness toward his family. He knew that Tryllos had begun behaving erratically over a year ago now, but he did not know the extent of Tryllos's troubled behavior. He didn't know that Tryllos was ready to plunge Kosundo headlong into a terrible war that would make the Great War seem like a minor skirmish.

Then there was the matter of Temeos. He had never liked him. Temeos had managed somehow to worm his way into being appointed the lord director, even though many thought that he was a lock for the position when it became open. Temeos had lied about him and his family's relationship with the emperor in order to secure the appointment by the Edvukaat, at least that is what he had been told and that is what he believed. So, instead of him becoming the lord director, he became just another Suvaten in an Edvukaat that saw its powers ever dwindling. Outside of the emperor, the only real power wielded in Doetora was wielded by the lord director. He was the executor of all imperial policy and had daily influence on the emperor. He believed he had reason not to like Temeos.

Still, Temeos did *seem* to be a good man. He certainly had nothing to gain and everything to lose by coming forward with information against the emperor. It seemed he had given Tryllos every benefit of the doubt until he felt he could not wait any longer to act. He had come away from the meeting with a newfound respect for the lord director.

On the other hand, his family owed a great deal to the imperial family. Not telling Cemyoz about the emperor's flunkies in the Edvukaat was not the same as telling the emperor himself. Cemyoz and Pitar should know who the flunkies are anyway, so why should he openly tell information that was told to him in confidence? That was no way to repay the emperor for confiding in him.

But what if neither Cemyoz nor Pitar nor Temeos knew all the names of the flunkies? What if by not telling Cemyoz what he knew, all of Kosundo suffered, including Doetora? What if Cemyoz and others suddenly had accidents staged by one of the emperor's henchmen?

Still, a man in Temeos's position should know if Pitar or Cemyoz doesn't. Why should he have to betray the emperor's confidence?

His stop was coming up, and he still wrestled with himself. Betraying the trust of the emperor or risking total war involving all of Kosundo; that was the choice. The overtrack stopped, and he got out and headed toward the Edvukaat. He was still undecided as he entered the lobby. He would have to make a decision once he reached the office area. He really didn't know whether he would go straight to his office or pay a visit to Cemyoz first. The decision was his, and he would have to live with the consequences. He just had to decide which choice was the right choice.

25
Mind Games

Beltram's eyes opened slowly. It was dark, but not completely dark. He could make out a white ceiling above him and white walls around him. The room was not familiar to him. He tried to move his arms and found that he could not move them. His arms were above his head and were being restrained at the wrists. He tried to move his legs and found them to be restrained at the ankle. The restraints were made of a soft material, but he found that he could not move his limbs more than a fraction of a bit.

As he became more aware, he found that his head ached and his muscles felt stiff. He then discovered that he could move his head, so he strained to lift his head. As he lifted his head, he saw the silhouette of his shoes. He was still dressed. He let his head fall back. The surface he was lying on was soft. It felt like it might be a bed.

His head pounded, and he was having a hard time orienting himself. He searched his pounding head for answers, but none came. Then blackness settled over his mind.

After some time had passed, his eyes opened again. The restraints, yes, he hadn't dreamed it. The restraints were real. His head still hurt but only a little now. How did he get here? He searched his mind for the answer. The last thing he could recall was…the sealed lab…he was in the sealed lab. His breathing grew frantic as he thought he remembered Degmer sticking a medical stick into Laysa's neck. He had reached for Laysa as she was falling, then felt a prick, and then…nothing. He remembered nothing after that. Degmer *must* have stuck him with a tranquilizer stick. Judging from the way he felt, a very potent tranquilizer stick. Why had she done that? And why was he now restrained? How much time had passed? Question after question filled his frantic mind, but no answers could be found.

Suddenly, the room filled with light. The light hurt his eyes. He first closed his eyes and then squinted through them. He could hear someone walking toward him in soft-soled shoes. Degmer and Laysa had both worn soft-soled shoes. He thought it might be one of the girls. Then he heard a rather deep voice say, "I noticed you were awake, so I thought I would come in and check up on you. How are you feeling this morning, Beltram?"

He strained to open his eye's enough to be able to see who it was that was talking to him. At first, all he saw was a dark blur; and then his eyes focused enough to reveal a tall man dressed in a white lab coat. The man had pale blonde hair and darker skin. He blinked his eyes, thinking he must have seen wrong. The man surely had gray hair, not blonde. After he refocused, his eyes still saw blonde hair, pale, but definitely blonde. He managed to say, "Who are you?"

"I am a doctor here at the complex," said the man.

It occurred to him that the man had called him by his first name. "Do I know you?" he asked.

"No, I do not believe that we have met before," was the reply.

"How it is that you called me by my first name then?" he asked.

"I did not know of another name to call you. Degmer only told me your first name," said the man nonchalantly.

"My last name is Chaf. You can call me Har Chaf," he said indignantly. "I am the site administrator of this complex. How is it that I do not know you?"

"I am new here. My name is Arstas, Arstas Upfar," the man said, pointing to a partially obscured ID badge. "You can call me Doctor Upfar, Har Chaf," said the man, seemingly unimpressed.

"Well, Doctor Upfar, how do you know Degmer Medchad?" he probed.

"Medchad is Degmer's last name? I did not know that either. I only met her when she dropped you off. You were out cold. She said that you were out of your mind and that she had to sedate you. That must have been some sedative. You were out for nearly a full day. We took the precaution of restraining you in case you were still not lucid when you awoke," explained the man.

He jerked his head up. "But you said it was morning."

"Oh, it is, Har Chaf. It is Diotiri morning," replied the man.

"Diotiri? What happened to eKureaki?" he demanded.

"Perhaps you are still not feeling well, Har Chaf. You seem rather beside yourself. I have already told you that you were out for nearly a full day," said the man.

"I am feeling fine," he growled. "It is Degmer who should be restrained. She's the one who stuck me with a medical stick for no reason. And she stuck Laysa too. Doctor, did Degmer bring in a young woman by the name of Laysa, Laysa Froe?"

"I did not see any young woman with Degmer. She did mention that you were raving about her kidnapping a woman though. Degmer says that you were alone with her yesterday when you started raving. Are you sure you are feeling all right?" asked the man as he studied his face.

"I don't know if she was trying to kidnap Laysa," he said, "but she certainly did stick her with a medical stick. She stuck her in the neck."

"Hmm. That is where she stuck *you*, Har Chaf. Are you sure you are not confused?" asked the man again.

"No, I am *not* confused. I am the site administrator. Look up my records. I have no history of mental problems. Stop asking me if I am sure. I assure you that I am quite sure!" he snarled.

"I will stop asking when I am as sure as you are," said the man. He started to walk away and then stopped. "There is a way that I can check your mind to see if everything is as it should be," began the man. The man then paused as if thinking to himself.

He closed his eyes, sighed, and said, "What are you talking about?"

"The method I use is rather unconventional." The man held up two small darkly colored glass lenses. "I can use these to see into your mind," he said.

"What are those? Lenses? How can lenses help you see into my mind?" he scoffed.

"The lenses do not help *me*. They are a safety precaution. I wear the lenses, so there is no risk to *you*," said the man.

He sighed again. "Axi. If it can get me out of here, go ahead and *look into my mind.*" He had said the last few words mockingly.

The man then turned his back to him. It appeared to him as if the man were putting the lenses into his eyes. The man turned back around and said, "I am now ready. You must look directly into my eyes." The man bent close to his face.

He looked into the man's eyes. It was like looking into a dark void. "I ... I have never," he gasped as he spoke.

"You have never what?" asked the man, still focusing his eyes on his eyes.

"I've never seen eyes like yours before," he whispered.

"Do not be alarmed. It is the lenses that make them look that way. Just keep looking into my eyes for a moment longer," said the man in a soothing voice.

He stared into the man's eyes and thought he might get lost in them. He was relieved when the man stood back up after only a tic or two. "So, doctor, what's the verdict?" he said hoarsely.

"I am not sure. It will take a longer session to be absolutely certain. I did see some things that could be of concern," said the man.

"I have to stay then?" he asked.

"For a little while longer, I think," said the man as he turned away. "I will be back shortly. I have other patients. Perhaps after a longer session I can be confident enough to release your restraints."

He heard the man's soft-soled shoes walk away, and then he heard a door open and close. The man was gone. He was left wondering if perhaps he really was going crazy.

In another room, Laysa's eyes opened slowly. It was dark but not completely dark. She could make out a white ceiling above her and white walls around her. The room was not familiar to her. She tried to move her arms and found that she could not move them. Her arms were above her head and were being restrained at the wrists. She tried to move her legs and found them to be restrained at the ankle. The restraints were made of a soft material, but she found that she could not move her limbs more than a fraction of a bit.

As she became more aware, she found that her head ached and her muscles felt stiff. She then discovered that she could move her head, so she strained to lift her head. As she lifted her head, she saw the silhouette of her feet. She could not tell for sure if any other of her clothing had been removed. She let her head fall back. The surface she was lying on was soft. It felt like it might be a bed.

Her head pounded and she was having a hard time orienting herself. She searched her pounding head for answers, but none came. Then blackness settled over her mind.

After some time had passed, her eyes opened again. She tried to move but she couldn't. She then remembered the restraints. The last thing she remembered was being in the sealed labs with Degmer and Beltram. She had just entered what Degmer had called the main lab. There was a wadded piece of paper that Degmer threw away. She remembered retrieving the paper, smoothing it, and reading it. The next thing she could remember was when she awoke the first time. She tried to remember what the paper had said. It said something about the last of a species. She couldn't seem to remember much more than that, except there was one thought the she connected to the paper. *It's not a to-do note.* Her head was not yet clear enough to remember more.

She lifted her shoulders off of the bed as far as her arms would allow her to lift them. She was able to keep them up a little longer now. Still, she could not see anything past a few dets. It was just too dark in the room to make out more. It didn't appear that there was any other furniture in the room other than the bed, but some pieces of furniture might be hidden by the darkness. She could see well enough now to see that she still had on her pink blouse. The sight of the blouse relieved her mind a bit. She relaxed her stomach muscles, and her shoulders fell back to the bed.

After laying there for a few moments, her mind seemed to clear. Her thoughts led her to the paper again. It said something about being the last of a species. She then remembered. It said, "I am the last surviving member of a species that was callously cut off by an inferior species called humanity." She also remembered starting to tell Degmer that the paper wasn't a to-do note. Then she remembered something that made her breath catch. She had felt a small prick in her neck. Someone had injected her with a medical stick, and that someone would have to have been Degmer. She was the only one close enough to her to have done it. She didn't want to believe it, but it had to be true.

Questions began to fill her mind. What was in that medical stick? Why would Degmer do that? Why had Degmer lied about the note? Who wrote the note? When was the note written?

It was the last question that gave her pause. The ink on the note was not faded in the least. That note could have been written anytime within the last few months. It could have been written today, if today was still eKureaki any way. If the note was written recently and if the voice that Degmer heard was more than a figment of an overactive imagination, there could be little doubt who had written the note.

Just then, she heard someone walking outside her room. There was a rubbing noise in the footsteps that told her that the person was wearing soft-soled shoes. She lay very still, hardly breathing, hoping that the footsteps that she heard belonged to Degmer. She heard the door open, and light from the outside poured into the room. Then light was everywhere in the room. Someone had turned on the lights in the room. The brightness of the light seared into her sight, blinding her for the moment. She turned her head to one side, closed her eyes, and then opened them just a sliver. She could make out a white wall to her left. There was a table against the wall with a single chair next to it. Then she heard a voice far too deep to be Degmer's voice.

"Sorry about the light, Laysa. My name is Doctor Upfar," said the voice.

Her heart pounded. She did not look in the direction of the voice. "Are you?" she said quietly.

"Well, yes. It says so here on my badge," replied the voice.

"This is a medical clinic then?" she asked, still not turning her head.

"Yes, you are in the clinic," said the voice.

She closed her eyes. "Why I am restrained?" she asked.

"You were having a seizure of some sort. We feared you might hurt yourself," said the voice.

She opened her eyes again and fixed her gaze on the table by the wall. "I am not having a seizure now. Have you come to release my restraints?" she asked.

The voice did not answer immediately. She heard soft-soled shoes shifting on the floor. "You can be released once we are sure you will not have a relapse," said the voice finally.

She continued to stare at the table. "I see," she said. Then she added, "I have been to the clinic for checkups many times.

All the tables that I have seen in the clinic have rounded edges and corners. I asked a nurse why the edges and corners were rounded. She said that the clinic only used tables with rounded edges and corners in case someone was to fall and hit their head against the table. She said that the roundness reduces the chance of head injuries. Why doesn't that table have rounded edges and corners, especially since I have recently proven to be prone to seizures? Or, maybe I am not so prone to seizures. Maybe I've never had a seizure in my life. Maybe I didn't have a seizure at all. What do you think, *Neaotomo?*" She turned her head to face the voice. She saw what appeared to be a tall man. He had blonde hair that was nearly white and darker skin. He was grinning at her. The grin made her skin crawl.

"I can see that my act does not fool you. I applaud your awareness, particularly after you have just awakened from the influence of a very potent drug. You have heard my name before. I suppose Degmer mentioned it to you," said Neaotomo.

She nodded slowly. "It appears that my awareness has not served me well enough to keep me from being bound to this bed." She managed a nervous smile.

Neaotomo shrugged his shoulders. "You would have had no way of knowing that I would be able to survive the gas and remain alive all this time. It was an ability that even I did not know I possessed until I needed to use it. It was not your fault that Degmer heard me cry out when I awoke. It was not your fault that Degmer chose to try to deal with me by herself instead of enlisting more help. I believe you are a victim of circumstances beyond your control, as was I."

"So, where does my circumstance leave me?" she asked.

Neaotomo smiled. "That is entirely up to you. We share the same goal. You want to leave this lab free. So do I. Perhaps we can find a way to make that happen for both of us."

Now she smiled as she spoke boldly. "You would have me believe that all you want is your freedom. What would you do with it? Would you try to live a normal life? I am not sure that would be possible for you. Your note said, 'I am the last surviving member of a species that was callously cut off by an inferior species called humanity.' It is clear what your opinion is of the human race. Do you really want me to believe that you are capable of living peaceably with a race that killed the rest of your kind? Could you meekly live a normal life with a race that you consider inferior?"

"Your candor surprises me, Laysa. Not too many humans in your position would dare to speak so boldly. I believe I can grow to admire you. However, since we are being candid, I am not sure your candor serves you well at this moment." He came closer to the bed where she was laying. "You see, I have the advantage. I am stronger than you are. You cannot overpower me. You are tied to a bed." he leaned over to finger the straps that held her to the bed. "These straps do not seem like they would be that strong, but once you are strapped into them tightly, with your arms and legs extended as they are, there is no hope of breaking them. Working your hands or feet free is impossible as well. The straps are ingeniously designed to tighten around your wrists and ankles if you try to wriggle out of them. They were designed to hold me and my kind. You will not get free. If you choose not to help me, I need only to leave you where you are. You will die in days."

She shuddered inside when she heard how nonchalantly he spoke of her death. "I will not help you, Neaotomo. You can be certain of that. Whether I live or die is not the issue," she said. Then she closed her eyes and took a deep breath. When she reopened her eyes, she looked determinedly at him.

"Perhaps your life or death is not the issue as you say, but I have no wish to end your life. I am afraid that we are getting off to a bad start. We have not even had the chance to get to know each other. Perhaps you will find that I am not the monster you think me to be. Let's start over without the pretenses and see where that leads us.

"Hello. My name is Neaotomo. I was formed in this lab by a team of scientists lead by Doctor Arstas Upfar." He pointed to the ID badge on his lab coat. "My parents are a genetically altered pair of sperm and egg. I was designed to be quite strong, intelligent, and handsome. I was also designed to be unique, thus my hair and skin combination. I had no childhood to speak of, but most humans seem to be glad when they grow past childhood anyway. I have several mental abilities and can heal very rapidly. Would you like to tell me a little about yourself now, Laysa?"

She exhaled sharply, letting out a quick, grunting noise, and then drew a sigh and said, "Axi. I will play along. My name is Laysa Froe. I was born and raised in Aturla. I was raised by two wonderful humans who loved me very much. I grew interested in genetic disease prevention in middle school and eventually obtained a degree in genetics. I came to work in the Dricho Genetics Foundation twenty-two years ago at the age of thirty-two. I am now fifty-four years old, and I am currently being held in bondage by someone the likes of which I never knew existed until very recently."

Neaotomo gave a laugh at the last part of her introduction. "I see you have a sense of humor. I have found many humans like to use humor to relieve stress. I imagine that you are feeling stress right now, am I right?"

He looked at her for a response, but Laysa only looked away. He shrugged.

"Maybe you are not feeling stress. After all, we are now getting to know each other, and now you know what a civil person I am. I would like to get to know the inner you, Laysa. To do that, I need to probe your mind."

She immediately started shaking her head violently as she said, "No. You cannot probe my mind. I refuse to let you."

"My, my. What a fuss you are making," said Neaotomo soothingly as he reached down and began to stroke her brown hair.

She recoiled at his touch.

He removed his hand. "I am only asking to probe your mind to take a look around. I will not touch anything. I just want to look. Besides, there is nothing you can do to stop me if I decide to probe. I am only asking to give you a chance to make the probe comfortable for you. If you cooperate, it goes much easier for both of us. All you have to do is look into my eyes," he said as he bent over close to her face.

She closed her eyes, shouting, "No! Stay away! No! No!"

He stood up and sighed. "Very well. We will do it the hard way." He then reached down and grabbed her head with his hands on either side. Then he bent down and put his forehead in contact with her forehead. She still had her eyes closed and was now whimpering no's. He closed his eyes. She began to scream.

Neaotomo did not hear her screams. He was inside her mind. He searched for the barrier that he knew would be there. Laysa's mind was in turmoil because of his presence. It really was much harder to navigate in a mind that he had to force open. Every move he made in a forced open mind was met with resistance from the mind. Every time he forced himself further in the mind, great pain was felt by the mind's owner— in this case, Laysa. No physical damage was being done to her brain, but her brain and her mind were two different things. A person could have a perfectly good brain and still not be able to function if their mind was severely damaged. Likewise, a person could be quite capable of functioning within their mind even if their brain was damaged enough so that communication with other persons was impossible. The brain was just a repository for thought, a place for the mind to put thoughts when the mind was not actively using them. Right now, he was risking damaging Laysa's mind; but he knew if he got in and out quickly, there was less chance of permanent damage. He cleared one obstacle after the other that her mind threw at him. Finally, he saw the barrier and examined it. It was solid, no fluctuations, no pulsating, no weaknesses at all. Neaotomo sighed within himself. He had seen this kind of barrier twice before. Despite his best efforts, he was never able to break across this kind of barrier. It was as if the barrier was being reinforced by a strong force from outside of the human mind. He would not be able to turn Laysa's will.

He frowned, opened his eyes, and released his hold on Laysa's head. He just then became aware of her screams. It was too bad. She would scream like that for a while longer until her mind managed to repair itself. He could not imagine the pain that she was experiencing right now, but she had brought that on herself. Still, he felt what he supposed was pity for her—not for the pain of the probe, but for how he would have to use her. He may not be able to imprint his will on her mind, but he may be able to force her to take action against her will. He would let her mind calm down and let her rest for a short time, and then he would return. Now it was time to give Har Chaf his longer session. He had big plans for him.

He left Laysa to her screaming and went down to the other end of the hall to Beltram's room. He could still hear her screams clearly as he approached the room, but he was not sure if Beltram would be able to hear them inside the room. The rooms were designed to muffle sound, but the rooms could not hide Laysa's screams from his hearing.

As he entered, he said, "I now have the time to take a more thorough look in that mind of yours, Har Chaf."

Beltram looked uneasy. "I thought I heard a woman screaming a moment ago and again when you opened the door," he said.

He put on a look that he had seen the real Doctor Upfar demonstrate when the doctor had explained to him why he heard screaming and said, "It is unfortunate that you had to hear that. We have a very disturbed woman down the hall from your room. Did it disturb you terribly?"

Beltram looked away from him and said, "No, Doctor. It just made me curious. That's all." Beltram looked at him once again and said, "Once you complete this search of my mind, you will see that it is quite sound and we can dispense with all this nonsense."

He nodded. "I believe you might be right, Har Chaf." He turned and pretended to put the dark lenses in his eyes. In fact, the lenses remained in his hand. As he turned back to face Beltram, he deftly put the lenses in his lab coat pocket. Beltram was none the wiser. He then said in a clinical tone, "For this test, I will need to probe deep into your mind. I will need your utmost cooperation. It is a delicate thing to probe so deeply."

A look of concern crossed Beltram's face. "Will it hurt, Doctor?"

He looked closer into Beltram's eyes and said, "You will feel some unusual sensations in your mind, but it will not hurt if you do exactly as I say. Do you understand?"

Beltram took a deep breath and said, "I understand, Doctor Upfar. I will do as you say."

He straightened away from Beltram's face a little and said, "Good. Har Chaf, do you think of yourself as Beltram or Har Chaf?"

"I think of myself as Beltram," was the reply.

"Then may I call you Beltram during this probe?" he asked.

"Yes, you may call me by my first name," said Beltram.

"Excellent," he said. He bent down and said, "Beltram, look into my eyes."

Beltram's arms fidgeted slightly, but he responded by looking directly into his eyes.

He now moved freely in Beltram's mind. No obstacles existed as they did when he forced his way into Laysa's mind. There was only a smooth movement of thought. He traversed through the random thoughts that were currently in Beltram's mind. Some thoughts had fear attached to them. These thoughts came, went quickly across his mind, and then vanished through the barrier that his mind had formed; or sometimes they rebounded back to cross his mind again. Other thoughts meandered much slower through the mind. These thoughts would stop now and again, indicating that Beltram was dealing with that particular thought. These thoughts, like the quick ones would eventually disappear behind the veil of the barrier. Still other thoughts did not seem ever to move at all. They were much dimmer than the other thoughts most of the time; but occasionally, they would become bright when brought into focus by the mind's owner.

There was one such thought in Beltram's mind just now. Neaotomo's curiosity overcame him, and he accessed the thought with his mind. The thought was of a woman's smiling face. It was an active memory, not a new thought. A couple of mixed emotions were prevalent with this memory: a sense of happiness combined with lust, and a sense of excitement coupled with fear. He did not have to access informational thoughts regarding this woman. The emotions told the story. He had seen it many times before. The woman was what was called a lover, not his soza. As he looked at the thought, he saw it connected to a weak point in Beltram's barrier. This weak spot had many other thoughts connected to it as well. This was a good place to start. He looked at other thoughts that connected to other weak spots in the barrier and took note of the thoughts. It seemed to him that this process took nearly a parz; but he knew that in the physical world the process took only a few tics, so he was in no hurry. It was more important now to be thorough. He looked at all the weak spots and made sure he had mentally recorded at least one thought that was connected to each spot. After he finished with the searching of thoughts, he pieced together what each weak spot thought seemed to have in common. He was now ready to confront Beltram's barrier.

He communicated directly with Beltram's mind through his thoughts. *Beltram, you have broken your word many times before. You do not value your word. You have broken your word to the company many times, most recently on eKureaki by opening the sealed lab. You have broken your word to your friends when you let them down by not being there for them or not acting as you said you would. You have broken your word to your soza upon many occasions, most recently with this woman.*

As he went through the examples of Beltram's broken promises, he tapped into the related thoughts and memories and flashed them through Beltram's mind. Then he sent this thought to Beltram. *Let me help you, Beltram. I will give you the ability to keep your word. Let me help you, Beltram. I will give you many other abilities that you cannot imagine. Let me help you,*

Beltram. Let me decide how best to keep your word. I will deliver on my word.

One of the weak spots in Beltram's barrier popped out of existence, leaving a hole in the barrier where the weak spot was. He felt Beltram's head jerk slightly with the pop. He knew that the entire barrier could collapse soon. The inability of Beltram to keep his word was a predominant theme in many of the weak spot thoughts. He continued, emphasizing a different yet common theme. *You will be a greater man, Beltram. I can give you strength. I can help you control your destiny. Let my thoughts rule your will. Let me in, Beltram. Let my will be your will. Let me enter into the place where your thoughts begin, Beltram. Take down all barriers between us, Beltram. Let us be one.*

Beltram's barrier grew weaker with every word of thought. One by one, the weak spots gave way until the entire barrier in Beltram's mind gave way with one great pop. He no longer needed to look into Beltram's eyes for access to his mind. Beltram had surrendered quite easily in his opinion, but that was to be expected. His mind barrier already had many weak spots. All he had needed to do was to nudge at the spots slightly. Degmer's barrier would not surrender so easily. That is why he planned to use Laysa to assist him in overcoming Degmer's barrier. What you can't break, you must bend.

As Neaotomo straightened away from Beltram's face, he noticed that Beltram's eyes were wide, yet empty, and his mouth hung open. It apparently was quite a shock to the human mind to lose its barrier. The astonished look would last for only a few moments, but the emptiness of the eyes would occur whenever he sent thought to Beltram directly. It was the same emptiness people saw in his eyes when they looked deep into them.

He closed his eyes and concentrated on Beltram's mind. The barrier was gone. The barrier was what humans called their will. He could now see the part of the mind where thoughts formed. This place is what the will was protecting. He believed that this place was what the humans called a soul. He just called it the hidden place. While the other part of the mind, the conscious mind, was a finite level plain, this part of the mind, the hidden place, seemed to have no beginning and no end, no up and no down. It seemed to stretch forever in all directions.

No thoughts were being formed right now in the hidden place. The removal of the barrier had thrown the organization of the mind into chaos. There was no direction for thought, so the mind created no thoughts. This accounted for the blank look of astonishment on Beltram's face. The barrier that had separated the hidden mind from the conscious mind did more than just separate. It acted as a catalyst for thought. It was the active consciousness for humans. Neaotomo knew that his mind had no barrier and therefore had no hidden place. When he had probed the minds of ones like him, he found a very large, level plain, larger than that of humans; but it had no infinite hidden place. According to those who had probed his mind, his mind had the largest level plain compared to all of the other plains within the minds of his kind; but still, his mind had no infinite hidden place. In minds like his, the plain formed the thoughts. The plain and the thoughts of the plain were all that existed. The humans had missed something when they created his kind's mind. He had no barrier, no hidden place, no soul.

He thought of the human barrier as its own living thing. When the barrier popped out of a human's mind, it did not cease to exist. It existed on another level of existence, a level that Neaotomo was unable to detect. For all appearances, it appeared right now that Beltram's barrier, his will, had ceased to exist. He knew that Beltram's barrier, his will, would eventually come back. There would be one large difference in the barrier that returned to a mind that he had imprinted. The barrier would not keep him out of the mind's hidden place.

He learned, through the study of the minds of others of his kind, that only a certain part of his conscious mind, what he thought of as his plain, created thought. Once the part of the plain that created thought was identified, it was only a matter of learning the weave of the pattern that made up that area of the mind. He had learned how to weave his will by practicing weaving other wills like his own. He could see the pattern of the others when probing their minds, and he knew that his pattern would be similar but different. As he grew more intuitive, he was able to discern a base weave and another more subtle weave in the patterns that he observed. All of the base weaves were the same. It was only the subtle intertwining of the other weaves that varied. After he learned how his subtle weave differed from all other subtle weaves, he simply combined the familiar base weave with his subtle weave to obtain the weave of his will. He mentally weaved the pattern of his will to fit Beltram's mind and imprinted the pattern over Beltram's plain.

As soon as the pattern was placed, he saw that thoughts were being created again in Beltram's hidden place. These thoughts were being initiated according to his will that was imprinted on Beltram's conscious mind. The thoughts were Beltram's, but the catalyst was now Neaotomo's will. Soon after Beltram's mind began creating thoughts again, his barrier came back into his mind. It appeared that it came out of nowhere to Neaotomo. The barrier was whole, with no weak spots; but it fluctuated wildly. He had no problem piercing the barrier and viewing Beltram's hidden place. The thoughts that now were being produced in the hidden place were being produced by Beltram's barrier; but the barrier now produced thoughts that were consistent to the weave on the plain, Neaotomo's weave. The plain-influenced thoughts passed through the barrier to enter Beltram's conscious mind. However, the hidden place thoughts hung on the precipice of the barrier and could not enter Beltram's conscious mind fully.

Since Neaotomo had full access to the hidden place of Beltram's mind, he could also implant thoughts directly into the hidden place. These thoughts traveled to Beltram's conscious mind freely. He had only one thought that he wanted to implant right now: *Do not tell anyone about anything that happened in the sealed lab.* He implanted the thought simply by projecting the thought into Beltram's hidden place. Beltram's mind accepted the thought as its own. Chances were Beltram's plain would spawn thoughts that would ensure Neaotomo's anonymity on its own, but implanting the thought ensured that the thought would be clear. It would also cause other related thoughts to be spawned in Beltram's hidden place by his imprinted conscious mind. Implanting a thought gave the thought priority in his mind.

Neaotomo opened his eyes. He was out of Beltram's mind, and he was now aware of his physical surroundings again. At once, he noticed that he no longer heard Laysa screaming. He wanted to go back to Laysa soon, while the agony she had just endured was fresh on her mind. Time had a way of numbing some pains of the past, especially physical pains. First, he needed to get Beltram back to his office before his absence drew any suspicion.

"Good news, Har Chaf. You can be released. It appears that you are not suffering from any mental abnormalities," he said to Beltram.

Beltram's expression was no longer blank or astonished. Outwardly, he appeared normal. His head was sweaty, but he could wipe the sweat off. Unless someone looked at his eyes closely when he was in contact with Beltram, Beltram would appear as if nothing happened to him. He would act that way too. He was still Beltram, still able to recall the memories of his past; the only part of him that had changed was his will. It was no longer his own.

As Neaotomo busied himself loosing the bed restraints, Beltram replied, "You see. I told you there was nothing wrong with me."

He smiled, "No. Nothing is wrong. I apologize for suspecting that your mind was unclear. You are free to go. Oh, and you had better go straight to your office. You are due there by 3:50, and it is already 3:42."

"So it is. What day is it again, Doctor?" asked Beltram.

"I see that our little session disoriented you a bit. It is Diotiri, Har Chaf. Have a good day. I will be in contact. Oh. Do not forget to erase your exit from the airlock from the system's memory," he said.

"Of course. Can't let anyone know about this place. Thanks for the reminder," said Beltram cheerfully. He gave a wave and was out the door.

He followed to see that Beltram found his way to the airlock and to make sure the airlock still registered Beltram as human by watching the airlock lights. The lights indicated that Beltram successfully exited the airlock. He was pretty sure that the physical enhancements that he had given to Beltram would not alter his base genome, and now the scanner in the airlock confirmed it. His base genome remained the same, yet Beltram's mind and body responded to his influence and pattern. Beltram was still Beltram, and yet he wasn't. Once Beltram left, he headed for Laysa's room.

Laysa was panting, trying to catch her breath, as he entered the room. She didn't know exactly what he had done to her, but she had never experienced such extreme pain before. The baffling thing was that now that the pain had stopped she couldn't point to any part of her body as the source of the pain, although her voice was raw from screaming. She had thought for a while that she might lose her mind because of the pain. For all that, she was thankful when she found she still had her mind; but seeing Neaotomo again sent her into a cold sweat. She began quivering so much that a hoarse whimper was coming from her lungs involuntarily.

Neaotomo came to the edge of the bed and smiled down on her. After a moment, a look of concern came through his smile, and he said, "Why, Laysa, you are trembling, and you sound hoarse. I know that my probe was quite painful for you, but I did ask you to cooperate. If you had done so, the probe would have been quite painless. Sometimes a little harmless cooperation can save a lot of pain."

She was breathing hard and still whimpering. She knew that she was helpless against Neaotomo, but she would show him that she was not just a pawn he could do with as he pleased. "I will never cooperate with you," she blurted hoarsely.

Neaotomo walked around the bed toward the wall, where the chair and table stood. He picked up the chair, dropped it near the bed, faced it toward her face, and sat down. He shook his head and said, "I have read many books authored by humans. One such book warned against using universal negatives. It seems that the author felt that the use of a universal negative implies that a person has knowledge that a person could not have. In your case, I believe the use of the word *never* implies that you know what you are going to do in the future, according to the author. The author suggests that a person avoid the use of these universal negatives. Perhaps a better way to state your point would be to say, 'I do not intend to cooperate with you.' I understand what you are saying. You are saying that no matter what I do to you, you intend not to cooperate with me," Neaotomo paused and then slowly nodded. "I believe that that is quite possibly true. You have shown great resolve, and I admire you for it.

"Nevertheless, I know something that you do not know. I know that in about a half of a parz, your friend Degmer will be coming back here. I know this because I gave her little choice but to obey me, and I told her to come back here at four parzes this morning. Perhaps you are wondering exactly how this information affects you." Neaotomo paused and redirected his focus directly at her. "I will tell you—Every time you refuse to cooperate, I will punish Degmer. And I assure you that Degmer will not enjoy the punishments that I can administer. Now, would you like to revise your statement?"

She thought of her friend. They had spent a lot of time together over the years and knew each other quite well. If Degmer was coming back here, it was probably because Neaotomo was using her as leverage against Degmer. Her breathing had slowed, although she was still trembling. She lifted her head and said as clearly as her throat would allow, "Have you no conscience?"

Neaotomo sat forward in his chair to get closer to her. He said coolly, "No, I do not. I came into existence without one. I am also missing some other things that humans have. I am missing what you humans call a soul. I make decisions based on what is best for me. I have no capacity for the emotion humans call remorse or guilt." After he finished, he sat back in his chair again.

Her heart sank. Now she knew what she had suspected all along. Neaotomo was capable of anything from cruelty to kindness, but he had no capacity to care for anyone but himself. He could feel fondness; but fondness would not stop him from his ultimate goal, even if it meant destroying the object of his fondness. He had said it himself. He had no soul. He was soulless. That thought shook her to the core. She didn't read the Levra as regularly as she should, but she remembered that there was a prophecy in the Levra about the soulless. She couldn't remember the details, but she knew that the prophecy was in regard to what the Levra called the last days. Funny. She had always thought that prophecy was just talking metaphorically about wicked people in that prophecy. It appears that the prophecy was more literal than she could have imagined. Neaotomo was still looking at her, waiting for an answer. She managed to say, "I will obey as long as my actions do not hurt anyone other than you or me."

Neaotomo didn't say anything right away. He just sat there, staring at her. After a while, he got up and moved the chair back to the table. He then circled the foot of the bed and came to stand very close by the other side of the bed. He bent down and drew his face very close to hers.

She tried not to blink, but it was difficult. At least she managed not to tremble.

"I think that you are trying to trick me," he said.

She tried to protest, but Neaotomo clamped his hand firmly over her mouth.

Her body began to tremble again, and her lungs seemed to demand that she take in more air. She found herself breathing heavily through her nose.

"You know that if I agree to your condition, you will be able to demand proof that your actions will not end up indirectly hurting someone somewhere in the future. That would leave me in an untenable position. You are quite clever, but remember to whom you are talking. I can be quite clever as well. Now... are we done playing games?" growled Neaotomo.

Her eyes were wide open as she nodded her head. She really had not intended to trick Neaotomo, but she understood his point. She would have to be very careful in choosing her words when talking to him.

Neaotomo took his hand away from her mouth and straightened himself. He remained very close to the bed, glaring angrily at her. His stare was making her feel very uncomfortable, very vulnerable. After a moment, his countenance softened, and he spoke.

"Very well. I ask you then. Will you obey me if I do not give you a command that directly results in someone getting hurt?"

She realized that she didn't have much room to maneuver in this agreement. Still, judging by Neaotomo's reaction to her vague assertion, he placed value on his word, so she decided to push him for a promise concerning Degmer. As she was about to speak, a thought occurred to her. *What about Beltram?* It took a moment before she realized that she had said that aloud.

Neaotomo drew a breath in disgust. "Beltram was happy to cooperate. I am sure he is busy in his office right now. He is not at issue here."

She was surprised at that answer. Could Beltram have been conspiring with Neaotomo all along? "You let Beltram go?" she asked.

"That surprises you? I keep my word, Laysa. Beltram cooperated, and I let him go back to work. I am sorry that that is no longer an option for you and Degmer," said Neaotomo impatiently.

"But you let Degmer leave. Why?"

"Since she was the only person left conscious yesterday, I had little choice. There were some tasks that I needed her to accomplish," he said, visibly trying to contain his anger.

She knew that Neaotomo's patience was running thin, but she dared another question. "Aren't you afraid that she may have informed the authorities about you?"

"No!" shouted Neaotomo, "I am not afraid!" He had bent down and shouted into her face.

She responded by closing her eyes and moving her head away from him as far as her bonds would allow.

Neaotomo stood up and regained his composure. He then said in an almost calm voice, "You are trying my patience, Laysa. I will not answer any more questions until you answer mine. Will you obey me if I do not give you a command that directly results in someone getting hurt?"

She still could not bring herself to promise without an assurance from Neaotomo that he would not harm Degmer. She blurted hoarsely, "I promise I will obey you if you promise not to hurt Degmer unless I disobey you."

Neaotomo stepped back and turned away from her for what seemed to be a long time. He seemed to be debating something within himself. When he turned around, he said, "I will not physically hurt Degmer unless you disobey me. I will not give you a command that will directly hurt anyone else but either you or me. Agreed?"

The addition of the word *physically* disturbed her, considering what she had just endured. She thought she might be able to push Neaotomo just a little bit further, so she asked in a hoarse voice, "Agreed, if you agree to two more points. You will not knowingly torture Degmer by mental means, and you will not end Degmer's life as a result of my disobedience."

Neaotomo hesitated for a moment and then said, "I agree. Now I want to hear you say that we have an agreement."

She hesitated, but she couldn't think of any other conditions that she dared to bring up. "We have an agreement," she said in a whisper. Her voice was nearly gone now.

Neaotomo chuckled and said, "It is a good thing that I have very good hearing or I wouldn't have understood that." Then his face grew serious, and he said, "You will not tell anyone about the consequences if you break our agreement by disobeying me. That is your first command. The second command is not to talk to anyone without me being present. Now, I am going to test your obedience. I am going to probe your mind again. Look into my eyes." Neaotomo bent over toward her until his nose nearly touched hers.

Her breath caught. She wanted to close her eyes and turned her head, but she had made the agreement. She took a deep breath and forced herself to look into Neaotomo's eyes. She saw emptiness, vast emptiness, as she gazed deep into Neaotomo's eyes. The emptiness seemed to swallow her whole. Soon, all she saw was black nothingness. Laysa felt her pulse quicken. The darkness was overwhelming. She felt fear welling up from inside her. As her pulse quickened, her breathing slowed. She felt beads of sweat forming and trickling down the sides of her face from her hair. She felt the urge to take a deep breath but could not. It was as if she was drowning in air. She could see nothing, and now she felt nothing. No. She felt something. Although, where she felt it she couldn't say. It was hard to describe. It was as if she felt something that could not be felt. It was only a feeling of being felt, sort of like a feeling that you are being watched. She was lost in darkness that didn't seem to exist and feeling a feeling that was not being felt. Yet she could take no action because she was unaware that her body existed outside the darkness. Still, she had the sense that her head had jerked a couple of times in the darkness. How could that be though? She had no body here.

Then there was light. A white light enveloped her. The feeling that wasn't a feeling was gone, but she could not sense anything outside of the light. The light was all there was. She needed to take a breath, but she could not. She was now drowning in light.

Then she wasn't. She wasn't drowning. She wasn't enveloped in light. She was staring at the ceiling. She could see again. She felt sweat on her face. She felt. It was a wonderful feeling to feel again. Her heart was exhilarated by just being somewhere again. Then she saw Neaotomo, and the exhilaration faded.

He had a frown on his face. However, his face did not show anger. His look was more like disappointment. He seemed to be deep in thought. After a moment, he seemed to realize that she was looking at him; and his look became more cheerful.

"Now that wasn't so bad, was it? I told you it would be much better if you cooperated," he said.

She took a deep breath and said in a little stronger voice than before, "Well, it wasn't as bad as before, but I can't say that I enjoyed it."

"Then I have good news for you. I will not be probing your mind anymore unless you give me reason to mistrust you. I have discovered what I wished to know," said Neaotomo casually.

She closed her eyes and said a prayer of thanks to Thaoi silently. She said, "Thank you," softly to Neaotomo. She certainly didn't want him messing with her mind anymore. She would have to make sure that she didn't give Neaotomo any reason to mistrust her.

"I thought that might make you happy," said Neaotomo. "I have more good news. You will be leaving this room soon. I have readied a small suite for you. It formally belonged to one of the others of my kind. It has a few furnishings and a bathroom. It also has an adjoining exercise room. I noticed that you have good muscle tone, so you must be used to exercising. Once I have settled you into your quarters, I will bring you something to eat. You must be hungry. I found quite a few dried meal packs in the commissary. Now that the power is back on, the water works as well. I can offer you a reconstituted meal and some water. I have been surviving quite nicely on them for the last week."

"That is kind of you," she said.

"Kind? Perhaps. However, it is also convenient for me. Your quarters have security doors, so you will no longer need to be restrained. That will be convenient for both of us," said Neaotomo, sounding perhaps a bit too nonchalant. He then reached down and released her restraints. "You may sit up now if you wish," he said, backing away.

She sat up on the bed and rubbed her wrists and then reached down and rubbed her legs. Her legs had become quite stiff, having been restrained that long.

"If you wish, I could massage your legs for you. I have read about how to relax muscles with a massage, and I am sure I could make your legs feel better," said Neaotomo.

She flushed at the idea and quickly said, "No." The no came out in a bit of a squeak. It seemed her voice was not quite recovered from her screaming yet. Neaotomo actually hung his head and turned away. She realized that she might have answered a little too harshly so she added, "But thank you for the offer, Neaotomo. I have a bit of knowledge about massage myself. I prefer to massage my own legs."

He turned back toward her and said something that shocked her. He said, "I am sorry. I did not mean to be too forward. I was merely trying to be ... kind."

She didn't know how to respond to that. Just a few spens ago, Neaotomo had put her in agony. Now he was apologizing, not for the tremendous pain he had caused her but for being too forward. Sometimes he was an uncaring monster, and sometimes he was like a schoolboy. She was overcoming her fear of Neaotomo somewhat now and was becoming curious. She stopped rubbing her legs and looked up at him. "How did you survive for seventy years in a sealed lab? There wouldn't have been enough oxygen to support you since the air circulation system was not operating." Her voice was fading in and out, but Neaotomo seemed to hear her without a problem.

"Sleep," said Neaotomo. "A deep sleep. I put myself in a state of near death."

She nodded thoughtfully. "And that was also how you escaped the gas."

He nodded.

"Not counting the seventy years of comatose existence, how old are you?" Her voice cracked badly on the *are*. She saw Neaotomo grin.

"I was told I came into being on the first day of the year 4443 MENS," stated Neaotomo, still grinning.

She ignored the grin and stopped to think. *It is* 4520 *MENS now. If the lab was sealed seventy years ago ...* "You are only seven years old!" she squeaked. "How can that be?"

"Accelerated maturity is what Doctor Upfar called it. I matured to the equivalent of an eighteen-year-old human in my first year. So, being physiologically accurate, I am the equivalent of a twenty-four-year-old human," he said. He was in a full smile now. Her voice seemed to be quite the entertainment for him.

"That is still quite young," she rasped.

"I am even younger than you think. Doctor Upfar said that I would live to be over three hundred years old," he boasted.

She waved her hand as if to dismiss his boast and said, "Many Cirrians live to be more than three hundred years old, and they are not even genetically engineered." Her voice sounded like it was stuck in a fog bank now.

Neaotomo frowned and said in a pout, "You will not live to be three hundred years old."

She wondered for a moment if that was a threat but then decided that he was just acting like a seven-year-old and said, "No. I suppose I won't." Life expectancy in Dricho was just over two hundred years old. Her father used to tell her that Cirrians lived to be longer because, as a nation, they kept the old way. Other countries had abandoned the old way long ago. She and her family tried to keep the old way, but it seemed that it was harder all the time. She looked at Neaotomo. It appeared that her admission that he would live longer than her took the pout off of his face. If she didn't know better, she would say that Neaotomo was trying to show off to her. She wondered if he was becoming fond of her. If so, she wondered if that could help her in some way. He had talked about Doctor Upfar and had used his ID when he was masquerading earlier. She wondered if he had been fond of him. Doctor Upfar was long dead now. If Neaotomo had been fond of him, it didn't do Doctor Upfar any good. Thinking of the death of Doctor Upfar gave her a gruesome thought. "Are there still dead bodies in the labs?" she asked.

Neaotomo shrugged. "There are many skeletons, but do not worry. I put the skeleton that was in your quarters in one of the labs. I suppose that the skeletons can be disposed of now that the power is back on. The trash pulverizer unit should be working now."

Now that was a thought she didn't want to dwell on. A body had died and decomposed in her quarters. She shivered when she thought of it.

"Are you cold? I thought it was a nice temperature in here. Oh well. It is time for us to get you into your quarters anyway," said Neaotomo while picking up her shoes and handing them to her. "You can take a nice hot shower. I will turn up the temperature a bit in your quarters. Do not get dressed after your shower. I want to do some sketching in the lab by your quarters. You will come there after you shower," said Neaotomo without changing his pleasant tone.

She couldn't help it. Her immediate response was, "I will do no such thing."

Neaotomo shook his head. "That refusal will cost Degmer some pain, I am afraid. I will tell you again. You will come undressed into the lab after you shower. Think before you speak. You don't want to ruin Degmer's day completely."

She was stunned. Where did that come from? He was being quite civil; and then, out of nowhere, he blindsided her with a command that he knew would get a refusal. She didn't see that coming. What had she done? She had made an agreement with a creature with no conscience. She knew that she would end up paying for it, but she had hoped to spare Degmer. Now she had already broken the agreement, and Degmer would suffer. She definitely should put Degmer before her own embarrassment. It was no choice at all really.

She answered meekly, "Axi, Neaotomo. I will do as you say."

"You're late, Zlux," hissed Nenavis. "You were supposed to report in last night."

"I am truly sorry, my master," groveled Zlux. "I was unavoidably detained."

He smirked. Zlux's faded appearance told him that he was still partially in a human mind. "Why is it you are still in the redhead's mind, Zlux?" he asked coyly.

Zlux delayed answering but knew that he could not conceal that fact that he had been trapped in the redhead's mind by the abomination. It had been embarrassingly easy for the creature to trap him. It was sudden and unexpected. "I, uh, cannot leave, my master."

Nenavis laughed heartily, partially because of Zlux's plight and partially because he was ecstatic that the abomination lived. "So, the abomination lives," he roared triumphantly.

Zlux saw that it was apparent that Nenavis knew about the abomination's abilities before he was sent on this assignment, and it irritated him. "You knew of the ability of this abomination?" he asked angrily.

Nenavis assumed an ominous visage and towered over him.

Zlux prostrated himself before Nenavis.

"Yes, I knew of this abomination's abilities, and I did not tell you. You have done nothing yet to earn my trust since your last deception," growled Nenavis. "I will tell you now that you will not gain your freedom from the trap that the abomination has created. I cannot even free you from that trap without gaining control of the human, and I am not inclined to attempt control of the human at the moment. You will stay put and inform me of the actions of this abomination. I have other things to put into motion before I deal with this creature.

But I will call all the D'Yavoly to take targets of opportunity within the reach of the abomination in the next few days. You already acquired your target, Zlux." He stopped and laughed derisively. "I will warn them to stay away from direct contact with the abomination for now. I cannot afford to have all my D'Yavoly in your situation." He laughed again. As he laughed, his visage grew and grew over Zlux until it nearly enveloped him. "I will find a suitable human after I am satisfied that the humans in Kosundo are in disarray. Once their inventions can no longer help them, they will be no match for the legions that I shall command. Soon, I will be able to bring Kosundo to its knees before me, and I will wrest full control of this world from the Other One."

Nenavis restored himself to his normal form and dismissed Zlux by saying, "Now go, and bring me daily reports on this abomination. If your reports prove useful, I might grant you your freedom from the human's mind. But beware, Zlux. I will not tolerate any deceptions."

Zlux withdrew himself from Nenavis's presence and put his concentration on his presence in the human's mind once again. The woman was preparing to go back to the sealed lab. It was fortunate for the abomination that the woman's curiosity and lack of clear thinking concerning her companions kept her from revealing the abomination's presence to the authorities. It seemed that it was also lucky for him at the moment. Nenavis would not be pleased if his prize creature was taken away from him.

26
To Trust or Not to Trust

"Well," said Dizkuh, "I cannot think of anyone else that shouldn't be contacted today about the full session. We have gone through the list of the eleven Suvatens who weren't present at Temeos's meeting several times. I'm satisfied."

Pitar sat back in his chair with his hands clasped upon the bald top of his head. Cemyoz, Dizkuh, and he were about to conclude an early morning meeting in Cemyoz's office. They were trying to be careful not to tip their hand to the emperor before tomorrow's session. "We have to be sure. Our heads are on the line here, after all. Maybe we should just tell all of them at the last moment possible," he said, only half-kidding.

"I share your sentiments, Pitar," said Cemyoz, "but I'm afraid that is not very practical. You can bet that whoever we do not inform today will be very hesitant to vote in favor of no confidence in the emperor tomorrow. I believe that we have found five Suvatens very likely to inform the emperor if they are told of the purpose of the full session. Their voting history on the emperor's initiatives is one-sided in favor of the emperor. They all seem overly anxious to please the emperor."

"Read the names again, Dizkuh," said Pitar, sitting up on the edge of his chair again. "I need to see if another name pops up in my mind."

"Axi," said Dizkuh tiredly. He read the names, pausing between each one, "The names are Kryse...Stodzh...Usradum...Devaranu...and...Felshivke."

"Hmm. Stodzh is a nice guy. But his voting record does seems to indicate a definite bias," said Pitar. "That's my only thought. No new names popped in my head."

Cemyoz started to get up when his secretary, Tersha, buzzed the office comm. "I apologize, sir, but Suvaten Shipunke is here to see you. He says that he has a matter to discuss with you that cannot wait. Shall I tell him to wait until your meeting is over?"

Cemyoz hit a button on the comm and said, "Shipunke? No. Tell him to come in," said Cemyoz. He turned to Pitar and Dizkuh and said, "Shipunke is not one to arrive early like this. I think I'd better see him. It might be important. You can stay. I can always take him into my sitting room if he needs to talk with me privately."

Just then, Tersha entered the room and announced, "Suvaten Shipunke, sir."

"Thank you, Tersha," said Cemyoz as he got up to greet Shipunke.

Tersha nodded, left the room, and closed the door behind her.

"Shipunke, what brings you here so early this morning? Sit down. Sit down." Cemyoz extended his arm, and Shipunke clasped it briefly and then sat down in the chair to which Cemyoz had gestured.

Shipunke briefly acknowledged Pitar and Dizkuh. He then looked at Cemyoz. "I assume you gentlemen are meeting this morning to decide which of the Suvatens should be left in the dark about the session until tomorrow," he said.

"We are," said Cemyoz.

Shipunke shifted his weight in the chair uncomfortably and then resumed. "There is something that you need to hear before you tell anyone about the reason for the session." Shipunke became aware of all of the other six eyes in the room looking at him intently. Shipunke averted his eyes downward and took a deep breath. "The emperor has always had enough votes to pass even his most outrageous proposals and always manages to defeat any measure that he wishes. The Edvukaat has been that way for quite some time, making the small powers that the Edvukaat retains dwindle to nearly nothing," he said.

"This much we know, Shipunke, but we have real evidence of the emperor's lack of rational thought along with the intent to wreak havoc on his own empire. I know the emperor has some lackeys on his payroll, but this evidence will make everyone else side with us to vote no confidence in the emperor," stated Pitar emphatically. "Are you getting cold feet, Shipunke?" he asked.

Shipunke looked Pitar in the eye. "No," he stated. "I am about to be bolder than I have been in my entire life, Pitar."

Now all of the other six eyes showed intense interest as they gazed at Shipunke.

Shipunke paused for a moment to think how he should best begin; then he decided just to say it. "The emperor has had enough pawns in the Edvukaat to sway any vote his way. It is just that all of them have never voted together. This has been done to deflect suspicion away and keep the other Suvatens from guessing who all of his pawns are." He paused, and all eyes drew to him more intently. He then said what he had come to say. "There are seven pawns in the Edvukaat, and I am one of them."

Dizkuh just looked blankly ahead as if he were awaiting execution.

Pitar's red head signaled that he was ready to charge him at any time.

Cemyoz looked surprised but kept his composure. He looked at Shipunke and said calmly, "That is quite a revelation, Shipunke. But if you are a pawn of the emperor, as you say, why are we not already in prison, and why are you telling us this?"

Shipunke stood up and walked behind his chair; then he started to explain. "Unlike the other stooges in the Edvukaat, I did not cooperate with the emperor because I was bribed to do so. I have cooperated with the emperor. This is true, but I have done so out of a sense of obligation. You see, this line of emperors has shown great kindness to my family for generations. I was taught that our family owed special allegiance to the emperor as a youth. I have colluded with the emperor to make sure that his wishes were carried out in the Edvukaat for my entire term of seventy-nine years. However, I am here because the meeting with Temeos made me reconsider the blind oaths of allegiance I swore to the emperor. I am here to let you know that you can count on my vote tomorrow. I also can name the six paid pawns. I do this for the sake of my conscience and for your sakes."

Dizkuh shook his head and said, "But, Shipunke, your voting record does not show an overly consistent support of the emperor. How is it you colluded?"

Shipunke looked at Dizkuh and simply said, "I have always made sure there were seven votes that sided with the Emperor for every vote that the emperor considered important. If there were seven votes other than mine, I voted my conscience..."

"And if there weren't at least seven votes, you voted with the emperor," said Pitar, finishing Shipunke's sentence.

Shipunke nodded. "Others have voted the same way."

Cemyoz contemplated about Shipunke's words for a moment and then said, "Very well, Shipunke. What are the names of the pawns?"

Shipunke nodded and began. "I will name the ones that are obvious first. You no doubt have already discussed them: Kryse, Stodzh, Usradum, and Felshivke."

Cemyoz was surprised at the omission of Devaranu and said, "We discussed those four, plus a fifth: Devaranu."

Shipunke shook his head, "Devaranu is a coward, but he is not a pawn. He will come around if he can be assured that we have the votes to remove the emperor. I believe that I can manage to do that simply by telling him what I know. Otherwise, he is just as likely not to show up for the session, full session or not."

Dizkuh said, "Axi, Shipunke. Who are the other two?"

Shipunke started pacing back and forth as he said, "The other two are going to surprise you. As I have, they have hidden their collusion with the emperor well. The other two pawns of the emperor are Slipar and Khenzhe."

There was no reaction other than silence for what seemed like quite while. Finally, Cemyoz spoke. "How do you know who is being paid to support the emperor?"

Shipunke circled to the front of his chair and sat down. "There are bonuses to being one of the very few people on the Doetoran continent who come by loyalty to this emperor naturally. The emperor took me into his confidence," he said.

"Well then that's good enough for me," said Pitar and started to stand.

Cemyoz motioned to Pitar to wait and then said, "Before we do what we must do today, let us first give thanks to our friend, Shipunke. He might have very well saved our lives this morning."

In unison, Dizkuh, Pitar, and Cemyoz got up, faced Shipunke, and bowed deeply. At the top of their bow, they said, "We bestow to you our honor and thanks."

Shipunke felt a tinge of joy. He was not sure how he would be received after he made his revelations this morning. He stood and placed himself where he could see all three of his fellow Suvatens. He then returned their bow and said, "I am honored, but thanks be to Thaoi."

"Thanks be to Thaoi!" was the return reply from each of the other Suvatens.

Then all four of them shouted it together. "Thanks be to Thaoi!"

Cemyoz then walked to Shipunke, clasped his arm, and said, "This could not have been an easy decision for you. I, for one, believe that you did the right thing."

"Yes, yes," said Pitar. "I too agree."

"As do I," said Dizkuh.

He was grateful for their encouragement; and deep down, he knew they were right. He was just having a hard time with breaking his word to the emperor. If all worked out well, he would be glad; but he would still owe Tryllos an apology. Tryllos would not accept it, of course; but he would give it nonetheless. He hoped that Cemyoz was successful. Reprisals were sure to follow if he was not. Still, perhaps after tomorrow, things wouldn't be the same in Doetora. It would change things for all of Kosundo really. He thought about that and smiled. That might well be a welcome change indeed.

There was a time in the history of Kosundo where acts of good conscience were commonplace despite the difficulty or consequence that they might bring. But in this moment of history, Shipunke's act shone brightly. It was a beacon of hope for the darkening world in which he lived.

Kosundo would need many more brightly shining beacons to stem the darkness that had swelled unnoticed. People in the world of Kosundo would have to choose for themselves. Some would choose what they viewed as the easy path, the path that would let the darkness increase, but a few brave souls would choose to become a radiant light that cut through the darkness. Each of these courageous souls would dare to believe that they could become a beacon of hope for a world beset with an unrelenting darkness.

Glossary

AGRODYNE
An enclosed biosphere for the purpose of raising crops or livestock. It was first used in the cave cities of Cirri.

AIRCRAFT
A transport vehicle of any size that flies using a combination of displacement fields.

AWGG
Base Kosundoan unit of weight. It is approximately equivalent to 14 earth grains.

AXI
Shortened, universally accepted, colloquialism of the old tongue word antexai, which means all right. It is an affirmative response that can indicate agreement or a satisfactory condition. It is used much like okay is used on Earth.

BIT
Base Kosundoan unit of distance. It is equal to a little less than two-thirds of an Earth inch.

BUMVOCE
Multipurpose congratulatory exclamation that is unique to Cirri.

CEFA
Drink that is usually served hot and is made from ground ceceo beans. It has a smooth taste and is a very popular drink everywhere in Kosundo.

CERECI
Snail dish similar to escargot but with unique Kosundoan spices and sauce.

CHE
Hot or cold drink made by running water through hurtale leaves.

CHOMILE
Device invented by Agap and programmed by Yotux. It is used exclusively in Bojoa's living complex. It uses concentrated energy fields to simulate matter.

CIRRIAN
Adjective used to describe a noun as being of the country of Cirri. It can also refer to a race of people with blonde hair and very fair complexion or pale skin.

COMM
Visual or non visual communications device often capable of functions other than communications.

COMMTERM
Kind of communications device that displays images.

COMPUTING TERM
Visual computing device with multiple capabilities.

CORNI
Common meat dish featuring the meat of koh.

CUMA
Male part of a Cirrian union. It literally means the giver of a vow in the old tongue.

DATATERM
Visual device used primarily for displaying data.

DET
Unit of distance equal to 10 bits.

Glossary

Diotiri
First day of the week.

Drus
Popular slang word indicating excitement, agreement, or approval.

Ducim
Twelfth month of the year.

Earpiece
Small audio communications device that fits in a person's ear. It is widely used by the military and news crews. It is also used, at times, by the general public.

Ecayta
Female part of a Cirrian union. It literally means the receiver of a vow in the old tongue.

eKureaki
Last day of the week and is also called the weekend.

Erith
Negative exclamation indicating disappointment or anger, or in some cases, a neutral exclamation indicating surprise.

Fet
Unit of distance equal to 100 dets.

Firocryl
Composite material consisting of iri, pirru, and polymers that is very strong at colder temperatures.

Gelinhe
Flightless bird about twice the size of a chicken. It is indigenous to northern Grasso.

Griphas
General term for the writings contained in the Levra.

Ispra
Race of people that is characterized by pale skin but without the fair complexion of a Cirrian.

Kliste
Larger and closer of Kosundo's two moons.

Koh
One or more very large grazing animals that run in very large herds in warmer climates. The animal is widely domesticated for meat and leather products. Koh reproduce prolifically, although their meat is perceived as lower in quality. It is the meat of the common Kosundoan.

Kosundo
Earthlike planet that is said by some to be the sixth world that mankind has inhabited.

Kosundoan degree(°K)
Unit of temperature on the Kosundoan scale. This scale measures the freezing point of water as 0 K and the boiling point of water as 222.8 K.

Levra
Collection of books believed by many to be supernatural in origin. The book is respected in Kosundo for its wisdom, and many consider it as a guide to daily living. The prophecies of the Levra have also proven to be amazingly accurate.

Levra scholar
Person who has formally studied the Levra and typically holds local proclamation services.

Lib
Unit of weight equal to 1,000 awggs. It is approximately equal to two Earth pounds.

Lotan
Metal alloy whose yellow luster is darker than that of gold. It is widely used in decorative pieces.

Mekry
Smaller of the two moons of Kosundo. Its orbit is larger and faster than that of the larger moon.

Glossary

MIGOTERM
Very large display for any kind of communications or computing device.

MILLENNIUM GENERATOR
Fifth-generation fusion device capable of creating huge amounts of energy with a very small amount of fuel. The name is indicative of the belief that this generator can sustain a constant flow of power for a thousand years without refueling.

MOLARE
Small pack animal slightly larger than an earth mule.

MUGMI
Race of people that have a mixture of traits from other races.

NECKWRAP
Decorative neck piece for Cirrian men. It is generally used in formal or professional settings.

NONATERM
Small display device that is sometimes used for computing but most often used for organizing data, displaying reading material, or playing multimedia files. It is widely used to take notes during a meeting. Many times, it is simply referred to as a nona.

OIKSITH
Flowering, red, decorative plant with a bright red blossom.

OLD TONGUE
Original language of Kosundo before the breaking apart of the land masses.

OVERTRACK
Mass transportation system or single conveyance in the system. Conveyances are of various lengths but consistent widths. They are propelled just above metal rails at high speeds.

PARASKEVI
Fourth day of the week.

PARZ
> *Unit of time equal to 100 spens and is exactly one-tenth of a Kosundoan day.*

PFARD
> *Large, fast-moving animal suitable for burden with great endurance. It is willing to carry large loads of cargo, but it resists being ridden.*

PHUSEN
> *Unit of light intensity approximately equal to one earth lumen.*

PIRRU
> *Common metal alloy used in manufacturing and building. Its strength is similar to the earth alloy steel, but it does not oxidize as easily.*

PRATESBEGES
> *Large, black berry that is grown widely in Cirri.*

PRINCAMPRE
> *Head waiter or host of an upscale restaurant.*

PROCLAMATION SERVICE
> *Meeting held by a Levra scholar centering around the worship of Thaoi. Meetings are not held at a specific time, but rather when announced by a Levra scholar.*

PT
> *Personal term used to received visual programming. The programming can be informational or entertaining. Certain PTs are capable of three-dimensional displays.*

SARK
> *Simple pullover shirt traditional in Cirri, although some sarks now bear decorative embellishments.*

SCHWAIN
> *One or more large, rutting animals that tend to grow fat and are a coveted meat source.*

SETMI
> *Seventh month of the year.*

Glossary

SOZA
Female of a union or marriage. The term is somewhat interchangeable with the term wife everywhere except in Cirri.

SOZO
Male of a union or marriage. The term is somewhat interchangeable with the term husband everywhere except in Cirri.

SPEN
Unit of time equal to 100 tics.

STET
Unit of distance equal to 100 fets.

SUND
Standard measure of depth equal in depth to the length of 10 dets.

TERM
Word referring to a viewing screen or an entire viewing or computing device.

THAOI
Spiritual being believed to be the creator of Kosundo and the entire universe.

THOUGHT WAVES
Radiated energy of active thought, whether generated biologically or artificially. The exact nature of the energy is still under debate, but it is believed that thought waves are able to bridge dimensions as they travel.

TIC
Base unit of time equal to a little less than an earth second.

TITARTI
The third day of the week.

TOWRUS
One or more large, two-horned, grazing animals that are a little larger than an Earth buffalo.

TRANSLIFT
Type of elevator unique to Bojoa capable of multidirectional movement through tubes and on suspended wires.

TRANSPORT
General term for any vehicle used to move people and/or cargo.

TRANSPORTER
Device used to instantly transport material from one place to another.

TRETI
The second day of the week.

TWR
Thought wave receiver, a device capable of receiving and identifying thought waves.

UCHUM
Eighth month of the year.

WEEK OF REMEMBRANCE
Holiday week added to the Kosundoan calendar once every twenty years between the eleventh and twelfth months of the year.

Appendix

The Calendar of Kosundo

In a Kosundo calendar year, there are fifteen twenty-four-day months plus a holiday week, which is called the week of feasts. Another holiday week, which only comes every twenty years, is called the Week of Remembrance. It occurs between the months of Uncim and Ducim and adds a week to the northern hemisphere's winter and the southern hemisphere's summer.

Names of Months
(Season in North, Season in South)

Onum (Summer, Winter)
Dusmi (Summer, Winter)
Trismi (Summer, Winter)
Coetru (Fall, Spring)
Cencam (Fall, Spring)
Sismi (Fall, Spring)
Setmi (Fall, Spring)
Uchum (Winter, Summer)
Noivi (Winter, Summer)

Dezmi (Winter, Summer)
*Uncim (Winter, Summer)
*Ducim (Spring, Fall)
Trisim (Spring, Fall)
Cotarci (Spring, Fall)
Week of Feasts (Spring, Fall)
Kencim (Summer, Winter)

* Week of remembrance occurs between these months once every twenty years.

Names of Days
Diotiri: first day of week
Treti: second day of week
Titarti: third day of week
Paraskevi: fourth day of week
eKureaki: fifth day of week (also called the weekend)

Kosundo Systems of Measurement

Units of Volume
An oggi is a little more than one twelfth of an Earth ounce.
1 pinte = 100 oggis
gelun = 100 pintes
remp = 100 geluns [or about ten Earth casks (640 Earth gallons)]

Units of Weight
1 awgg = 14 Earth grains
1 lib = 1,000 awggs = 2 Earth pounds
1 tun = 1,000 libs = 1 Earth ton

Appendix

Units of Distance

base unit is a Bit, which is about 0.6336 Earth inches.
10 bits = 1 det (a little over a half Earth foot)
100 dets = 1 fet (about 17.6 Earth yards or 52.8 Earth feet)
100 fets = 1 stet (about 1760 Earth yards or 1 Earth mile)
A sund is the standard measure of depth. 1 sund = 10 dets or about 5.28 Earth feet

Units of Area

1 stramme = 100,000 sq dets
10 strammes = 1 akler
1 stramme = 0.64 Earth acres
1 akler = 6.4 Earth acres or 2.59 Earth hectares

Unit of Light Intensity

1 phusin = 1 lumen

Unit of Power

1 donem = 1.08 Earth joules

Units of Temperature

temperature is in Kosundoan degrees (°K)
To covert from Fahrenheit to Kosundoan, use this formula:
$K = (F-32) \times 10/9$
To convert from Kosundoan to Fahrenheit, use this formula:
$F = K \times 9/10 + 32$

Units of Time

100 tics = 1 spen
1 tic = 0.864 Earth seconds
100 spens = 1 parz
1 spen = about 1.44 Earth minutes
10 parz = 1 day
1 parz = about 144 Earth minutes or 2.4 Earth hours

Approximate Time of Day Conversions (Kosundo to Earth)

1:00 (spoken as "one parz") = 2:24 a.m.
6:00 (spoken as "six parzes") = 2:24 p.m.
2:00 (spoken as "two parzes") = 4:48 a.m.
7:00 (spoken as "seven parzes") = 4:48 p.m.
3:00 (spoken as "three parzes") = 7:12 a.m.
8:00 (spoken as "eight parzes") = 7:12 p.m.
4:00 (spoken as "four parzes") = 9:36 a.m.
9:00 (spoken as "nine parzes") = 9:36 p.m.
5:00 (spoken as "the fifth parz or noon") = noon
10:00 (spoken as "the tenth parz or midnight") = midnight